WINTER JOURNEYS

Atlas Anti-Classics 18

First edition of 2000 copies.

GEORGES PEREC AND THE OULIPO

Winter Journeys

MICHÈLE AUDIN • MARCEL BÉNABOU • JACQUES BENS • PAUL BRAFFORT • FRANÇOIS CARADEC • FRÉDÉRIC FORTE • PAUL FOURNEL • MIKHAÏL GORLIOUK • MICHELLE GRANGAUD • REINE HAUGURE • JACQUES JOUET • ÉTIENNE LÉCROART • HERVÉ LE TELLIER • DANIEL LEVIN BECKER • HARRY MATHEWS • IAN MONK • JACQUES ROUBAUD • HUGO VERNIER • TRANSLATIONS BY IAN MONK • HARRY MATHEWS • JOHN STURROCK •

ATLAS PRESS, LONDON

Published by Atlas Press,
27 Old Gloucester st., London WC1N 3XX
This edition ©2013, Atlas Press
Translations ©2013, Ian Monk, Harry Mathews & John Sturrock
French texts ©2013, The Oulipo
Copyright of individual texts remains with the authors
All rights reserved
The translation of *Le Voyage d'hiver* is
© John Sturrock, 1997, 1999 and is reprinted
from Georges Perec *Species of Spaces and Other Pieces*
and is reproduced by permission of Penguin Books Ltd.
Printed by Antony Rowe ltd., Chippenham
A CIP record for this book is available from the British Library
ISBN: 1-900565-64-1
ISBN-13: 978-1-900565-64-6
We are pleased to thank the Arts Council of England
for their financial assistance with the first version of this book,
and the Centre national du livre for their financial assistance
with the present edition.

CONTENTS

INTRODUCTION

● The "Bibliothèque oulipienne" currently consists of more than 200 small fascicles, each of around 32 pages, and privately published in a numbered edition of 150 copies by the group of mainly French writers known as the Oulipo. Essentially they constitute the group's "research papers", and are mostly given to members of the group and to friends. The present book consists of translations of those shown opposite, preceded by a short narrative by Georges Perec.

Is it still necessary to explain the Oulipo to English readers? Perhaps so, despite its longevity as a group (some 52 years) and the appearance of so many of its members' books in English (not to mention in magazines, such as the recent special issue of McSweeney's). The name stands for *Ouvroir de littérature potentielle*, which roughly translates as "Workshop for Potential Literature". It was founded in 1960 by a writer (and amateur mathematician), Raymond Queneau, and a professional scientist (and amateur everything else), François Le Lionnais. Their intention was to explore the connections between mathematics and literature, but their field of research was quickly expanded to explore all voluntarily assumed constraints within literary production — everything from poetic structures (one of the simplest being the sonnet) to constraints such as the lipogram, the voluntary omission of certain letters from a text (which provided the main constraint for Georges Perec's most notorious novel, *La Disparition*, which does not use words containing the letter *e*).

Although such works are now known as "Oulipian", this in fact ignores the stated aim of the group, specifically its concept of "potentiality". The Oulipo was founded not to actually produce literature, but to provide tools for its construction, to codify and invent constraints that could be used for producing literary texts. This penchant for pure research (which means not all of its members are actual writers, and the Oulipo continues to recruit mathematicians) derives in part from its origins as a branch of the Collège de 'Pataphysique, which also means that its approach has not been quite so po-faced or astringently theoretical as might otherwise have been the case. The narratives here demonstrate very well that the writers attracted to the Oulipo tended to balance theory with a more ludic approach to literature.

Perec's short story "Le Voyage d'hiver" first appeared in 1979 and became his most oft-reprinted text, especially after his early death three years later. It was some years before the first Oulipian sequel appeared, by Jacques Roubaud, in 1992, and this set the precedent of using a homophonic version of the original title to influence the content of the text. Roubaud's was followed by the texts published here, up until Harry Mathews's *Le Voyage des verres* of 1999, which brought the first sequence to a close. Indeed one suspects his narrative was intended to kill off the possibility of any further sequels. It was then that Atlas Press approached the Oulipo to publish these texts, several of which (by Grangaud, Caradec, Haugure and Mathews) had not yet appeared in French (indeed there has never been a French collected edition of the Journeys). We published this first version of *Winter Journeys* in 2001 in an edition of 1000 copies (bibliophiles should note that we still have a few for sale on our website at www.atlaspress.co.uk).

Harry Mathews's attempted curtailment of the series proved unsuccessful, and over recent years yet more sequels have appeared, making this a very long-lived literary experiment (or hyper-novel, as some Oulipians refer to it): 20 texts between 1979 and this year. As will become clear to the reader, the Journeys have assumed certain specific functions within the group. They have become a sort of entry ritual for new members (membership is by invitation, but see too the text by "Hugo Vernier") who often take the opportunity to push the series in new directions (thus, for example, Étienne Lécroart undertakes to show that this same Hugo Vernier was also an anticipatory plagiarist of several well-known authors of comic books). The Journeys also constitute an ongoing entertainment for members, who often appear in each other's narratives, and on occasion, they are the place for a little mild criticism of one another. There are, therefore, a few "in" references that needed footnoting in the translation (indicated by an asterisk), and it also seems helpful to supply here a complete list of members of the Oulipo, past and present: Noël Arnaud, Michèle Audin, Valérie Beaudouin, Marcel Bénabou, Jacques Bens, Claude Berge, André Blavier, Paul Braffort, Italo Calvino, François Caradec, Bernard Cerquiglini, Ross Chambers, Stanley Chapman, Marcel Duchamp, Jacques Duchateau, Luc Étienne, Frédéric Forte, Paul Fournel, Anne F. Garréta, Michelle Grangaud, Jacques Jouet, Latis, Étienne Lécroart, François Le Lionnais, Jean Lescure, Hervé Le Tellier, Daniel Levin Becker, Harry Mathews, Michèle Métail, Ian Monk, Oskar Pastior, Georges Perec, Raymond Queneau, Jean Queval, Pierre Rosenstiehl, Jacques Roubaud, Olivier Salon and Albert-Marie Schmidt.

Readers will notice that some of the authors of texts here are not included in the list above, but they should have no trouble in working out who is responsible for them. Biographical and other information regarding the activities of the Oulipo may be found in three other English publications: *Oulipo: A Primer of Potential Literature*, by Warren Motte (new edition, Dalkey Archive Press, 1998); *Oulipo Compendium*, edited by Harry Mathews and myself (Atlas Press, revised edition, 2005); and Daniel Levin Becker's recent *Many Subtle Channels* (Harvard University Press, 2012).

The texts are complete translations, which means that certain repetitions are inevitable, especially in the earlier ones, but we decided not to edit anything out. We have, too, followed the original layouts of the Bibliothèque oulipienne, although a certain amount of typographical unification has been applied.

Alastair Brotchie

GEORGES PEREC

The Winter Journey

Le Voyage d'hiver

Translated by John Sturrock

1979

● In the last week of August 1939, as the talk of war invaded Paris, a young literature teacher, Vincent Degraël, was invited to spend a few days at the place outside Le Havre belonging to the parents of one of his colleagues, Denis Borrade. The day before his departure, while exploring his hosts' shelves in search of one of those books one has always promised oneself one will read, but that one will generally only have time to leaf inattentively through beside the fire before going to make up a fourth at bridge, Degraël lit upon a slim volume entitled *The Winter Journey*, whose author, Hugo Vernier, was quite unknown to him but whose opening pages made so strong an impression on him that he barely found time to make his excuses to his friend and his parents before going up to his room to read it.

The Winter Journey was a sort of narrative written in the first person, and set in a semi-imaginary country whose heavy skies, gloomy forests, mild hills and canals transected by greenish locks evoked with an insidious insistence the landscapes of Flanders and the Ardennes. The book was divided into two parts. The first, shorter part retraced in sybilline terms a journey which had all the appearances of an initiation, whose every stage seemed certainly to have been marked by a failure, and at the end of which the anonymous hero, a man whom everything gave one to suppose was young, arrived beside a lake that was submerged in a thick mist; there, a ferryman was waiting for him, who took him to a steep-sided, small island in the middle of which there rose a tall, gloomy building; hardly had the young man set foot on the narrow pontoon that afforded the only access to the island when a strange-looking couple appeared: an old man and an old woman, both clad in long black capes, who seemed to rise up out of the fog and who came and placed themselves on either side of him, took him by the elbows and pressed themselves as tightly as they could against his sides; welded together almost, they scaled a rock-strewn path, entered the house, climbed a wooden staircase and came to a chamber. There, as inexplicably as they had appeared, the old people vanished, leaving the young man alone in the middle of the room. It was perfunctorily furnished: a bed covered with a flowery cretonne, a table, a chair. A fire was blazing in the fireplace. On the table a meal had been laid: bean soup, a shoulder of beef. Through the tall window of the room, the young man watched the full moon emerging from the clouds; then he sat down at the table and began to eat. This solitary supper brought the first part to an end.

The second part alone formed nearly four-fifths of the book and it quickly appeared that the brief narrative preceding it was merely an anecdotal pretext. It was a long confession of an exacerbated lyricism, mixed in with poems, with enigmatic maxims, with blasphemous incantations. Hardly had he begun reading it before Vincent Degraël felt a sense of unease that he found it impossible to define exactly, but which only grew more pronounced as he turned the pages of the volume with an increasingly shaky hand; it was as if the phrases he had in front of him had become suddenly familiar, were starting irresistibly to remind him of something, as if on to each one that he read there had been imposed, or rather superimposed, the at once precise yet blurred memory of a phrase almost identical to it that he had perhaps already read somewhere else; as if these words, more tender than a caress or more treacherous than a poison, words that were alternately limpid and hermetic, obscene and cordial, dazzling, labyrinthine, endlessly swinging like the frantic needle of a compass between a hallucinated violence and a fabulous serenity, formed the outline of a vague configuration in which could be found, jumbled together, Germain Nouveau and Tristan Corbière, Rimbaud and Verhaeren, Charles Cros and Léon Bloy.

These were the very authors with whom Vincent Degraël was concerned — for several years he had been working on a thesis on "The Evolution of French Poetry from the Parnassians to the Symbolists" — and his first thought was that he might well have chanced to read this book as part of his researches, then, more likely, that he was the victim of an illusory *déjà vu* in which, as when the simple taste of a sip of tea suddenly carries you back thirty years to England, a mere trifle had succeeded, a sound, a smell, a gesture — perhaps the moment's hesitation he had noticed before taking the book from the shelf where it had been arranged between Verhaeren and Viélé-Griffin, or else the eager way in which he had perused the opening pages — for the false memory of a previous reading to superimpose itself and so to disturb his present reading as to render it impossible. Soon, however, doubt was no longer possible and Degraël had to yield to the evidence. Perhaps his memory was playing tricks on him, perhaps it was only by chance that Vernier seemed to have borrowed his "solitary jackal haunting stone sepulchres" from Catulle Mendès, perhaps it should be put down to a fortuitous convergence, to a parading of influence, a deliberate homage, unconscious copying, wilful pastiche, a liking for quotation, a fortunate coincidence, perhaps expressions such as "the flight of time", "winter fogs", "dim horizon", "deep eaves", "vaporous fountains", "uncertain light of the wild undergrowth" should be seen as belonging by right to all poets so that it was just as normal to meet with them in a paragraph by Hugo Vernier as in the stanzas of Jean Moréas, but it was quite impossible not to recognise, word for word, or almost, reading at random, in one place a fragment from Rimbaud ("I readily could see a mosque in place of a factory, a drum school built by angels") or Mallarmé ("the lucid winter, the season of serene art"), in another Lautréamont ("I gazed in a mirror at that mouth bruised by my own volition"), Gustave Kahn ("Let the song expire… my heart weeps / A bistre crawls around the brightness. The solemn / silence has risen slowly, it frightens / The familiar sounds of the shadowy staff") or, only slightly modified, Verlaine ("in the interminable tedium of the plain, the snow gleamed like sand. The sky was the colour of copper. The train slid without a murmur…"), etc.

It was four o'clock in the morning when Degraël finished reading *The Winter Journey*. He had pinpointed some thirty borrowings. There were certainly others. Hugo Vernier's book seemed to be nothing more than a prodigious compilation from the poets of the end of the nineteenth century, a disproportionate cento, a mosaic almost every piece of which was the work of someone else. But at the same time as he was struggling to imagine this unknown author who had wanted to extract the very substance of his own text from the books of others, when he was attempting to picture this admirable and senseless project to himself in its entirety, Degraël felt a wild suspicion arise in him: he had just remembered that in taking the book from the shelf he had automatically made a note of the date, impelled by that reflex of the young researcher who never consults a work without remarking the bibliographical details. Perhaps he had made a mistake, but he certainly thought he had read 1864. He checked it, his heart pounding. He had read it correctly. That would mean Vernier had "quoted" a line of Mallarmé two years in advance, had plagiarised Verlaine ten years before his "Forgotten Ariettas", had written some Gustave Kahn nearly a quarter of a century before Kahn did! It would mean that Lautréamont, Germain Nouveau, Rimbaud, Corbière and quite a few others were merely the copyists of an unrecognised poet of genius who, in a single work, had been able to bring together the very substance off which three or four generations would be feeding after him!

Unless, obviously, the printer's date that appeared on the book were wrong. But Degraël refused to entertain that hypothesis: his discovery was too beautiful, too obvious, too necessary not to be true, and he was already imagining the vertiginous consequences it would provoke: the prodigious scandal that the public revelation of this "premonitory anthology" would occasion, the extent of the fallout, the enormous doubt that would be cast on all that the critics and literary historians had been imperturbably teaching for years and years. Such was his impatience that, abandoning sleep once and for all, he dashed down to the library to try and find out a little more about this Vernier and his work.

He found nothing. The few dictionaries and directories to be found in the Borrades' library knew nothing of the existence of Hugo Vernier. Neither Denis nor his parents were able to tell him anything further; the book had been bought at an auction, ten years before, in Honfleur; they had looked through it without paying it much attention.

All through the day, with Denis's help, Degraël proceeded to make a systematic examination of the book, going to look up its splintered shards in dozens of anthologies and collections. They found almost three hundred and fifty, shared among almost thirty authors: the most celebrated along with the most obscure poets of the *fin de siècle*, and sometimes even a few prose writers (Léon Bloy, Ernest Hello) seemed to have used *The Winter Journey* as a bible from which they had extracted the best of themselves: Banville, Richepin, Huysmans, Charles Cros, Léon Valade rubbed shoulders with Mallarmé and Verlaine and others now fallen into oblivion whose names were Charles de Pomairols, Hippolyte Vaillant, Maurice Rollinat (the godson of George Sand), Laprade, Albert Mérat, Charles Morice or Antony Valabrègue.

Degraël made a careful note of the list of authors and the source of their borrowings and returned to Paris, fully determined to continue his researches the very next day in the Bibliothèque Nationale. But events did not allow him to. In Paris his call-up papers were waiting for him. Joining his unit in Compiègne, he found himself, without really having had the time to understand why, in Saint-Jean-de-Luz, passed over into Spain and from there to England, and only came back to France in 1945. Throughout the war he had carried his notebook with him and had miraculously succeeded in not losing it. His researches had obviously not progressed much, but he had made one, for him capital, discovery all the same. In the British Museum he had been able to consult the *Catalogue général de la librairie française* and the *Bibliographie de la France* and had been able to confirm his tremendous hypothesis: *The Winter Journey*, by Vernier (Hugo), had indeed been published in 1864, at Valenciennes, by Hervé Frères, Publishers and Booksellers, had been registered legally like all books published in France, and had been deposited in the Bibliothèque Nationale, where it had been given the shelfmark Z87912.

Appointed to a teaching post in Beauvais, Vincent Degraël henceforth devoted all his free time to *The Winter Journey*.

Going thoroughly into the private journals and correspondence of most of the poets of the end of the nineteenth century quickly convinced him that, in his day, Hugo Vernier had known the celebrity he deserved: notes such as "received a letter from Hugo today", or "wrote Hugo a long letter", "read V.H. all night", or even Valentin Havercamp's celebrated "Hugo, Hugo alone" definitely did not refer to Victor Hugo, but to this doomed poet whose brief *œuvre* had apparently inflamed all those who had held it in their hands. Glaring contradictions which criticism and literary history had never been able to explain thus found their one logical solution; it was obviously with Hugo Vernier in mind and what they owed to his *Winter Journey* that Rimbaud had written "I is another" and Lautréamont "Poetry should be made by all and not by one."

But the more he established the preponderant place that Hugo Vernier was going to have to occupy in the literary history of late nineteenth-century France, the less was he in a position to furnish tangible proof, for he was never able again to lay his hands on a copy of *The Winter Journey*. The one that he had consulted had been destroyed — along with the villa — during the bombing of Le Havre; the copy deposited in the Bibliothèque Nationale wasn't there when he asked for it and it was only after long enquiries that he was able to learn that, in 1926, the book had been sent to a binder who had never received it. All the researches that he caused to be undertaken by dozens, by hundreds of librarians, archivists and booksellers proved fruitless, and Degraël soon persuaded himself that the edition of five hundred copies had been deliberately destroyed by the very people who had been so directly inspired by it.

Of Hugo Vernier's life, Vincent Degraël learnt nothing, or next to nothing. An unlooked-for brief mention, unearthed in an obscure *Biographie des hommes remarquables de la France du Nord et de la Belgique* (Verviers, 1882) informed him that he had been born in Vimy (Pas-de-Calais) on 3 September 1836. But the records of the Vimy registry office had been burned in 1916, along with duplicate copies lodged in the prefecture in Arras. No death certificate seemed ever to have been made out.

For close on thirty years, Vincent Degraël strove in vain to assemble proof of the existence of this poet and of his work. When he died, in the psychiatric hospital in Verrières, a few of his former pupils undertook to sort the vast pile of documents and manuscripts he had left behind. Among them figured a thick register bound in black cloth whose label bore, carefully and ornamentally inscribed, "*The Winter Journey*". The first eight pages retraced the history of his fruitless researches; the other 392 pages were blank.

JACQUES ROUBAUD

Yesterday's Journey

Le Voyage d'hier

Translated by Ian Monk

Bibliothèque oulipienne 53

1992

"What if these yesterdays consumed our fine tomorrows?"
Hugo Vernier

● On the last Friday before the 1980 Easter holidays, Dennis Borrade Jr., a young associate professor of French literature in the Romance Languages department of the University of John Hopkins at Baltimore, arrived as was his custom in the Milton Eisenhower University Library as soon as the doors opened. There, he was fortunate enough to possess that highest point of intellectual comfort that consists of an isolated, peaceful office in the basement, just a few yards away from a photocopier. He spent most of his time in this tunnel of paper (the library was open every day, from eight a.m. until midnight).

But, that morning, he found it impossible to read. His head raced with thoughts of the journey he was to make the next morning to Iowa, one of the ten states that possess a slice of the Mississippi, and thus associated in his mind with two of his favourite childhood books, *The Adventures of Tom Sawyer* and *Huckleberry Finn*. He was going to a symposium on Romanticism, where he was to speak on his special subject, Théophile Gautier.

A snowstorm was in the air. The windows of the almost deserted periodicals room of the library were level with the lawns and, above the grass, the whitish-grey sky looked expectant and hesitant, as though composed of one huge cloud with its edges hanging down over the horizon and the roof. He watched a few flakes tumble down in flurries.

Absent-mindedly he had picked up from the table a small review whose title, *Saisons*, seemed particularly appropriate given this strange circumstance of watching the sudden return of snow in the middle of spring in what was practically a southern state. The review in fact consisted of a slim collection of four short stories, originally published in the magazine *Hachette Informations* and here brought together by Nicole

Vitoux in a special limited edition of 1000 copies, of which he was now holding (and heaven knows how it had ended up here) copy number 0644. The fourth of these stories was by Georges Perec and was entitled "Le Voyage d'hiver".

He started to read it. When he reached the fifth line of the text, he was astonished to see his own name — or, rather, that of his father, Denis Borrade. This could certainly be no coincidence. The "place outside Le Havre", the "villa" mentioned in the story, was obviously the one that had once belonged to his family (and which had been destroyed in the bombing that occurred in the last few months of the Second World War). What is more, the story it told was far from fictional, despite the tone of the writing. Vincent Degraël's incredible discovery and tragically romantic fate had been recounted to him by his mother when he was twelve years old and had played no small part in deciding his vocation.

As we know, in "Le Voyage d'hiver" Georges Perec tells of how a "young literature teacher", Vincent Degraël, was invited during the "last week of August 1939" to the country house belonging to the parents of one of his colleagues, Denis Borrade (i.e. Dennis Borrade's paternal grandparents), and there, in his hosts' library, happened upon a slim volume of verse by a certain Hugo Vernier which was also entitled *Le Voyage d'hiver*. This book had been published in Valenciennes in 1864. So far, nothing of great interest. But the incredible, stupefying fact that was to determine Degraël's destiny was that this book actually consisted of a huge "anticipatory plagiary" of all of late-nineteenth-century France's great poetic *œuvres*. "The most celebrated along with the most obscure poets … seemed to have used *The Winter Journey* as a bible from which they had extracted the best of themselves: Banville, Richepin, Huysmans, Charles Cros, Léon Valade rubbed shoulders with Mallarmé and Verlaine … Lautréamont, Germain Nouveau, Rimbaud, Corbière … were merely the copyists of an unrecognised poet of genius", Hugo Vernier.

The young associate professor read Perec's "short story" eagerly through to the end. Everything in it was just as he remembered. Nothing, absolutely nothing, had been invented: neither the disappearance of all the known copies of Hugo Vernier's book, nor Degraël's increasingly obsessive and maniacal pursuit of what would turn out to be an unreachable Grail — a proof, the slightest piece of hard evidence that this revelation had really happened. In 1973, during his only trip to France in a quarter of a century, Borrade senior had visited Degraël in the psychiatric hospital of Verrières. Degraël had gone utterly insane. He did not even recognise him.

Dennis Borrade put *Saisons* thoughtfully back down on to the coffee table in front of him. Outside, large woolly flakes of snow were now falling, already covering the earth in a thick shroud. He quietly analysed Perec's *tour de force*, which was even subtler than that of Hugo von Hofmannsthal, the author of "Marshal de Bassompierre's Adventure". It seemed to him that one of the secrets of the Romantic short story, be it Pushkin's "The Captain's Daughter" or Kleist's "The Marquise of O", was to draw on the apparently inexhaustible stock of private destinies and on the documents that enshrined them: "memoirs", "written accounts" and "personal letters". However, the craftiest technique in this class of fiction, the one adopted by Hofmannsthal and, before him, by De Quincey in his "The Last Days of Immanuel Kant" and "The Spanish Military Nun", consisted in using adventures that had actually happened to real people and magnifying them, adding here or taking away there, and thus magically transforming them into works of art. But, in each of these examples, a visible model existed. De Quincey, Hofmannsthal and a few others had, like the potter seizing his clay or the goldsmith his ingots, exploited real lives. They had, by digging over the soil of the past, turned up buried but existing texts, which admittedly were little known but still quite readily accessible to a determined scholar, thereby allowing devotees the delicious pleasure of comparing them word by word, and exposing these demiurges of prose in their "Machiavellian moments" of creation.

But it seemed to Dennis that Perec had gone even further. Not only had he managed to make a perfectly true story read as though it were a splendid piece of fiction, but he had also chosen a "source" for his subject that would remain forever invisible. Perec had, so to speak, not only hiked himself up to the pinnacle of prose creation by his own boot-laces, but had also pulled up the ladder behind him. However, as he himself was aware of the true story, he wondered how these events had come to the attention of the author of *A Void*. It occurred to him that he should write to Perec and ask, but in the end he did not.

Vincent Degraël was not the only man to be mobilised during the last fateful days of September 1939. At the same time, his colleague Denis Borrade also received his "marching orders", as they used to say. Being an English scholar, he then worked as an interpreter between the British and French armies and thus found himself, early one morning in May 1940, on the sands of Dunkirk. As soon as he arrived on English soil, he put himself at the disposal of that crazy general who meant to continue the struggle against Hitler, and was parachuted on several occasions into occupied France on missions to liaise with the Resistance. He escaped from the Gestapo ten times. But then, a few weeks before the liberation of Grenoble, he was dropped at the head of a twelve-man commando (five Britons, three Canadians, one New Zealander, two Frenchmen and one Lebanese) in the *maquis* of the Massif de la Grande Chartreuse. After the Maquis had suffered a surprise attack by the Germans, they took refuge for two days in a cave where, at dawn on the third day, they were suddenly surrounded by Vichy militiamen and massacred almost to a man. Borrade was captured, along with a certain Louviers, and handed over to the Gestapo. He was tortured, but remained heroically silent, was then sent to Buchenwald, and survived. His old grandmother, broken by the ordeal of the Occupation (his parents had died during the bombing of Le Havre), barely recognised the virtual skeleton that arrived at the Hôtel Lutétia in early May 1945. After having been occupied by the Gestapo, this was now the place where families and friends would come day after day in the hope of identifying loved ones who had been "deported" and had returned to France. It was six months before he looked human again.

He became obsessed by one idea: to avenge his murdered comrades and unmask the traitor. For the commando had certainly been betrayed. Only two people had known about the meeting place, the cave near the site where weapons were to be dropped after a "personal announcement" from Radio London. He could still hear that message ringing in his ears: "This year, the month of May will have fifty-three days, I repeat, this year, the month of May will have fifty-three days". Only two people, himself and "Louviers". "Louviers" was the traitor. He had no difficulty locating him; thanks to being a "Resistance hero" he had thrived. Robert Serval[1] was well known, famous and powerful.

Borrade spoke out, but was not taken seriously. A conspiracy of silence protected Serval. For two years he struggled to expose the truth. Then, realising that nothing would come of his efforts, he accepted the unexpected offer of a teaching post in an obscure college in the Mid-West, which had been passed on to him by an English friend from his days in London, and decided to turn a page on his past. There was nothing left for him in France. His grandmother had died shortly after his return. His little sister had perished along with his parents. The family house by the edge of a wood in Normandy was in ruins. He left. He threw himself eagerly into his new life. Within a few years, he had written an astonishing and brilliantly argued thesis on Barnabe Barnes, an extravagant Elizabethan who was at once a Baroque poet, the virtuoso author of a triple sestina, and a poisoner. It immediately won him a post at a prestigious university on the west coast. A beautiful student, who was fascinated by this dark, brilliant, tormented lecturer, married him. Dennis was born in 1953.

Borrade had intended to eliminate France completely from his life and from his memory. The first name he chose for his son was clear proof of this. It was, and yet was not, his own. The presence of the second *n* ("Dennis" instead of "Denis") symbolised that essential "translation", that definitive crossing-over from French to English. Dennis was raised as a little Californian. He played with a frisbee and not *le jeu de barres*. While young, he did not even know his father's native country, or the part his father had played in that war which was still recent, but seemed so far away to the population of the Pacific seaboard. It was his mother who told him the story. She it was who recounted to him the marvellous tale of Vincent Degraël and of Hugo Vernier, the mysterious poet. It marked him profoundly. When Dennis suddenly decided to study French literature during his first year at Harvard, his father put up violent opposition. But he was not to be moved.

Father and son had not exactly fallen out, but their relationship had grown more distant. So, on the last day of the autumn semester of 1980 (just one week before his departure for Australia) when Dennis dropped in to see his secretary after his seminar

1. Of course I cannot reveal his real name.

on Baudelaire and was told that someone was waiting for him in his office, he was rather surprised to find himself face to face with his father, who had just arrived from Vancouver (where he had retired the year before). He looked aged, tired and confused. After a rather taciturn lunch at the Faculty Club, his father took out a red cardboard folder, secured with a strap, from his briefcase and handed it to him, saying: "Would you mind reading this, please?"

The file contained a typescript, three notebooks (one orange, one blue and one white) and a few jotters containing scattered annotations. The typewritten text was the beginning of a complex detective story. The notebooks and jottings made up, roughly in order, an account of the Chartreuse story and a narration of those events. The victim in the novel was the traitor in the notes: Robert Serval. It had a title: *The Month of May will have Fifty-Three Days*. The novel was unfinished and Dennis was incapable of working out the end of the plot or of deciding who was supposed to be the murderer.

A worrying thought suddenly occurred to him and, however hard he tried, he could not convince himself of its absurdity. What if his father had, after all these years of stubborn silence, suddenly decided to revenge himself and his fallen comrades, not leaving Serval's crime unpunished, and taking the law into his own hands? He feared lest the typed manuscript now before him were a sort of anticipatory confession, or else (given its unfinished state) a cry for help to his son: "Stop me before it's too late!" But his mother (when he finally managed to have her to himself on the telephone) put his mind to rest. She told him (something he had not heard about, being more involved in nineteenth-century France than its contemporary descendant (barring his trips to the Bibliothèque Nationale in Paris)) that Robert Serval had died (in his sleep, honoured and honourable) over six months ago. "Your father," she went on, "had become obsessed once more by that old story. He wanted to publish the truth, but without any risk of being sued for libel. And this was the approach he adopted. But I think he finally abandoned the idea. I don't know why he gave all that to you. So as to tell you what really happened, I suppose. He can't seem to talk to you about it directly." Reassured, Dennis took that strange gift of a red folder with him in the aeroplane that flew him to Brisbane, Australia.

Now that summer, Australia had a writer who was already famous as its guest for several weeks: Georges Perec. Dennis Borrade attended the informal seminar, which was half chat, half writer's workshop, that Perec organised for university students and where he introduced them to the mysteries of restrictive composition and the sometimes rather austere charms of Oulipian exercises. Then one day, after much hesitation, Dennis asked him about "Le Voyage d'hiver". Perec replied quite openly, saying that there was no mystery about it. His "short story" had been written in homage to Vincent Degraël, a teacher he had had at the age of seventeen at the Lycée d'Étampes. Some time after the publication of *Things*, which had earned him the Prix Renaudot in 1965, he received a letter from Degraël that recounted, more or less, the story in his tale ("I took nothing away, invented nothing, changed nothing," he said. "I know," answered Dennis.). The letter came with a request: if Degraël, despite all his efforts, died before finding the proof he was looking for (he mentioned a possible lead involving an eccentric bibliophile, a certain H.M., who lived sometimes in Hamburg, sometimes in the Vercors, occasionally in Houston and from time to time in Vendôme, who might, perhaps, possess a copy of Vernier's work), he wanted Perec, whose book he had greatly admired, to give "these formless notes form" so that later he would be accredited with the discovery when the day of confirmation finally came. His life would then have been lived not entirely in vain. "I gave him my promise and kept my word to the letter," Perec added. "But," said Dennis, "do you think his story was true? Do you believe that Vernier's book, which Degraël had in his hands for just one night, really contains the seeds of all of the major innovations in late-nineteenth-century French poetry?" "Yes," said Perec, "I do. I can assure you that, in 1966, Degraël was not mad. I went to see him. He knew perfectly well what he had read. I have no doubt on that score."

After this conversation, Perec and Borrade Jr. became friends. They had many a drink together (and not just Australian beer, but also shots of vodka, Vouvray, Rhenish vino (Hock) and the list goes on — the evenings are long in Brisbane!). They went around the outskirts of the town together in search of kangaroos (Perec claimed that these animals did not really exist but had been invented by naturalists and then marketed by travel agents). Dennis greatly admired *Life a User's Manual* and Perec revealed to him certain of the secrets of its construction (including some, by the way, that have not yet been unearthed or analysed by professional Perecians). Perec spoke to him about the novel he was then writing, in which the work of Stendhal, and in particular *The Charterhouse of Parma*, was to play a role that he left undefined. He was working hard on it but seemed to be finding it difficult to construct. One day, emboldened by the increasingly intimate tone of their conversations, and replying to Perec's curiosity about the fate of one of the characters in the "short story", Vincent Degraël's "colleague", Denis Borrade Sr., he decided to tell him the whole story, with the idea that the writer might one day do for his father what he had done for Degraël. He thus gave him a copy of the notes and of the rough drafts that made up Denis Borrade's unfinished "novel", *The Month of May will have Fifty-Three Days*. At the beginning of September, Perec returned to Paris. As for Dennis, he was preparing to move back to California where he had just won, after a bitter struggle, his first post as a tenured professor in the very same prestigious university where his father had taught for so long.

The reader may recall (the fact has been duly underlined) that Borrade (senior) had a little sister who was also present in the villa in Normandy during that fateful weekend in 1939. This young lady (who was then a girl aged seventeen) was called Virginie Hélène. We have also pointed out that Dennis Borrade, when reading "Le Voyage d'hiver" (the Degraël/Perec version and not, for obvious reasons, Hugo Vernier's volume of poems), had been struck by the exactitude of the events as related by the novelist. But this simply means that what Perec had written matched what Dennis's mother remembered about the episode, that is to say what she had been told by her husband concerning events that had for obvious reasons remained forever engraved in his own memory. However, certain points in this account now need to be corrected.

To begin with, Borrade was not just Degraël's colleague, he was his best friend. They saw a lot of each other and something resembling the beginnings of a love affair had sparked up between Virginie and that young man whom her brother admired and who was also extremely handsome. As for Degraël, he had not remained utterly indifferent to Virginie's almost Nordic blondeness and, during that famous weekend, we can imagine that they occasionally held hands in secret and exchanged a few furtive kisses. It must then be added (and here Degraël's memory played tricks with him) that Borrade's parents, the owners of the villa, were absent during the day. The young people were left alone. This point may sound trivial but, as we shall see, it is vital.

For the copy of Vernier's work which destiny led Vincent Degraël to take down from the shelves of the library in that large house had not at all "been bought at an auction, ten years before, in Honfleur". It had always belonged to the Borrade family. Even more than this, *it was the reason for the family's very existence*.

But let us return to 1939 once more. The shock of the declaration of war at once made the Borrade family forget all about the problem of identifying Hugo Vernier, which means that Virginie Hélène had no reason to doubt that the book was a recent acquisition (and it lay amidst a batch of books of little importance, proof that the parents had no idea themselves of the significance of a volume which they had inherited from grandfather Borrade, a grumpy old man who had started the family fortune (they were quite rich) from nothing, as a self-made man, a success story and so on and so forth, during the years around the turn of the century). Virginie exchanged a few tender letters with Vincent during the "phoney war", but immediately lost touch with him after the defeat of France. They never saw each other again. (Enrolled in the Free French Army, under de Gaulle, Degraël was sent almost at once to Equatorial Africa and did not know that Borrade had also crossed over to England.) Like her brother and her lost lover, Virginie joined the Resistance. The house in Normandy became a refuge for British pilots who fell (intentionally or unintentionally) out of the sky. One of these was a gallant Australian RAF pilot called Roger Wedderburn. They fell in love. As soon as France was liberated, they set out to look for each other and finally met again in Athens after a series of incredible adventures which lie beyond the scope of this story. They married and went to live in Australia. Before leaving France, Virginie found a small suitcase containing family papers in the cellar of the bombed-out villa (under which her parents had perished) and took it with her to the Antipodes. In her memory, Vincent Degraël was now no more than an adolescent "fling", as they used to say before the war. She had completely forgotten about Hugo Vernier.

Her brother thought that she had died along with their parents. She had heard that he had been killed by the Gestapo in the Alps. It was only much later, after the name Borrade had by chance been mentioned in the local press (to announce his presence at the university during the spring semester) and when she finally had a spare moment from her duties as mother, wife, lawyer and recent grandmother (oh yes, many years had gone by!), that Virginia Helen Wedderburn, née Virginie Hélène Borrade, picked up her phone, called the department of French Studies and unexpectedly discovered herself to be in possession of a nephew.

As for Dennis, he was delighted to find out that he had (as the symmetry of their relationship dictated) an aunt. He spoke about his life, about himself. He spoke about his father's adventures, which had Virginia in tears and made Mr. Wedderburn chew hard on his pipe as he remembered those dreadful years. He also spoke, in private (for he was a discreet and diplomatic young fellow), about the quest, madness and death of Vincent Degraël, which had her once more in tears, but of a rather different sort from those shed above, for what might have been and never was.

It was only on the penultimate day of her nephew's stay that she suddenly remembered grandfather Borrade's papers, which had been dumped in a drawer and left untouched for thirty years (except to show photographs of the olden days and pictures of France to her own children). She remembered a vague, long-suppressed feeling. And her memory proved perfectly correct. Hugo Vernier's name was mentioned therein.

It all begins with this moving letter, at once awkward and sober, which the apprentice poet sent to an illustrious master in 1853:

Besançon (Franche-Comté), 24 May 1853
To Mr. Théophile Gautier, rue de la Grange-Batelière, Paris

My dear Master,
These writings are by a young, a very young man, whose spirit has developed in obscurity. I am seventeen years of age. One is not serious at the age of seventeen.
If I am sending you some of my verses then it is because I adore the true romantic and true

poet that you are. In two years' time, perhaps I shall be in Paris. Do not turn your nose up too far, dear Master, when reading these verses.

Oh! Mad ambition!

Hugo Vernier

Now, the letter in the possession of Virginia-Virginie Wedderburn-Borrade, which Dennis removed from its yellowed envelope with understandable emotion, was an original and not a copy. A fairly long (and completely unpublished) correspondence then followed between Gautier and his young admirer, both sides of which were now for some inexplicable reason in his possession. These exchanges also contained numerous poems by Hugo Vernier. Dennis read them and was just as astonished as Vincent Degraël had been. But everything in good time.

The letters to and from Gautier stopped after a few months and a second correspondence started up, between Vernier and another person living in the Gautier household. Théophile's eldest and favourite daughter, Judith, was then just seven years old. She had just left the convent, where she had been so unhappy, to live once more with her father and mother in their flat on the Rue de la Grange-Batelière. This precocious, lively child was helping her father to revise *The Romance of the Mummy*, which he was then writing. Judith had a governess. This governess was seventeen. She was beautiful and blonde ("blonde with dark eyes"). Her name was Virginie Huet. The letters and papers belonging to Hugo Vernier, in the folder that another Virginie now gave to her nephew, were hers.

With the aid of these words, with their indefinable aura of a distant past, of a bygone age, which gave off a strange odour in what were for him the peculiar scents of Australian nights that wafted in through the open window of his small office in the university, Dennis had no difficulty in reconstructing the story up to its inevitable conclusion.

Encouraged by Gautier, Hugo came to Paris (where, in order to survive while awaiting glory, he worked as a shop boy in a bookshop, first on Rue Helder, then on Rue Vivienne) and started frequenting his master's house. In it, there were of course Judith, and Virginie. And Virginie at once meant everything to him. Their exchanges, which are intelligent, passionate and poetic (Virginie was a keen but also cool-headed critic of Vernier's work which, since she had entered his life, had undergone a quite startling development), soon became tender, then fervent and finally simply passionate. They had fallen in love.

What happened next? If the results are clear enough, the causes and circumstances remain rather obscure (and were to remain so until the end for our young couple, Virginie and Hugo). The best approach is no doubt to summarise briefly the contents of the poet's first book, *Les Poésies d'Hugo Vernier*, the first and only edition of which numbered 317 copies, was never put on sale, but instead was completely destroyed by its author, except for Virginie Huet's personal copy, which was preserved in the bundle. The book was due to appear on 23 June 1857 "at the author's address". The printer, for reasons unknown, was a few days late and this fatal delay made publication impossible.

This volume, which is slim in appearance but weighty in substance (and Vernier was only just twenty-one!), starts with four poems, entitled "Plusieurs Sonnets". Then comes "Premiers Poèmes", next a section called "Autres Poèmes", some "Hommages & Tombeaux", and so on.[2]

Take, for example, this sonnet written in his early youth:

> À travers la vapeur splendide du nuage,
> Loin du noir océan de l'immonde cité,
> L'air brisé, la stupeur, la morne volupté,
> Les plus riches cités, le plus grand paysage,
>
> Les esprits que dévore une douleur sauvage
> Dans une ténébreuse et profonde unité,
> Comme un divin remède à notre impureté,
> Le tonnerre et la pluie ont fait un tel ravage.
>
> Les morts, les pauvres morts, ont de grandes douleurs,

2. Just over fifty pages in all. Professor Borrade and I shall analyse the collection in a subsequent article.

Au milieu de l'azur, des vagues, des splendeurs,
Les parfums, les couleurs et les sons se répondent.

Au fond d'un monument construit en marbre noir,
Les sons et les parfums tournent dans l'air du soir,
Comme de longs échos qui de loin se confondent.[3]

This poem contains an outpouring of memorable lines and a constant verbal, rhythmic and musical inventiveness. But probably the most original section of Hugo Vernier's book comes at the end. It begins as a simple list of thirty-four lines, divided into seven groups, all the lines in each group rhyming with one another. As follows:

14

a – **ants**

Les singes, les scorpions, les vautours, les serpents,
Les monstres glapissants, hurlants, grognants, rampants,
(Ces êtres singuliers, décrépits et charmants)
Les lèvres sans couleur, les mâchoires sans dents
De peine, de sueur et de soleil cuisants
Le silence, l'espace affreux et captivant
Dans nos cœurs sanglotants, dans nos cœurs ruisselants

3. Because of the documentary interest of this poem and of other extracts from Vernier's opus they have been left in the original French. We here provide in the footnotes a strictly Nabokovian crib, with no literary pretensions, for the benefit of the non-French-reading public. [Trans. note]

Through the splendid vapour of the cloud, / Far from the dark ocean of the squalid city, / The broken air, the stupor, the gloomy ecstasy, / The richest cities, the largest landscape,

The spirits devoured by a wild agony / In a shadowy and deep unity, / Like a divine cure for our impurity, / The thunder and the rain have made such devastation.

The dead, the poor dead, have such agonies, / In the midst of the azure, of waves, of splendours, / Scents, colours and sounds answer one another.

In the depths of a monument built of black marble, / Sounds and scents turn in the evening air, / Like long echoes mingling in the distance.

Dans les canaux étroits des colosses puissants
Suivant des rythmes doux, et paresseux, et lents
À travers les lueurs que tourmentent les vents
Avec leurs gros bouquets, leurs mouchoirs et leurs gants
Comme d'ambre, de musc, de benjoin et d'encens
Comme des chariots ou des chocs déchirants
Ô monstruosités pleurant leurs vêtements![4]

7

b - **ique**

Les yeux illuminés ainsi que des boutiques
Les cocotiers absents des superbes Afriques
Le sommeil et le don des rêves extatiques
Comme les sons nombreux des syllabes antiques
Ô pauvres amoureux des pays chimériques
Beaux écrins sans joyaux, médaillons sans reliques
Comme d'autres esprits voguent sur les musiques[5]

4

c - **eurs**

Les rires effrénés mêlés aux sombres pleurs
Au milieu de l'azur, des vagues, des splendeurs

4. *The monkeys, the scorpions, the vultures, the snakes, / Monsters yapping, screaming, groaning, crawling, / (These singular, decrepit, charming creatures), / Colourless lips, toothless jaws / Burning with pain, with sweat, with the sun / The silence, the terrifying, enthralling space / In our sobbing hearts, in our streaming hearts / In the narrow channels of powerful colossi / Following smooth, lazy, slow rhythms / Through the gleam, tormented by the winds / With their large bouquets, their handkerchiefs and gloves / Like amber, musk, benzoin and incense / Like chariots or harrowing shocks / O monstrosities weeping for their clothes!*

5. *Eyes lit up like shops / The absent palm trees of wonderful Africas / Sleep and the gift of ecstatic dreams / Like the numerous sounds of ancient syllables / O poor lovers from imaginary lands / Beautiful cases with no jewels, medals without relics / As other spirits wander to the musics.*

Comme l'azur au ciel, les oiseaux et les fleurs,
Les morts, les pauvres morts ont de grandes douleurs[6]

3
d - ère
Les amoureux fervents et les savants austères
Les choses où les sons se mêlent aux lumières
Citadins, campagnards, vagabonds, sédentaires[7]

2
e - té
À travers le chaos des vivantes cités
Comme un divin remède à nos impuretés[8]

f - ondent
Les parfums, les couleurs et les sons se répondent
Comme de longs échos qui de loin se confondent[9]

g - oir
Au fond d'un monument construit en marbre noir
Les sons et les parfums tournent dans l'air du soir.[10]

At the end came these simple words of explanation:

6. *Wild laughter mixed with dark tears / In the midst of the azure, of waves, of splendours / Like azure in the sky, the birds and the flowers, / The dead, the poor dead, have such agonies.*

7. *Fervent lovers and the austere learned / Things in which sounds mix with lights / City people, country folk, vagabonds, stick-in-the-muds.*

8. *Through the chaos of the living cities / Like a divine cure for our impurities.*

9. *Scents, colours and sounds answer one another / Like long echoes mingling in the distance.*

10. *In the depths of a monument built of black marble / Sounds and scents turn in the evening air.*

One after the other, these lines majestically imposed themselves on the mind of the poet, who simply wrote them down as though taking dictation from a dream, a sibyl or a phantom. Each of them is a line. Each of them is the line: the line which, by means of a few terms, reinvents an entire word, making it new, a stranger to our tongue, like an incantation.

From each of these "words" make a poem. Take them as you wish, take them where you wish, so long as they rhyme. From two to fourteen lines, any poem is possible and any rhyme scheme is possible. Someone who is a better arithmetician than I shall say how many there are.[11]

Some will say that the path I have chosen has already been marked out, already ploughed deep by many of my illustrious predecessors, such as Meschinot, Puteanus, Kenellios and Kuhlmann. This is true. By simply writing down ten apparent sonnets I could have given you the potential gift of a hundred billion of them. I could have done, but have not. And yet nobody, truly nobody before me has thought to give to the winds of posterity such a mass of sonorous melodies, such a profusion of contrasting timbres.

I intend, if the breath of God remains with me, to go farther in this direction: to give, according to this very principle of absolute interchangeability, each of the rhymes in our language the lines they deserve and thus compose, by so doing, its incomparable song of glory.

Such was the book that never saw the light of day. On 25 June 1857, two days after the planned publication of *Les Poésies d'Hugo Vernier*, the first edition of Charles Baudelaire's *Les Fleurs du Mal* went on sale in Paris. Now, all of the lines, yes all of the lines in Vernier's book appear (occasionally with slight variations) in *Les Fleurs du Mal*. It is a case of blatant plagiary. But who was the plagiarist? Baudelaire, without a shadow of a doubt. The correspondence between Hugo and Virginie is enlightening on this point. In her absolute naïveté, Virginie speaks (in her diary) of Baudelaire's "borrowing" Vernier's manuscripts throughout the years 1854, 1855 and 1856, then returning them with hypocritical expressions of his deepest admiration. The concealed double meaning, at once perverse and sinister, of the title *Les Fleurs du Mal* suddenly becomes clear.

---

11. See the article mentioned above for an exact calculation of the number of poems produced by this "potential" work.

But, some may say, why did Vernier give up straight away, without putting up the slightest fight? Why did he not publish his work anyway? Why did he not immediately confront Baudelaire and the world with proof of this theft? Alas! Alas! the trap was perfect. Baudelaire would never have taken the risk of being exposed, and of ruining his reputation, without having first covered his tracks.

Baudelaire had easily supplanted Vernier in Gautier's affections. The Parisian dandy had eclipsed the awkward little provincial genius, fifteen years younger than himself. And he had cunningly taken the precaution of sending Gautier copies of all his poems, as soon as each one had been hastily concocted around lines stolen from his young rival. Thus, it was in utter good faith that Théophile did not believe Virginie when, red with indignation and brandishing the proof, she came to see him to denounce this plagiary. When she persisted, he threw her out of his house and closed his door to Vernier forever.

(Borrade thought parenthetically how this rather neatly explained the hitherto unexplained aversion that Judith Gautier felt towards Baudelaire, as recorded in her *Mémoires*; for example "the cat incident".[12] She was eleven at the time and the young couple had obviously confided in her.)

Virginie went back to her family. Hugo Vernier returned to his miserable existence as a shop boy. He almost gave up poetry for good. He spent two years without writing a line. Even the condemnation of Baudelaire on 20 August (for the wrong reasons, for

---

12. The anecdote is well known. One rainy March day, young Judith saw Baudelaire from the window as, superbly dressed as ever, he approached his master Gautier's house for a visit. On the pavement, in front of the basement window, sat a beautiful black cat, shivering and miaowing. Taking a run up, Baudelaire aimed a kick at the poor creature. He skidded and ended up flat on his back in the mud. Cursing and swearing, he rose to his feet and entered the house. Judith immediately scampered downstairs to see how he would account for the state of his clothes. Horrified, she heard him brag in bitter cynicism of having had a "wicked idea". (It is quite probable that he had spotted Judith at the window and did not want to risk telling a lie that might be exposed. We might also add that this anecdote should have attracted the attention of more Baudelaire scholars. As all poems, all works of art, faithfully reflect their author's personality, how is it that nobody has realised that Baudelaire can never have written "Les Chats"? The original of this poem, almost entirely plagiarised in *Les Fleurs du Mal*, can be found in Vernier's *Poésies* under the title "La Vieille Hélène". It is dedicated to Virginie's pussy-cat.)

a handful of so-called "erotic" pieces to which, it should be said, Vernier contributed nothing) was of no comfort to him. It is thanks to Virginie's love that he survived and regained confidence in himself.

Then, as he courageously went back to his poetic labours, that are "such a heavy weight",[13] he considered the pathways French poetry should take after *Les Fleurs du Mal*. It is from this profound and majestic contemplation that his anticipatory masterpiece arose, the very book that Degraël had the great misfortune to discover three-quarters of a century later. For what has been seen as Baudelaire's influence over the great names of turn-of-the-century French poetry is, in fact, Vernier's twofold influence: directly, through the camouflaged borrowings from his still unknown second book (just as Degraël had perceived); but also indirectly, since Mallarmé and Cros, Rimbaud, Corbière and Laforgue believed that they were reading Baudelaire in *Les Fleurs du Mal*, whereas they were once again reading Vernier. All of which is further proof that literary history is not a question of chance, but is absolutely coherent.

But the book that Vernier subsequently wrote was, first and foremost, a passionate love song. In the spring of the previous year, 1863, Virginie Huet and Hugo Vernier had married in secret. They honeymooned near Le Havre then modestly set up home with Hélène, their cat, in a small house in Vernon (in the Heure département). Hugo Vernier devoted himself to poetry. Virginie earned their bread by giving English and piano lessons. (Hugo continued to receive a tiny allowance from his father, Hippolyte Véron Vernier.)[14]

Their bliss was not to last long. His nerves and financial troubles undermined the poet's health. It was only thanks to his superhuman energy, plus the loving care of his young, blonde wife, that he was able to complete his task. Then, as soon as the last poem had been written and sent off to the printer, he went into a rapid decline. (His

---

13. As Vernier puts it in one of the poems in *Poésies*.

14. Co-author of a *Table of the Legal System of Weights and Measures* in 1846 (Bibliothèque Nationale: V1554 (2)) and of an *Arithmetic for Humanities Classes* (1830, BN: V54807). It is probably from him that the poet inherited his taste for permutations, which is so striking in his *Poésies*.

"last verses", which were not collected in the volume, show that his genius was still intact while death approached. Let us take, for example: "*Oh le printemps! — je voudrais paître!… / c'est drôle, est-ce pas: Les mourants / Font toujours ouvrir leur fenêtre / jaloux de leur part de printemps!*")[15] As a last pleasure, he just had time to breathe in the smell of the fresh printer's ink on the pages of his book, before passing away in Virginie's arms.

Virginie was pregnant. The child, a boy named Vincent, was born three months after his father's death. Two years later, the young widow married again, this time to a nice, reliable roadmender from Louviers. He gave her a son, who was baptised Denis. It will come as no surprise that her second husband's surname was Borrade.

In accordance with Hugo Vernier's last wishes, Virginie sent a copy of his book to the Bibliothèque Nationale (as we know, this copy has since vanished). She kept all of the other 316 copies. During the next few years, she sent them, one by one (apart from her own personal copy, containing the only known portrait of Hugo Vernier), to all of the great names in French poetry at the time. All of them read it. All of them copied it, then, presumably, destroyed it.

The fact that we have not referred to Hugo Vernier's book by its name in the preceding paragraphs is perfectly intentional. The title on the copy discovered by Degraël is in reality a printer's error. The real title was not *Le Voyage d'hiver* ("The Winter Journey") but *Le Voyage d'hier* ("Yesterday's Journey").[16] This "journey" stands at once for the lovers' journey described in the first poem, "Le Voyage du Havre", and an allegorical journey through French poetry which the poet imagines in the "future perfect" when, once his book has been rediscovered, his genius will be recognised.

---

15. *Oh, spring! — I want to graze!… / it's funny, isn't it: The dying / Always have their windows opened / to claim their part of the spring!*

16. Oddly enough, the opposite misprint in the original edition of Perec's short story fleetingly restored the original title (unless it was an intentional "clinamen" resulting from an intuition of the truth).

Additional note: I met Dennis Borrade Jr. in autumn 1992 in Colorado when, answering to an invitation from Professor Warren Motte (and thanks to the generosity of the Ministry of Foreign Affairs) I

participated, along with Paul Fournel of the Oulipo, in a worldwide writers' symposium. He gave me the text that I have herewith reproduced, after minor modifications, and the "folder" containing full details of the "Hugo Vernier affair", which we shall shortly publish in its entirety in a critical edition.

HERVÉ LE TELLIER

Hitler's Journey

Le Voyage d'Hitler

Translated by Ian Monk

·

Bibliothèque oulipienne 105

1999

● In the night of 10/11 January 1995, Wolfgang Gauger, a young lecturer at the University of Freiburg-im-Breisgau, got up to drink a glass of milk. He had acquired this nocturnal habit at the age of about sixteen and had no intention of giving it up. Normally, he managed to go back to sleep again at once, but, on this occasion, since it was already almost six o'clock in the morning, he decided not to return to his bedroom and the warmth of his blankets for such a short time.

At first, he paced around aimlessly in his flat, occasionally gazing out of the misty living-room window at the fine snow that was falling softly on the town. Then he sat down in an old, cracked, leather armchair, the colour of gingerbread, which he had purchased several years before in a tacky junk shop in Düsseldorf, and which now meant as much to him as a souvenir from his childhood. He glanced through yesterday's paper, then reached out for a pile of stapled pages. It was a photocopy of a short story written by a French author, Georges Perec, entitled "Le Voyage d'hiver", which had been given to him the day before by one of his female students.

Wolfgang Gauger taught contemporary French literature, so the name of Georges Perec was familiar to him, even if it had come to him late. He had read (in French) *Things*, then admired the virtuosity of *A Void*, but, put off by the imposing bulk of *Life A User's Manual*, had decided to wait for the German translation to come out.

As a fan of Schubert, his first thought was that "Le Voyage d'hiver" alluded to its namesake in German, *Winterreise*, a series of twenty-four lieder based on poems by Wilhelm Müller which was written in 1826 and was the undisputed jewel in the composer's crown. This *Winterreise*, composed by Schubert at the age of twenty-nine, was a dark and gloomy journey through the depths of the human soul. In the tragic suffering expressed by each lied, certain experts have seen signs of the physical torments caused by the venereal disease which was to kill Franz two years later.

However, once he had read Georges Perec's text, Wolfgang Gauger realised that it had nothing to do with Schubert. Instead, he discovered a fictional treatment of plagiary, which was of course a classic theme, but which was here developed so majestically that it attained the heights of a literary myth.

In "Le Voyage d'hiver", Georges Perec tells how a "a young literature teacher", Vincent Degraël, visits his friend Denis Borrade in Le Havre and, in the library, stumbles upon a volume entitled *Le Voyage d'hiver*, written by a certain Hugo Vernier. At first, Degraël assumes that he has identified borrowings from the greatest authors of the previous century, from Verlaine to Lautréamont, then to his astonishment he notices the publication date: 1864. Hugo Vernier could not then be a plagiarist. On the contrary, it appeared that "the most celebrated along with the most obscure poets … seemed to have used *The Winter Journey* as a bible from which they had extracted the best of themselves". Banville, Richepin, Huysmans, Charles Cros, Léon Valade, Rimbaud, Mallarmé and so on had lifted their poetry and their imagery from Hugo Vernier, this "unrecognised poet of genius". But then the Second World War broke out, which prevented Vincent Degraël from announcing his extraordinary discovery. When it ended, almost six years later, the only copy of *Le Voyage d'hiver* had vanished (and the Borrades' villa with it) during the terrible bombing of Le Havre. "For close on thirty years," according to Perec, "Vincent Degraël strove in vain to assemble proof of the existence of this poet and of his work. When he died, in the psychiatric hospital in Verrières," his former pupils (for he taught French) discovered "a thick register bound in black cloth whose label bore, carefully and ornamentally inscribed, 'The Winter Journey'". The first eight pages retraced the history of his fruitless researches; the other 392 pages were blank."

Perec's short story was extremely short and Wolfgang Gauger read it through in under fifteen minutes. Pensively, he laid down the photocopy, smiled and said to himself that he really must thank the young student who had given him such a delightful start to the day. It also occurred to him to include the text in his teaching programme, thus bringing up to date the well-worn course that he had been shamelessly recycling for the last three years — the myth of the *poète maudit*, who was robbed, sucked dry and finally obliterated by his contemporaries. This would make his students sit up and listen.

The young lecturer yawned, glanced at his watch then at the snow that was stubbornly refusing to melt on his window-sill, before finally deciding to have a shower. He was the sort of person for whom the day never really begins while he still feels dirty and unshaven. But then, while he was vigorously massaging his scalp, in an attempt to slow down his premature hair loss, the music of Vernier's name ran persistently through his mind. It was at the point when the foam of the shampoo was about to enter his left eye that he suddenly remembered where he had encountered it before.

He was practically certain that it had been when he was working on his thesis, soberly entitled: "Censors in France under the Third Reich: an historical study of the creation of the lists of banned books". He rapidly, and only partially rinsed his hair and rushed over to his computer. When the right window at last came up on the screen, he typed in "Hugo Vernier" and pressed enter.

Before going on, it would perhaps be appropriate to remind the reader — in passing — of the nature of these lists of banned books, which Wolfgang Gauger had studied.

As soon as France was occupied in August 1940, the German authorities ordered that one hundred and forty-four books, "of a political nature", be seized — books they had picked out from those published in France and indexed in a four-page document known as the "Bernhard List".

This list began with:

1. ** Paul: *J.A.!* Éditions des lettres françaises, 21, Place des Vosges, Paris.
2. ALLARD Paul: *Quand Hitler espionne la France.* Les Éditions de la France, Paris.
3. ALLARD Paul: *L'Allemagne parle. Que veut-elle?* Paillard, Paris, 1934.

and finished with:

142. WEILL Georges: *Race et nation. Série: Erreurs et Vérité.* Éditions Albin Michel, Paris.

143. WOODMAN Dorothy: *Au seuil de la guerre.* Éditions du Carrefour, Paris.

144. (*Saemtliche Veroeffentlichungen von*) *Notre combat* (*publication hebdomadaire*). Éditions R. Denoël, Paris.

The man responsible for co-ordinating their confiscation from publishers, bookshops and libraries was Sonderführer Friedhelm Kaiser. Operations began on 27 August, at eight o'clock in the morning. In his report dated 31 August 1940, the head of the Paris operation, Feldpolizeikommissar Dr. Heinrich Niggemeyer, remarked: "The French police have been particularly zealous," being constantly "encouraged by their superiors to respect the instructions they have received. Their collaboration has been attentive and thorough."[1]

On just the first day, 10,944 copies of books on the list were seized, to which were added 9,150 other titles that were not on the list but had been spontaneously given up by librarians and booksellers, such as Bertrand de Jouvenel's *D'une guerre à l'autre*, or Jacques Bainville's *L'Allemagne*. The books were taken away in lorries and unloaded by a hundred prisoners of war into a huge warehouse on Avenue de la Grande-Armée. On 31 August, there were over one hundred tons of them. And by the end of September, nearly 750,000 books had been seized.

Nevertheless, the first list was rather limited. In October 1940 the Germans therefore issued a new version, known as the "Otto List", which was expanded on 24 March 1942 into a second edition containing more than 1,500 titles. Apart from works written by political opponents, this final list now featured:

1) translations of English and Polish works (with the exception of classics);
2) books written by Jews (with the exception of scientific works);
3) biographies of Jews, even when written by Aryans.

1. Report of 31 August 1940, Archives Nationales, AJ40 889, quoted by Pascal Fouché in *L'Édition française sous l'occupation*, Bibliothèque de la littérature contemporaine de l'Université de Paris 7, p.22.

The nature of this list was the logical consequence of the meeting held on 20 January 1942, the so-called Wannsee Conference, where Reinhard Heydrich, the heads of the S.S. and the Secretaries of State decided, just before going to lunch, to put into action their "final solution to the Jewish question in Europe". Some authors cited on the second Otto List because their names sounded suspect made it known to the authorities that they were not Jews and succeeded in having themselves removed.

It is now time to close this long digression and to discover the result of Wolfgang Gauger's word-search. Sure enough, on the last page of the "Bernhard List", between a book by VERMEIL Edmond, entitled *Le Racisme allemand* (Éd. Sorlot), and (*Unbekannt*), *Von Reichstagbrand zur Einfachung des Weltkriegsbrandes* (Hergest. unter der Redaktion v. G. Friedrich u. F. Lang. Éd. Prométhée, Paris), appeared:

139. VERNIER Hugo: *Le Voyage d'hiver.* Éditions Hervé Frères, Valenciennes, 1864.

Wolfgang Gauger was now face to face with an enigma: what was *Le Voyage d'hiver* doing on the Bernhard List? And, for that matter, what would he have said during the viva for his thesis if a member of the jury had asked him to explain? First of all, thanks to his natural composure, he would have smiled, then, because he hated being caught out, he would have come up with some evasive answer. For example, the author asks questions about the Aryan purity of Schubert, arguing that the rhythms and melodies of the famous lieder in the Austrian composer's *Winterreise* resembled certain traditional Yiddish airs. It was all nonsense, of course, but viva juries accept this sort of absurdity without batting an eyelid.

When compared with the other books on the list, *Le Voyage d'hiver* seemed incongruous. A book's title does not, of course, always directly reflect its content. To take just one example from French literature, *Scarlet and Black* could be justified only by means of vague symbolic relationships. But such an approach was futile. French publishers issued nearly twelve thousand new books per year and, for their initial selection, the Germans had simply chosen titles that were absolutely explicit: ones containing the words "Nazism", "Jew", "race", or else "war" or "peace". Apart from Hugo Vernier's mysterious volume, the only other book on the list that broke this rule was *La Haine*, Heinrich Mann's anti-Nazi pamphlet. What particularly bothered Wolfgang Gauger was how this strange state of affairs could have escaped his notice while he had been writing his thesis. But it must be admitted that he had paid more attention to the context of the drawing-up of the list, than to its contents, which had been thoroughly dealt with by others.

This moment of confusion no doubt explains why Wolfgang Gauger immediately became convinced of the authenticity of Perec's "short story". In his first wave of enthusiasm, it never occurred to him that the author might have studied the Bernhard and Otto Lists and picked out this title and this writer as the foundation stones of his fictional tale. And this is just as well, for otherwise our story would have ended here.

Thrilled by this discovery, the same morning Wolfgang Gauger phoned up at least ten of his friends in Paris, London and even one of his former students who was now assistant librarian in the highly prestigious Library of Congress. He managed to communicate his newly-discovered passion to them, and immediately acquired their full and unqualified assistance.

Less than an hour later, he had already received one incredible piece of confirmation: the "obscure" *Biographie des hommes remarquables de la France du Nord et de la Belgique*, which Georges Perec mentioned in his short story, really existed. It could be consulted at the Bibliothèque Nationale in Paris, and it did indeed include an entry for Hugo Vernier, born in Vimy (Pas-de-Calais) on 3 September 1836. Wolfgang Gauger immediately concluded that if Perec made no mention of the presence of *Le Voyage d'hiver* on the lists of banned books, then it was because he had known nothing about it.

What he now had to find out was who, among those who drew up the list, had decided to include *Le Voyage d'hiver*, and for what reason. Although the archives of the Literature Office (Amt Schrifttum)[2] and its 60,000 volumes had been almost completely destroyed during the carpet bombing of Berlin at the end of the war,

---

2. The translation of *Schrifttum* (writing) as "literature" is no doubt inadequate. Hugo von Hofmannsthal was the first to point out in a speech made in 1927 that *Schrifttum* is the "nation's spiritual space". It is ironic, in fact, that Perec's short story "Le Voyage d'hiver" is quite reminiscent of Hugo von Hofmannsthal's rather less subtle "Marshal de Bassompierre".

Wolfgang Gauger considered that he knew enough about its staff to be able to conduct his research rapidly.

It must be remembered that the Bernhard List was drawn up first in Leipzig, then in Berlin, by the Reich's Department for the Promotion of German literature (Reichstelle zur Förderung des deutschen Schrifttums). This department had been set up in 1933 by Hans Hagemeyer, an Inspekteur in the League for the Defence of German Culture (Kampfbund für die deutsche Kultur), and by 1940 it numbered almost one hundred and thirty civil servants and more than four hundred voluntary readers. The "French" section alone employed forty civil servants and about one hundred and twenty readers. It came under the direct supervision of the head of the "central readership" of the Amt Schrifttum, Dr. Bernhard Payr, who no doubt gave his first name to the list. It was, by the way, thanks to him that in 1939 the Führer received Robert Brasillach's novel *Comme le temps passe* as a birthday present.

Finally, the Amt Schrifttum itself reported to the Rosenberg Office (Einsatzstab Reichsleiters Rosenberg), directed by Alfred Rosenberg, the Nazi theoretician. In each occupied country, the local branch of the Rosenberg Office had the task of providing the Berlin headquarters with books to be evaluated (and also, at the same time, these expert judges organised the systematic plundering of Jewish belongings, but that is another story).

Of course, there were not many people now left for Wolfgang Gauger to question. The active heads of the "Permanent Circle for Literature Questions" were no longer with us.

Alfred Rosenberg had been executed in 1946, after the Nüremberg trials.

Georg Ebert, who had run the Paris branch of the Rosenberg Office until 1941, had died peacefully in his bed several years before, as too had Hans Hagemeyer.

Karl Epting, from the German Embassy in Paris and director of the German Institute, was also dead, but not before Steingüben had published his *The Golden Years of France* in 1962. So was Arbeitsführer Walther Schultz, from the Propaganda-Abteilung, who had passed away in 1957 in the little Bavarian town where he had become deputy mayor.

As for Bernhard Payr, who would certainly have been one of the best sources, he had totally vanished after the fall of the Reich and had never been heard of since. He would now have been a hundred-and-one years old.

But Wolfgang Gauger had his notes, his documentation and hundreds of papers accumulated during his thesis years, which he still kept religiously in some cardboard boxes. Before rummaging through them, he set about looking for VERNIER Hugo in the indexes of the reference books in his possession.

He lay down on the floor and spread out Ernst Loewy's massive *Literatur unter dem Hakenkreuz*, both volumes of Pascal Fouché's *L'Édition française sous l'occupation* and Gérard Loiseaux's *La Littérature de la défaite et de la collaboration*. The name of Hugo Vernier was mentioned neither in their bibliographies nor in their indexes.

Absent-mindedly, he leafed through the Fouché until he came to page 290 with its copy of the Bernhard List.

Wolfgang Gauger could not believe his eyes. It contained only one hundred and forty-three titles; the one hundred and thirty-ninth was:

139. (*Unbekannt*): *Von Reichstagbrand zur Einfachung des Weltkriegsbrandes*, Hergest. unter der Redaktion v. G. Friedrich u. F. Lang. Éd. Prométhée, Paris.

Le Voyage d'hiver was not there.

Stupefied, Gauger grabbed the Loewy, then the Loiseaux, which also contained copies of the list in their appendices. The blood rushed to the young man's face; the two lists made no mention of *Le Voyage d'hiver* either.

He carefully examined the lists. The three copies were absolutely identical. When laid one above the other, in front of a bright light, the words fitted together precisely, creating the impression that they all came from the same printing press.

What is more, were it not for the presence of *Le Voyage d'hiver*, given the absence of any imprint, it looked as though the "Gauger" version had come from the same run — the typography, the body, the leading and even the justification were identical. However, on the fourth page, tiny differences were detectable. For example, on the "Gauger" list (this is how we shall refer to our hero's version henceforth), entry 132 contained a typing mistake: "*éditions*" was spelt "*édtions*", whereas the mistake had been corrected in the official version.

"Corrected"? Gauger was not so sure. If a correction had been made to the official list, then this meant that it must be later than his version; which may mean that *Le Voyage d'hiver* had been deliberately erased. Or, on the other hand, had this mistake crept into his own version when the official list had been reprinted? Hugo Vernier's book might then have been added. Why not, indeed? After all, the official version did include a typing mistake which was absent from the Gauger version: entry 142 had "*erreusr*" instead of "*erreurs*".

The photo credits of the Bernhard Lists in the reference books said only "private collection". Wolfgang Gauger immediately contacted both Parisian historians and, after a long trail of telephone numbers, finally learnt that one of them had procured his copy from an important publishing house which had kept it in its archives (and which did not want to be named), and the other from a former high-ranking police officer. Despite the lack of a date, it was now obvious that this was the list used during the confiscations.

Wolfgang now felt certain that "his" list was unique; that it predated the official versions and contained a mystery that he alone, perhaps, was in a position to unravel.

But, before proceeding any further, it is necessary to go back a few years and so become better acquainted with Wolfgang Gauger's family.

If it is acknowledged that all men are born free, then it is none the less true that chance is a rare commodity. So it was that Wolfgang Gauger's choice of subject for his thesis owed very little to himself. For Heinrich Niggemeyer, one of the heads of the Bernhard operation, was not only the commissioner in the secret military police (Geheime Feldpolizei — GFP) whose report was quoted above. He was also Wolfgang Gauger's great-uncle.

In 1940, young Dr. Heinrich Niggemeyer was a highly conscientious Nazi; one is extremely serious at the age of twenty-seven. Although joining the party late, he managed to enter the secret services at the beginning of hostilities, rather than the Wehrmacht or the S.S. His hope was to avoid active service. Because of his reputed abilities, he was appointed to supervise the searching of publishing houses. He knew about the world of books. Had he not, before the war, co-authored an authoritative translation of folk tales from the Moluccas?[3]

In Paris, the City of Light, Heinrich Niggemeyer spent two "blissful" years as assistant to Sonderführer Gerhard Heller in the Propaganda-Staffel and as a special member of the Gruppe Schrifttum. The women were beautiful, the nights long and money plentiful; it came from the pulping of books. Heinrich lived stylishly, dining with Drieu La Rochelle, Louis Thomas, Jacques Chardonne and so on. He appreciated French writers and liked their *savoir faire*, one of his favourite French expressions. All the same, he felt ill at ease after an evening spent with Céline, whose violent gut-reaction anti-Semitism revolted and even terrified him. Céline wanted blood, so much blood.

But Heinrich Niggemeyer was to have his share of blood soon enough. In June 1942, he was transferred to Warsaw. After the armistice, he claimed that his had been a mere office job, with responsibility for providing books for the troops at the front. However, in the east the Geheime Feldpolizei had been working with the Einsatzgruppen for two years with the aim of exterminating the Jews, and it is hardly credible that Dr. Niggemeyer did not take part in any "special missions" (*Sonderaufträge*). He was later denounced anonymously and, in 1950, brought to trial. During the hearing, which lasted less than a month, he claimed that he had always acted without "particular excess" (*besondere Ausschreitungen*). Fortunately for him, he lived in the American zone. The United States had just declared war against Korea and had other fish to fry. "Denazification" had turned into a tragic farce and, guilty or innocent, Heinrich Niggemeyer was acquitted for lack of "hard evidence". He immediately went back to his post as a lecturer in the department of Oriental Languages at Frankfurt University.

As far as Wolfgang Gauger had been concerned, the honourable Herr Doktor was an affectionate great-uncle and a gifted story-teller who knew hundreds of tales crammed to the brim with fairies and magic. Meanwhile, the old man, who had had no children of his own, became attached to this lad, with his finely-drawn features,

3. *Volkserzählungen von der Molukken-Inseln*. Ceram. gesammelt u. bearb. v. Ad. E. Jensen u. H. Niggemeyer. Frankfurt a. M. 1939.

studious expression and quiet ways. When Wolfgang had become a student and was hesitating about a subject for his thesis — he was considering studying French translations of Rainer Maria Rilke's poetry — he went to ask the retired professor's advice. Heinrich Niggemeyer lived an isolated existence in a chalet in the Black Forest with only a housekeeper for company. The conversation got round to the war and the part he had played in it. For once, the Doktor was not evasive. He spoke about the censorship, the repression, the expropriations, the killings. Then he gave his copy of the Bernhard List to Wolfgang, who was speechless at these revelations, and thus rather unwittingly decided his great-nephew's research subject.

This was in 1989. Wolfgang did not want to see his great-uncle again, who was to die of throat cancer a few months later, at the age of seventy-six. He granted life tenancy of his forest chalet, his "dacha", to his housekeeper Frau Jägers.

In the grip of an intuition, Wolfgang Gauger thought of the old woman and picked up the telephone. After ten rings, she finally answered. She was ill and expecting her grand-daughter, who was to bring round her dinner, but he nevertheless pressed her with questions. He quickly found out what he wanted to know. As he suspected, she had thrown or given away most of his great-uncle's possessions, but there was still a large, padlocked trunk in the attic which she had not dared break open. His imagination flared up. He rather impolitely told her that he would be there in half an hour's time, then hung up without waiting for an answer.

When Wolfgang reached the chalet, a young brunette in an orange anorak was waiting for him on the snow-covered steps. She was furious with him for disturbing her grandmother, and Wolfgang allowed the storm to blow over before trying to explain himself. Little by little, her green eyes softened. She knew almost nothing about French literature, but the story intrigued her. When she learnt that he meant to unravel the mysteries of this Doktor's murky past, curiosity finally got the better of her anger. And Klara Jägers — Wolfgang had managed to get her to reveal her first name — smiled as she let him into the house.

The attic was covered with grime. He wanted to take the trunk downstairs, but it weighed a ton. So, instead, Wolfgang broke open the lock under the yellowish gleam of the light bulb. The lid crashed down on to the floor in a whirlwind of dust. The trunk was full of books, files and notepads.

Wolfgang examined the books one by one. His hope of finding *Le Voyage d'hiver* soon proved to be in vain. The trunk contained a dozen books in Malay, several fifty-year-old Nazi propaganda manuals, which were not mentioned in the catalogue held on the ground floor of the library, and a few more recent ones, such as Gerhard Heller's *A German in Paris*, published in 1981. Klara absent-mindedly opened it. She browsed through it for a moment, then her expression became fixed. She handed it to Wolfgang.

Page three bore a signed dedication. The handwriting was fine, the wording friendly and the reference intriguing:

> *From Gerhard Heller,*
> *to his learned friend Heinrich Niggemeyer,*
> *in remembrance of a happier time*
> *and of the Hugo Gruppe.*

As though hypnotised, Wolfgang re-read the sentence several times. "Hugo Gruppe". When researching his thesis he had never come across the slightest allusion to such an organisation. Klara suggested that it might have something to do with Victor Hugo, but Wolfgang shook his head pensively. Nazi codes were almost always first names: Bernhard, Otto, Matthias; or else the heroes of Aryanism, such as Siegfried, Barbarossa and Walküre. Hugo could of course have been von Hofmannsthal, but naturally Wolfgang and Klara both secretly hoped that this Hugo was another.

Excited by their discovery, the two of them took the files and notepads down to the living-room in order to work more comfortably. Before long, they came across some yellowed papers in the file dated 1940 each of which was marked "Hugo Gr." in the top left-hand corner.

They were the minutes of meetings. Each set began with the number of the meeting and a list of those present. Wolfgang quite easily recognised certain names.

Those present at the HG3 meeting of 24/08/1940 were:

Gerhard Utikal, ERR (Utikal was the head of the Rosenberg Office in France),

Gerhard Heller, P-S. (i.e. representing the Propaganda-Staffel),

Bernhard Payr, Schr. (i.e. representing the Schrifttum),

Heinrich Niggemeyer, GFP-K (i.e. Geheime Feldpolizei Kommissar).

Then came the names of three subordinate officers, Karl Brethauer, Rudolf Ganshofer (we cannot reveal his real name) and Friedrich Heinemann, all from the GFP.

The same names could be found each time, even if Utikal and Payr sometimes sent a deputy.

Klara and Wolfgang had great difficulty deciphering Niggemeyer's handwriting, which was full of personal abbreviations. The poor quality of the paper and the fading ink added to their problems. Even worse, the notes were so patchy and disjointed that they were almost totally incomprehensible. But, whenever they found a legible sentence or clearly identifiable word, Klara noted it down in a school exercise-book.

Suddenly, Wolfgang caught his breath. In one margin, his great-uncle had written in a firm hand and in capital letters the name BORRADE. Borrade, Denis Borrade, whose library in Le Havre had once contained the copy of *Le Voyage d'hiver* which Vincent Degraël had discovered!

Wolfgang Gauger was triumphant. He had thus proved not only that this "Hugo Gruppe" did indeed refer to Hugo Vernier, but also that George Perec's text was not fictional. Klara, in a fit of almost childlike glee, affectionately squeezed his arm.

The "Hugo Gr." papers contained further confirmation. Hugo Vernier's name was mentioned three times between 1941 and 1942. The title *Le Voyage d'hiver* appeared, clearly written out, on 13 January 1941. During the meeting of 21/04/1942, there was even talk of a book entitled *Les Poésies d'Hugo Vernier*, which Gauger had never heard of.

Once the initial excitement had worn off, they came down to earth. They had no real lead to help them find that legendary book.

The real questions remained unanswered: why had the Propaganda-Staffel been so interested in *Le Voyage d'hiver* that they had set up this mysterious "Hugo Gruppe"? And why had this book been included in the Bernhard List, then removed at the last moment?

It was getting late. Klara and Wolfgang patiently went through Heinrich

Niggemeyer's address books in the hope of finding the names of the people mentioned in the minutes: Friedrich Heinemann, Karl Brethauer and Rudolf Ganshofer. They found nothing.

The day had clearly given up all the discoveries it had in store. Night was falling and Wolfgang invited Klara to dinner. With scarcely a blush, she accepted.

We must here leave a long pause for, despite all their research, the Vernier affair did not progress for two whole years. Wolfgang consulted Gerhard Heller's archives in Hamburg, then, in Berlin, that part of the GFP records which had been made available to researchers. In vain. On the internet, he launched a web-search for all the names of the protagonists of the story. The net was swarming with Nazi and revisionist sites but, to the question "Hugo Vernier", it came up with only one answer: "Le Voyage d'hiver" by Georges Perec.

Wolfgang and Klara had dinner together on several occasions, before deciding to link their destinies for a time. When the Vernier affair resurfaced, like a whale bursting up from the depths of the ocean to fill its lungs, Wolfgang had just obtained a teaching post in Hamburg and had set up home there with Klara, in a flat scarcely bigger than the one in Freiburg.

Klara had recently been taken on as an IT engineer at Lufthansa's head office. It should be pointed out that she was a specialist in "cognitive science" and was working for the airline on developing an "intelligent" co-ordination of its customer files. On 15 April 1997, during a validation test, she typed into the system a surname and forename that she thought she had made up. Memory plays tricks on all of us: the name Klara typed in was "Rudolf Ganshofer". Two years before, she and Wolfgang had vainly looked for this name (and all the others, too) in every available electronic directory. She smiled and launched the search anyway.

Her eyes widened. So far as Lufthansa was concerned, Rudolf Ganshofer did exist. The cells in the table listed all the flights he had taken over the last twenty years. An average of 5,000 km. per year, with a preference for Paris and Austria. Almost every year he had reserved his seat on the Hamburg-Salzburg flight on the morning of 19 April, with the return on the evening of the 21st, or sometimes the 22nd.

Now in Braunau, to the north of Salzburg, on 20 April 1889 (as Klara well knew) a baby had been born whose name was to become famous: Adolf Hitler. And, every 20 April, this small town has the largely unenvied privilege of welcoming, under close police protection, those people in Germany and Austria who remain nostalgic for the Third Reich.

Within a few minutes, Klara had collected all the information that her company had gathered regarding Rudolf Ganshofer. Since his sixtieth birthday on 10 May 1980, he had had a reduction on the tickets he always reserved two months in advance and had sent to him by registered post to his address on Bismarkstrasse in Mamstorf, a small town to the south-west of Hamburg. His telephone number was listed as well.

She informed Wolfgang at once. She had an idea. Better still, she had a plan.

On 19 April, at 9.30 a.m., a young woman on Lufthansa flight 5689 to Salzburg seemed deeply engrossed in a set of photographs in the centre pages of the rather dog-eared book she was reading.

"Miss?"

Klara raised her eyes with a smile. The old man in the window seat seemed extremely moved.

"I'm sorry to disturb you, Miss. But I noticed that you are reading Gerhard Heller's *A German in Paris.*"

Klara nodded her head charmingly. Rudolf Ganshofer — of course — hesitated, then went on:

"It is an… instructive book… one that many youngsters should read."

Klara gestured vaguely.

"Herr Heller was a close friend of my uncle."

She slipped a finger between the beautiful pages to reveal the inscription.

"My God… Heinrich Niggemeyer was your uncle?"

"Yes. He was a wonderful man."

She had rehearsed with Wolfgang thoroughly and learnt the words she should use. She added, in a whisper:

"The Americans caused him some problems after the defeat, because of those… Jews and communists. Did you know him?"

"Ah yes, I knew him…"

The old man sighed, then stared at Klara.

"That's right. I can see something of him in your eyes."

Klara smiled and closed the book. Then she suddenly became serious again and looked round with a conspiratorial expression on her face. She leant over to the old man and murmured:

"Are you… are you going… to where I think…"

Ganshofer looked worried. She purred, reassuringly:

"I'd like to go there one day myself, just to see. But there are so many policemen, and then there are all those stupid demonstrators outside, it makes me a bit scared…"

He shook his head in irritation and mumbled a few insults. Klara nodded silently and tapped a finger on Gerhard Heller's smiling face on the dust-jacket.

"Can I ask you a question, sir?"

"Ganshofer. Rudolf Ganshofer," her neighbour informed her affably. "Please do."

"It's about that inscription… I've asked my uncle's friends, the old members of the ERR."

"I can guess what you want to know. It's the 'Hugo Gruppe', isn't it? Would you like me to tell you about it?"

"Why? Do you know what it was?"

Ganshofer nodded his head proudly. He carefully removed his wallet from his jacket and, just opening it slightly so that nobody else could see, showed Klara a yellowed photograph. It showed Adolf Hitler surrounded by some friends, including an extremely young officer, who was just barely recognisable as the old man sitting next to her.

"It was taken in Berlin, in the bunker, in February 1945."

"Mein Gott, did you know the Führer?" Klara whispered with a distinct tone of admiration in her voice and, as though hypnotised, stared at him with her deep green eyes.

The trap sprang shut. Ganshofer started speaking. The cassette player had already been recording for several minutes.

As Jacques Roubaud points out in *Le Voyage d'hier*, his regrettably highly incomplete study of the Hugo Vernier affair, Denis Borrade found himself "on the sands of Dunkirk" in May 1940. The British and the French remained there for many days under the shelling and machine-gun fire of the Stukas. What none of them knew was that German spies, dressed in British and French uniforms, had infiltrated their ranks and were collecting all sorts of information.

Thus it was that Denis Borrade spoke to one of these agents about Hugo Vernier and *Le Voyage d'hiver* before embarking on a fishing boat. Almost immediately, the spy relayed this incredible story to his superiors.

No one should be astonished about the Nazi secret services' interest in such a purely literary matter. For many years, the Reich's theorists had been denouncing the "universal pretensions of French thought". "France," they said mockingly, "has been travelling first-class with a second-class ticket." If the Hugo Vernier affair were publicised, then it would kill off "French influence" for good and knock down that intelligentsia of "Jew-boys and Niggers" that was haughtily dismissing the new National Socialist civilisation.

German spies at once started looking for Vernier's book, but without success. All they knew about Borrade was his name, and they failed to track down his parents' house. As for the copy in the Bibliothèque Nationale, ref. Z87912, it had disappeared during the 1920s, just as Georges Perec says. On 20 August 1940, *Le Voyage d'hiver* was thus included in the first version of the Bernhard List, which was printed in Paris on 24 August under the supervision of the young commissioner Heinrich Niggemeyer.

But then Berlin sent a counter-order. It had occurred to the heads of Propaganda that, by attracting attention to this book, the result might be the opposite of the one they desired, and the book in question would be hidden rather than given up. The print run was pulped, apart from the single copy that, fortunately for history, Heinrich Niggemeyer decided to keep.

The "Hugo Gruppe" was set up shortly afterwards. Its mission was to find a copy of the book and to gather all possible information concerning its author. No fewer than thirty agents were mobilised. In Beauvais, one of them unearthed the note in the *Biographie des hommes remarquables de la France du Nord et de la Belgique* which has already been cited. Another found a solitary, undated school exercise-book belonging to a certain H. Vernier in the archives of the primary school in Vimy, the village where he was born. It was full of closely-written aphorisms and short poems, in what was already a mature hand, which meant nothing to the Schrifttum readers who examined it.

> *On ne tue pas le temps,*
> *Car c'est lui qui nous tue.*[4]

Or else:

> *On ne saurait rien de la vie*
> *Si Dieu n'avait avec génie*
> *Mis la naissance avant la mort.*[5]

But *Le Voyage d'hiver* remained elusive. Göbbels was furious, a sign that Hitler was even more so. In order to calm the Führer down, the idea of forging a copy was even mooted. But no one was possessed of sufficient literary skill to concoct a plausible *Voyage d'hiver*.

In early 1943, the "Hugo Gruppe" was broken up, its activities became dormant and some of its members were sent to the eastern front. The inevitable defeat at Stalingrad became a turning-point in the war.

On 29 July 1944 — as Jacques Roubaud rightly says — Borrade was captured in the Vercors, where he was taking part in a Resistance uprising. He was tortured then handed over to the Gestapo. But, contrary to what Jacques Roubaud claims, it is untrue that Borrade "remained heroically silent". In the cell where his torturers threw his pain-racked body, he revealed his name and stammered a few words about Le Havre and his parents. Louviers, the traitor mentioned in *Le Voyage d'hier*, was also present.

---

4. *We do not kill time, / It is time that kills us.*

5. *We would know nothing of life / If God had not, in his genius, / Placed birth before death.*

This information was immediately relayed to Berlin, where Borrade's forgotten file was taken out of the cabinet and the Nazi secret services, which were not yet completely disorganised, managed to set up the burglary of the villa in Le Havre.

On 7 August, the unique copy of *Le Voyage d'hiver* left for Berlin under close escort. Then, the Borrades' house was blown up. Perec was thus wrong to attribute its destruction to the Allies' bombing.

At the Schrifttum, five French literature specialists went through the work carefully. At once, like Vincent Degraël, they were astonished to find the "*cet interminable ennui de la plaine*" stolen by Verlaine, the "*l'hiver lucide, saison de l'art serein*" plagiarised by Mallarmé, and the "*l'orage te sacra suprême poésie*" that was plundered by Rimbaud.

Suddenly, one of them stopped at a passage which had a familiar ring to it:

> *L'homme! L'homme! L'homme!*
> *Voilà ce qu'il nous faut surmonter.*
> *Mais qu'avez-vous fait pour le surmonter?*[6]

The Schrifttum reader blanched. This passage, or at least a variant of it, was by Nietzsche from his *Thus Spake Zarathustra* of 1883. And what of this one? asked a second professor:

> *Elle était comme un fruit de miel et de ténèbres,*[7]

whose was this, if not Rilke's? Gripped by an almost holy dread, the readers flicked through the pages. One of them found some Wedekind, another some Stefan Georg, and yet another some Hugo von Hofmannsthal. Finally, one of them pointed a trembling finger at the following simple alexandrine:

6. *Mankind! Mankind! Mankind! / That is what we have to surmount. / But what have you done to surmount it?*
7. *She was like a fruit of honey and shadows.*

L'amour resplendissant, la mort pleine de joie.[8]

And, aghast, he muttered:

"*Siegfried...* by Richard Wagner."

Wagner... The terrorised Schrifttum readers closed *Le Voyage d'hiver*, never to open it again.

Over four months passed before the Führer demanded to see the book. The accompanying report prudently made no mention of the thefts committed by German poets, writers and artists.

The Führer had the book sent to him in his bunker, beneath the Chancellery in Berlin, which he now never left. It was Rudolf Ganshofer's task to deliver it. Hitler was drunk and at once attempted to read it aloud to his mistress, Eva Braun, in an appalling French accent and clearly without understanding a single word. Then he slumped down on to a couch and fell asleep.

As the weeks went by, the Führer became increasingly insane. One chill March night, he staggered out of the bunker, half-naked, holding a glass of sekt and chanting amidst the falling bombs to the tune of "Lili Marlene": "*Laisse expirer la chanson... mon cœur pleure;*"[9] which Hugo Vernier had written long before Gustave Kahn.

Finally, on 30 April, while the Führer was leafing feverishly through *Le Voyage d'hiver* for the thousandth time, two pages that had long ago become stuck together delicately drifted apart. On the left-hand side, an inscription appeared, written in sepia ink in Hugo Vernier's tormented hand. It read:

To my dearest mother, Sarah Judith Singer,
from her son, Hugo.

During the night of 30 April/1 May, Hitler committed suicide, along with the

8. *Resplendent love, death full of joy.*

9. *Let the song expire... my heart is weeping.*

other ten people present in the bunker. Soldiers from the Red Army discovered their charred bodies. Not a single Soviet report mentions Hugo Vernier's book.

The original Bernhard List (Gauger collection):

— 4 —

124. RHODES Fernand : *Lettre courtoise à Monsieur Hitler.* (Documents sur l'Allemagne). Paris : Ed. F. Sorlot.
125. ROUBAUD Louis : *La croisade gammée.* Paris : Ed. Denoël 1939.

126. SERRIGNY Général : *l'Allemagne face à la guerre totale.* Paris : Ed. B. Grasset.
127. SORBETS Gaston : *Le péril extérieur : Hitlérisme.* Coll. „Documents sur l'Allemagne." Paris : Ed. F. Sorlot.
128. SOWINSKY Commandant : *Journal d'un défenseur de Varsovie.* Paris : Ed. B. Grasset.
129. STOFFEL Grete : *La dictature du fascisme allemand.* Paris : Les Editions internationales.
130. STRASSER Otto : *Hitler et moi.* Paris : Ed. B. Grasset.
131. STRASSER Otto : *Saemtliche Werke.* (Toutes les œuvres.)

132. TURROU Léon G. : *Espions nazis aux Etats-Unis.* (Traduit de l'anglais par P. F. Caillé. Paris : Les éditions de France.

133. VALAYER Paul : *L'Allemagne fera-t-elle sombrer l'Europe?* Paris : Ed. Hachette 1935.
134. VERMEIL Edmond : *L'Hitlérisme.* Comité de vigilance des intellectuels antifascistes. Paris : 5, Place Jussieu.
135. VERMEIL Edmond : *Les doctrines du national-socialisme.* Paris : Ed. F. Sorlot.
136. VERMEIL Edmond : *Le racisme allemand.* Coll. „Les carnets d'Actualité". Paris : Ed. F. Sorlot.
137. VERMEIL Edmond : *Pangermanisme et Racisme. Le racisme allemand.* Coll. „Documents sur l'Allemagne". Paris : Ed. F. Sorlot.
138. VERMEIL Edmond : *Le racisme allemand. Essai de mise au point. Coup d'oeil d'ensemble sur l'histoire des idées racistes en Allemagne.* Coll. „Races et racisme". Paris : Ed. F. Sorlot.
139. VERNIER Hugo : *Le Voyage d'hiver.* Valenciennes : Ed. Hervé Frères. 1864.

140. (Unbekannt). : *Vom Reichstagsbrand zur Entfachung des Weltkriegsbrandes.* Hergest. unter der Redaktion v. G. Friedrich u. F. Lang. Paris : Ed. Prométhée 1939.
141. (Unbekannt) : *Warum Judenfrage? Rueckfall ins Mittelalter oder...* Paris : Ed. Prométhée 1939.

142. WEILL Georges : *Race et Nation.* Série : Erreurs et Vérités. Paris : Ed. Albin Michel.
143. WOODMAN Dorothy : *Au seuil de la guerre.* Paris : Ed. du Carrefour.
144. Saemtliche Veroeffentlichungen von „Notre Combat" (publication hebdomadaire). Paris : Ed. R. Denoël.

Das gesamte PROPAGANDAMATERIAL folgender VERLAGE :

Editions du Carrefour, Paris
Editions „La Lutte Socialiste" Paris
Editions Nouvelles Littéraires, Paris
Monr-Verlag, Zuerich, Paris
Verlag des 10. Mai Paris.
Verlag fuer soziale Literatur, Zuerich-Paris.
Editions Prométhée, Strasbourg-Paris

JACQUES JOUET

Hinterreise

Hinterreise

Translated by Ian Monk

Bibliothèque oulipienne 108

1999

● During the night of 21-23 January 1717, Ignazius Stoßfest, a printer in Weimar, finished publishing a considerable work which should have been hailed as a masterpiece.

The reader should not be put out by the apparent absurdity of the preceding phrase "during the night of 21-23 January". The explanation is that on 22 January the population of Weimar was fortunate enough to see a solar eclipse in perfect conditions which, so to speak, made the most of a sunny period that broke through the otherwise grey, rain-laden sky that hung over the town immediately after and before it. Hence the recollection of a night that lasted thirty-six hours.

So, Stoßfest the printer finished publishing a considerable work which should have been hailed as a masterpiece, if, that is… But everything in good time.

One evening in 1999 in Russia, Mikhaïl Gorliouk, a young teacher of French language and literature at the University of Kaliningrad, had just received a slim volume entitled *Le Voyage d'Hitler*, which had been sent to him by a Parisian poet whom he had met during a brief stay in France. Gorliouk eagerly read through its twenty-odd pages and had to admit that he would be able to make little sense of it without having also read "Le Voyage d'hiver" and *Le Voyage d'hier*, two texts which are explicitly referred to in *Le Voyage d'Hitler*.

Gorliouk informed his Parisian friend of his desire to read back to the source of this story and, a few days later, he was in possession of the entire "Vernierian corpus", as his writer friend put it with ironic grandiloquence.

Whilst reading through the first two texts, Gorliouk felt that the excitement he had experienced while reading the third one had now been fully confirmed. So why did they leave him with a feeling of incompleteness? He at once realised that he had been caught up in the net of the story and was thus joining a sort of intellectual community, which included Vernier, Borrade, Degraël, and also Gauger, Virginie Huet and Klara Jägers; he also realised that, come what may, he would never be able to forget Rudolf Ganshofer, the traitor Louviers, and certainly not the calamitous chancellor of the Third Reich who had perhaps dragged down with him the extraordinary book which had been the inspiration for those Gorliouk had just read.

At this time of the year, Mikhaïl Gorliouk was not exactly idle, but he had more or less completed his programme of work on "The Retreat from Moscow in the Novels of Balzac", and in particular the story "Adieu", one of the *Études Philosophiques*, in which he had spotted an anticipatory plagiary of Italo Calvino, a "countess perched" in the trees, who had lost her wits when crossing the Berezina, only to regain them again fleetingly, and fatally, during a therapeutic reconstitution of that terrible crossing in a private garden in the suburbs of Paris.

So, Gorliouk had a good deal of free time and decided to look into this Hugo Vernier who would surely provide him with a territory that was frequented far less often by his colleagues than Balzac.

But where to start? Hervé Le Tellier had shown that the original *Voyage d'hiver* (Vernier's, not Perec's) had been in the bunker during the twilight of the Nazis, so it was not entirely inconceivable that the Red Army had made off with it. In that case, if the official records made no mention of it, perhaps the book had survived somewhere as part of the wartime treasure of an army officer, whose children had now forgotten all about it.

Gorliouk imagined himself in possession of the book and causing a sensation in Paris, first in Perecian circles, then before a more general public.

With methodical persistence, he went round all the army veterans in the Kaliningrad region. Without success. Then, he ventured as far as Moscow where one lead pointed to another: "Go and see so-and-so... He'll send you to see what's-his-name..." Gorliouk's interviews became increasingly promising, until finally they produced something solid, as is shown in the following dialogue: "The bunker, the bunkers, there were bunkers everywhere! All the leading Nazis were buried in bunkers!" — "Yes, but the one in Berlin! *The* bunker!" — "There were several in Berlin" — "Yes, but Hitler's one!" — "Ah, you mean Hitler's one… Kramponov's the only man I know who went inside. Say I sent you. He's old, but still alive. What's more, oddly enough, he's of French extraction, I think, on his father's side at least. Anyway, he spoke French very well, and read it a lot, too."

It seemed to Mikhaïl Gorliouk that he was nearing his objective, and his heart was beating fit to burst when he rang on Commandant Kramponov's door, in a cold but well-kept building in the Moscow suburbs. Kramponov welcomed him in the full dress uniform of the Red Army, with all his decorations. He was very old and tired, but his memories of Berlin in 1945 remained crystal clear. Along with a few other officers, he had entered the bunker. Before going inside, he had seen the charred bodies in the courtyard of the Chancellery. He had held three books in his hands, no more no fewer, then had taken them out of the bunker with a heap of documents, military maps, dispatches, letters and so on. Before putting the whole lot in sealed files, he had had time to see that two of the three books were occult works in German, printed in Gothic letters, concerning a future life after death which would be perfectly glorious. The third, rather slim volume was an anthology of French poetry.

"An anthology?" asked Gorliouk, feeling rather deflated, until he remembered how Georges Perec had spoken of a "premonitory anthology" when referring to *Le Voyage d'hiver*. "An anthology? Are you sure?"

"So far as I remember," Kramponov replied. "When I was young, I read a lot of French literature, and in this book I recognised many famous quotations that I knew almost by heart."

"Did it say 'anthology' on the cover?"

"I wouldn't know."

"Was there an author's name?"

Kramponov hesitated.

"I honestly can't remember."

"Try."

"I can't recall very much about the cover… But, inside, I can clearly remember a poem… It was called 'Marche funèbre' and it had a two-line refrain that I shall never forget, because it seemed to stand as a perfect epitaph for my comrades who had fallen on the way to Berlin. I can still recall it today. It went:

> *Compagnons des mauvais jours*
> *Je vous souhaite une bonne nuit."*[1]

The old commandant recited these two lines over and over, then broke down in tears. Gorliouk supposed that he was not going to get anything more out of him, but then Kramponov produced a small, battered notepad, in which two other lines had been copied down from the work in question. They were:

> *et qu'à l'est*
> *les salue le jais noir de la toute-jeunesse*[2]

"Yes, that was my youth," Kramponov concluded, with his tear-stained face. "My youth, that came from the east."

Gorliouk tried to find out what had happened to the objects taken from the bunker in Berlin by the Red Army and placed in sealed files. Two months' research cost him, in bribes, one month's salary and did not produce the slightest serious lead.

So Gorliouk took his meagre plunder back to Kaliningrad. He thought about the two pairs of lines quoted by Kramponov. The first couplet came from a poem by Jacques Prévert, entitled "Le concert n'a pas été réussi" ("The Concert was no Success") from the collection *Paroles* (1946 for the book, but after checking he found that the song had been registered with the SACEM by Prévert and Kosma in 1939); then two lines by Georges Perec himself from *Épithalames* (1982). How very odd! The dates of the Perec and Prévert proved that the book which Commandant Kramponov had glimpsed could hardly have been an anthology of poems that had not yet been

---

1. *Comrades of evil days / I wish you good night.*

2. *And that in the east / the black jet of youth salutes them.*

written (in the case of Perec) or were not yet famous (in the case of Prévert). What it did seem to suggest was that both Perec and Prévert had once had the book in their possession, and had had no more qualms about borrowing from it than their illustrious predecessors. This evidently gave more credence to Vincent Degraël's testimony and also shed a fresh light on Georges Perec's own *Voyage d'hiver*!

Gorliouk's excitement dwindled before the huge obstacles that he would have to overcome if he really wanted to recover Vernier's book. He decided to let the matter rest there for a while and turn to other concerns, until another sign might lead him back into the heart of this strange pursuit.

As soon as he could, after acquitting himself of his unavoidable and rather dull university responsibilities, Gorliouk took the train to Berlin. He had long wanted to visit the historic cities of Thüringen, Eisenach, Leipzig, Weimar and so on.

In Weimar, he casually glanced at the programme of concerts and noticed a performance of lieder: Jorg Demus, piano, and Jürgen Retti, baritone, in a concert which included, by a happy coincidence, the *Winterreise* that Schubert had composed in 1827 based on poems by Wilhelm Müller, as Hervé Le Tellier rightly reminds us in his *Voyage d'Hitler*. Gorliouk reserved a seat, fully determined to resume his investigations, if the opportunity arose. The awaited sign came at once, in the first lied. The concert programme gave the title: "Gute Nacht". Good night… just as in the Prévert poem and in the anticipatory plagiary in the book that Commandant Kramponov had seen. In the Schubert, the narrator-singer abandons his fiancée, because love adores "*das Wandern*" (how to translate? wandering, departure, flight…). He tells her "*Gute Nacht*". He writes to her "*Gute Nacht*". It is a final farewell.

It occurred to Gorliouk that he had discovered a lead which he had never dreamt of, obsessed as he had been by the rather fanciful idea of finding the book. The Schubert angle had been neglected, in particular by Wolfgang Gauger. It should now be explored. Why had Hugo Vernier called his book *Le Voyage d'hiver*? Did he know Schubert's work? The presence of that "*bonne nuit*" might give some credence to the hypothesis. And didn't the fact that Vernier's mother had been called Singer, apart from revealing his Jewishness, point more towards an exploration of the world of song, rather than of sewing-machines? Mikhaïl Gorliouk moved heaven and earth to get back-stage in order to quiz the baritone and congratulate him heartily. Retti was tired and happy to lap up this praise, then invited Gorliouk to dinner the following evening.

Jürgen Retti told Gorliouk that Schubert's works would certainly have been listened to in mid-nineteenth-century France in the musically advanced circles around César Franck, Duparc and Fauré.

But when, in the hope of resolving the mystery of the missing link between Schubert and Vernier, Gorliouk asked the singer what the Schubertian "*Gute Nacht*" reminded him of, Retti immediately replied:

"What that '*Gute Nacht*' reminds me of? Papageno's, of course!"

Gorliouk, who had had in mind Jacques Prévert, or at least someone in the future, felt a touch put out about having to retreat into the past.

"Papageno?" he repeated.

"Of course. In Act II, scene 29 of Mozart's *Zauberflöte*, Papageno's courage totally deserts him and he decides to commit suicide. Quite simply, if, at the count of three, nobody comes to rescue him, then he will hang himself. The tone of this passage is farcical. But when he has counted '*ein, zwei, drei*' and nothing has happened, the music abandons its farcical tone and becomes more serious. Papageno then sings:

> *Nun, wohlan, es bleibt dabei!*
> *Weil mich nichts zurücke hält;*
> *Gute Nacht, du falsche Welt!*"[3]

The baritone then effortlessly intoned Papageno's aria. It was sublime. He added:

"This moment in *Die Zauberflöte* is difficult to pull off because the music (even though it does not become frankly tragic) underlines the *opera seria* sincerity of the *opera buffa* character that is Papageno who is, in fact, on the verge of an initiatory death... and yet at the same time there is a hint of parody! What approach to adopt? Well, never mind, let's move on to other matters, for I have more to tell you," said Jürgen Retti. "Mozart knew Johann Sebastian Bach well. Now, in Cantata BWV 82,

---

3. *So, since that's the way it is, / As nothing now holds me back, / Good night, false world!*

Ich habe genug, which is a sort of '*nunc dimittis*' (it does not mean 'I've had enough', but 'I am fulfilled'), old Simeon, who has held the baby Jesus in his arms, says that he can now die happy. In the recitative, he sings:

> *Der Abschied ist gemacht. Welt, gute Nacht.*[4]

Once again this bidding of a 'good night', which is also a litotes, a casual way of saying farewell to those who remain behind, whereas logically it should really be the world, which continues on its course, that says good night to those who are leaving it for unknown darkness. This is, in fact, how it is used in the other Schubertian and Müllerian occurrence of '*Gute Nacht*', in the final lied of *Schöne Müllerin*, where it is the stream that bids good night to the dead miller."

Mikhaïl Gorliouk had rediscovered the thrill of the chase. He noted down on the paper tablecloth all the information that the singer had given him and then, in passing, he asked another question:

"And Schubert's *Winterreise* was written in 1827, wasn't it?"

"Exactly."

"And the *Ich habe genug* cantata?"

"1727," said Retti with a smile.

Gorliouk went pale.

"The Lutheran office of Sunday 2 February 1727. *Haben Sie genug?*" Retti asked, while paying the bill.

"Plenty, for the moment."

"Listen, I'll tell you a story about the Bach family. It was told to me by Georges Kolebka, a highly witty French writer. The Bach family, which is extremely large, is about to have dinner. The children are playing outside. So papa Bach booms out in a voice that carries to the end of the garden: 'Carl, Philipp, Emanuel, come here all three of you!' Ha! Ha! Ha!"

Gorliouk was so dazed that he left his dinner partner to laugh at his joke alone. He

---

4. *I take my leave. World, good night.*

was on the track once more. He decided to go back to Berlin and undertake a thorough search of the libraries there. He read all that was humanly possible to read about Schubert, about Mozart, about Johann Sebastian Bach. Biographies. Monographs. He examined Bach's sacred and secular works. He went through the cantatas. His mind was assailed on all sides by questions. Did the three "*Gute Nachts*" indicated by Jürgen Retti have musical points in common? He regretted not having asked him. He telephoned him, but without success. The baritone was on tour. He applied elsewhere.

"No," Michel Puig replied.

"No," David Pendrous agreed.

So it was Schikaneder and Wilhelm Müller alone that had plagiarised Bach's anonymous librettist! But who had Bach's anonymous librettist recycled to make this "*Gute Nacht*" into a commonplace in German poetry? Was the presence of that "*bonne nuit*" in Vernier to be explained only by Schubert? Was Vernier a German scholar? Jacques Roubaud did mention that he referred to Quirinus Kuhlmann. And so on, and so forth.

Suddenly, in the collections of period correspondence, which he was rather desperately ploughing through, Gorliouk happened upon a carefully preserved dog-eared manuscript note, dated 12 February 1723, and addressed to Bach, who was then at the court of Köthen, and signed by a certain Ignazius Stoßfest. In the middle of this brief note, Gorliouk thought he recognised the name Vernier, then wondered if he had not in fact read "Wernier". Gorliouk's magnifying glass was powerful and effective. The note simply read:

Ich erinnere mich an U. Wernier.[5]

This scrap of paper had the look of an anonymous letter, the smell and the style of an anonymous letter. It resembled an anonymous letter in every way, but it was not anonymous. It sounded like a threat. The note was not included in selections of

5. *I remember U. Wernier.*

correspondence addressed to Bach. It had apparently never been noticed before, or commented on.

Gorliouk then looked into this Stoßfest, a printer in Weimar, whose catalogue of publications proved easy to find. Among them figured a work by a certain Ugo Wernier, entitled *Hinterreise, weltliche Kantate* ("The Backward", or "Reverse Journey, secular cantatas"), Weimar Municipal Archives, Bd CVII, 2843. Gorliouk screamed out a triple cry of victory in the library, even though he did not exactly know what he had gained. Fifty disapproving faces turned to stare at his broad grin. He stammered out an apology, before rushing to Weimar, filling out a form to order the book from the reserves and receiving a large binding ("Very poor state of conservation" said the slip). It contained only one page with a list of contents and a scrap of the preface. The rest of the volume had obviously been pulled apart and sold off, page by page. The list of contents mentioned a series of secular cantatas dealing with spring, vineyards, the vintner's journey (*Winzerreise!*), the farmyard, the miller's wife, a stream, yesterday, winter, drunkenness, the bird-catcher, departing on a journey, different sorts of suicide and childhood. Then came a preface which, according to the contents, was six pages long. Most of it was missing.

Gorliouk carefully copied out the page, numbered 3, which had miraculously survived. It read:

must indeed consider composing music using the letters that stand for the notes in German. For example, a musician could with great advantage write a fugue on the notes corresponding to the letters of his name, if with good fortune they fall between A and H; and if the motif could turn back on itself, that would give an even better formal meaning to such a self-centred piece. Consider leaving aside subjects drawn from Greek or Latin mythology for the plots of secular operas and instead write on contemporary subjects. Do not forget the dramatisation of silence. Consider dealing with German mythology, for example the Niebelungenlied. And do not forget the poetic flyting of Wartburg. In a love song, treat the "du" and "und" as a dialogue. Why not repeat motifs that would guide the listener through an opera? Motifs that corresponded to a feeling, a sentiment, etc. In a song, repeat four times over the name of the colour blue, for example: "Azure, azure, azure, azure" in order to indicate that one can be haunted by it. Consider using

in a series the twelve tones of the chromatic scale. Consider sitting down to work on the
programme that now has been decided upon for the years to come. This first work is ca

An amazed Gorliouk saw the work of Bach, the subject of the *Querelle des Bouffons*,
Beethoven, many of Wagner's inventions, and much more besides stream past his eyes
in a virtual flood.

Gorliouk photographed the book, and checked the age of the ink and paper. He
took out another book dating from the same period to see if their states of
conservation were similar.

All of this was fine, and extremely interesting, but why had the printer Stoßfest felt
the need to write to Bach, six years after the publication of Ugo Wernier's book, to
remind him in such a threatening way that *"Ich erinnere mich an U. Wernier"*?

The answer lay in a libellous diatribe against Johann Sebastian Bach, which
Gorliouk had not bothered to read because all the serious biographers were
unanimous in qualifying it as being an absolutely unfounded piece of malicious
slander. Now that he had accepted the idea that Bach had been the subject of some
controversy it suddenly came back to his mind. In this short pamphlet, which this time
is indeed anonymous, called *Bach's ABC* (*Abc von dem Bach*, Leipzig, 1724) Gorliouk
found the following passage:

May the greatest glory on earth and in heaven be reserved for the great fury of the Cantor,
which made him so generous that he acquired all of the copies of the Hinterreise, *to make bricks*
of paper from them and so light his earthenware stove and heat himself and his large family
during the greater part of the winter of 1717 in Weimar. Has no one wondered why the Cantor
murmured "If I were Catholic, I should confess," when the publisher of the Hinterreise, *who*
was then on his death bed, reminded him of this terrible memory? And was it at this moment
that he decided to leave the urbane paradise of the court of Köthen (with its music-loving patron,
and great musicians) for the ascetic atmosphere of Leipzig, through a desire for self-humiliation,
in shame at having destroyed the Hinterreise, *which he has continued to pillage ever since to*
the delight of Leipzig?

Gorliouk came down to earth with a crash. It seemed to him that, if all this were true, then Bach had not been so daring as his reputation suggested. Unless, that is, his feelings of penitence had prevented him from overly exploiting that mine of ideas and propositions, which he had been in the best position to understand at the time.

He wondered if Stoßfest had not finally republished the *Hinterreise* and then proceeded like Virginie Borrade, *née* Huet, to send copies to Bach's colleagues, who had also despoiled them before burning them. There could now be no doubt that the Hugo Vernier of Hervé Frères had known this whole story. It was clear that Hugo Vernier, like Wagner and Schoenberg, must have come across a surviving copy of the book. It was clear that he must have decided to imitate his near namesake's approach. Hugo Vernier had understood his anticipatory destiny when he had learnt of this pioneer's adventures!

Gorliouk was greatly struck by the situation which Jacques Roubaud had described as follows: a young, frail author, and a poet sure of his gifts, wonders how to break new ground. He answers, in the light of history, by not being in the avant-garde, but in the present, conceived as the point of arrival of a backwards journey, a reverse journey, a *Hinterreise*, a *Voyage d'hier*, or a *Voyage à rebours* (as Gorliouk now decided to translate the title, with reference to Huysmans), realising that if one really wanted to go back to Vernier, it would then be necessary to go back a further one hundred and fifty years to find Wernier.

Who knows if the "Hugo Gruppe", which Hervé Le Tellier mentions, did not have a previous manifestation in search of a copy of the *Hinterreise*, which was already considered to be a dangerous attack on the originality of great established names, and then, in 1940, began looking for *Le Voyage d'hiver*?

Gorliouk had asked for the assistance of many researchers during this return to the source. Just when he was putting the finishing touches to the lecture he was going to give in San Francisco during a symposium organised by the Alliance Française on "The Day Before Yesterday's Day After Tomorrow: Motifs of Borrowings", he received a note from a young lady archivist in Leipzig, who had been rather taken by the subject of the research and by the researcher himself. She had found a long letter written by Stoßfest concerning this affair. From the end of 1716 to the beginning of

1717, Stoßfest had employed a young apprentice typesetter, who was in fact a promising musician known under the pseudonym of Hugo Wernier. The previous year in Chemnitz he had paid from his own purse for the performance, under his real name, of a cantata called *Winterreise*, which had shocked the public. When he arrived in Weimar, after failing an interview in Lübeck with the inevitable Buxtehude, he decided to publish a larger collection of his work, under the same title. This is why he found himself a job in Ignazius Stoßfest's printing works. When he was setting the title, which was initially to be:

HUGO WERNIER, *WINTERREISE*

the printer's devil realised that there was only one capital W in the font he had selected. He said to himself that he simply could not fall back on the mysterious:

HUGO .ERNIER, *WINTERREISE*

and it was then that, turning adversity to his advantage, he had a stroke of genius and composed the title as it has come down to us:

UGO WERNIER, *HINTERREISE*

Stoßfest tells how his apprentice was extremely agitated. He completed publication of his work then, soon after, returned to his family in the east, where terrible accusations of the ritual murder of Christian children were making life dangerous for Jewish families. He was never heard of again. He came from Poland and his name was Peretz.

IAN MONK

Hoover's Journey

Le Voyage d'Hoover

Translated by Ian Monk

Bibliothèque oulipienne 110

1999

● At the break of dawn on 10 June 1946, J. Edgar Hoover, the head of the FBI, left the club where he had just attended an all-night orgy with a few close friends and assorted party animals. Back home, he was in too much of a hurry to take a shower, so he slipped a white shirt and grey suit over his corset, silk stockings and suspender belt. He then went down to the car park and told his driver to take him to the airport. As soon as he was comfortably ensconced in a seat in his private plane, he tried to sleep. But the state of excitement caused by the top-secret mission he was about to undertake, plus the charms of the steward's seductively rounded physique, kept him awake during the long crossing of the Atlantic until his arrival in West Berlin.

On another 10 June, fifty-three years later, John Scale awoke as usual at around nine o'clock, made himself some tea and looked through his mail. The articles he had been expecting for the last few days on the cyclical composition of French medieval epics had still not arrived, presumably because of another postal strike in France. Feeling irritated, he got his breakfast ready and wondered how he was going to spend the rest of the day. As he had little else to do, he decided to go to a book sale organised by his university.

The sale took place in a small room in the Students' Union. He arrived and started to browse through the rows of books. Most of them did not interest him in the slightest. This sort of sale was an opportunity for teachers and students to rid themselves of books they no longer wanted. He glanced absent-mindedly at the old, dusty editions of classics and outdated critical works, then happened upon a set of four slim volumes, going as a job lot at a bargain price of £5.50: *Le Voyage d'hiver* by

Georges Perec, *Le Voyage d'hier* by Jacques Roubaud, *Le Voyage d'Hitler* by Hervé Le Tellier and *Hinterreise* by Jacques Jouet. None of the authors' names meant anything to him, not even Georges Perec, for this young French lecturer at London University was interested only in twelfth-century works. From what he could remember from school, French literature came vaguely to a halt in about 1950 with Sartre and Camus. He looked through his find and discovered that these four authors belonged to the Oulipo. He suddenly remembered an article that he had read in *The Times* a few weeks before, which had explained that the Oulipo had been a group of crazy writers and mathematicians during the 1960s, and that it was largely speaking their fault if French literature was now the laughing-stock of the world. This harsh judgement excited his curiosity and, looking forward to a pleasantly inane read, he paid up and left.

Back in his armchair, he read straight through the four brief texts and found them rather amusing. It seemed to him that, if these were typical Oulipian products, then the group was simply a bunch of harmless jokers and the journalist on *The Times* had been a tad severe. He put them away in one of his bookcases and that is where the matter would have rested if, the next day, he had not received a letter from his aunt, Agnes Scale, asking him to come and see her as soon as possible. He took the first available train.

She welcomed him on the threshold of her detached house in London's leafy suburb of Purley. After making some tea, she explained the reason for her letter: she had just discovered a large trunk belonging to her recently-deceased husband, Peter, who had thus also been John's uncle. In his youth, Peter Scale had worked as an assistant to Michael Ventris. It is a well-known fact that this brilliant archaeologist and linguist managed to decipher, with the help of John Chadwick, one of the ancient Cretan scripts, known as Linear B, after he had realised that its syllabic structure in fact concealed an early version of Classical Greek. So much for his public career. What is less well known is his work on ENIGMA. With the help of other experts, he deciphered the Germans' communication code. A notable example of this success was that the Allies knew that the Nazis were not expecting them on D-Day, or on the beaches where they had decided to begin the landings. Michael Ventris died in a car accident in 1956. Even though John was neither a Greek scholar nor a code-breaker, his aunt thought that he might be interested in the papers she had found in the trunk. After all, he was now the only member of the family who was keen on "that kind of thing" (by this, she meant foreign languages). John was of course delighted to be able to learn more about his uncle and, with his aunt's agreement, he took the trunk home.

The following weekend, John Scale devoted most of his free time to examining its contents. First of all, he found several drafts of failed attempts to decipher Linear B before the final breakthrough. He then read through the notes his uncle had taken while working on ENIGMA. Finally, at the bottom of the trunk, he came across a batch of papers that dealt with a different subject. He flicked through several pages of apparently meaningless jottings, until the following entry stopped him dead in his tracks:

9 May 1945
Have collected the Hugo Gruppe's three gems. Await further instructions.

His hands trembled. He had naturally supposed that the Hugo Gruppe, which Hervé Le Tellier mentions in his text, was as imaginary as the rest of this "Vernierian corpus". But he now seemed to have proof that the group had really existed. And if the Hugo Gruppe was real, then these four texts were no longer simply the mind games of a Parisian literary clique, but a genuine exploration through the dark labyrinths of history and of the imagination.

He made some tea, smoked three roll-ups, pulled himself together and started to examine the little batch of papers systematically. He knew that his uncle had participated in the decipherment of ENIGMA, but why was there a message (presumably deciphered, too) among his papers dated one day after the Armistice, given that this code had not been used again after 8 May? A close study of the notes raised more questions than it answered. All that seemed sure was that they dealt once again with the breaking of a code, but not of ENIGMA. There were several pages of incomprehensible figures, interspersed with messages that were for the most part just as baffling.

That night, he was unable to sleep and so read and re-read the texts again and again until he knew them by heart. Then, he re-examined his uncle's papers. As dawn broke, he decided to go back and quiz his aunt. In an advanced state of nervous excitement, he took the early morning train.

Back in his aunt's living-room, he stammered out a series of confused questions about Peter Scale's activities immediately before and after the Armistice.

"Sorry, but your uncle never spoke to me very much about that part of his work," said Agnes. "He used to say the less I knew the better. But I do remember that, just before the end of the war, he started learning Russian. He told me that he was now going to work for the Americans and that I shouldn't tell a soul about it. But, he's dead now, isn't he, so what difference does it make? Since the ENIGMA project had been such a success, the Americans wanted him to help them break the Soviet communication code. It was called VENONA, if my memory serves me right."

"And I suppose that the name Hugo Vernier doesn't ring any bells?"

"Who was he? A politician? A general?"

"No, a nineteenth-century French poet," John answered, suddenly feeling rather foolish.

Agnes thought for a moment then smiled:

"In that case, I might be able to help you. One of your uncle's jobs was to follow the traces of works of art. At that time, there was an incredible number of paintings, sculptures, antique furnishings and old books that were circulating either under the counter, or else openly among high-ranking members of the Nazi party. Then, after the end of the war, Peter went on doing the same sort of thing, but this time watching what the Russians were up to. In the USSR, there was a flourishing black market and also a number of semi-official bodies looking out for works of art that had been stolen by the Nazis. If Peter mentions a poet in his notes, then it's probably because he was after some valuable first edition. He was much more open about that part of his job. For one thing, I've always been more interested in art than in politics. And then I suppose he thought that this sort of intelligence data was not particularly dangerous. For example, I remember him telling me that the Soviets were intending to make use of certain works to prove that 'bourgeois art' was corrupt. I suppose they must have got hold of some saucy books, if you see what I mean."

"I'm sorry, but I'm not expressing myself very clearly. He doesn't mention a book in his notes, but an organisation called the Hugo Gruppe. Does that name mean anything to you?"

"No, I'm afraid it doesn't."

They shared another pot of tea, then John politely refused her invitation to lunch and returned home.

On the train, he tried to assemble the pieces of the jigsaw. If Hervé Le Tellier was right in saying that *Le Voyage d'hiver* was not mentioned in any Soviet report, this did not prove that the Red Army had not recovered it from Hitler's bunker. What is more, according to Gorliouk in Jacques Jouet's contribution, Commandant Kramponov claimed that he had removed the anticipatory anthology himself from the bunker, along with some other papers and books. One hypothesis that could explain the presence of this mysterious message in his uncle's papers was that the Russians were aware of the activities of the Hugo Gruppe, of the Rosenberg Office and of the black market. They had accordingly decided to lay their hands on Hugo Vernier's work as well as two others. But which? Surely not the two books of occult gobbledygook mentioned by Kramponov. These would scarcely have been described as "gems". The next day, an officer would have sent a short message telling his superiors that the mission had been successful, then this message had been immediately destroyed to prevent its falling into the hands of a double agent working on the black market. Another possible reason for such precautions was the importance of the discovery. *Le Voyage d'hiver* would indeed have been an excellent way for Stalin to prove that "bourgeois art" was corrupt, just as the *Hinterreise* could have been used in the same way for European music — assuming that it had been one of the other two "gems". But fortunately for us, the Americans had intercepted the message before it was destroyed. Thus, thanks to his uncle's work on VENONA, the only proof that Hugo Vernier's work had survived lay among the papers in the trunk and not in the Red Army's official reports. The only proof? Perhaps not. There had to be other traces in the archives of the FBI or of the OSS. The problem was now simple: how could he gain access to these archives?

Like any self-respecting young researcher, John Scale was a regular internet-user.

He decided to start out by trying a web-search. But he soon realised that, unless he became a brilliant hacker, this approach was not going to take him very far. The archives he wanted to examine had not been made available to researchers. So, one evening, he too tried all the names of the various people mentioned as protagonists in the story, and discovered that Dennis Borrade still lived in the United States, where he now occupied a post as emeritus professor at Princeton University. His hands trembled as he emailed him a message telling him of his discoveries. An answer came back at once. Borrade was delighted to hear of this new lead and invited Scale to come and see him in Princeton as soon as he had a moment to spare.

He flew to New York the next Friday. When he arrived in the large house where Borrade and his wife lived, he felt so overwhelmed that he had to swallow a couple of shots of bourbon before he was able to get his tongue round his questions. The two men took refuge in Dennis's study. Borrade told him at once that he had not made much progress since receiving his message. He, too, had unsuccessfully tried to consult the archives of the FBI and OSS, and was now convinced that the only place where they would find any additional information about the decoded messages dealing with the activities of the Hugo Gruppe and of its Soviet equivalent was in the personal records of J. Edgar Hoover, the head of the FBI at the time.

"Why so?" John asked.

"Because he was the only person to practise cultural imperialism to the extent of being interested in such matters. But I don't think even he would have been particularly bothered about a book which proved that the great nineteenth-century French poets were plagiarists. There must have been something else."

"Maybe the *Hinterreise* was one of the batch, despite what Kramponov said. Was Hoover a music-lover?"

Borrade grinned. "Yes, but not of the classical sort. No, I reckon that the answer to the puzzle lies in one of the other books mentioned in the message."

"So how are we going to gain access to his archives?"

"I might have an idea."

The next day they drove to Washington in Borrade's car. When they had arrived, instead of heading for the Library of Congress, or a government department, Borrade took Scale to a small, seedy bar.

"Here's where we're going to start," he said.

"But I thought we were going to try and examine Hoover's archives!"

"That's exactly what we are going to do. When I said 'personal records', I didn't mean bundles of papers, but living archives. Hoover's toy-boys, who are now old and neglected. This was one of his regular dives. And there are plenty more."

From bar to bar, and from nightclub to nightclub, they followed Hoover's distant steps, listening out for a sign from Hugo Vernier. Borrade was extremely generous with his dollars and they heard numerous fascinating stories, which unfortunately lie outside the scope of this account. At last, after the umpteenth tale of debauchery and flagellation, they encountered a decayed but elegantly made-up old man who smiled at their questions and said:

"Allow me to introduce myself: the name's Dolly Haze. Though I once had a different name. Now, what was it?… I haven't the slightest idea… But as regards your character, there, I remember him like it was yesterday. I was just a kid at the time and I'd met Johnny, as we used to call him round here, only a few days before. Now, that evening, he was really going some. He'd come back from Berlin all puffed up and got the whole gang round to Arthur's place. But you wouldn't know Arthur, would you? Too bad. Anyway, they'd gotten together one of their extravaganzas with drag-queen *cancan* dancers, only *sans culottes*, guys dressed up like Groucho Marx, but in *liederhosen* [*sic*], and blacks done up in Elizabethan costumes, you know, with tights, codpieces, the whole works. And one of the guys told me that this had been organised to celebrate a discovery Johnny had made during his trip to Berlin. During the party, there was a poetry reading. It was the only time they included a number like that in one of their shows. It was really something. I couldn't quote you metre and verse, but I do remember that it was like old poems talking about a big black guy who was buggering the poet and his pal. Or something along those lines anyway."

"But," said Borrade, who was trembling slightly, "why does the name Hugo Vernier bring all of this back to you?"

"That's not what you asked me. You said 'Hugo Group'. And that's just how Johnny introduced the show: *Ladies and gentlemen, I give you the Hugo Group.*"

"Can you tell us anything more about that evening? Who else was there?"

"Well, there were loads of us Johnny groupies, and then there was the guy who did the reading. He was called Moses, I think."

Borrade thanked him with a few extra dollars, then the two researchers returned to Princeton.

As they drove back, Borrade said to Scale:

"Now we're going to have to find this Moses. He's our only chance."

Perhaps, but how to proceed? Scale soon had to go back to England and was thus unable to contribute to their research. As for Borrade, he persisted in his nocturnal wanderings. But nothing solid came of them. If a few regulars of Washington's nightlife did vaguely remember someone who went by the name of Moses, nobody had seen him in years.

As is so often the case, it was just at the moment when they had more or less decided to drop the entire business that Scale received an email message headed "Moses", requesting his presence that evening in a Soho pub.

He arrived early, ordered a pint of London Pride and peered round at the rest of the clientele with increasing curiosity. At the precise time that had been indicated, an old man sat down in front of him and introduced himself: around fifty years ago he had used the assumed name "Moses", but had dropped it several years later and, no, he was not going to reveal his true identity.

"How did you know I was looking for you?"

"You and your American pal have been stirring such shit with your questions that my old friends are starting to get scared. Most of them don't want their links with Hoover to be made public. I didn't either, in fact. But now I couldn't give a damn any more. That's why I came looking for you. This way, the two of you are going to be able to give my friends a break. Now, listen good. The story I'm going to tell you is highly instructive and I don't like having to repeat myself."

Scale took a swig from his beer and nodded.

Being both a spy and a transvestite, Moses had been a member of Hoover's inner circle. He spoke English, French, German, Russian and Hebrew. As we now know, thanks to the deciphering of the ENIGMA code the Americans and the British were extremely well informed concerning the Germans' activities. Among other things, they kept an eye on the operations of the Rosenberg Office, which was confiscating Jewish property, and of the mysterious Hugo Gruppe. Then, as soon as the defeat of the Nazis had become certain, they started spying on the Russians. Many people thought, and Hoover more than most, that the war would go on immediately after the surrender of Germany, and that it would be between the United States and her western allies on one side, and the USSR and eastern Europe on the other. This explains why the FBI and OSS knew about the discovery of certain books in Hitler's bunker: *Le Voyage d'hiver*, which, it must be admitted, did not particularly interest them; a book of German esotericism, which did not interest them in the slightest; and a third volume, which Hoover was willing to move heaven and earth to get hold of. For Kramponov's memory was faulty. Only one of the other two books was printed in Gothic script, the other was in Hebrew. The fact that a Jewish book had been found in Hitler's bunker was already sufficiently odd to whip up the curiosity of a man like Hoover. What is more, once they had compared its title with the reports issued by the Hugo Gruppe, they knew what it was about.

It goes without saying that there were precious few Hebrew scholars still working in Germany at the time, but the Nazis had managed to unearth one: an old Catholic monk, known as Brother Hans, who lived in a monastery near Heidelberg. This monk wrote readers' reports on the Jewish books which the Rosenberg Office and the Hugo Gruppe sent to him, and sometimes even provided translations. For Hervé Le Tellier is mistaken when he claims that this organisation was "broken up in early 1943". Having initially failed to find *Le Voyage d'hiver*, some of its members were indeed sent to the eastern front, while others set out to find other literary gems. They discovered at least two. The one that concerns us here was an extremely old, bound manuscript, dated 1444, which had been stolen by members of the Hugo Gruppe from an ancient Jewish family living in Belgium, where it had emigrated from Spain during the Inquisition. According to Brother Hans, this manuscript was entitled: *The Winter's Tale, an epic story in prose and verse*, and signed by two initials: *Waw He* (or W.H.). The first scene took place on a desert island, where a sorcerer called Prozepero lived with his daughter Mathilda. He cast a spell to raise a tempest, thus causing a ship to blow on to the coast of the island. Among the survivors of the wreck were a prince and his servant, who both had, unbeknown to themselves, a twin brother. The reader will no doubt have already recognised the beginnings of *The Tempest* and of *The Comedy of Errors* which certain experts consider to be respectively the last and the first of Shakespeare's plays. Then, as in a *roman à tiroirs*, nearly all of Shakespeare's plays were recounted until the final scene when Prozepero "drowns his book". The history plays did not obey this rule, for obvious chronological reasons, but the work did include a version of the life of King John, and most of the others had been replaced by tales dealing with similar historical events. But the resemblance did not stop at the plots. Even in the monk's summary, which was obviously written in German, a large number of Shakespearian quotations emerged, including the immortal "To be or not to be". It also contained numerous extracts from the history plays, placed as we have seen in other contexts. For example, this line from a tale of the siege of Jerusalem in 1099: *Once more unto the gate, dear friends*, which was also (or nearly) spoken by Henry V in front of Harfleur, in the play that had so inspired the British during their resistance against Hitler. Even worse, the story that later became *Othello* was preceded by another tale which told of a homosexual *ménage à trois* featuring an aristocrat, a poet and a Moorish soldier, who was experiencing a moment of sexual indecision before finally falling passionately in love with a princess. This tale was told in sonnets and clearly formed the basis of Shakespeare's sonnet sequence. The English poet had simply changed the Moorish soldier into a "dark lady", altered the progression of the sequence as a result, and suppressed a large number of poems of an extremely erotic nature that would have appalled his readers (what Dolly Haze remembered was a reading of a translation of these poems that had been hastily drafted for Hoover's show). There was of course nothing very new about the idea that Shakespeare had been a plagiarist, but nobody had imagined that he had taken things quite so far. For it was now clear that Shakespeare had not copied Cinthio, Lodge, Kyd, etc., but that everybody had pillaged W.H., this mysterious figure who had succeeded in assembling a varied selection of stories drawn from ancient sources, such as Plautus and Saxo Grammaticus, as well as his own original tales and poetry. What is more, everybody had always considered the sonnets to be pure Shakespeare, whereas they were now relegated to being mere adaptations. Thomas Thorpe, the first printer of these poems, was obviously in on this literary theft and had placed a clue in the dedication of the 1609 quarto: *To the onlie begetter of these insuing sonnets Mr. W.H.* If this W.H. had never been satisfactorily identified, it is because scholars had taken him to be the subject of the poems and not the original author. At first, Hitler had hoped to make use of this manuscript as anti-British propaganda, but the fact that the true genius behind Shakespeare had not only been a Jew, but had also celebrated unnatural intercourse with a black, put it definitely beyond the pale. He nevertheless found it horribly fascinating and kept the manuscript with him in the bunker, along with the notes drafted by Brother Hans.

There were several reasons why Hoover wanted to get his hands on this book so badly. Firstly, he distrusted the British and was also considering using it as a threat: if the British refused to follow America's lead, then he would reveal that their national poet had been nothing but a vulgar thief. Secondly, he did not want the Russians to be able to use it to demonstrate that "bourgeois art" was corrupt. According to his sources, Stalin had already ordered some academics to prepare critical editions of *The Winter's Tale*, of *Le Voyage d'hiver* and also of certain other discoveries. Thirdly, he could hardly resist such a homosexually explicit masterpiece. He put his best spies on the case and, a year later, had a better result than he had hoped for. A university professor, called Slonim, who had been given the job of preparing the critical edition of *The Winter's Tale*, wanted to defect to the West and, for several thousand dollars and a new identity, he was willing to make off with *The Winter's Tale*, *Le Voyage d'hiver*, plus a third book called *Hinterreise*, which seemed to show that famous composers were just as dishonest as famous poets. The latter did not come from the papers found in Hitler's bunker, but directly from a Soviet source. Hoover took out the necessary sum from the federal reserve and flew to Berlin in order to take personal reception of the books. Once back in Washington, he organised the party which Dolly Haze remembered so well.

"And where are these books now?"

"God knows. It sounds incredible, but we all drank so much that night, that everyone fell asleep on the spot. The next day, the books had vanished. Hoover put his best agents on the case, but they were never heard of again."

"And did you keep your translation? Do you remember anything about *Le Voyage d'hiver*?"

"I still have the notes I took. I'll give you them if you want. As for Hugo Vernier's collection, I only had it to myself for a few minutes. Obviously, I recognised the quotations from Baudelaire, from Mallarmé and so many others. But I was also struck by two others: '*Au vert remué où tendent tes bas rouges*', and '*Le féticheur se signe / non sans verser quelques gouttes d'eau-de-vie*',[1] maybe because of the red stockings I was wearing that evening and because we definitely did overdo the hooch."

"There's still something I don't understand. Was the Hugo Gruppe's third 'gem' in fact the *Hinterreise*, even though it was not in Hitler's bunker?"

"No, it wasn't. As I've already told you, it came directly from a Soviet source. Though I never knew exactly who from. Literature was my speciality, not music. According to the messages we intercepted, the Hugo Gruppe's third literary gem was also in the bunker and came from Göbbels's personal papers. But Hoover didn't manage to get his hands on it."

"What was its title?"

"*Homer's Vision.*"

Scale shuddered, but preferred not to think about the possible implications of this revelation. Instead, he asked his last question:

"So, why are you telling me all of this now?"

"As I told you, I used to be scared. But now I'm old, I've been HIV positive for years and I know my time is definitely nearly up."

I.M. I met John Scale during my last trip to London, and he entrusted me with a photocopy of the notes and translations given to him by his mysterious informer. They

1. To the shifting green, where your red stockings lead; The fetishist signs himself / not forgetting to pour a few drops of hooch.

These two quotations seem to come from Jacques Roubaud ∈ 2.1.2 (GO 73) and from Jacques Jouet (*Le Chantier*, "Zou") respectively, except that in the second case, the "*eau-de-vie*" has become "Johnnie Walker". Do these two poets know more than they are letting on, or are they subject to post-anticipatory plagiarism?

will shortly appear in a critical edition. Meanwhile, I append the basic structure of *The Winter's Tale*, as it appears in Moses's notes:

Story of a shipwreck (*The Tempest* — beginning)
Story of lost twin brothers (*The Comedy of Errors*)
Story of a postponed marriage (*Love's Labour's Lost*)
Story of a man who courts his best friend's fiancée (*The Two Gentlemen of Verona*)
Story of a weak king dominated by his barons (similar to *Henry VI*)
Story of a powerful, evil king who dominates his barons (similar to *Richard III*)
Story of a king held prisoner (similar to *Richard II*)
Story of two lovers from rival families (*Romeo and Juliet*)
Story of a man transformed into an ass (*A Midsummer Night's Dream*)
Story of King John
Story of a Spanish grandee disguised as a bandit (*Hernani?*)
Story of a pawnbroker (*The Merchant of Venice*)
Story of an independent woman who finally marries (*The Taming of the Shrew*)
Story of a civil war in Spain (similar to *Henry IV*)
Story of the First Crusade (similar to *Henry V*)
Story of a fool who courts two women at the same time (*The Merry Wives of Windsor*)
Story of a cynic who falls in love (*Much Ado About Nothing*)
Story of Julius Caesar
Story of Tamburlaine
Story of an exiled duke (*As You Like It*)
Story of a shipwrecked woman disguised as a page (*Twelfth Night*)
Story of an unhappily married woman (*All's Well that Ends Well*)
Story of Troilus and Cressida
Story of a prince who hesitantly revenges his father (*Hamlet*)
Story of a duke disguised as a monk (*Measure for Measure*)
Story of a homosexual *ménage à trois* (*The Sonnets*)
Story of a jealous Moorish soldier (*Othello*)

Story of a king who divides his kingdom in three (*King Lear*)
Story of a baron who kills his king (*Macbeth*)
Story of Antony and Cleopatra
Story of Coriolanus
Story of a rich man who loses everything (*Timon of Athens*)
Story of a princess who marries against her parents' will (*Cymbeline*)
Story of a jealous king who loses his wife and daughter (*The Winter's Tale*)
Story of two shipwreck survivors vainly waiting on an island where one tree grows
(?)
Story of a sorcerer duke who gets his revenge (*The Tempest* — end)

Does this list definitively solve the problem of the chronological order in which Shakespeare's plays were written?

It is interesting to note the absence of *Titus Andronicus* and of *Pericles*, but the inclusion of what is apparently *Hernani* (by Victor Hugo), *Tamburlaine* (by Christopher Marlowe), as well as a story that strangely resembles *Waiting for Godot*, which was written six years after the drawing-up of this list.

JACQUES BENS

Arvers's Journey

Le Voyage d'Arvers

Translated by Ian Monk

Bibliothèque oulipienne 112

1999

for Jacques Beaumatin, great connoisseur of Arvers

0

● In the 1990s, a retired French teacher who was called Apollon and not Martin Dumoulin, lived in the Ventoux. He was passionately interested in antiquarian books, be they rare or simple curiosities. By doing the rounds of jumble sales and auctions he constantly made new acquisitions, with which he lined the walls of his large, old, beautiful house.

He was also rather keen on imitations, pastiches and parodies of Félix Arvers's famous "Sonnet",[1] and not just the numerous satirical examples produced during the second third of the nineteenth century, but all those that mischievous spirits have delighted in concocting over the last hundred and sixty years.

One day in July 1997, this hobby led him to make a rather momentous discovery which provided an unexpected answer to one of French literature's most famous enigmas.

This is what occurred, as it was recounted to me several days later.

I

While still teaching at the Collège Raspail in Carpentras, Apollon Dumoulin had befriended a father of one of his pupils, who had inherited a comfortable fortune from a line of Côte-du-Rhône wine merchants. Donatien Bourrassol lived in a beautiful

---

1. For the benefit of readers unfamiliar with this celebrated sonnet, the original together with a crib translation have been reproduced in an appendix at the end of this episode. [Trans. note]

eighteenth-century manor-house, pompously called Le Château de l'Hirondelle, which his great-grandfather had purchased towards the end of the reign of Louis XVI from an aristocrat ruined by an immoderate taste for womanising and gambling.

Bourrassol was another lover of antiquarian books and luxurious bindings, and so he appreciated Dumoulin's learning and conversation and often invited him to stay as a house-guest on Saturdays and Sundays. While sharing a pre-prandial drink, either under the plane trees on fine days, or else in the music-room during the rest of the year, they would compare their recent acquisitions and discuss their importance and rarity.

Dumoulin naturally had full access to his friend's library. That afternoon, which must have been Sunday 6 July, the day when we used to celebrate Saint Alphonse until the Vatican's absurd reform in 1963, he had gone there at around five o'clock in the afternoon.

This spacious room had two pairs of French windows which led out to a balcony overlooking the vineyards and truffle fields. All of the walls, with the exception of the doors, windows and fireplace, were covered with books which were clearly consulted with great care, for not one of them stood out of line.

In the middle of the room, four armchairs stood around a rectangular table, covered with an antique tapestry. On a small occasional table, between the two French windows, a few purple roses were wilting in a smoked-crystal Art Deco vase.

Dumoulin slowly paced round the shelves. He acknowledged the common stock of classical works that are inevitable parts of any civilised man's collection, with a pronounced preference for historical studies in this case. His attention was then drawn by a separate set of shelving (above the fireplace) consecrated to poetry. Why did his eye suddenly fall on that slim volume, squeezed in between Austin (Alfred) and Aveline (Claude)? Was it the faded green of the binding? The uneven line of gilt letters printed on its spine? Whatever the reason, he took it out absent-mindedly and started to peruse it.

It was a manuscript made up of twelve quarter-quires of slightly mottled laid paper, whose format was 11.5 by 17 (octavo foolscap), which had been roughly sewn together then clumsily bound into an ill-fitting cover. The text consisted of about sixty poems, carefully written out in black ink. The author's name was Hugues Auvernier, its title was *Estampes de Vaucluse*, its sub-title *Vers provençaux et français*, its place of publication Vacqueyras and the date 1827. Dumoulin started flicking through it.

On the first pages he read:

> *Dis un mas que s'escound au mitan di poumié.*[2]

Then:

> *Sus lis estello à soun declin*
> *Entre li petelin*
> *L'aubeto auro...*[3]

And then:

> *Cante uno chato de provènço...*[4]

Dumoulin started. He drew an armchair over to the French windows and made himself comfortable.

The poems in French formed the second part of the volume. As the house-guest turned the pages he chanced on:

> *J'écris sous un mur de forêt*
> *où le merle chante son lai doucement...*[5]

But also:

2. *I speak of a house hidden among apple trees.*

3. *Under the stars as they go down / Amid the terebinths / The dawn breeze...*

4. *I sing of a young girl of Provence...*

5. *I write under a forest wall / where the blackbird sweetly sings its lai.*

> *On n'a pas supporté la table blanche, dehors,*
> *quand le soleil est venu la frapper.*[6]

And also:

> *Tu t'es penchée à mon oreille, tu as juste glissé quelques mots amers, et tu es*
> *partie.*[7]

And then:

> *Cœur à l'instant saoul,*
> *reclus à trône inutile...*[8]

And finally:

> *Ma cave a son secret, mon cellier son mystère...*

This time, he fretfully read the poem through to the end:

> *Ma cave a son secret, mon cellier son mystère:*
> *Le code de mes crus, spécialement conçu.*
> *Chaque vin a sa clé, qu'il me convient de taire.*
> *Aucun de mes amis n'en a jamais rien su.*
>
> *Mes plus glorieux nectars passent inaperçus.*
> *Quand je leur fais honneur, dévot et solitaire,*
> *Débouchant les flacons qui dorment sous la terre,*
> *Je bénis Dionysos de les avoir reçus.*

6. *We could not bear the white table, outside, / when the sun began to strike it.*

7. *You leant to my ear, you simply whispered a few bitter words, and you were gone.*

8. *Heart at the instant of drunkenness / recluse with a useless throne.*

Parfois, un commensal, d'une voix douce et tendre,
M'implore de l'admettre en bas et, sans attendre,
Chez les chauves-souris il m'emboîte le pas.

Privé d'indications, devant faire fi d'elles,
Il se dira, goûtant près des battements d'ailes:
"Quel est ce millésime?" et ne trouvera pas.[9]

His heart full of strange presages, the retired French teacher began to feel decidedly perplexed.

II

A few minutes later, Apollon Dumoulin went to the vegetable patch, where his friend was picking runner beans for that evening's dinner. He showed him his find.

"Do you know this book?"

"I did browse it once, but I have never read it all the way through. The poems seem rather second-rate, don't you think? What is more, my Provençal is rather rusty."

"But it also contains poems written in French!"

"Does it?"

"Here, take a look at this, then tell me what you think."

Dumoulin handed him the book, open at the page containing the vinous sonnet.

---

9. *My cellar has its secret, my larder its mystery: / The code to my vintages especially conceived. / Each wine has its key, which I prudently keep concealed. / None of my friends is any the wiser.*

My most glorious nectars go unnoticed. / When, devout and alone, I pay them tribute, / Uncorking bottles that sleep beneath the earth, / I bless Dionysus for having accepted them.

Sometimes, a dinner guest, in a sweet and tender tone, / Begs me to be allowed below and, without waiting, / Dogs me down to the bats' domain.

With no indications, having to manage alone, / He will say to himself, while tasting amid beating wings: / "What is this vintage?" and will not find it.

Donatien put his basket down, wiped his hands on his cotton trousers and took the volume. One minute later, he gave a short whistle of surprise:

"Well," said he, "you seem to have made quite a discovery!"

"Perhaps."

"One second. Help me finish picking the beans. I'll take them to the kitchen, then we shall go and discuss this curious tome over a glass of Beaune muscat."

And so they did. Glass in hand, Apollon began:

"Who was this Auvernier? Have you ever heard of him? I mean, anywhere else than on the title-page of this manuscript?"

"Vaguely. I'll tell you everything I know. After that, we shall try to fathom out, or else guess, everything that we do not know."

"Good idea."

After a second shot of muscat, this is what our two friends came up with.

Some precious pieces of biographical information about Hugues Auvernier can be found in Jorgi Peiresc's indispensable *Portraits familiers des Écrivains du Comtat* (Aubanel, Avignon, 1863). This work is today extremely rare. The Inguimbertine Library in Carpentras has one copy, in a poor state of preservation, which it is chary about letting anybody consult.

According to Jorgi Peiresc, Hugues Auvernier was born on 2 February 1798, that is to say on Candlemas, in Font-Bonne, a hamlet near Vacqueyras. He was the third child (and only son) of an important family of landowners, who lived mostly off their vineyards, but also thanks to lavender, goats and olives. While remaining quite interested in viticulture, Hugues fell under the charm of the Muses and, from the age of fifteen, began singing the praises of grapes, cicadas, honey and the youngest of his neighbours' daughters in rather limp but touching verse. At the age of twenty, he sent several more finely crafted compositions, such as odes, elegies, complaints and pastoral poems, to the Montélimar *Moniteur*. His vocation was later to inspire at least one other member of his family, since, through his sister Delphine, he was the uncle of the poet Anselme Mathieu, known as "Le Marquis", who in May 1854 became one of the seven founder members of the Félibrige, a society for the promotion of Provençal literature.

In 1816, his father died of a brain haemorrhage. Since his two sisters had married respectively a merchant and a magistrate, he decided to take over the vineyard despite his young age. Then, during the months when the Earth slept, he frequented the Comtat's intellectual community where he succeeded in making a small reputation for himself. He died in 1827, at the age of twenty-nine, from what was called at the time "acute ague". His mother followed him a few years later. Since his two brothers-in-law were already firmly established in Orange and in Vaison-la-Romaine, and did not want to keep up the family home, the property was sold and its contents auctioned off.

None of the young poet's work was ever published during his lifetime but, as he freely gave out manuscript copies of his poems to whomever he considered might be capable of appreciating them, researchers and bibliophiles may still come across rare copies of his work in public sales and auctions.

"Very well," said Apollon Dumoulin, handing the Peiresc back to its owner. "But what of the relationship between Auvernier and your house?"

"We shall have to examine another source for that," Donatien replied. "One of my great-great-grandfathers on my mother's side, Victorin du Grès, kept a sort of visitors' book from 1817 until his death in 1854, which was common practice in wealthy houses at the time. It consists of five notebooks which have been carefully handed down in the family over the last five generations. In them, my ancestor, who was clearly a bit of a snob, made a note of all the more or less illustrious visitors that graced his manor with their presence. I should not be at all surprised if Auvernier appears there, and probably on several occasions, between say 1820 and 1827. I'll go through them this evening."

"Isn't that visitors' book providential!" Dumoulin remarked. "Especially since it may turn out that you will also find a trace in it of the famous imitator of this vintage sonnet, in about 1830 I should think."

"That is, in any case, what I shall endeavour to find out, my friend. I'll telephone you tomorrow morning to tell you."

"I'll await your call on tenterhooks."

A third drop of muscat helped to calm their emotions.

III

The next day, at about ten o'clock, Dumoulin's telephone rang.

"Good morning," a familiar voice said. "I've found what you were after. If you intend to stay in this morning, I'll be round in an hour's time."

"I'll be here, and waiting expectantly."

Fifty minutes later, Donatien rang the bell on the garden gate. Apollon went to let him in. They admired the fine olive tree, whose flowers were beginning to give way to tiny green pearls, then the oleander and the pomegranate tree. After that, they got down to serious business.

"This contains several answers to your questions. I have photocopied the most important pages. But you can consult the whole lot if you wish."

"Of course I do!"

Bourrassol gave his friend three notebooks bound in black boards. They each contained about one hundred pages, covered with a spidery, rather elegant handwriting.

"In the first two volumes, which cover the years 1823 to 1827 (each notebook generally covers two to three years), you will find the information concerning Auvernier. There is even a portrait of him, painted when he was about twenty-five, I imagine. The third, which is dated 1829, mentions Arvers. It is all rather odd, as you shall see. In broad terms, this is what happened…"

Victorin du Grès described the poet as being a tall, slim, young gentleman, who was shy and retiring, with a rather pale complexion and who blushed easily when questioned too directly. He sometimes gave his poems to his hosts, but refused to read them out loud himself or to have them recited in his presence. People found the poetry rather dull, but the poet so likable that he was a frequent guest. Women felt an almost maternal affection for him, which in no way made their husbands or suitors jealous. The sonnet about wine intrigued its readers so much that they tried to uncover its hidden meaning. They, of course, found several for even the most ordinary poem gives ample ground for such a pastime.

So it was that they amused themselves by making the cellar stand for a harem, and the bottles of wine for odalisques. Anybody who has indulged in such an exercise knows that, since language is such a rich domain, the most unexpected meanings can be mined from the most innocent texts. In the case of Auvernier's sonnet, the "each wine has its key" was reminiscent of a notorious medieval belt, "go unnoticed" of veils concealing hidden charms, "Dionysus" of Silenus, Priapus and the Satyrs, the "dinner guest" of any companion in debauchery, the "bats" of furies, demons, succubi and vampires, while the "beating" smacked of the sort of activity no civilised person could even think about.

The first time this interpretation was mentioned in Auvernier's presence, he almost fainted with embarrassment, all the more so because the distaff side of the group seemed particularly excited by this cunning and suggestive idea.

("Re-read it with that in mind," Donatien remarked, "and you'll be in for a surprise…")

However, this joke was rather a cruel one, for everybody knew that the poet had never experienced, or at least never shared, real passion. Since he was quite good-looking, the ladies suspected him of having some physical imperfection — which, as we all know, never greatly endears us to the fairer sex.

Hugues Auvernier's untimely death saddened his friends. His pleasantly discreet company was long missed. Some people, feeling rather paranoid before the term had been coined (forgive me for being pedantic, but the word was first used in French only in 1838), even felt guilty for having occasionally made fun of him. So they placed his little collection of manuscript poems among the precious books in the library, then forgot all about it.

IV

At first sight, Félix Arvers was quite the opposite of his Venaissin colleague: self-satisfied, confident and better looking, as all young men are when certain of their looks.

According to the ancient visitors' book, he was a guest at L'Hirondelle during the second week of October 1829. He had arrived in the region ten days beforehand with the idea of carrying out a sort of pilgrimage to the Fontaine-de-Vaucluse, in the steps of the great Petrarch. He had frequented some of Carpentras's finer minds, thanks to a Parisian friend who came originally from Monteux, and so this regular visitor to Paris's Bibliothèque de l'Arsenal was received at the Inguimbertine Library with caramels, nougat and tears of emotion. Then, as one thing generally leads to another, he had been introduced to the masters of the Château on the Mazan road, who had begged him to accept their hospitality.

He initiated this small society into some of the current practices of the Nodier literary circle, which allowed the inhabitants of Carpentras to feel less distant from the culture of the capital. But life meant more to him than socialising.

At the hour when the southerners were having their siesta, he explored the library, noting down rare or curious titles, copying out strange or evocative passages, and saying to himself that he was going to whet the appetites of his friends on Rue de Sully — and perhaps, since no one is perfect, planning to feed their anti-provincial prejudices.

"It is easy to imagine," Donatien Bourrassol went on, "how one day he stumbled upon Auvernier's collection and how much it marked him. Perhaps autumn rain was beating against the window-panes, which often makes young men with fiery imaginations melancholy. What is certainly true is that, on the morning of his departure, he gave the manuscript of an unpublished sonnet discreetly to my great-great-grandfather, who at once stuck it in his visitors' book. Look, here it is. It has been lying here undisturbed for the last hundred and sixty years, and few people other than us can have noticed it."

"Very good," Apollon remarked. "So much for the form, but what of the heart of the matter? What inspired Félix Arvers to this idea which has drawn tears from seven or eight generations of unrequited lovers? The rain and his romantic melancholy are inadequate explanations."

Donatien smiled:

"You're right, of course. And, if I have no real explanation, I do have an excellent hypothesis."

Upon which, he continued his presentation.

V

The family's youngest daughter, who had been baptised Stella (presumably out of some naïve romantic snobbery), had become partially paralysed several years before and had lost the use of her legs. The Comtat's most prestigious doctors had been incapable of explaining the cause of this disability, which rarely affects the young, and even more so of finding a cure. She thus spent her days in a wheelchair or in bed, but remained in quite good spirits since those around her, and those who visited her, did their utmost to distract her from her illness.

In accordance with the curious habits of the time, a nun belonging to the Sisters of Charity, who specialised in caring for the sick and bedridden, had been put at her disposal. This woman was aged about thirty, with bright, serious, fine features and a body whose vigorous nature was not entirely concealed by her grey robes. According to some gossip in the visitors' book, Félix Arvers had not been indifferent to the charms of Sister Fidèle de la Résurrection, even though he can scarcely have exchanged three words with her during his brief stay. It even seems that this attraction had been observed by those present, who had made a number of ambiguous and not always entirely innocent jokes about it (particularly the ladies).

VI

"And so this unexpected discovery has finally put paid to…"

"… the notion that the sonnet was dedicated to Marie Nodier…"

"… an idea that has, in fact, come in for a deal of criticism over the last few decades…"

"… from the finest experts."

"Take, for example, the opinion of Dr O'Followell, who wrote the splendid biography of Félix Arvers…"

"… published in Largentière (Ardèche) in 1947…"

"… and also a good twenty works as varied as *Local Anaesthesia Using Guaiacol and Gayacil*, Ollier, 1897…"

"… *Hygiene for Clerks and Tradesmen*, Munier, 1901…"

"… *Dressing New-Born Babies*, Le Lien Médical, 1926…"

"… *The Corset, Volume 1*, Maloine, 1905…"

"… *The Corset, Volume 2*, Maloine, 1910…"

"… and the superb *Bicycles and Genitalia* (3 figs.), Baillère, 1900…"

"… which gave this unstinting researcher a particular authority when it came to Marie Nodier…"

"… who wore corsets…"

"… had several children…"

"… but did not go cycling."

"In any case, we have no need of this worthy doctor to prove that there was no connection between Marie Nodier, who in the meantime had become Mme Jules Mennessier…"

"… as they used to say…"

"… for how could anyone imagine that a reference to that young nineteen-year-old wife…"

"… plainly in love with her sottish husband…"

"… could be found in the twelfth line of Félix's poem…"

" '*Piously faithful to austere duty*' ?"

"Many ladies…"

"… famous ones, at that…"

"… still considered conjugal obligations to be an 'austere duty'…"

"… but they did not generally brag about the fact to other people…"

"… and their husbands were offended by the slightest reference to this point in public."

"As for 'piously'…"

"Indeed. But it should not be forgotten that a prominent personage has commanded us to…"

" 'Go forth and multiply', I know…"

"… but let us proceed."

"There is still…"

"… last but not least! …"

"… the final hemistich!"

"That's correct, you write an impassioned sonnet to a lady…"

"… you write it down yourself in her copy-book…"

"… then you claim that she '*will not understand*'? Won't understand what?"

"That the sonnet was written especially for her, of course!"

"Absurd!"

"So, exit Marie Nodier."

"It is said that Adèle Hugo…"

"… presumably to annoy Sainte-Beuve…"

"… publicly claimed to be this famous sonnet's unknown woman…"

"… and pointed out that '*the first two rhymes in the final tercet…*"

"… *have the same assonance as her first name; only the initial letter is missing*'."

"But in Victorin du Grès's hypothesis nothing is missing!"

"And, with the advent of our nun, the word 'piously' can now be explained!"

"Which puts an end to the entire controversy."

A little out of breath, our two delighted friends stared at each other in wonderment then smiled.

Despite the sciatica in his leg, Apollon Dumoulin went down to the cellar to fetch a bottle of Châteauneuf-du-Pape, cuvée Anselme Mathieu, 1990: Hugues Auvernier's nephew fully deserved such fine homage.

VII

Wiping his chops with a broad sweep of his wrist, Apollon then observed:

"My friend, I think we will be done with this wonderful tale once we have quoted a remark made by Jacques Jouet about a certain Gorliouk, and which concerns Huysmans. Strangely enough, Jouet, who is generally extremely thorough in his undertakings, rather ignores one point which, it seems to me, deserves more ample treatment. I mean the striking similarity between that writer's *À rebours* and *Arvers*, which someone like Lacan would have turned into an entire series of seminars."

Donatien looked pensive.

"Do you really think we will be done?" he murmured. "I'm not so sure. There is no end to mysteries such as this one."

Then, as though giving himself the courage to wait, he took another full-throated swig of the "Marquis" vintage.

00

I was putting the finishing touches to my presentation of this astounding discovery, destined for a learned society of which I have long been a member, when my friend Dumoulin sent me a letter that he had just received from Donatien Bourrassol. Since it refers in a striking way to the preceding matter, I shall herewith reproduce it in full.

Dear Friend,

Since you are interested in the Venaissin origins of Arvers's "Sonnet", I simply have to communicate to you a marvellous piece of new evidence.

We missed something in Hugues Auvernier's collection. I seem to remember that your expert eye had noticed its ill-fitting binding. How right you were! For a thin sheet of parchment had been slipped in between the hide covering the inside back cover and the board. I shall not keep you waiting any longer, this is what it contains:

> *Quel est donc ce secret? quel est donc ce mystère?*
> *Un sonnet à écrire après l'avoir conçu?*
> *Moi qui fus si longtemps entraînée à me taire,*
> *Comment l'aurais-je fait? comment l'aurais-je su?*
>
> *Je suis une violette, un être inaperçu,*

Une pauvre esseulée et un cœur solitaire.
Je n'ai rien fait de bon, inutile sur terre,
Je n'aurai rien donné, je n'aurai rien reçu.

Ah! s'il était au monde une personne tendre
Qui pourrait une fois, rien qu'une fois, m'entendre!
M'est refusé l'ami vers qui porter mes pas!

C'est pourquoi j'aime tant, rassurante et fidèle,
Ma bêtise banale, épaisse et sûre d'elle.
Dieu m'a voulue ainsi: je ne le comprends pas.[10]

And who, do you think, penned this sonnet?

Sister Fidèle, of course! That, at least, was the view of Victorin du Grès, who was familiar with the nun's handwriting, and who pencilled in this attribution at the bottom of the page. What is more, is it not in fact signed at the end of the twelfth line?

Some of the expressions it contains do, of course, read strangely, such as "I have done nothing good" and "There is no friend for me to approach". But this can be put down to over-religious modesty.

Finally, is not the hiding-place chosen by the author an admission of the truth?

Yes, it can now be affirmed that, if Sister Fidèle inspired Arvers, it was our unfortunate Auvernier that had won her heart.

It all rather makes you think, doesn't it? Who can know what occurred in the unfortunate,

---

10. *So what is this secret? so what is this mystery? / A sonnet to be written after having been conceived? / I who was so long taught to be silent, / How was I to do it? How was I to know how?*

I am a violet, an unnoticed being, / A poor lonely woman and a solitary heart. / I have done nothing good, am useless on this Earth, / I shall have given nothing, I shall have received nothing.

Oh! if there were one tender person in the world / Who could once, just once, hear me! / There is no friend for me to approach!

That is why I so adore, reassuring and faithful, / My base stupidity, dense and sure of itself. / God wanted me this way: I cannot understand it.

and perhaps passionate, soul of a Sister of Charity in 1829?

You can be certain that Marie's hubby had no reason to worry. (Pity, really, don't you think? What a swine I am!)

Yours,

Donatien Bourrassol

All very well. But there is more to this than meets the eye. For this unexpected find raises a question which, to my mind, Donatien has answered rather too superficially, and which other scholars may solve in years to come. For nothing proves that Félix knew of Fidèle's sonnet. Of course it must predate his own one. (Hugues was two years dead when Arvers put in an appearance at the Château de l'Hirondelle. It is hardly likely that the love-stricken nun waited so long before slipping this pledge of her affection into the binding of his collection of poems; on the contrary, she must surely have done so while he was still alive, secretly hoping that he would discover it.) But the fact that something is possible does not prove that it actually happened, except in the firmly-held convictions of certain modern-day bloodhounds.

The path therefore lies open to other researchers — *ad augusta per angusta*, to quote a sublime play by a certain poet, V.H. of course!

11. (next page) *My soul has its secret, my life its mystery, / An eternal love conceived in an instant; / This pain is without cure, so I was forced to keep it silent / And she who caused it has never been any the wiser.*

Alas, I will have passed her by unnoticed, / Always by her side and yet alone, / And I will have lived out my time on the Earth, / Not daring to ask for anything and receiving nothing.

As for her, though God has made her sweet and tender, / She will go her way, distracted and without hearing / This murmur of love that rises where she walks.

Piously faithful to austere duty, / She will say, on reading these lines full of her: / "So who is this woman?" and will not understand.

APPENDIX

Le Sonnet d'Arvers

Mon âme a son secret, ma vie a son mystère,
Un amour éternel en un moment conçu;
Le mal est sans espoir, aussi j'ai dû le taire
Et celle qui l'a fait n'en a jamais rien su.

Hélas, j'aurai passé près d'elle inaperçu,
Toujours à ses côtés et pourtant solitaire,
Et j'aurai jusqu'au bout fait mon temps sur la terre,
N'osant rien demander et n'ayant rien reçu.

Pour elle, quoique Dieu l'ait faite douce et tendre,
Elle ira son chemin, distraite et sans entendre
Ce murmure d'amour élevé sur ses pas.

A l'austère devoir pieusement fidèle,
Elle dira, lisant ces vers tout remplis d'elle:
"Quelle est donc cette femme?" et ne comprendra pas.[11]

MICHELLE GRANGAUD

A Divergent Journey

Un Voyage divergent

Translated by Ian Monk

●

Bibliothèque oulipienne 113

2001

● On 22 September 1999, I received a package that has certainly changed my life, and will also doubtless be much talked of, given the new directions it creates in literary history. That day, I received from a distant cousin a letter which was impressive both for its bulk and the significance of its contents. The two of us are close more because of a common interest in anagrammatic poetry and literary games in general, than because of any blood tie. This letter will interest so many people (in fact, it is more of a document than a letter, given that it is almost totally impersonal) that it seems to me only right and proper to reproduce it here almost in full.

In it, my cousin, Antoine Huet, describes a discovery that has just been made in Kálamos, a large village on the plain of Marathon. These very names give us pause for thought. Marathon suggests, if I may be so bold, *a travail de longue haleine*. While Kálamos (the ancient instrument for writing, or the Greeks' ballpoint pen) is a word evocative of literature, even for those who have never studied Greek. These names are already redolent of adventure. For the life of anybody concerned with history is a perpetual journey — sometimes real, leading from libraries to archives, sometimes (and perhaps more often) imaginary: on a flying carpet from the *Thousand and One Nights,* the historian glides over the centuries and can sometimes reach almost virgin territories in distant eras. The tablets discovered at Kálamos have already pointed a crowd of explorers to a *terra* until now *incognita*, which extends backwards beyond Homeric poetry to reveal an absolutely stupefying vista of literary history. For, as my cousin puts it, what we had previously thought to be myths, fables and legends, containing at most some symbolic truth, now turn out to be absolutely historically accurate. The heroes and heroines who had been taken for products of the popular imagination are here revealed to have been people, who not only really existed, but who also left behind writings and their life stories. But the most surprising factor is that all of these autobiographical works, written as poetry, prose, or in diaries and letters, contain details and textures which irresistibly bring to mind real or imaginary characters in our own literature — I mean what is generally termed the western canon. (At this point in the letter, I came to a halt, saying to myself "he cannot be serious!", and I could not resist looking Kálamos up in my battered old atlas, just to check. It was there, next to Marathon. My confidence restored, I pressed on.)

To give you a clearer idea (my cousin went on), the best thing would be to provide you with some examples of what has been unearthed. For instance, Oedipus has left us a sort of journal — punctuated by a series of symbols that are not part of the text itself, and seem to be dates in some unknown calendar system — which is distinctly reminiscent of... No, I'm not going to tell you, sure as I am that you will see at once and understand what makes this text so strange:

> *Apollo 9, Moon 2.*
> *Everything has been going well, yes, fine, much better ever since I married Jocasta. It is even something of a metamorphosis for me. Since I am nervy, even cowardly at the best of times, and so unsure of my ability to make a life for myself, the Delphic oracle had left me in dread of what form the terrible threat would take. But now I feel reassured. The pythoness must have been mistaken. Or else, by force of will, I have managed to turn away a dreadful fate. For, who more than me could have felt obedience, respect and even tenderness for his parents? Now there is nothing more to be feared. My marriage with Jocasta assures my success. She is just the right wife for me. And the birth of the twins is a pledge from the gods, the guarantee of having heirs and descendants. I am already thinking about their education. We must develop their natural filial love, which is the source of all the virtues. This will not be very difficult, given that I am loved and respected by the entire town. The future looks glorious. My daughters will be courted by princes. And, for posterity, the couple formed by Jocasta and me will be the image of a rarely reached perfection.*
> *Moon 5, Apollo 9.*
> *Word has it that the Greek army has set siege to Troy. This afternoon went for a dip.*

And this is not an isolated case. *All* the tablets thus far deciphered contain the same sort of astonishing similarities and premonitory echoes. Phaedra, the daughter of Minos and Pasiphaë, has left us a text that could well be a letter and, although the beginning and end are missing, it is particularly relevant to the matter in hand:

> *There, I've said it now, I admit it, yes, I adore Hippolytus, the son of the Amazon and of my husband Theseus. I burn for a man far younger than me, even though I, oh ghastly thought, am old enough to be his mother, and this love, this passion, is directed at someone who is apparently unfeeling, as gifted with beauty as he is cold as marble.*
>
> *Desirous of knowing what would happen, I summoned Calchas the soothsayer, who is well known for his wily caution. He did not deign to answer my question directly, but he predicted that, in some future generation, a poet would be born who would make the story of my love famous, while interpreting my sorrows in a way that would be totally alien to me. For this John Rhizome (or Rhizos, I didn't really catch his name) will see my present misfortunes as a crime for which I am personally responsible and which must be expiated. Calchas then used a strange word. He spoke of the <u>repentance</u> that Rhizome the poet would attribute to me. I asked him what "repentance" was, but he just beat about the bush and didn't really seem to know what it meant himself. "Repentance", what an odd word! It has a dishonest ring to it, how singularly unappetising! I shall try to remember it, just for fun, at the moment of pleasure. Sighing a hypocritical sigh, I shall plaintively say: "Ah, this must be repentance coming!"*
>
> *Anyway, if this Rhizome individual, with his stupid tragedy, really is going to exist, then I wish him all the worst in the world.*

Narcissus's cantata (the letter goes on) is perhaps even more peculiar, given that it quotes the poetry of Paul Valéry almost directly. Yes, yes, I can already hear you crying out that this is all a scandalous forgery, but I can assure you that these tablets really exist, I have seen them, I helped translate them. What is more, these texts have been examined by dozens of specialists. And it is true that, apart from their historical interest, they have a definite literary worth. Narcissus's poem is particularly amusing since his sentences are written backwards, as though reflected in a mirror. But Echo then turns them back the right way by means of her own internal mirror. Here is their fascinating conversation:

Narcissus	*!love in am I you with, image my, O. you love I, myself, O*
Echo	*O, myself, I love you. O, my image, with you I am in love!*
Narcissus	*!me to cruel fountain O, animals to sweet, fountain O*
Echo	*O fountain, sweet to animals, O fountain cruel to me!*
Narcissus	*!agony is here everything, Narcissus unquiet For*
Echo	*For unquiet Narcissus, everything here is agony!*
Narcissus	*.wishes my accepting at wavers voice fresh My*
Echo	*My fresh voice wavers at accepting my wishes.*
Narcissus	*!sleeps clarity that where delight opaque the In*
Echo	*In the opaque delight where that clarity sleeps!*
Narcissus	*!valerian mysterious O, pole dazzling O*
Echo	*O dazzling pole, O mysterious valerian!*
Narcissus	*.say would Roubaud Jacques as forth so and on so And*
Echo	*And so on and so forth as Jacques Roubaud would say.*
Narcissus	*.tragically end must story my But*
Echo	*But my story must end tragically.*
Narcissus	*!reflection my embrace I if me take will Death*
Echo	*Death will take me if I embrace my reflection!*
Narcissus (exhorting himself)	*!wait, yourself for, prudence for, love for, longer little a Wait*
Echo	*Wait a little longer, for love, for prudence, for yourself, wait!*
Narcissus	*!executioner O, minute another Just*
Echo	*Just another minute, O executioner!*
Narcissus	*!sorrow of die shall I, you embrace not do I if But*
Echo	*But if I do not embrace you, I shall die of sorrow!*

But not all of these texts are so tragic. There is one in particular (which is at once a sort of family register, private diary and chronicle) that comes across as a joke.

Although it is unsigned, numerous indications suggest that Penelope was the author, as you will see for yourself in the following anthology piece which I shall transcribe next, as it seems almost to have been written for you:

If anyone asked what a husband's absence is like, I would certainly answer: it's his ideal presence. Never has O [evidently standing for Odysseus] been so close to me than since he left. I find him everywhere. Wherever I go, memories of him parade like familiar images by my side. However, I am not wrapped up in some sort of preparatory mourning; I am neither plunged in austere loneliness, nor obsessed by my memories of him. O will or will not return. Time will tell. I am waiting for him, but have become accustomed to my present condition, being able to manage my existence and my household as I wish. And to kill the time spent waiting, I invite round my friends. Together, we form a rather pleasant company. They are far from morose, and that is why I like them so much. Each week we get together for a light supper. Ideas run riot, laughter and conversation are the order of the day. We are serious in our humour, discussing the news and the well-being of the town, the State and all of Greece. My philosophers bring me back news from all over the world. A certain Pythagoras has discovered a formula: it allows one to calculate the hypotenuse of any right-angled triangle. This is a marvellous invention, which should go down well with the architects. Regarding cooking and culinary pleasures, it seems that a new beverage has been invented in India, a nectar with an agreeable odour, making those who drink it feel euphoric. This marvel is called wine. Thanks to my delightful guests, I have also been informed of the latest gossip in Greece. I heard that Agamemnon was murdered by his wife Clytemnestra, who in turn was murdered by their son Orestes. What an unhappy family.

But, it is always good to be informed about what is happening in the world. I note down everything in a logbook, which my philosophers have nicknamed my "tapestry", for such meticulous work seems typically feminine to them.

After Penelope, I cannot resist sending you another extract, which does not appear in the *Odyssey*, but which was presumably written by Odysseus himself:

The Eros Company has started researching its next show, which will be on a singularly original subject: what is Love? [written on the tablet with a capital L as though it were a town or country] *My answer from this island, where I have spent so long with an extremely charming Nymph, would be simple. It's Calypso. Or else, to go back a bit, it would be Circe. Or even the Song of the Sirens. But what happened yesterday reminded me of something else, of a much older love, and quite different from those capricious gods who play at piercing the hearts of humans (and even more so of seductive inhumans) and deranging their minds. What occurred yesterday opens up a quite different perspective. I was walking on a pebbly beach, when suddenly I was invaded by a strange and powerful sensation which brought me to a halt. It was a sensation of intense happiness apparently caused by a simple pebble, which I had disturbed while walking and had tipped over under my foot. Now, during my childhood there was just such a stone at the entrance to the palace, which tipped over in exactly the same way when you trod on it.*

A little farther on, near the stream, a breeze was making the reeds rustle, and at once the same sensation spread irresistibly through my heart, bringing with it a vision of a distant past, which returned in all its freshness, even though it had long since vanished from my memory.

It was like a summons, a bearer of nostalgia, but also an order demanding instant execution. I immediately decided to go back to Ithaca. And I want to mark this journey, to make a rhapsody of my return. I want that sensation of intense happiness to leave a trace, or perhaps a poem, in human memory. Cannot such an experience also be termed love? Is it not will, desire, tension that push us to look for pleasure and fertility at the same instant? If the ever-gracious Athene lets me achieve this, then I know my life will not have been lived in vain.

In the same mannered, almost grandiose style, with an unexpected solemnity, we have also found some poetry by Helen of Troy among the tablets:

> *The world knows I am fair,*
> *Everyone, but me,*
> *For the Fates now declare*
> *I am a cold beauty.*

By candlelight when you are elderly,
A gallant fool averred,
Though a poet far greater than any
Listener has overheard.

. . . .

I feel, as my fairness is just a word,
The pain of my beauty.

And now for the apotheosis of the unlikely: the Orphic songs "faithfully transcribed", according to the text engraved on the tablets, "by Eugophernes [Εὐγοηερνης] his servant". Here are a few highlights:

Respect in the beast its wilful movement,
This love song that will start over again,
It raises our hearts, assuages our pain,
Alone in itself, and in one sole instant.

Or else:

Perfume, harmony, maidenhead;
Happiness passed by, it has fled.

Or else:

When the hecatomb lies in its stable,
As though etherised upon a table,
Our future time is perhaps time present
And our pasts contained in that same instant.

Or else:

Even the Aborigine
Knows that the credulous spider

Has bled itself with a razor
For the love of an ancient flea.

Or else misogynous Orpheus's song, or rather hymn *par excellence*:

Contemplate how that legion squirms,
A thousand legs, a hundred eyes,
Cockroaches, cochineals, worms
Scarabs that cause me more surprise
Than seven wonders that will be
Or beautiful Eurydice.

Here the plagiary is blatant. Our national poets, and others too perhaps, parade before our eyes. You hear Nerval's melancholia, the young Verlaine's evanescence, and the obtusely angled fury that was to pierce our poetry and give us Apollinaire. But the question is: who is plagiarising whom?

I have my own theory, but before concluding (provisionally, at least, as always) I would like to add two more extracts. You will see how charming they are. The first work is in strange synchrony with the Orphic, or perhaps Eugophernian corpus. It is a complaint that tells of the woes of poor Io. Even though it is written in the third person, this speaking animal may well be the real author:

She runs, she runs, pursued by a gadfly / Poor Io, alas, alas / No time to rest / Poor Io / Pursued by a prionodont horde / Who track poor Io / Who feed her bones / And make her a cannibal / Who milk her for their cornflakes / Of modified maize / Who eat her, who eat her / Though her brains turned to sponge / Who mince and place her between two buns / Poor Io, poor Io / [etc.]

Finally, I give you Tiresias, a character that can be found in numerous texts and whose dugs were celebrated by Apollinaire, among others. You will see how he tells his story. On the tablets, the text is written in dialogue form, or rather as though it were an interview in which only the answers are heard. The various paragraphs are separated by what we suppose are questions, which are represented or perhaps symbolised by various indecipherable signs. The limitations of my Mac mean that I can give you only a distant echo of them but, for your amusement's sake, I shall try all the same:

Yes, I have double nationality. In general this is extremely handy, especially for daily business. I cross the border whenever I want.

aqwaz / SxÛ%Yf!

Yes, being a citizen of the north is, indeed, rather pleasant. You have authority and power, influence over the world and supreme control over everything around you. You are important, people listen when you speak, you are the boss, the number one. Yes, yes, it is nice to be from the north.

mΔ®c®ß

Ah yes, things are rather different in the south. Life is much more flexible there. There are fewer limitations, and fewer barriers, you will always find a turning that leads where you want to go, no matter which direction that might be. And then you are no longer endlessly concerned with your self-image, as you are in the north. You don't have to wonder if you're well placed or not. The more carefree you are, the more comfortable you are.

soeifnn(^vvvPdda

Which do I prefer? Ah well, that's the story of my life, that is. Did you know that Zeus and his wife Hera had a row about that? Not about my opinion, of course, but about whether being a citizen of the north was more pleasurable than being a citizen of the south. It was one hell of an argument, with each of them claiming that whichever nationality he or she didn't have was the better one. What's the point of living on Olympus if you can't even answer such a basic question as that? To cut a long story short, they called me in and asked my opinion. So I gave them a straight answer. When it comes to pleasure, I declared, then being a southerner is ten times better than being a northerner. Hera was furious about my verdict and struck me blind in punishment. Yes, it's since then that I've been as blind as a bat. But Zeus, in his glee at having beaten Hera, was good enough to give me the gift of prophecy to make up for it. I lost the light of day, but gained *the illumination of knowledge. And that's how you can become a wise man from having been caught up in a godly row.*

Do you know (Antoine went on) that some people have put forward a hypothesis concerning the story of Tiresias, which is extremely interesting though rather daring? The texts discovered on the tablets at Kálamos are all by Tiresias. This hypothesis would explain the quotations from authors living in far later periods which we have found in these texts. And it does seem rather fitting. It is interesting that the only person not to be caught up in a web of quotation is Tiresias himself, who thus comes across as being separate from the rest, in the wings as it were, as a sort of potential author. What is more, lexical analysis demonstrates that his style is far more modern than the others. On the other hand, the snag with this theory is that it would imply that Tiresias really did have the gift of prophecy, which unfortunately adds an irrational element to our scenario. I am sure that there must be a logical explanation. Science (linguistics, genetics, historiography) will perhaps unlock this mystery one day. What's your opinion?

My opinion, my dear Antoine? What is my opinion? Well first of all, I tried to contact you, but this is apparently impossible at the moment. It seems that you are travelling and not just in the realms of the imagination. So, all alone, I'm going to have to pull myself together and think things through. It seems to me that both of us have our own explanation for this story. For you, it is Tiresias, but I would lean towards Eugophernes, hence the documents I am enclosing with my letter.[1] You will see (but this is perhaps a mere coincidence) that the maiden name of the wife of Hugo Vernier, the poet referred to in all of the texts I am sending you, was Huet, the same as your surname. But this coincidence is perhaps not very significant. I've checked in the phonebook, and there are three columns of Huets in the city of Paris alone. But the resemblances between the names (could Hugo Vernier be a descendant of Eugophernes?) and the evident similarities between their writings are far more striking. It all makes my head spin. I impatiently await your answer.

1. Enclosed with the letter are: Perec's *Le Voyage d'hiver*, Roubaud's *Le Voyage d'hier*, Le Tellier's *Le Voyage d'Hitler*, Jouet's *Hinterreise*, Monk's *Le Voyage d'Hoover* and Bens's *Le Voyage d'Arvers*.

FRANÇOIS CARADEC

The Worm's Journey

Le Voyage du ver

Translated by Ian Monk

Bibliothèque oulipienne 114

2001

Das ist die Hegelsche Philosophie
Das ist der Bücher tiefster Sinn!
Ich hab' sie begriffen, weil ich gescheit,
Und weil ich ein guter Tambour bin.

H.H.[1]

---

1. *That is the philosophy of Hegel / That is the books' meaning in sum! / I've grasped them because I'm clever, / And also play a splendid drum.*

● I was born at nightfall on 5 June 1944 in a scantling in the bell-tower of Sainte-Mère-Église, which my family had been occupying since the reign of "Good King Louis", as my grandmother used to say. Which King Louis? Even my grandmother had no idea. I think she must have been mixing him up with our old Duke William, you know, the Conqueror.

However, one thing that's certain is that my parents and grandparents had been bashing away for ages at that broad old beam, as thick as two short planks it was, with little cones of sawdust rising up five metres below. Occasionally, some of our ample progeny would extricate themselves from our homeland and nose off for scantlings new. This is what our many detractors call worming one's way out of a situation, or "vermifuge".

Hardly had my mother finished laying another clutch, including me and my brothers and sisters, at the end of a deep dead-end shaft, than dawn rose over the horrors of war. Our home was on fire!

After a moment's panic, followed by the reassurance that we would not be drowned by the firemen, who had other fish to fry in their own station and with their neighbours, our lives were saved when the scantling and the rest of the church roof plunged down on to the village square. The fire, caught unawares by the violence of the impact, suddenly went out.

But what a crowd was milling around down there! Our wood was trampled under foot, crushed by the caterpillar tracks (quite an ironic fate for worms!) of army tanks, which no longer seemed to be driven by Germans, whose lingo was now familiar to my parents, but by men employing a different tongue and who, to terrorise us, emitted the terrible cry of the cricket. (I have since heard that it's also one of their games.)

During the battle, I lost a large number of my brothers and sisters who had been born at the same time as me, but there were so many of us that my mother didn't notice, and I discreetly avoided mentioning their absence.

But let us skate over this tragic period. My father joined the Resistance by means of a box of matches, which he craftily ignited inside an Oberleutnant's pocket, but died during the course of his action, crushed between the thumb and index finger of his charred-buttocked victim. My mother, overcome with grief and smoking like a trooper, soon followed him into the grave: she had imprudently taken refuge in the cork filter of a NAAFI cigarette.

Now orphaned, I undertook a rapid course of studies with my paternal uncle, an old Anobion, who started by teaching me that though I was a coleopter, it was nothing to beetle my brows about. I was born xylophagous and remain so, despite a slight leaning towards necrophagy. This is, after all, the strict diet of worms.

Did you know that, according to the old Anobion, genealogists have found one of our ancestors in the Lias? But he was so flattened and dry that he was hardly presentable. It was only later, during the Tertiary, that a large number of our predecessors chose a career as fossils. Every day, you can find intact elytra hidden away in the rock just waiting to spring out on you.

One last thing about my tree, and then we'll move on. I must tell you that my great-grandfather on my father's side occupied for some time the position of "death watch" in the woodwork of a convent in the Calvados. I never met him, being too young, but according to the elder generation he was the life and soul of the party. His favourite pastime was winding up the nuns in the convent where he worked by springing up under the ticking of their wooden beds.

"Tick!" he used to go. "Tock!" And then: "Tick tock!"

As he'd become a little effeminate in the company of all those God-botherers, his neighbours nicknamed him the "Limp wrist watch".

Nor have I forgotten another of my Breton uncles, a scholastic Scolytid to whom I owe my taste for books. The old tomes he used to leave behind after his winter visits were illuminated under their barks with exquisitely fine engravings, lacework galleries carved out on the surface of the wood, which I have long ago given up trying to match. I am a simple borer, more of a nihilist than a niellist.

Finally, a word or two about my terrible cousins, the weevils. I was quite simply told to ignore them, and think no weevil, see no weevil and hear no weevil.

And now that I've introduced myself, let's turn to my journey, since that's what you came to hear about.

You no doubt suppose that I had to leave my log when the battle was over. How wrong you are. During the months and years that followed my eventful birth, I found myself on several occasions up against the perilous teeth of hacksaws until my native beam had been reduced to a mere plank.

Brutally dumped in a van, I was deported some twenty kilometres outside Rouen, to Barentin, or to be quite exact, the Château de Latréaumont. This ancient Borrade property was a rather dilapidated ancestral pile, which had been occupied by the Todt Organisation until 1944, then for a few days by a group of rosy-cheeked S.S. After them came some loud Americans, Texan cowboys for the most part, while rumours of peace were starting to invade France. Finally, some F.T.P. who were promptly disarmed and volunteered for the 1st Army, thus becoming part of the militant military. The château was purchased by a local farmer, who prudently stocked his dung in it, given the excellent airing it received thanks to the fact that the various soldierly individuals referred to above had, like any self-respecting active army, smashed all the windows, gutted the armchairs, torn down the curtains, without forgetting to defecate thoroughly in all of the drawers before leaving.

One chill March evening, the new owner, a friend of the deceased Comte d'Auray de Saint-Pois and, like him, originally from Pavilly, the head town of the region, decided to throw everything out into the courtyard, the disjointed armchairs, smashed chests-of-drawers, broken beds, battered tables, demolished desk, ripped carpets, cracked china — everything went out and was turned into a bonfire! The bedbugs had a pretty hot time of it, the poor things. I was starting to feel the heat too when, to my great surprise, he kept hold of my plank.

"Good bit of shelving this," said he.

I carefully folded away my antennae, deciding to play dead as I'd been told to do, if anyone ever spotted me inside my hole.

But he didn't. H(I don't know his name, only his initials, H.M., which appear on his *ex-libris*)e picked up my plank, plus a second uninhabited one, and placed them on brackets nailed to the living-room wall.

Then he bent down over a pile of books that had been dumped in the corner ("books should not be burnt," he mumbled between his teeth), and placed them in alphabetical order on the two shelves.

I, who had been born in a church on a day of celestial fireworks, could easily have taken umbrage at thus being turned into part of the fixtures and fittings.

Instead, that evening, I realised that a new career lay before me.

Before arriving in this providential manor, I had been thinking of joining the Forestry Commission, despite possible massacre by chainsaw. Up until then, I had worked all my life on wood. Would I now be able to live off paper? But if you're not an adult by the time you're three, you never will be. It was time I chose a career, and this man had presented me with a golden opportunity. Instead of the plank that was already riddled with my family past, he was offering me the chance to become a bookworm, with my own admittedly modest library, but it could certainly stand me in good stead if ever I wanted to join the lending library in Le Havre in the course of a purchase or donation. As yet, I had seen nothing of the items weighing down on my plank. But my hopes were high.

Before diving into the unknown, with the same uncertainty and enthusiasm as Professor Lidenbrock had when jumping into the crater of the Sneffels, I pondered the whole thing deeply.

Firstly, I'd have to leave my native joist. A new departure in life always involves a certain anxiety. I was leaving those cosy shafts, so warm and redolent of maternal shavings, in order to shoot up perpendicularly towards the surface of the wood, which is the toughest and most hostile, and then leap into the unknown. For the first time in my life, my antennae were trembling with fear, when by some miracle they encountered the leather binding of the first book placed at the far left of the shelf formed by the plank I had just abandoned after a final push. All I had to do now was slither inside (this took two months) before starting my Grand Tour from left to right, in the same direction in which you are reading.

I wasn't used to paper. I had scarcely ever nibbled any, except once when I accidentally nibbled a communion wafer, thus inventing the Polo mint. I was surprised by its texture, how supple and yet tough each sheet was, then by the variety of different tastes: from the finest rag paper, to single or double-faced coated paper with its kaolin that cracks between your jaws; from smooth calendered paper, to slightly aromatic dyed paper; from the delicacy of China paper to the sonorous stiffness of Japanese vellum. After years of experience, my favourite paper is still a heavy Lafuma Navarre which bulks well, is so thick that you can spend days inside it, and all a curious eye would see was an indecipherable watermark, from which not even Champollion could worm out any sense.

I set to work according to a carefully prepared plan. I would start with the first volume in alphabetical order, and finish with the last, with no funny business and no turning back, by working eight hours a day, including breaks, but with no days off. However, I was soon to realise that my initial intention to bore one book per year was unrealistic. I had not taken into account the difference in textures (which I have just mentioned), and especially not the bindings… and God knows, there are bindings and bindings (the best to my taste is an eighteenth-century calf skin). It sometimes took me months to reach the flyleaf. How much time I wasted before crossing those great works of the mind! But I tried to make myself patient by remembering the words of my old uncle Anobion: "Patience up there! Not all of us can be called Marathon!" No, really, writers have no idea of how wronged they are by bookbinders.

Still to this day I can remember how moving *my first book* was. It was a July morning in 1947. The weather was wonderful. The sun was flooding into the lounge and you would even have thought that this apparently incongruous collection of books had not just been put there to hide the damp marks on the wall. The sweet warmth of summer titillated my nervous system and made me extraordinarily peckish and ready to fill my guts with this novel sawdust. Paper, at last! Paper!

Like that person in a famous book, with his lantern tied to the end of a rope delving into the opening of the martyrs' bone orchard, I hesitated for a moment. My delicately deployed antennae shifted to the right, then to the left, before choosing the best angle of attack, then crack! I bit into my first page.

It was the title-page of Félix Arvers's *Mes Heures perdues*, which was a good sign. From what I've been told, it is a rare enough thing these days to begin by encountering a Romantic first edition in a library. I must admit that this one was probably not worth the effort it took me. When you heard its gilded cover crack between H.M.'s fingers, as he looked for the famous *Sonnet* (*an imitation of the Italian, a likely story!*), it was obvious that the book had never been opened, either since 1833, or else since it had been rebound.

The other poems in the collection seemed rather hard to digest, which explains the hangover I had the morning after my first paper feast.

Hugues Auvernier was hardly any better. His *Vers provençaux et français*, dated 1827, may have been the work of a precursor, but they were already as sickeningly romantic as the movement which was to be reborn about a century later. His garlicky rhymes gave me repeaters.

I then penetrated from one side to the other a paperback published by Poulet Malassis in 1857. The date and the publisher reminded me of something. But what? I was still munching through the last pages of those *Odes funambulesques* by Théodore de Banville (what a clown this poet was, to be sure, he who would later receive a bouquet of flowers from the young Arthur Rimbaud) when I came across the same date and same publisher once again. It was the first edition of Charles Baudelaire's *Les Fleurs du Mal*. In this same collection, with its thin cover and dense content, I deliciously discovered debauchery.

I was still in a tizzy from these unexpected thrills when I tumbled into a dark pit. Léon Bloy! Holy Jesus, was it possible that such a foul blasphemer ever existed? I made my way rapidly through a cheap octavo edition of *Le Désespéré* with its poor-quality yellowed paper, which crumbled into dust. The sod didn't deserve any better.

Luckily, I was better treated by my sixth and seventh books, both dated 1873 — which, when I reached the letter R, I later realised was quite a year. Tristan Corbière read like someone who likes the wood of casks, which my species avoids for fear of cirrhosis. But you can't trust appearances, and I now think that our adorable Charles Cros's tendency for sound and fury was rather down to his alcoholism.

In the end, so far I really couldn't complain. I had gobbled up the works of three of our greatest poets. I had already spotted a fourth, Théophile Gautier, whose *Émaux et Camées* I was looking forward to, but I first had to swallow the terrible Albertus, which sped in front of my eyes on the wings of a storm, while waiting to get into his daughter Judith's fine novel *Les Mémoires d'un Éléphant blanc*, which had also been a thundering success in 1893.

I had gone thus far when, massed behind Stefan Georg, I came across some German occult tomes, printed in Gothic letters, among which I'm happy to say were Hugo von Hofmannsthal, Nietzsche (*Also sprach Tzarathruster*), Rilke (*Die Weise von Liebe und Tod des Cornets Christoph Rilke*, a thirty-six page-booklet, published by Insel-Bücherei in 1941), a batch of Wagner scores, and a Wedekind in such poor condition that I still wonder what there was in it for me.

Phew! I now thought that I'd got through the major part of my library, which I'd enjoyed more or less. The Germans in particular had put me out. It isn't easy to hack your way through texts written in Gothic characters, known as Fraktur, which that extraordinary blockhead Adolf Hitler had ordered to be replaced by the Roman script, because he thought the Gothic alphabet had been invented by a Jew! I'd now been working in that château for twenty-two years and, saving a few yells from the courtyard telling us that we should "keep up the fight!", the events of the century had pretty well passed me by.

There I was, at the end of my shelf, and at the beginning of the letter H, which was represented by a single massive tome by Ernest Hello. Things were running as smoothly as an iambic pentameter when, suddenly, in horror, I realised that I was not going to be able to devour the books from A to Z as planned…

Oh no. The second shelf, like the first, was arranged from left to right, and here I was at the right… Unless I made my way back to where I'd started, I was not poised above the first, but the last book on the second shelf.

Thus was I constrained, after vertically perforating my native plank, to do a U-turn before continuing with

(the worm turns)

"Of course, you dimwit! I used to work in ecclesiastical libraries before ending up in a missal and, believe you me, in the lives of saints you come across some extremely odd monikers. Take Vital, the saint who's celebrated on 10 July, for example. It's both a surname (Rue Vital in Paris was named after the former owner of the land) and a first name, like Vital Hocquet who contributed to *Le Chat noir* under the pseudonym Narcisse Lebeau. And what about Valéry Vernier who in 1857 (another good year) published his *Aline*, referred to by Sainte-Beuve on Monday 3 July 1865 (in those days, literary critics took the time to read), was Valéry his surname or his first name?

"For Vernier is in fact a first name. It belongs to a saint honoured in the diocese of Auxerre. According to Lorédan Larchey, who also had one hell of a moniker, the probable meaning of Vernier is quite simply 'Verne', and the *verne* is the alder. (The Erl King was apparently Jules Verne.)

"If Vincent Degraël never found Hugo Vernier again, then it is because he was looking for him under V and not H. In the same way, there's no point looking through birth registers for a name you'll never find. Our Vernier Hugo was not born in Vimy in 1836, but in Besançon in 1802. He was Victor Hugo's twin brother.

"As united as all identical twins, they wrote their monolithically colossal *œuvre* together — Victor wrote the prose works and Vernier the verse — under the common initial of their two first names: V. Hugo. (Wasn't the phoney letter these two fifty-year-olds sent to Théophile Gautier posted from Besançon? Nobody has ever noticed this allusion.) And only this book . . ."

"*Le Voyage d'hiver*?"

"Yes, *Le Voyage d'hiver* is the only book that bears the first name Vernier, all of the others were signed V. or Victor."

In the year 2000, I reached the end of my initiatory journey. In *Le Voyage d'hiver* we are now raising a clutch of baby worms. They have already reduced large chunks of it to dust and soon, thanks to them, you will never hear another word about *Le Voyage d'hiver* or Hugo Vernier.

(*Translated from the Japanese*)

began. Huysmans, I must confess that I skimmed rather rapidly through *À Rebours*...

What a title, and what a coincidence for a gobbler-up of books such as I, thus constrained to read the books on the shelf... in reverse from V to H.

Then it was that I saw the last volume to be eaten through and yelled in triumph.

There before me lay... the last pages of *Le Voyage d'hiver*.

I was heading for the title-page when I thought I heard a faint sound of nibbling. There was no doubt about it. *Someone had got there before me* and was taking care of *Le Voyage d'hiver*. I advanced cautiously through the publication date (Hervé Frères, Valenciennes, 1864, limited edition of 499 copies, this being number 7). From 1947 to that instant I had crossed a good forty paperbacks and hardbacks in sweat and torment, twenty-two years on the first shelf, thirty-one on the second, to arrive at my life's objective — and someone had beaten me to it. ''This unexpected discovery raises serious questions,'' I said to myself.

I was so engrossed by this strange intrusion that it was only when I reached the third page of Hugo Vernier's book that I noticed that, instead of being placed at the far end of the shelf, next to Verlaine, it had been mistakenly filed under his first name, in the letter H.

And it was at that precise moment that our antennae met. What a surprise. It was not a male, but a charming female. Without a moment's hesitation, we rolled round each other so tightly that nobody could have undone the knot of our union without killing us.

When weariness undid us, I leant over my sweet partner and softly asked her how she had managed to reach the first page of *Le Voyage d'hiver* before me.

''It's perfectly simple[!]'' she said. ''It's thanks to an old lady aged seventy-eight, called Madame Virginie, who used to keep me in her missal until she laid it for a moment on the shelf. As you can imagine, I grabbed the chance to leave all of that Holy Joe crap behind and leap into a profane volume.''

''Virginie? You mean Borrade's sister?''

''The very same. And that's when I realised that this book had been correctly filed away, despite what you think.''

''Correctly filed? Under H?''

dog-eared volume of whose *Stances* I was now absorbing. I remembered how he said, one lucid evening:'"I have no opinion about God before having lunch."

A little nibble at Albert Mérat's *Triolets des Parisiennes de Paris* (published by Monsieur Lemerre, if you please) and there I was in Catulle Mendès with (how can I put it?) an odd feeling of *déjà lu*. But where? There was quite a choice, I know, and maybe I was just a bit jealous of the smooth way he glided through the octosyllabics of his *Soirs moroses*, far more easily than I did through paper.

… then suddenly my head span. An abyss had opened out in front of me, as deep as a poem by Jean Lahor: Stéphane Mallarmé's *Poésies*. How to resist the call of the Great Dice. For poets, too, have their Big Bangs. Ah, then I was cast from the pit of an obscure word, not found in any dictionary, through the thirty-two pages of the 8th edition (November 1940) of *Un coup de dés!* … Just a mouthful of paper, but what a mouthful!

Can one write a line about the *Chants de Maldoror* without saying "I"? Me even less than anybody else, since I live all year round in the Château de Lautréamont, from which Isidore Ducasse bodged his pen-name. So, was Isidore dyslexic? I've no idea, but his prose singed my antennae. I sped through the six *Chants* backwards, from last to first, with my sphincter clasped shut…

On the other hand, I encountered books that were so limp, so boring, that I imagined their authors yawning as they wrote them. Such as Victor de Laprade, of the same family as the Ratisbonnes and Lacaussades. Just hear him in his *Odes et poèmes* sobbing over the "death of an oak":

When the man struck thee, with his coward blow…

So? How else did he expect people to make paper?

I preferred Gustave Kahn, in his *Palais nomades*, despite the free verse which made my head spin, before crossing an extremely recent fascicle, number 107 of the Bibliothèque oulipienne, namely Jacques Jouet's *La Redonde*, which made it spin even faster!

It was with relief that I struck into my penultimate book before the year 2000

Then came Émile Verhaeren's *Les Villes tentaculaires*, Léon Valade's *À Mi-Côte*, Antony Valabrègue's *Petits Poèmes parisiens*, and then a sheet of pink card, a "ghost" marking the place of a book that had been borrowed but never returned (some Hippolyte Vaillant, no doubt).

Trente-et-un au cube by Jacques Roubaud (Gallimard, 1973, poetry collection, inscribed to H.M.) came before Maurice Rollinat, whose *Névroses* (in a modest 1905 edition) gave me nightmares for several months. Rimbaud seemed less dangerous, even if *Une Saison en Enfer* can torment a less hard-skinned reader than me. But it didn't keep me for long, since it was the booklet published by Poot in 1873 (an excellent year) which Rimbaud had evidently not destroyed, and which good bookdealers have since set about making even rarer. So there was no surprise finding one here in Barentin.

Jean Richepin's *La Chanson des Gueux*, in a full edition containing the items removed after he had been sentenced to a month's imprisonment, stood next to a book by Jacques Prévert, dating from before my departure and which had been greatly recommended to me. And yet... "Dead leaves are not *shovelled up*," the château gardener corrected, "they are *forked up!*" Anyway, I was about to dig into it when I was surprised to discover beneath the cover of the 1946 *Paroles* the text of Paul Géraldy's *Toi et Moi!* So I immediately got stuck into Charles de Pomairols's *Lamartine*, which came next, before delving into *La Disparition*.

La Disparition was no easy meat. So I gave myself an additional constraint. I would cross only by means of the letter *o*. This wasn't hard. There was even one in the title. In fact, I was a little disappointed. I'd heard about Perec. He's the guy who wrote a whole novel without once using the letter *e*, people said. So what? Just try writing the words "*la disparition*" with an *e*...

Germain Nouveau brought me out of the letter P, and as I read the slim volume in Louis Forestier's collection, *Les Poètes d'Aujourd'hui*, I had the pleasant sensation of nearing M, L, K, J and the second part of H, which lay at the end of the shelf.

I liked Charles Morice, because he'd created *Lutèce* with Léo Trézenik, but I was disappointed to learn from a critical comment by Walch that "he'd converted to Catholicism like Rimbaud...". That would never have happened to Jean Moréas, a

Eve future by Villiers de l'Isle-Adam, in the charming Club du Meilleur Livre edition, based on a design by Janine Fricker. H.M. in fact sometimes, but rarely, topped up my shelves with books bought by mail order, because he couldn't be bothered to go into town, and this one had arrived just ten years after my perusal of Arvers.

This edition of *Eve future* was one of the most tiring books I have ever crossed. And yet, I noticed that the first reading of supposedly arduous texts is always the right one, and there's no point going back. I managed to slip inside the front cover, under a sheet of protective plastic, and there I was plunged into the delights of a red velvet binding. When I reached the beginning of this fine novel, I was stopped in my tracks by a four-page cellophane brochure containing the various stages of an exploding view by Hadaly. What could I do? One way or the other, I was going to have to get round this obstacle. Via the headband, I slipped through its spine, which was neither easy nor consistent with the rules I had made for myself when it came to crossing the books on the shelves from the first volume's first page to the last one's last...

Apart from a few snags, such as that *Eve future*, I must say that I had quite an easy time of it. H.M. left me alone and it never occurred to him to replace my two shelves with a more elegant bookcase. All I had to do was avoid being inside the book he'd decided to browse, for if he found me between the pages, then I'd be in for a squashing! Luckily, most of the tides didn't interest him in the slightest. He'd set up home once and for all in Barentin to raise his goats. He was such a stick-in-the-mud that he had no plans to move and thus disturb my patient labours. People who move home a lot don't like books. Which wasn't the case with him, or with me.

Things returned to normal with the 1895 edition of *Cueille d'Avril* by Francis Vielé-Griffin, an American from Touraine who thought in italics:

The proud Loire slowly slips from isle to isle
Tying and untying its watered silk...

Verlaine at last! That was something else. His *Romances sans paroles* were here, in a clean edition unfortunately lacking in any apparent interest for bibliophiles, were it not for its rarity value in two or three hundred years' time.

REINE HAUGURE

Verse's Journey

Le Voyage du vers

Translated by Ian Monk

●

Bibliothèque oulipienne 117

2001

● By Reine Haugure, Secretary of the *Association des Amis d'Hugo Vernier* (53, rue Hugo Vernier, Paris 17ème). Winner of the first Prix Hugo Vernier, 1999. Paper read at the first Congress of the International Association of Vernierian Studies, Princeton, February 2000.

1. If the 1979 publication of Georges Perec's "Le Voyage d'hiver" in a privately printed limited edition did not set the world of French nineteenth-century poetic scholarship alight, Jacques Roubaud's *Voyage d'hier* (1992) was like a bolt from a previously calm sky.

2. Professor Borrade's discovery of the only surviving copy of Hugo Vernier's supposedly lost opus, as well as *Les Poésies d'Hugo Vernier*,[1] created what has now become an academic industry. Professorships of Vernierian Studies are mushrooming across the campuses of the USA and the halls of European Universities. There is talk of a forthcoming *Bulletin des Études Verniériennes* and of a *Hugo Vernier Review*, to name only those with the most prestigious names (apart from Dennis Borrade[2] himself, Bernard Magné, Warren Motte, David Bellos, Marcel Bénabou, etc.) on their editorial

---

1. Unfortunately we are still waiting for the promised critical edition of Vernier's *œuvre*, which will finally put a stop to certain nonsense.

2. Still working in spring 2000 as I write, and not an "emeritus" professor, as Ian Monk (of the Oulipo) wrongly says [*Mea culpa* — translator].

committees or advisory boards.

3. In such a ferment, certain absurdities were bound to occur. We think it our duty to point out a few of them.

4. The revelation of the derivative nature (to put it mildly) of most of the great works of late-nineteenth-century French poetry (at least from *Les Fleurs du Mal* onwards) has turned critical thought on its head. Instead of bringing out a work's *originality* or *newness*, instead of going into raptures over the breaks, leaps forward and "revolutions of the poetic discourse", we have now (given that all of the supposedly "original" characteristics of Baudelaire, Rimbaud, Mallarmé and many others have now been shown to be non-existent) set about emphasising the continuity of tradition, formal repetitions and, above all, plagiary (as Lautréamont pointed out, when copying Vernier);[3] the major plagiary being, of course, that of Vernier's work.

5. But we have perhaps gone too far in this direction. Articles have recently been published by certain authors who attempt to give fresh lustre to works whose reputations were beginning to fade by claims that they derive from *Le Voyage d'hiver* or from *Les Poésies*.[4] But it should be clearly stated that there is not the slightest Vernierian echo in René Char, Saint-John Perse, Madame de Noailles or Henri Michaux.

6. Some poets have even published their own work under Vernier's name! It is sufficient to cite Arthur Silent, Olivier Cadot and Pierre Alféri. This is also the case with Denis Roche, who apparently wants to conceal the fact that he has started writing poetry again (or that he has never actually stopped). We are witnessing an epidemic of new counterfeiters. But these ones do not try to hide their borrowings and thefts, instead they pretend that they have plagiarised VH or PO.

---

3. "Plagiary is necessary; progress implies it!"

4. A title which was knowingly recycled by Isidore Ducasse. These two books shall henceforth be referred to in this article by the abbreviations VH and PO respectively. We should mention in passing that they can now be consulted on microfilm (requests should be addressed to Professor Borrade or to JR (of the Oulipo)). Oulipian writers will also be referred to by their initials.

7. Studies published by several members of the Oulipo (HLT, JJ, IM, JB, MG and FC),[5] which are not always as serious (see below) as one might have hoped, have unfortunately inspired a horde of imitators. Attempts have been made to detect Hugo Vernier's hand in countless works of every description, from the recent to the distant past. In most cases, the technique consists in spotting the initials **H.V.** or **V.H.** in an entry in a dictionary or encyclopædia, and then deducing by various far-fetched arguments that Hugo Vernier is in fact lurking behind it.

8. Vernier has seen himself in the guise of: **V**ítezslav **H**álek, the Czech poet and storywriter; **V**ictor **R**ául **H**aya de la Torre, the Peruvian politician (died 1979); **V**ictor **H**ess, the American physicist originally from Austria; the poet **V**ladimir **H**olan; **V**ictor **H**orta, the Belgian architect and designer; the painter **H**ugo **V**an der Goes; **H**arold **V**armus (a biologist); **H**enry **V**aughan, the English metaphysical poet; **H**orace **V**ernet; **H**enri **V**ieuxtemps; **H**eitor **V**illa-Lobos, etc.[6][7]

9. An even stranger form of "reasoning" has led some scholars (inspired, alas, by certain tendencies manifested by a few of the Oulipians cited above) to add to the Vernierian nebula names with the initials **H.W.** or **W.H.** They argue that since the letter **W** is not a "**double U**" in French but a "**double V**", it is twice as **V**-like as the simple letter **V**, and thus even more suggestive of a hidden code.

10. Hence the supposed "Vernierism" of Hugo Wolf's *Lieder*, the mathematician Sir William Hamilton's quaternions, William Harvey, Warren Hastings (the British colonial administrator and governor of India in the early nineteenth century), William Hazlitt, Werner Karl Heisenberg (Vernier would thus be the true inventor of the

---

5. To which must be added Bernard Magné's *Voyages divers* and Julien Bouchard's *Voyages d'envers*, respectively the pre- and postface of a joint republication of GP's and JR's texts.

6. A complete survey (to date) of these "critical fantasies" can be found in the article by L. Jeanpace & P. Desmeyeurs to be published shortly in the *Revue d'Histoire Littéraire de la France*.

7. The attribution of Plutarch's *Parallel Lives* to Vernier simply because its French title is *Les Vies des hommes illustres* is clearly grotesque. We should also point out that the *Vacances de Monsieur Hulot* has nothing to do with VH.

uncertainty principle), Wilhelm Von Humboldt, etc.[8]

11. The case of William Randolph Hearst deserves a special mention. It was when reading VH (which had been delivered to him by the Holy Ghost in person, we imagine!) that Orson Welles is supposed to have decided to use the figure of this American press baron as his model in *Citizen Kane*.

A Verniereal Disease

12. In all such work can be seen traces of what might be termed a *Verniereal disease*. One of the symptoms manifested by the more seriously afflicted critics is the title they choose for their papers.

13. Many of them (and particularly the Oulipians) go out of their way to retain elements of the verbal (rather than graphic) sonority of George Perec's original title.

14. We have seen published a *Voyage d'avers* ("Flipside Journey"), a *Voyage du vert* ("Green Journey"), a *Voyage d'Auvers*,[9] a *Voyage du verbe* ("Verb's Journey"), a certain *Voyage du Vair* ("Journey of the Fur/Glass Slipper" — Hugo Vernier is alleged to have plagiarised Perrault's fairy-tales), a *Voyage pervers* ("Perverse Journey" — Vernier plagiarising Sacher-Masoch and Sade),[10] and so on.

15. (I was unable to obtain a copy of Algernon D. Clifford's recently published *Voyage d'Hilbert* in time to include it in this paper. I shall return to it later.)

16. It will be noticed that all but one of the titles I have mentioned keep the "*voyage*" and a d ("*d'* " or "*du*"), and most of them also retain the "*v*" (except HLT who instead keeps the "*i*", while others try to approach it by using a *u*). As for JJ, he has slipped into

---

8. We point out in passing that **W**alter **H**enry, the pseudonym (if such it is) of the specialist in the work of Paul Braffort (of the Oulipo), was evidently selected with this in mind.

9. This particular example, which its author presents as an unpublished text by Raymond Queneau (of the Oulipo) and which shows that Vernier painted Van Gogh's pictures, is a blatant forgery.

10. *Le Voyage Bouvard*, by Jacques Neefs, which indicates some (rather suggestive) passages in Flaubert's manuscripts, remains rather loosely argued and the title is distinctly distant from the original!

German. His title contains *Reise* ("journey"). He then attempts to justify the shift from *Winter* to *Hinter* by some monkey business with a printer which seems to us highly dubious.

17. MG is the only one (apart from Bernard Magné) to keep the entirety of "*voyage diver*", but with an additional syllable, "*-gent*", which breaks the metrical/rhythmic harmony (the hemistich of an alexandrine) that we find in all of the other French titles.[11]

REMARKS ON THE OULIPIAN CONTRIBUTIONS TO THE ELUCIDATION OF THE VERNIERIAN CORPUS[12]

18. Let us first state that, after due examination of all the data (and despite the serious mistakes and lapses in the second work, which is far inferior to the first one) **practically all of the information provided by GP and JR is true. It is on this data that all future analysis must be based.** We shall now succinctly examine in sequence the contributions made to Vernierian studies by HLT, JJ, IM, JB, MG and FC.

19. HLT's *Le Voyage d'Hitler* adds a new element of considerable importance to what might be termed the history of "Vernier after Vernier": the identification of the famous "Hugo Gruppe" and its role in the history of the Second World War.

20. The tale is lively, well told, though sometimes rather clumsily written (as JJ has indicated to me in a private communication). The "precious directives" of FLL, the President/Founder of the Oulipo, insisting upon the necessity of aiming for the highest level of literary excellence in Oulipian works, have not been respected to the letter.

21. HLT occasionally allows himself to be carried away into narrating events "as a fly on the wall" and the final scene in Hitler's bunker seems to us to have sprung from the

---

11. The shift in this title from a pattern of six metrical syllables to seven is perhaps a subtle allusion (typical of the author) to Verlaine, as we show below, and to the famous "*et pour cela préfère l'impair*" ("and for that reason prefer uneven numbers").

12. This expression has been taken from JJ.

author's own imagination rather than from an eye-witness account.

22. HLT also feels the need to cast doubt over JR's assertion that Borrade heroically resisted torture and revealed nothing to the Gestapo. But such scepticism is groundless. It is an established fact that Louviers, in whom Borrade had confided, told the Gestapo what they wanted to know and then covered his tracks.

23. Despite these inevitable quibbles, we must say that our examination of *Le Voyage d'Hitler* leaves us with a generally positive opinion.

24. It was doubtless the spectacular nature of HLT's discoveries that encouraged JJ, and subsequently IM, to carry out the research they have set down respectively in *Hinterreise* and *Le Voyage d'Hoover*.

25. We were perhaps involuntarily biased against JJ before weighing up his contribution,[13] but it quickly became clear to us that the musical angle almost certainly has nothing to do with VH. After due investigation we think we have proved that Ugo Wernier's work was not known to Hugo Vernier. The indisputable presence of *Le Voyage d'hier* in Hitler's bunker masked the additional presence of *Hinterreise*, which the Hugo Gruppe had hunted down for other reasons that had nothing to do with French poetry. The Schubertian reference in the title (and only the title, which came about, as we now know, from a misprint) is a pure coincidence. This of course does not detract from the importance of Gorliouk's work, but it is only of secondary interest in Vernierian studies.

26. The revelations in *Le Voyage d'Hoover* are equally sensational. Although it is true, as IM himself points out, that there is nothing new about the idea that Shakespeare was a plagiarist, the indisputable confirmation of the extent and the nature of these "borrowings" will have a considerable impact on Shakespearian studies, which are at present languishing in a rut. IM has, unfortunately, allowed himself to be led astray by

---

13. When we told JJ of our astonishment at the fact that Gorliouk did not seem to know that the real title of Vernier's work was *Le Voyage d'hier*, he replied rather glibly (tape-recorded interview, 9.9.99) that so far as he was concerned nothing proved that this title was genuine. Has he even read the rest of the corpus?

JJ, so that part of his contribution is totally irrelevant. But what remains is of the utmost importance. It is to be regretted that a decisive clue seems to have escaped his attention. The famous and mysterious W.H., the phantom recipient of the *Sonnets*, was indeed, as he shows, the author of the old manuscript that Shakespeare pillaged. But Shakespeare himself, in a mixture of cynicism and insolently narcissistic sleight of hand, even admits the fact. For W.H., as we know, should be read "*Will Himself*".

27. Let us pause for a moment at this point in our textual navigations. The eight short texts under examination can be naturally divided into three sub-sets (which are not numerically equal, nor do they form a cardinal progression, thus making the lack of a ninth cruelly felt, for the separation in that case would be either $3+3+3$ or $2+3+4$).

28. There is, first and foremost, the pair *Voyage d'hiver* (GP) and *Voyage d'hier* (JR) — then secondly the contributions of HLT, JJ and IM, which we have just examined. Finally, there are three others, in the chronological order of their composition:

    A - *Le Voyage d'Arvers* by JB
    B - *Un Voyage divergent* by MG
    C - *Le Voyage du ver* by FC.

29. We have little to say about **B**; leaving aside the famous and enigmatic *Homer's Vision*, referred to by IM at the end of *Le Voyage d'Hoover*, the only link between *Un Voyage divergent* and the matter in hand is *Eugophernes*, whom MG wants to associate with our Hugo V. In fact, the implications of the discoveries at Kálamos are so huge that they surpass my faculties. MG uses the adjective "divergent" to describe the journey she takes us on. But if the revelations she presents were to be confirmed by the specialists, then it would be more appropriate to call it a *convergent journey*.

30. A poses a particular problem and it took me some time to grasp its true significance. The text apparently recounts a "parallel life" to that of the prototypic Hugo Vernier. Very well, but what light does it shed on the Vernier affair? Does JB mean to imply that Vernier "copied" his own life from that of Hugues Auvernier, whose manuscript poems, *Vers provençaux et français*, are dated 1827, that is to say nine years before his birth (in 1836 (I take this opportunity to point out that 1836 is the *centenary by anticipation* of the birth of Georges Perec, and that this astonishing fact seems to have escaped the notice of all other Perecologists))? Without a doubt; and this would be just like the author, whose modesty is unrivalled. But we feel that there is a different explanation for this Bensian discretion. Is it not rather a piece of preventive medicine, aimed at diverting the critical gaze from the fact that the Bens of *Chanson vécue* and the "Irrational Sonnets" is perhaps less original than has been thought?

31. C — the worm whose memoirs FC has taken down is of course not the first animal to have its adventures translated into a human tongue;[14] but it is probably the first among members of the *Dermestidae*. This account, which is in the end a marvellous love story, is moving and utterly convincing. But should we trust the final revelation which the worm places in his darling's mouth? Does it not rather prove her charming naïveté? For the arrangement of the library's books (so convenient for this dermestid hypothesis), on which the whole reasoning actually depends, and which suggests (ingeniously but fallaciously) that Vernier is a first name, and thus the name of Victor Hugo's twin brother (until now utterly unheard of by Hugo scholars),[15] is in fact due to a human agent, the notorious H.M. And do not these initials in fact conceal an author (whom we shall leave unnamed) who played on our heroine's credulity for his own unstated (but easily fathomable) ends?

32. Although unfortunately mistaken, the dermestid hypothesis translated by FC does have the merit of drawing our attention back to literature, and in particular to post-Baudelaire French poetry[16] which is, after all, central to the entire affair. Considerations about the Hugo Gruppe, the history of music, Shakespearian studies, Homer or Arvers's Sonnet, though fascinating, have tended to draw us away from this

14. We can cite, among others (list taken from Paul Braffort's *Bibliothèque animale*): *The Memoirs of a Donkey*, *Mother Goose's Tales*, *Of Mice and Men*, *Monsieur Séguin's Goat*, *The Barbel of Seville* (and not "Barber", as Julia Kristeva has shown), *The Maltese Falcon*, Charles Baudelaire's "Albatross", *Steppenwolf*, Joseph Kessel's *Lion*, Italo Calvino (of the Oulipo)'s "Argentine Ant", "The Gold Bug" and *The Hound of the Baskervilles*.

15. We insist on the adverb utterly. We have been through the entire bibliography of Hugo Studies using a web worm of our own invention.

16. We leave aside Vernier's prose, which researchers have so far almost completely ignored.

fact. But it must be said that much remains to be done in this field, and progress in Vernierism has been rather sluggish.

33. We shall conclude this paper, which has already grown over-long, by broaching a subject that requires in-depth treatment. It is clear that a large number of poets have copied Vernier. But it is also clear that their entire *œuvres* cannot be straightforward plagiary. Simple quantitative reasoning demonstrates this point. So how to distinguish the lines in Heredia, Mallarmé or Richepin that were copied from those which were simply influenced by Vernier, and also from those (far more mediocre) passages which bear the marks of each author's purely individual endeavours? Can we establish a *measure of Verniericity* that would be as equally valid for Verlaine as for Rimbaud, and for Apollinaire as for Corbière? In this vital task that we have undertaken, we have adopted the strategy already developed by HV[17] in her analysis of the composition of Shakespeare's *Sonnets* (in particular Sonnet 20 in which IM might have found additional proof of his argument).

34. Our demonstration will here be simply sketched out using a few examples taken from the work of Paul Verlaine (perhaps the most Vernierian of all poets).

35. Let us take the line by Hugo Vernier which this poet has grafted into his poem "Nevermore" in the collection *Poèmes saturniens*:

> *Souvenir, souvenir, que me veux-tu? L'automne.*[18]

Let us now write out this line again highlighting certain letters:

> *Sou**VENIR**, souv**EniR**, que me veux-tu? L'automne.*

We can thus see that it contains, by pragmatic dissemination, the name of Vernier, who thus signed it in a way the plagiarist overlooked.

36. Let us now turn to "Clair de Lune", the first poem in the same "author's" *Fêtes galantes*. It contains twelve lines. Lines 6, "*L'amour vainqueur et la vie opportune*", 10, "*Qui*

17. Helen Vendler, *The Art of Shakespeare's Sonnets*, Harvard University Press, 1997, pp.127-132.
18. *Memory, memory, what do you want from me? Autumn.*

fait rêver les oiseaux dans les arbres" and 12, "*Les grands jets d'eau sveltes parmi les marbres*"[19] are by Hugo Vernier[20] and also contain his "signature", as explained above.

37. In the first two lines of the poem "Les Ingénus", in the same collection:

> *Les **H**a**U**ts tal**O**ns lutta**IE**nt a**VE**c les lo**NG**ues jupes,*
> *En sorte que, selon le te**RR**ain et le vent,*[21]

we find his entire name: HUGO VERNIER.

38. Lines 51-2 of "En patinant":

> *Vint nous corriger, bref et sec*
> *De nos mauvaises habitudes*[22]

also contain it. And the second of these two lines conceals his initials, HV.

39. It should be pointed out that these last two lines are not as famous as the preceding examples. However, they are extremely beautiful, as can be seen from the axiom: **that which is beautiful is Vernierian, and that which is Vernierian is beautiful**.

40. Other lines published by Verlaine, and which are not by Vernier, of course contain some of the letters of the plagiarised poet's name. *But they do not contain them all.* As the name's subliminal presence influenced the plagiarist more or less, they contain a correspondingly large or small proportion. We can thus construct our *scale of Verniericity*, which is also (because of the axiom given above) a scale of aesthetic value: **the less a line has been influenced by Vernier, the less beautiful it is**.

41. This observation, ladies and gentlemen, brings my paper to an end. Thank you for your patience and attention. Any questions?

---

19. *Conquering love and seasonable life; Which makes the birds in the trees dream; The large fountains, slight amid the marble.*

20. Quotations that we have been able to check on the microfilm of the original edition of *Le Voyage d'hier*, thanks to the kind co-operation of Professor Borrade.

21. *The high heels struggled with the long skirts, / So that, according to the land and the wind.*

22. *Correct us, swiftly and dryly, / From our bad habits.*

HARRY MATHEWS

A Journey Amidst Glasses

Le Voyage des verres

Translated by the author

Bibliothèque oulipienne 118

2001

● Key West, on one of those late-April evenings when happiness infuses the air — lukewarm air laced with a touch of jasmine — in a world emptied of winter visitors and cruise ship tourists. My last evening as a single man: my wife would return from Paris the next day. I had worked late on a narrative eodermdrome that was both appealing and hard, so I decided to eat out, and here I was at 10 p.m. seated at the outdoor bar at Mangoes. The delightful T.K. had already poured me a glass of Pinot Grigio; Amy, the no less delightful owner, had slid two Marlboros on to the ashtray in front of me; and I was about to order something to eat when a stranger settled on the stool to my right. He straightaway ordered a glass of Californian Merlot.

I later learned that he was well into his seventies. No one could have guessed it from looking at him: a tall, muscular man, with newly tanned features that were pronounced without being plain, greying hair still thick, and a look sharp enough to inspire uneasiness.

Key West is a friendly town. I naturally introduced myself.

"Harry."

"My given name doesn't matter. I'm known as Parsifal. Or sometimes Parsifal III."

"You're of German origin? Or maybe a Wagnerite?"

"No, no. My grandparents were Belgian. A Jewish family from Antwerp. My last name is Bartlstand."

"How do you spell it?"

He spelled it out as I've written it down.

He remarked to me, "*Je n'aime pas les œufs.*" He was consulting the menu.

"At this time of day they're not something I'd recommend."

"You misunderstand. *Je n'aime pas les e.* I don't like *e*s. I got rid of mine. Our name is normally written 'Bartelstand'."

"No kidding. Well, if you don't like *e*s, there's a book you should read —"

Looking me straight in the eye, he said, "It was thanks to Georges Perec that I changed my name. As a matter of fact, my first name is Perès, although that has nothing to do with it. But how did you hear of the book?"

"I was a friend of Perec's. And I also belong to a group called the Oul–"

"You don't say? Then, if I'm not mistaken, you must be Mathews. The only Oulipian from America," he chuckled, not unkindly. We each ordered another glass of the same wine, together with a dish both simple and substantial. Parsifal was making me nervous. I asked him,

"Were you a friend of Georges's?"

"I certainly was." I lighted my second Marlboro; he drew a pack of American Spirit from the breast pocket of his sports shirt. "Are you really a member of the Oulipo? You don't look like an Oulipian. Not one bit."

"Let's say I'm the token cowboy." I told him about the eodermdrome I was working on.

"OK, OK, I believe you. You see, there's this business that's been going on for more than twenty years now, and I'm starting to get fed up with it. Not long ago I brought it up with Caradec in a vague way. I think he caught on."

Our food arrived. The terrace was almost empty, so we took our dishes to an out-of-the-way table — grilled tuna for him, Jamaican jerk chicken for me.

"What would you say to a bottle of Châteauneuf?" I nodded agreement. "It's weird all the same, finding you here three thousand miles from the scene of the crime."

"The crime?"

"It wasn't a crime. Something was done that offended me. Not even offended: annoyed me."

"If you're in the mood for talking…"

Fresh glasses were brought; the Châteauneuf was served.

"It'll be the first time ever. Not counting Borrade. But he was in on it from the beginning."

"Borrade? Denis Borrade?"

"Dennis Borrade. His son." He smiled at me condescendingly. "Listen, this may take a little while. But you won't be bored."

"I can believe that." I was divided between anticipation and anxiety. He began his tale.

The Bartelstands, he explained, settled in Antwerp early in the 18th century. Starting out as modest retailers of produce, they eventually specialised in the wine trade. They owed their increasing success in particular to competition — forthright but intense — between two branches of the family: one imported the wines of Bordeaux by sea, the other those of Burgundy by land. By the beginning of the 19th century the Bartelstands' fortune was made. Their interests soon extended to banking, manufacture, even the cultivation of cutting-flowers.

The family's prosperity grew further during the opening decades of the 20th century. Early in 1929, Perès Bartlstand's grandfather had the prescience or the good luck to retire from all commercial and financial activity. At the age of forty, he was the possessor of an immense fortune, which he divided with his children. The grandfather was the first to be given the nickname Parsifal: he had a penchant for extravagant, "impossible" undertakings. He gave full rein to this penchant after 1934. He wanted, he declared, to undermine the Third Reich through ridicule. For instance, with the help of qualified artisans he devoted himself to concocting a fake 18th-century volume that would prove that the greatest German music, from Bach to Wagner, owed its existence to the ideas of a poor Jewish musician from Poland. He managed to introduce the book into the reserves of a Berlin library, although too late to affect Hitler's wholesale takeover of German culture.

His son, who was to become Parsifal II, supported his father in combatting the Nazis, albeit by very different means. He got in touch with the British secret services, who provided him with a new and, of course, "Aryan" identity; thanks to which, in the summer of 1939, he set out in the guise of a rich dilettante with an enthusiam for watercolours on a prolonged tour of German ports. A tiny camera ensconced in his easel enabled him to provide the British with valuable information about naval preparations then under way. (Afterwards, he had his watercolours fashioned into elaborate jigsaw puzzles that would challenge the talents of Bartelstands old and young.)

Before the end of the same year, the entire family moved to England, with the exception of Parsifal II: he hoped to continue working for the British. Soon after the occupation of Belgium and its neighbours, he began helping to organise the first Resistance groups. In 1942 he was given the task of establishing links with networks in northern France. It was then that he met Denis Borrade, a principal figure in the Resistance in Pas-de-Calais. Thanks to their partnership, one of the most effective subversive organisations in all Europe came into being. It so worried the German authorities that they set up an office whose sole purpose was to counter and destroy their network. (The office was called the Hugo Gruppe, in memory of Hugo von Krakl, the ruthless governor of Belgium during World War I.)

In December 1944 the Hugo Gruppe finally succeeded in arresting Denis Borrade. It was then that Parsifal II fully earned the right to his name. Disguised as a colonel in the Wehrmacht and accompanied solely by two comrades similarly disguised, he brought off the unimaginable exploit of getting Borrade out of captivity. It is safe to say that from this time on the two men's loyalty as comrades in arms was transformed into durable friendship. Several months later, thanks to the British decoding of German messages, they had the satisfaction of supervising the capture of the French and Belgian collaborationists who had betrayed them.

Parsifal III paused and asked, "How about a small grappa to speed things on their way?"

"Fine. But it's better across the street."

We paid our bill, crossed Duval Street in one direction and Angela Street in the other, and soon were seated at the bar at Antonia's. After setting two snifters in front of us, the imperturbable Tiffany poured us generous helpings of Nardini grappa. Parsifal III resumed his story.

In 1947, at the urging of the American government, Parsifal II and Denis Borrade emigrated with their families to the United States. They both worked not only for the various intelligence services that replaced the OSS but as well — and above all — for a highly secret Franco-American counter-intelligence group formed at the outset of the Cold War. Their sons, Dennis (with two *n*s) and Perès (aka Parsifal III), had been profoundly impressed by their fathers' wartime careers when they re-emerged in 1945, and no less so by the example they set, day after day, of indissoluble friendship. After graduating from college, they decided to follow in the traces of Denis and Parsifal II. They applied for admission to what was to become the CIA, and after two years of training in America and abroad, they succeeded, thanks to their fathers' influence, in being assigned to the same service as they.

Parsifal III was posted to Paris. It was decisive for what later happened that his first cover was an appointment as English teacher at the lycée in Étampes. There he became acquainted with Georges Perec, one of his students and only ten years his junior. A lively sympathy sprang up between them, fuelled by their first, brief accounts of their childhood experiences. It was only in Paris, much later, that they truly became friends, during a night on guard duty at the Writers Union (for so, in the month of May, 1968, the building belonging to the Société des Gens de Lettres had been renamed). As the dawn gradually illuminated the acacias, rhododendrons and quince of that lovely garden, Georges and Perès each told his story, one about his mother, the other about his father.

"Georges also told me about his latest book, not yet published: *A Void*. By the end of that summer I'd already deleted the *e* from my last name."

The two friends met several times after that, always manifesting a real if discreet affection for one another. But such occasions were rare, since Parsifal III had been transferred to Brussels in 1970. It was there, eight years later, that he received his copy of *Life A User's Manual*. The book was warmly inscribed and accompanied by a note from the author apologising for not asking permission before making use of the story of Parsifal III's father. There was no questioning the note's sincerity; it was all the same rather abrupt, and it left Parsifal III in a state of undeniable irritation.

After changing our glasses for some unaccountable reason, Tiffany had already replenished our ration of grappa.

"You see, the real problem wasn't that he'd appropriated my father's exploit without breathing a word of it to me, but that he'd turned this example of unbelievable daring — a Jew risking his life day after day — into the gratuitous pastime of an idle English gentleman. And then, dammit, he even kept his name! Bartel becomes Bartle, Parsifal becomes Perceval, that's really subtle, and stand — what does *stand* mean in French if not booth? Then, to top it off, he justified the name with the ghosts of Melville and Valéry Larbaud! You can understand why I was pissed off.

"Not for long — the book was too inspiring; and after all, poor Bartlebooth does get his comeuppance. So I was able to write him a sincerely enthusiastic letter."

Parsifal III was nevertheless left feeling slightly bitter. He decided that he should take his "revenge"; a revenge in no way vindictive but none the less effective at the level at which he had been "offended"; in other words, a literary revenge.

It was past midnight. The last customers left the restaurant. Tiffany could not altogether conceal her relief when we signalled for the bill. We walked up Duval Street as far as Diva's.

"Have you got a good mescal?" Parsifal asked the barman, someone unknown to me. He murmured Spanish sounds; Parsifal was satisfied. "No ice, lime on the side."

Two tall glasses; two consequential portions of the golden liquor.

"So: a literary revenge. Early in '79 I wrote Georges a long letter. It was 'Degraël's letter', so to speak, but it was no way sent after the publication of *Things*, and likewise no way by Degraël. Degraël never existed. Poor Roubaud swallowed the story whole, just like Georges! But in it I talked about Degraël, of course, and about Vernier and Borrade and so forth. I knew my buddy all too well, and I invented an elegant hoax that I was sure he couldn't resist. He thanked me by return mail and said he was getting straight to work on composing "Le Voyage d'hiver". And what do you know, the piece came out before the year was over."

"That's impossible. Degraël was one of his teachers in Étampes."

"No kidding. Anyone ever find the shred of a trace of him? Anyway, would Georges have talked about him, and even written his piece in homage to him, without mentioning his being there? No. He says, 'appointed to a teaching post in Beauvais,' and that's all."

"You can't honestly tell me that the whole story was made up."

"Not the whole story. Just the important parts. I should have explained one thing to you: Dennis Borrade was in on my project from the start. In fact we made up the story part of *Le Voyage d'hiver* together. (I thought it showed a certain flair for fiction writing.) On the one hand, I wanted his opinion; he found the whole thing altogether entertaining, deserved, and free of any possibly harmful consequences. On the other hand, I didn't know where it was all going to take me. I might need logistic and other kinds of support (and I was certainly right about that). In any case, it's true that Dennis was in Australia at the same time as Georges. It gave him a chance to supply him with some prime supplementary disinformation. Later on there were Gauger, and Gorliouk, and finally John Scale, all people just as real as you and me. Well — I often have doubts concerning my own reality. Don't you?"

"Especially right now."

"But those people are what I'd call coincidental pawns. They did nothing to alter the fictitious facts, if you'll pardon the expression."

"And the principal pawns?"

"Why, Georges, of course, and then you — the members of the Oulipo. But you came much later."

More mescal had been poured into our tall glasses.

"1982. I'd planned to tell him sooner or later. It wasn't just that. When he died, a whole world of sport and joy went with him. I naturally expected to drop the project. It had become absolutely pointless. And then, and then... There was his posthumous fame, and especially the unbelievable hullaballoo over the Oulipian structures of *Life A User's Manual*. I watched the book and its heartbreaking eloquence dropping out of sight. So I went back to my plan, only now with the Oulipo as my target. Everything was back on track when Roubaud met Borrade in Colorado in 1992."

"Exactly. You can't make me believe that you got Roubaud, who wasn't born yesterday, to swallow what was nothing more than a pack of lies."

"He took the bait all by himself! Only three years after *"53 Days"* came out, how could he resist the idea that the Louviers story was based on fact? Although in my opinion what really hooked him was learning that Vernier's father was the author of *Arithmetic for Humanities Classes*. But think of the mistakes he made, which only over-enthusiasm can explain. Georges had already mentioned the Louviers episode in the sketches for *"53 Days"* he'd made before he left for Australia and his meeting with

Borrade. And then Roubaud says the trip took place in 1980, when we know it was in 1981. It's preposterous."

"Vernier's book existed all the same. There's documentary proof of its publication."

"You think I didn't make sure that every sign of it had disappeared? Some day maybe they'll find a copy. It won't be the same book, or the same author."

"It's simply not possible. Let's get down to facts — I mean, the people you admit really exist. Gauger to start with—"

"Gauger had already been under restricted surveillance for years because of his uncle (a real shit, by the way — we even thought of eliminating him, with a little help from Mossad). And then — I haven't told you this crucial fact — the whole Oulipo was under surveillance from 1990 on. Phone taps, mail intercepts, tails if needed. With everything Dennis and I had at our disposal, it was child's-play. So Le Tellier, who likes womankind as much as you do, or almost (don't argue, I know everything), starts something with a pretty young German woman who is a student of Gauger's. She goes home with a xerox of *Le Voyage d'hiver* that's been dropped off at her hotel by 'Hervé Le Tellier', aka Parsifal III. I wasn't sure of what would happen next, it was like throwing a bottle in the sea. But what happened next was glorious, as you know. Here's something you don't know.

"Gauger had written his thesis in '83, still in the days of typewriters. Later, a secretary in his department transferred it to microfilm, and later still to a computer. So all we had to do was enter Vernier's book in the final digital version to lay our trap. (It was probably in checking this version that he happened to notice Vernier's name, which obviously didn't appear on the other lists.) It was likely that sooner or later he would want to inspect his uncle's archives. We were waiting for him. Years before we'd recruited Klara along with her mother to keep an eye on the old man. So Klara let us get to the trunk and the papers we had to tamper with. I should point out that they already contained references to the 'Hugo Gruppe' and 'Borrade', for obvious reasons — after all, they were fighting each other tooth and nail. The only name missing was Vernier's.

"I was sort of disappointed that things stopped there. In time Gauger's romance with Klara took care of that. I know that money and love can mix, and Klara was paid well enough, but I frankly didn't expect it. Later I was worried she might spill the beans to her husband, but it was also true that I had the goods on her, a little case of swindling ten years earlier. The business with Lufthansa and Ganshofer was shooting fish in a barrel. It wasn't Ganshofer who was suckered, though; it was Gauger and Le Tellier. The German wasted no time passing on all his 'discoveries' to his old student's friend. There was no plane trip, no Ganshofer, no anything aside from a man's voice on a tape recorder saying things sure to make Gauger and every last Oulipian jump for joy. Although I was astounded that you could seriously accept the idea that the Nazis would take such trouble to discredit French poetry. They wouldn't have assigned a single man to a mission as silly as that. I wouldn't say no to a beer."

I had more than one reason to feel dizzy; still, I was able to suggest we walk down Duval Street almost to its lower end. It was a little far, but we would be rewarded at last by the excellent draught beers at Wax. We talked little on the way. There were quite enough words seething inside my skull, heated no doubt by drink but even more by these upsetting revelations. I did my best not to believe them, since all the work slowly amassed by my Oulipian companions was in danger of crumbling to dust; but Parsifal was bursting with confidence and, above all, with knowledge. I could only dread what our further conversations might bring.

It was after two when our glasses — more like vases — were set in front of us, one filled with Bass, the other with Samuel Adams. I girded up my loins and asked the ineluctable question, "So what about Gorliouk and Kramponov? I suppose you recruited them, too?"

"Kramponov, yes; Gorliouk — Gorliouk was manna from heaven. And the whole *Hinterreise* episode that followed was pure joy. It's true our Oulipian surveillance had put us on to Jouet meeting Gorliouk in Paris and then sending him the *Voyage d'Hitler* in Kaliningrad and later the other elements of your story. But we didn't expect much to come of it. The minute we learned that Gorliouk was looking for men who'd gone inside Hitler's bunker in Berlin, we got to Kramponov long before he did. We'd been interested in the question from the start, as you can imagine, and we were positive that Kramponov was the only one of those people who'd survived. It would be exaggerating to say we recruited him: we rented him for the occasion. The poor guy!

After the '98 devaluation his pension wasn't worth peanuts. He was only too happy to learn what he was supposed to say. I think it was rather brilliant to have introduced verses by Georges himself."

"But Retti was a long way from being broke. How did you manage to turn him around, as they say in your business?"

"Not only Retti but Gorliouk's whole trip to Germany was a gift of fate. Once the Russian had settled on a musical hypothesis, my one and only desire was to lead him to the 'book published by Stoßfest'. We kept a tail on Gorliouk day after day. I was prepared to have a fake scholarly article published in a musicological review that I'd have him 'accidentally' find, so he'd learn about the note Stoßfest is supposed to have sent to Bach. No need: we found out what documents he was researching and slipped the note into the pile, and sure enough he found it. The rest took care of itself. I can't describe how I felt when Gorliouk and then Jouet discovered the *Hinterreise* and its annex, the *Abc du Bach*, both of them fabricated by my grandfather sixty years earlier and forgotten ever since. How I laughed when I read Reine Haugure's comment — 'the musical angle almost certainly has nothing to do with Hugo Vernier' — when that's what provided the model for my whole design! Hugo Vernier is merely a remake of Peretz, the Jew who anticipated Bach, Beethoven and Wagner."

"Then John Scale was another 'gift of fate', since he went to Borrade on his own initiative?"

"Let's say he caused us no major problems. There was a minor problem: we had no idea he'd show up; and farther down the line, there was a somewhat bigger problem, at least a potential one. If he'd actively followed up the matter of the Hugo Gruppe, he might have discovered its historical reality, and that would have jeopardised everything I'd done. But he quite naturally came across the name 'Dennis Borrade', and as soon as he'd contacted him, he was a piece of cake. Our agents, in fact, had a ball, 'Dolly Haze' in Washington, and 'Moses' in London. We gave them little set-pieces they could enjoy acting out. You know, a secret agent's life is often, as we say, 'stressful'. As soon as Waw Hé's book in Hebrew was presented (purely as hearsay), with its plots of Shakespeare's plays, Scale swallowed it, Ian Monk swallowed it, once again you all swallowed it!" Parsifal III emitted a rather Niebelungian giggle. "Let me remind you that the whole story had no source except for Moses's assertions. The series of translations and outlines he passed on to Scale afterwards were typed by my own happy hands."

More beer was proposed to us. I could not face the prospect. Parsifal III pointed out, on a shelf behind the bar, a prodigious assortment of single-malt whiskies. I picked a fifteen-year-old Cragganmore, and he a Glenmorangie dating no doubt from the Hundred Years War. At my request they were served in wine glasses.

"If what you've told is true," I said, "you have taken extravagant measures for a project even less important than 'discrediting French poetry.' It's not believable."

"You're wrong. The surveillance, both Dennis's and my own, was virtually managed in off-hours. When you come down to it, there were very few extras (so to speak): Klara; a man to record a cassette; Kramponov; a librarian; and finally Dolly and Moses. That makes six in all, for twenty years of shenanigans. (Dennis obviously doesn't count. He's like a brother.) I'll tell you about it some other time, but I've performed some fairly useful services for France and the US. I was getting close to retirement. No one bothered me, I could take all the time I wanted."

"And what about the other Oulipians?"

"The others are special cases. I certainly have nothing to say about Bens."

"How come?"

"First of all, he's a reactionary Catholic–"

"You're totally insane!"

"Oh, yeah? How do you explain his emphasis on the feast days of the Holy Mother Church — St. Alphonse's Day, Candlemas, and Lord knows what else? Or the fact that he refers to 'the Vatican's absurd reform in 1963'?"

"No, no, no, no, no! You're wrong. You're absolutely wrong."

"Maybe. In any case he's your typical southerner, a real nuisance, the kind that's always trying to hog the limelight. His contribution to the subject is nothing more than a belated attempt — once again! — to give precedence to Provence, the Mother of All Poetry. The fact that he writes charmingly does nothing to alter what I say." After a pause: "'Hugues Auvernier'! For Christ's sake!"

There was no denying it: the malt whisky was doing me good. We had another glass of it. My irritation subsided. I mentioned Michelle Grangaud.

"I don't know what to think. I had nothing to do with that, in any case. I think she may have wanted to set herself apart, but I'm in no position to say, because Classical literature — of the Graeco-Roman variety, I mean — has always bored me to tears. It seems to me, though, that she may have possibly been trying to, I don't know, broaden the context, to make all these episodes seem less like instalments in a serial. Perhaps she caught on, at least partially. And you — you believe her story?"

I no longer had any notion of what I might believe. I asked him:

"But what about Eugophernes?"

"She's very clever."

"Well, Caradec's no dope, either."

"Exactly. With François it's a whole other matter. You understand, I've been dragging this business around with me for twenty years now. I know there was a break after Georges died, but it's still been pretty long. Especially when I see this nutcase, Reine Haugure, coming to the boil with her mythical Hugo Vernier Association, her *Bulletin of Verniereal Studies*, and other disasters. It's never been my intention to drag the whole of academia into an interminable hoax. I have to say, too, that I was a little wary of François. I said to myself: he knows his stuff; he may not take the bait as eagerly as the rest of you. So I told him a little bit about it, nothing substantial, just suggesting it was time to stop the rot. I don't know what he made of it. In any case I think he rose to the occasion. You don't agree?"

No word issued from my mouth. Parsifal III asked me, "A little one for the road? It's fabulous how this brew warms you up."

"It's not cold."

"Part of us always feels cold."

After a final glass we started home. It was close to four, the hour at which every drinking spot in Key West shuts its doors, until the Schooner Bar opens three hours later. We went back up Duval Street as far as Mangoes, where I retrieved my bike. I walked Parsifal III to the Merlin Inn on Simonton Street, and there we took cordial leave of one another and emphatically expressed our hopes of meeting again the next day. At last I set out for my house in Grinnell Street, still on foot — an attempt to swing my leg over the bicycle saddle had led to a dizzy spell that counselled prudence.

The following afternoon the desk clerk and manager of Merlin Inn assured me that they had taken in no one by the name of Bartlstand, nor had they seen any gentleman whose description corresponded to the one I gave them. I have not heard from him since.

Around five p.m. I drove our car (its licence plate reads OULIPO) to the town's little airport to meet my wife. Her plane was for once on time. We were overjoyed to be together again.

While waiting for her luggage, Marie said to me, "I have news for you. They've found a copy of the *Voyage d'hiver*. It's not at all what you thought. Hugo Vernier went to Egypt with an Egyptologist friend in December, 1860 — the book's an account of his trip and especially of the digs he saw. He also talks about his affairs with local boys. That's why his family bought up the entire edition and had it destroyed. They found the copy in Alexandria; it belonged to the descendant of one of those lovers. He must have sent a few copies back."

"And it was published in 1864?"

"Oh yes, it all fits. The most interesting thing is his description of the digs. For instance, they found a second-millennium-B.C. manuscript scroll that seems to be a kind of novel. There are some pretty funny stories in it: four kings who mutually conspire against each other while their wives are putting up preserves; a writer who composes an entire book by explaining that he's incapable of writing; small talk between men who meet to drink in public places; a man encased in clay who makes his best friend die of fright; a machine that assembles discoloured teeth into mosaics—"

"OK, OK. You can tell me all about it later."

"Very well. I've saved the article about it from *Le Monde*. Just one thing. Guess the name of the scribe who was responsible for all this."

"No! I don't want to know. I'm fed up with this business myself."

MIKHAÏL GORLIOUK

If on a Night a Winter's Traveller

Si par une Nuit un Voyageur d'Hiver

Translated by Ian Monk

Bibliothèque oulipienne 129

2003

Jacques Jouet has communicated a letter he has received to the Bibliothèque oulipienne. We are delighted to publish it here.

Kaliningrad, 9 September 2003

From: Professor Mikhaïl Gorliouk

Institute of French Language and Literature
Kaliningrad University
Federation of Russia

● To: M. Jacques Jouet, Oulipo, Paris

My dear Monsieur Jouet,

I hardly know where to begin. I suppose you must be surprised to receive a letter from me, and perhaps even furious, or else baffled by the fact that I never thanked you for (or even acknowledged receipt of) your *Hinterreise* (Bibliothèque oulipienne 108), which even though it dates back to 1999 still seems as fresh as ever and sums up, with a remarkable sense of concision and in a dazzling style, the essential points contained in the modest discoveries you so honestly credit me with, and which, when we met, I gave you permission to make public. I cannot deny the fact that, as you may no doubt imagine, I have rather neglected Vernierian studies during the past four years (above all in order to devote my time to Makhambet Utemissov, a nineteenth-century Kazakh poet, who deserves greater attention, as you shall soon see when I send you the work I have done on him).

To try to make amends for my long silence, I shall describe to you in detail how, a short time ago, I was to become once more embroiled in this enigma (or, as you shall see, what I now consider to be a pseudo-enigma) involving this business that so concerns you and your Oulipian friends. I of course mean the *Voyage d'hiver* affair. And I do mean *Hiver* and not *Hier*.

Last 4 August, Jacqueline Wedderburn, a young trainee research assistant in French literature (and who will remain so for some time I think), lurking behind the pseudonym Reine Haugure, was introduced to me in Graz over drinks during a rather dull symposium devoted to "The Herring Paradigm in the works of Ibsen". My first contact with Mademoiselle Haugure was quite warm, the second utterly icy. I shall pass rapidly over the warmth, which was largely down to the heat-wave, for my initial excitement was incapable of standing up to the barbs of a particularly heated intellectual disagreement, in particular over the business that concerns us.

My name, of course, was not unknown to the little idiot and, as soon as she had brought it back to mind, after a long period of absence, which was scarcely to her credit but which none the less suited her, scorn could clearly be read on her face. We had words.

She spoke to me about her slim tome, *Le Voyage du vers*, as well as other recent publications which you have been good enough to send to me regularly, but which I am ashamed to admit I only flicked through at the time. This has since been corrected. In the dispute between you and Mademoiselle Haugure you can of course count on my total support, and I should herewith like to provide you with a few arguments, assuming that you are in need of any. What in fact does Jacques Roubaud say about *Le Voyage d'hiver*? I quote: "As we know, in "Le Voyage d'hiver" Georges Perec tells of how a 'young literature teacher', Vincent Degraël, […] in his hosts' library, happened upon a slim volume of verse by a certain Hugo Vernier which was also entitled *Le Voyage d'hiver*." Let us compare this with what Perec actually wrote: "*The Winter Journey* was a sort of **narrative** written in the first person […] The second part […] was a long **confession** of an exacerbated lyricism, mixed in with poems, with enigmatic maxims, with blasphemous incantations." [The bold print is mine, M.G.] Hardly what, in 1864, would have been called a "slim volume of verse"! But no matter… According to Mademoiselle Haugure, following on from Jacques Roubaud, the real title of *Le Voyage d'hiver* by Hugo Vernier should have been *Le Voyage d'hier*. In her opinion, this is her mentor's most important contribution, which everyone else has ignored since. What a totally unfounded claim! And was such an eye-catching piece of publicity really necessary in order to advance the (in itself interesting) discovery that Vernier mastered combinatorics? It would seem that Reine Haugure, blinded by her admiration for Jacques Roubaud, had not read Georges Perec's short story with any more attention than her apparent paymaster. In particular, what does she make of certain extracts from

Vernier's book, which Vincent Degraël read in late August 1939 at Denis Borrade's house on the outskirts of Le Havre? I shall quote Perec once more: "winter fogs"; "the lucid winter, the season of serene art"; "the snow gleamed like sand"; "the train slid without a murmur", etc. Blinded by their apodictic approach, Haugure and Roubaud presumably think that we should read: "**yesterday's** fogs" or "the lucid **yesterday**", or that the **snow** in question has melted as much as that of yesteryear… Mademoiselle, Monsieur, be serious! This is what I told Reine Haugure in forthright tones, and the way she paled at once confirmed that I had touched a nerve.

I should like to pause for a moment to discuss the silent train Perec mentions, "the train slid without a murmur". *Un train traverse la nuit* ("a train crosses the night")… you know better than I this "alexandrine of variable length" which a rather more inspired Jacques Roubaud once heard pronounced by Jean Queval, and which then led to the formulation of his AOVL theory. So why did this phrase "the train slid without a murmur", which Vincent Degraël read in Vernier's book, leave a mental trace whose true significance would only occur to me later? But all in good time…

I let this vague impression lie for a few days, before receiving a flash of inspiration thanks to a certain Walter Henry (whose name, I think, is not unknown to you). He was also in Graz and his paper "From Ibsen's Rollmops to Nabokov's Butterflies" was a ray of sunshine in this dreary symposium. And yet, after accepting my congratulations, Henry flatly refused to talk to me about Vernier or the Oulipo because of his "recent occultation in solidarity with a well-known occultator who had just re-occultated himself, after his own disoccultation" (I am not quite sure what he meant by all this). Nevertheless, Walter Henry slipped me the address of his website as discreetly as if it were a pornographic photo. When I looked it up, the results were fruitful. Attracted by one of the site's tabs, *Invisible Libraries*, and preoccupied as I was by that "season of lucid art" (which seems to me to have been perfectly coined for the Oulipo; for a Chinese portrait, if asked "If the Oulipo were a season, which would it be?", wouldn't the answer be **winter**?), I clicked on the "Seasonal Libraries" menu, combined it with a search for "journey" and strangely enough arrived at a sub-menu entitled "Winter Sports Library" which led me to your excellent short story "Bonnet Blanc", and then the real miracle happened: the site's visuals flashed up on the screen

Italo Calvino's mighty *If on a Winter's Night a Traveller* into whose pages Georges Perec's tiny *Voyage d'hiver* then slipped like a clove of garlic into a leg of lamb! I said to myself in French, a language which is not unknown to me: why had this never occurred to me?

Without losing a second, I pinpointed the dates. Amazingly, *Se una notte d'inverno un viaggiatore* was published in Italy "*al principio dell'estate 1979*" (see *Romanzi e raconti* II, Mondadori, Milan, 1992, p.1381), with its railway station in a bottle set in a desolate landscape... *Le Voyage d'hiver* was published in the winter of 1979, on 20 December, in *Saisons, nouvelles* by Hachette. "Seasons" once again... Georges Perec's story had been written for this seasonal publication, while Rezvani, Jean Freustié and Jacques Chessex had dealt respectively with spring ("Dernier printemps"), summer ("L'été lointain") and autumn ("Octobre est le plus beau mois") (a point about which Reine Haugure presumably is ignorant), its entirety quite clearly forming a sort of remake of the *Four Seasons* of Nicolas Poussin, Vivaldi or Stuart Merrill.

Thus the leg of lamb and the clove of garlic appeared during the same year, at an interval of only a few months. They were cousins at the very least. And what if they had been cooked so that their tastes may be enjoyed together?

I then remembered something which you had happened to tell me during our meeting (and to which Harry Mathews alludes in his *Voyage des verres*, because we met only once (and this did not occur in Paris, as you can tell him from me, if you have not already done so, but in the charming village of Saint-Julien-Molin-Molette)). Do you remember? You told me that at a workshop in Royaumont, in August 1978, Georges Perec told the participants, you amongst them, about a project for a tetra-lingual novel in Italian, English, French and Spanish, featuring such authors as Italo Calvino, Harry Mathews, Perec himself and possibly Julio Cortázar — but had the latter even been informed? Oddly enough, Jacques Roubaud, who was, it's true, not yet an established novelist, had not been included in this foursome, even though it would soon become well known that he had a fictional project, and that he could well have written in Provençal, or even Japanese!

After re-reading Italo Calvino's *If on a Winter's Night a Traveller*, followed by Georges Perec's *Voyage d'hiver*, I acquired the conviction — and this is the revelation I want to share with you — that the two authors had indeed considered this collective project, seeing to it that the first two chapters — one long and in Italian, the other short and in French — would be published at approximately the same time and would be set on the same, pre-established field. For this novel is indeed a 'hyper-novel', as defined by Italo Calvino in his *Six Memos for the Next Millennium* as a "machine for multiplying stories". Other examples are *Life a User's Manual*, *If on a Winter's Night a Traveller* and *Winter Journeys*. Let me take a little more of your time, if I may, in order to prove it.

As early as page 3 of Calvino's novel we find: "[…] for-the-books-we-have–already-read-there's-no-need-to-open-them-because-they-belong-to-the-category-of-being-already-read-even-before-they've-been-written". If this is not a clear allusion to those books by the French poets spotted by Degraël, as soon as he had opened Vernier's book, then I shall become occulted too, in solidarity with Walter Henry! Once again, in Calvino, at the beginning of the first novel within the novel, we find: "Reader, you have already seen me beneath the glass ceiling in a railway station, eyes fixed on the points of an old, round clock's hands, which are pierced like halberds, trying in vain to make them turn back and pass back through the cemetery of past moments, laid out inanimately in their circular pantheon." I can just imagine Mademoiselle Haugure pursing her lips with an "I told you so" imagining that this corroborated her master's theories about Yesterday. She would have been quite right. But perhaps she had not understood the meaning of *Hinterreise* in German. But let it pass. I shall now press on.

You know how Italo Calvino, in an article entitled "Se une notte d'inverno un narratore", published in the review *Alphabeta* in December 1979, pointed out that the ten beginnings of the novels in the novel all obey the same narrative schema; well the same applies to the framework fiction, with the story of the two readers. He describes this schema as follows: "A masculine character narrating in the first person finds himself adopting a role which is not his, in a situation where the attraction exercised by a female character and a vague threat posed by a group of enemies envelope him irrevocably."

Calvino compares this outline to Raymond Queneau's *Exercises in Style* and explains how he has treated it in ten different ways: "a fog novel, a physical experience novel, a symbolic-interpretative novel, a politico-existential novel, a clinical-brutal novel, an anxiety novel, a logico-geometric novel, a perversion novel, a telluric-primordial novel and an apocalyptic novel."

I would like to open a parenthesis to point out that it would perhaps be better to leave aside this information, which is a piece of wool-pulling, so to speak, if you want to read *If on a Winter's Night a Traveller* seriously. Close of parenthesis.

At first sight, Georges Perec's *Voyage d'hiver* hardly conforms to this narrative structure. You might even say that he takes a wicked delight in utterly avoiding it. The story is not told in the first person, it cannot really be said that Vincent Degraël plays a role which is not his, there is no female character (except for Denis Borrade's mother, whose existence can be deduced from the phrase "the parents of […] Denis Borrade"), nor is there a vague threat from a group of enemies, unless you want to include the Luftwaffe.

As usual, Perec's text is full of ruses and clinamens. What does Perec say about *Le Voyage d'hiver*, and I mean Vernier's text, not his own? "*The Winter Journey* was a sort of narrative written in the first person…" Ah! The first element in the Calvinian specifications. Degraël's destiny is also a tragic one. How would you describe otherwise the 500 or so swine who burnt the edition of Hugo Vernier's book down to its penultimate copy, than as the vague threat from a group of enemies, as Calvino put it, and that this threat then had a knock-on effect on Degraël after destroying Vernier himself?

It is now that we come to the fourth musketeer in this trio, thus joining Harry Mathews (who certainly took his time about it). This fourth man, after the disappearance of Julio Cortázar, is none other than Jacques Roubaud. We are now in 1992. He too has taken his time. Calvino's novel had been available in French for over ten years. Why continue such a fastidious multi-lingual project, which would demand similar linguistic skills from its readers? Thus, *Le Voyage d'hier* is the third section of the collective novel, into which Roubaud has entered by force. He knows the Calvinian specifications. Since Perec had decided that Vernier's *Voyage d'hiver* was narrated in the first person, Roubaud decided against narrating *Le Voyage d'hier* in the same voice. On the other hand, the absence of any female characters worries him so much that he adds two: Denis Borrade's little sister, Virginie Hélène (note also the initials V.H.), while forcing the reader, by an extraordinary sleight of hand, to remember her existence: "The reader may recall (the fact has been duly underlined) [which is a downright lie and ethically indefensible, I must add, signed M.G.] that Borrade [i.e. Denis] had a little sister…". Then, later on, we have Virginie Huet, the governess of Judith Gautier, the daughter of Théophile (note once again the initials V.H.). Sure enough, obeying Italo Calvino, Jacques Roubaud gives us a Hugo Vernier who:

1) is attracted by a female character, Virginie Huet;

2) must also adopt a role which is not his, that of the plagiarist of Baudelaire, while Baudelaire had plagiarised him;

3) finds himself the target, with no escape, of a vague threat from a group of enemies, in other words Baudelaire once again, as the first of all the poetasters of Gautier's acquaintance, then later bards who were to pillage so tragically his work.

Here, I must give credit to Jacques Roubaud for a certain skill, which makes the bitterness he expresses via the foolish Haugure in *Le Voyage du vers* seem all the more absurd. It is true that he could have become annoyed at seeing the, in fact, rather touching spectacle of Hervé Le Tellier, yourself Jacques Jouet, Ian Monk, Jacques Bens, Michelle Grangaud and François Caradec all failing to see the Calvinian-Perecian-Mathewsian root behind all these *Voyages*, while at the same time having no fear in making their flights of fancy about Vernier in such magnificently naïve ways.

I am not sure that this Roubaldian ill-humour haugurs well or that the Reine he has found is the best spokesperson to shake up the whole affair. But this has had at least one good effect: shaking Harry Mathews out of his long lethargy (it is true that he did also have *Cigarettes* to write which is, I think, a hyper-novel too), for like Perec and Calvino, Mathews was at the origins of this project. Not knowing what approach to take, in his *Voyage des verres*, after having waited so long, Mathews then revealed a little of the secret by inventing his deus-ex-machination of a Bartlstand, thus denouncing a truly baffling plot (though not the right one!) and thus trying to bring this literary adventure to a close at last.

Allow me, my dear Jacques Jouet, to conclude by noting that this conclusion (and do please inform your colleagues of it) will not now be down to Harry Mathews, but instead to a modest French literature teacher in Kaliningrad. If you want, in these uncertain times, you can see it is a revenge for my country, which is neither holy nor eternal. I mean of course the unholy and ephemeral Russia.

Signed,

Mikhaïl Gorliouk

FRÉDÉRIC FORTE

The Journey of Dreams

Le Voyage des rêves

Translated by Ian Monk

Bibliothèque oulipienne 139

2005

● On 12 September 2004, I visited Jacques Jouet in his Paris flat. At a certain moment in our conversation we started discussing the various *Voyages*. Yes, of course I was interested… Then I blurted out my intention of writing to Mikhaïl Gorliouk, at the University of Kaliningrad. This was untrue, of course; I hadn't thought of doing any such thing even two seconds before. Jacques made no attempt to find out any more. He quite simply looked amused, went "Well, well, well!" in a fake southwest accent, then poured me another cup of his excellent green tea. We turned to other matters.[1]

A few hours later, I was finding it hard to fall asleep in the night train taking me back to Toulouse. What on Earth could have made me invent this idea of writing a letter to Gorliouk? Of course, I had been extremely impressed by his *Si par une Nuit un Voyageur d'Hiver*… but why claim that I was going to write to him? This conversation with JJ seemed to have awakened something. I would understand what this "something" was while crossing the night, that night. And this "something" concerned Harry Mathews.

The following evening, I took down the eleven *Voyages* from my shelves and spread them out on my bed, with the firm intention of re-reading them all, one after the other. This took quite a while. Once again I slept little and badly, my slumbers cluttered with "Hugo-Vernierian" dreams.

1. His project to write poems on the trees in the Jardin des Plantes, I think.

• • •

I'm lying on the sofa in my parents' dining-room, and there are four people sitting around the table. I recognise Jacques Roubaud, who is staring at me with a squint. I can hear my mother busying herself in the kitchen. I feel extremely weary and incapable of sitting up, let alone understanding what is being said at table. I get the highly unpleasant feeling that something important is happening *under my own roof* and that it is all escaping me.

I'm sitting and holding in my hands a green cardboard box-file, on which is written: A HARSH WINTER JOURNEY.
   My father is standing beside me and says:
   "You see, that's it, that's what I wanted to do…"
   Then I notice that in fact it's Georges Perec.[2] //★

• • •

I'm with Ian Monk and Jean-Marie Duffourc (doctor and friend) on the terrace of Le Gambetta, on Rue Gambetta, in Toulouse, opposite the Harmonia Mundi shop where I've been working for some time. We're drinking coffee. I draw a grid on the tablecloth.

The shop is decorated as though for Christmas, even though

2. That evening, I had noticed on reading the original *Voyage d'hiver* that, at a distance of 115 years, Hugo Vernier had the same birthday as my father: 3 September. Adopting this same rationale, and for my own personal satisfaction, I consider that Hugo Vernier died on a 29 January (in 1864 if Jacques Roubaud's sources are correct).

★ Forte uses // to indicate that a part of the dream has been omitted. Note too that the box-file carries a variant on the title of a novel by Queneau, *Un Rude Hiver*.

apparently it is springtime.

IM (who, in my mind, is Dennis Borrade / John Scale) says to me:

"Harmonia Mundi is *HM*."

He repeats the sentence several times gravely.

Jean-Marie tells us (though it seems to me that IM/DB/JS has vanished) that he's going to earn lots of money treating the wives of emirs in Yemen. Then he hums an operatic air.

· · ·

I spent the next day biting at the bit, constantly thinking about the letter that I now keenly desired to send to Mikhaïl Gorliouk. It was impossible for me to tell anyone else what I had to say to him. Reine Haugure could also have been a possible addressee, but I said to myself that, as a loyal Roubaldian, she would never reply to my letter. I also had the vague sensation that it was out of the question that a member of the Oulipo should get hold of what I called "my hypothesis".

Here is what I wrote to Gorliouk:

Dear Sir,

[…]

The revelations that you made to Jacques Jouet in your letter, the "exposure" of the Calvino-Perecian hyper-novel in particular, seem to me to be of a capital importance. Like you, I can only wonder how all this could have remained unknown so long… However, if I may, I'd like to make a remark. In your brilliant exposé, you place Hugo Vernier's Voyage d'hiver *on a purely conceptual level, and the original book discovered by Vincent Degraël vanishes into thin air during such a demonstration! Perhaps I'm being naïve, and I almost certainly am, but I remain persuaded that the Borrade copy of the* Voyage *really exists. And I think I know who has it…*

Here, I paused. Something wasn't quite right. What I was going to say, quite obviously, was that Harry Mathews was in possession of *Le Voyage d'hiver.*

Jacques Roubaud clearly hinted at this in *Le Voyage d'hier*: "[…] (he mentioned a possible lead involving an eccentric bibliophile, a certain H.M., who lived sometimes in Hamburg [Berlin?], sometimes in the Vercors [!!], occasionally in Houston [New York?] and from time to time in Vendôme, who might, perhaps, possess a copy of Vernier's work) […]"

And didn't François Caradec then bring this point up again in *Le Voyage du ver*? "H(I don't know his name, only his initials, H.M., which appear on his *ex-libris*)e…" Even Reine Haugure (and how else could she have known if Jacques Roubaud hadn't told her?) raked over the same coals in *Le Voyage du vers*: "[…] a human agent, the notorious H.M. And do not these initials in fact conceal *an author (whom we shall leave unnamed)* who played […] for his own unstated *(but easily fathomable) ends* [my italics]?"

It was only by taking into account this factor, the concrete existence of a copy of *Le Voyage d'hiver*, in Harry Mathews's possession, that we can explain H.M.'s determined attempt to conclude the cycle. This was the sole aim of the pseudo-revelations of the providential Bartlstand — what a man! — (because dissimulating the hyper-novel project, in which Mathews was supposed to participate, seemed secondary to me).

But something didn't seem quite right. Why had such transparent allusions by JR, FC and subsequently Reine Haugure not been taken further? Above all: why had Harry Mathews, who was so quick to pick up on the slightest imprecision, especially those of Jacques Roubaud in *Le Voyage d'hier* (e.g. his barbed (and groundless) remark concerning the date of Perec's trip to Australia), not bothered to answer such an obvious insinuation (based on his own initials!) coming from the very same Jacques Roubaud in the above-mentioned *Voyage*? It was barely credible!

My head was spinning. At regular intervals I got up from my chair and paced around the tiny space that constituted my flat. To calm down, I decided to fix myself an infusion, something I hadn't done for a very long time but which seemed like a natural solution just then.

Why had none of the Oulipians taken this revelation to its logical conclusion? I started to glimpse an answer, but didn't dare put it into words. This perhaps explained why I wanted this letter to travel far away, to Russia, and with a bit of luck get lost on the way.

I went back to bed with my stack of *Voyages*. I had to be sure. Re-read them calmly, I said to myself, don't get carried away… And so it was that I fell asleep and had another dream, the kind of dream you rarely have.[3]

● ● ●

I'm walking through the corridors of a huge house, constructed like a maze. Music can be heard coming from an upper storey. I know that it's a piece by Robert Schumann.

The doors to the right and left are ajar. I really want to open them completely, but stop myself.

I go into a room. It's the store where Olivier Salon keeps the volumes of the *Bibliothèque oulipienne*. There's a single bed and a wall covered with shelves full of the *Bibliothèque*. I absolutely want to find a particular number: it's 166. I find it, on the floor, at my feet. On the cover there is the author // and the title //.

Inside, I see isolated lines of poetry, which look like they have

3. I remember once dreaming that I was floating in space: the Earth forming this region (?) was an orange circle representing an embryo inside a placenta. Later, I was on the Moon. A huge hammer and sickle had been sculpted into the grey dust of the surface. We cosmonauts had rather charmless rooms, rather like in a university residence. We were not sure if we were going to be able to leave again. To do so, it would be necessary to climb aboard an inflatable lifeboat which would be propelled towards the Earth using a sort of cannon. Months later, I went back to the Moon and, this time, the air was breathable and there was a town like a Northern Venice. In the streets and then the lift of a townhouse, the inhabitants were wearing white carnival masks.

ten or twelve syllables. One line I remember is:

While I was still at school the weather was set fair

I'm with OS in his living-room. He's showing me what he can do
with a mask. He puts it on, takes it off and then says:
   "It's easier like that."

I'm holding in my hands the volume I found in the room
downstairs. OS says to me:
   "That one's *Le Voyage des rêves*, but that's not what I'm
supposed to do."
   And I:
   "Really? And what are you supposed to do, then?"
   He removes a small black book from his bookcase, which is not
a volume of the *Bibliothèque oulipienne* at all, and shows it to me.
It's *Le Voyage d'hiver*.

· · ·

I spent the next day feeling incredibly down. I wanted to drop everything, both the
Voyages, and my letter to Gorliouk…

On Thursday, which, thank God, was my day off, I woke up in an excellent mood.
While I was putting some water on to heat for my tea (smoked, a Lapsang Souchong),
my eyes fell on *Le Voyage d'Hoover*, which was still there on the edge of the table. I
opened it automatically, without any real conviction…

On page 14, Ian Monk had written: "*The Winter's Tale, an epic story in prose and verse,*
and signed by two initials: *Waw He* (or *W.H.*)."

W.H.… A Hebrew text… I turned the book round and saw in front of me: H.M.! W.H. when rotated was H.M.![4] Ian Monk, remembering *W or the Memory of Childhood*, and the Hebrew letter *Mem*, invented by Perec, had slipped in another allusion to Harry Mathews, but hidden this time, dissimulating there under the noses of the other Oulipans. And then, a little further down, didn't the "immortal 'To be or not to be'" refer to HM's "35 Variations on a Theme from Shakespeare"?

I immediately went back to the draft of my letter to Gorliouk:

[…] *Reine Haugure, when waxing ironic about the strange "reasoning" that makes certain people "add to the Vernierian nebula names with the initials H.W. or W.H.", has quite missed the point, that much is sure.*

As for you, when you mention Harry Mathews's "denouncing a truly baffling plot (though not the right one!)" you're on the right track, but I don't think that you've quite put your finger on the central conspiracy: i.e. that Harry Mathews is keeping possession of Le Voyage d'hiver **with** *the complicity of the Oulipo, or at least some of the group.*

I know that this may sound outrageous, but I think that the sole aim of the entire cycle of the Voyages *is to mask the truth while pretending to reveal it. A certain number of things would then be explained: readers attentive to the slightest sign cannot have failed to notice the famous initials HM in both* Le Voyage d'hier *and* du ver. *By subtly dosing truth and lies, realism and fantasy, the Oulipo is having fun leading its readers off into different dimensions. For example, Mathews hints that Caradec "knows his stuff", but when FC makes his revelation, it is with an innocent look on his face thanks to his (quaint but oh how ingenious) use of a worm, thus tipping the balance towards an animal tale, or just a big joke.*

The role of both Un Voyage Divergent *and* d'Arvers *can be understood in the same way: they lead the cycle on to other plains, clearly telling us that this is just Literature and that* Le Voyage d'hiver *doesn't exist 'in reality', thus disturbing the overly perfect linearity and historicity of the first five volumes that "reveal" (and which are thus necessarily off the point). Ian Monk apparently then intended to send a signal to the reader, or else play with the other*

4. But I don't think that Walter Henry has anything to do with this story. Otherwise Michelle Grangaud could equally well be lurking behind Mikhaïl Gorliouk's pen.

Oulipians.[5]

As for Harry Mathews, he acts as a lightning conductor, if necessary bringing the thunder down upon himself and thus protecting the Oulipo…

I stopped once again. This all sounded fine, but there wasn't a shred of proof for my thesis. If I openly questioned JJ for example, or IM, they would almost certainly deny outright any participation in an 'Oulipian plot'. They'd remain polite and say that they, in any case, had not the slightest idea about all that; I'd look ridiculous. And Mikhaïl Gorliouk probably wouldn't swallow it either: Monk's formula takes us no further than a Schubert polynomial…

Once again, I abandoned my letter. I had other things in mind: the following weekend, I was going on holiday with Louise, to her native Scotland. On Saturday evening, I took the plane to join her in Paris; by Sunday afternoon we were driving towards Calais. As for all those revelations, we'd see when I got back.

On Friday 24 September, a few days after an underground crossing of the Channel, then taking the road north while admiring the green English countryside and the English clouds, after suffering the Travelodges and experiencing the Little Chefs, after contemplating the Cumbrian Mountains in the Lake District (and in the mist), after arriving in Scotland and in Ayr, where Louise's parents lived, after following the traces of Robert Burns's "Tam O'Shanter" fleeing the witches of Alloway Kirk as far as the Old Bridge overlooking the Doon, on Friday 24 September, then, we took the ferry to Ardrossan, to spend a day on Arran.

---

5. As is well known, the Oulipians are players. In this way, HLT signs the text of his *Voyage d'Hitler* twice. If we accept that *Le Voyage d'hier* = *Le Voyage d'Hitler*, then by simplifying letter by letter we obtain: $v = tl$. It can thus be seen that "Hervé Le Tellier" can be spelt with the letters of the word "Hitler" (in which tl is also the equivalent of v). Such offbeat humour can only be praised.

The weather was wonderful. We disembarked at Brodick and went for a long cycle ride, following the east coast of the island. At the end of the afternoon, we decided to have dinner at the Brodick Bar, the main pub in the town, before taking the ferry back. First of all, we ordered two large white coffees, then Louise went off to make a phone call. I took the book I'd chosen for the trip out of my bag: Julio Cortázar's *Hopscotch*.

While I was endeavouring to get back into my reading, I suddenly sensed that someone was staring at me (it is always odd to 'sense' this kind of thing, and in such cases it is hard to say which of our senses 'sense' it, personally I really wouldn't know… In any case, I clearly sensed that two eyes were now focused on me). When I raised my head, an alert man sitting at a neighbouring table leaned towards me and said, in excellent French:

"Excuse me but… I see that you're reading Cortázar… Do you like it?"

Surprised, I said:

"Oh… Yes, yes… You know Cortázar?"

"Yes, and well in fact… He was a very good friend of mine," he said with a satisfied smile.

He was a man aged between seventy and eighty, with a round face, thick white hair, dense darker eyebrows, and looking at me with amusement. His appearance made quite an effect.

I found it incredible, in this place, as remote as could be from where I lived, a place where I had never been before, an island whose population could barely exceed 5,000 inhabitants, to come across a man who had known well a writer who had died twenty years before, and who I was reading for the first time… But, after all, and perhaps for that reason in fact, this trip was so new and exotic to my eyes that I saw no reason why it shouldn't be true.

Louise came back at that moment and saw that I was disconcerted. I stammered:

"Eh… This is my friend, Louise Maxwell… And you are…?"

"Bauld, Douglas Bauld. You must be astonished by what I've just said, young man. But I must say in turn that I don't bump into someone reading Cortázar every day! During the fifteen years I've been on this island, it hasn't ever happened once!"

I explained the situation to Louise.

"And you really knew him well?" I asked Douglas Bauld.

"Of course! We met in Paris… It was in, wait a second… 1955. We were both working for UNESCO as translators. I was much younger than him, but certain things brought us together…"

He fell silent, then went on:

"In *Hopscotch*, you've come across the mother of Gregorovius?"

I nodded. I was in the middle of the book.

"Well, she's my mother… I mean, Julio based it all on my story, you see… Like Gregorovius, I was born in Glasgow… and my mother brought me up on her own. My father left when I was two… He wasn't a 'sailor' as Cortázar puts it, but he behaved like one. That's what brought Julio and I together… the fact that our fathers had… abandoned us. We told each other about our childhoods one evening, in a café in the Latin Quarter… after that we became very close."

He paused for a while, then continued:

"Have you read *Cronopios and Famas*, perhaps?

"No… not yet."

"Well, in *Cronopios and Famas*, Julio alludes to a Scottish legend I'd told him, it's one of the 'instructions'. He did modify it a bit, as you'll see. It's a story about the blank page and about death… It was his way of honouring his friends. He was exceptional, if only you'd known him…"

Mr. Bauld was clearly deeply moved; we were too. Then he smiled and said: "Well! Dinner time."

And he invited us to join him. In any case, we'd just missed the 7 p.m. ferry, which left us two hours until the next one. We all ordered fish and chips.

Douglas told us how he'd finished his career with UNESCO in New York in the 1970s and '80s, and since then had been living in a cottage he'd bought in Corrie, a small village on the northeast of the island, and which we had passed through earlier that afternoon. He was a widower and came regularly to the Brodick Bar for a chat and to socialise. He didn't often have the chance to speak French. It must be said that Louise and I were all ears — Louise because she was Scottish and Francophile, me because meeting someone who was almost a character out of a Cortázar novel was completely fascinating.

Louise had ordered haddock, Douglas Bauld a fish whose name I can't remember, and me monkfish. I dipped my chips in the brown sauce. I was far from home. It was perfect.

We talked about Scotland, Paris and literature and I quite naturally mentioned *Le Voyage d'hiver*. It was all I'd been thinking about the week before, and hadn't Julio Cortázar featured in Mikhaïl Gorliouk's letter? I summed up the story for Bauld, as best I could. He went pale, so much so that I thought for a moment that he had a fish bone caught in his throat. I had never seen before, and no doubt will never see again, a man react in such a way to something I'd just said. He had to take a good swig from his pint before recovering his fine Arran colours. What he told me next came as something of a surprise.

So, in June 1978, Julio Cortázar visited Douglas Bauld in New York. There was nothing exceptional about that. In the previous few years, Cortázar had visited NYC on a regular basis, for literary or political reasons, and had been put up by his Scottish friend almost every time. On this occasion, Bauld told us, the main reason for the trip was to see his New York publisher, Pantheon, who was to bring out *A Manual for Manuel* the following September… Cortázar also told Douglas that he had arranged to meet a friend from Paris that evening, a writer who was also staying in town for a few days. He suggested that Douglas came along with him.

A few hours later, the two men were sitting at a coffee table, in a disco bar in Manhattan, face to face with Georges Perec and Harry Mathews, who had not initially been invited but had come along too, and they were all savouring a round of Arran single malt Bauld had ordered. The atmosphere was warm, a bit too 'disco' for Julio Cortázar perhaps, but the two Oulipians were having a hell of a time. Perec told them that he was in New York to check out locations. With a director friend, he was working on a project for a film called *Ellis Island*. As for Mathews, he was currently teaching in Vermont and had come to see Georges for the weekend. As the evening wore on, the two rogues became increasingly animated. It was Georges Perec who started the ball rolling. He wanted to talk to Julio about a project, a project for a "multi-lingual hyper-novel", something he had planned with Harry Mathews and Italo Calvino. Perec and Calvino had made considerable progress in their respective parts. But as Calvino was not present, it was difficult for them to explain what he was doing. It was a highly complex novel, which, Perec felt certain, would greatly appeal to Julio. His own part was more modest. It was a short story based on a tale that one of his former teachers had told him. And he presented the outline of what was to become *Le Voyage d'hiver*. But that was not all…

"We'd all drunk quite a lot of whisky, and we were rather merry. Perec and Mathews were looking at each other every three seconds and sniggering. They were obviously enjoying the surprise they were going to create. Harry Mathews had a briefcase with him, which he'd been clutching since the beginning of the evening. He then removed a book from it, which he solemnly handed to Cortázar. It was a slim volume, and looked old… Julio started leafing through it, and then did so more and more feverishly. When I leant towards my friend to see what he was reading, I soon understood what he was holding in his hands. The alcohol made this all seem completely natural, while giving me the impression of being in some ways a… a character in a novel, if you see what I mean? An incredulous Julio handed the book back to Mathews and asked: '¿Cómo?'. Mathews then told us a strange tale: he had found the book in the post one morning, a few months before, when he was in his New York apartment. *Le Voyage d'hiver* was accompanied by an anonymous letter, he said. He didn't have it with him, but basically it said that he should show the book to Georges Perec, and no one else, until he received further instructions. He also informed us that there was a P.S. advising him to take this whole business 'extremely seriously', and that 'they' were not joking. 'Just like a secret message from the CIA, in fact!' he said, laughing. The extravagant side of this story seemed rather to amuse him. But he had since been rather disappointed as he had not received any subsequent letters.

" 'And you should have seen Georges when I showed him the book!… I don't think I've ever seen such an expression before!'

"Cortázar picked up the book again, flicked through a few pages and I heard him murmur: 'No… no, Mallarmé…' In the end, Perec invited Julio to participate in the project, which I'd been expecting him to say for some time, as you can imagine. But my friend's answer surprised me:

" 'Listen, Georges… I really don't know.'

"That rather ruined the atmosphere. Perec and Mathews now looked slightly awkward. Julio told them, not very convincingly, that he'd think about it. And, as it was late, we decided to go home. I think that Julio felt somewhat overwhelmed… We never talked about the matter again, in any case. And I didn't know whether anything had happened subsequently. But what I do know, my lad, is that *Le Voyage d'hiver* really exists. Or at least it did in June 1978."

Louise reminded me that the ferry was about to depart. It was time to go. We quickly exchanged addresses, then Louise and I had to run. We were the last ones on board.

Night had fallen. My head was spinning after this day on the island, the sea air, the sprint to the ferry and above all Douglas Bauld's revelations. Comfortably seated inside, we soon fell asleep.

• • •

I'm on the deck of the ferry. The weather is wonderful. The boat leaves the bay of Brodick. Louise is standing on the quay and we wave at each other. I know it's the last time I'll see her.[6] The seagulls are plunging into the waves like stones in order to fish, which looks suicidal.

Inside the ferry, Douglas Bauld and I are sitting in chairs. Night has fallen. He's reading a tourist brochure: "*WHy Arran?*"

"Yes, why?" I ask him.

Douglas, who is now Harry Mathews, says:

"It's because they're dead. Perec, Calvino, Cortázar… We can't go back in time."

"Is that why you're keeping *Le Voyage d'hiver* secret?"

---

6. I was wrong in my dream. I did see Louise again, a few months later, in Brussels, Julio Cortázar's place of birth.

He answers:

"You're in the Oulipo now[7]... and you... must understand... If it turned out that *Le Voyage d'hiver* really did exist, *you wouldn't have been able to write what you're going to write*... No Oulipian would be able to write what they should write... The perpetual novel initiated by Georges Perec would stop and probably, with it, the *in vivo* novel by Raymond Queneau... And you wouldn't want that, would you?"

"No, of course not."

"Fine... What we know about *Le Voyage d'hiver* is shut up in a box... just like Schrödinger's cat, you see? Our collective novel is in that box, describing but not showing its interior... In there, *Le Voyage d'hiver does (not) exist.*

He doesn't answer

and I remain

indefinitely

suspended

waiting

for this

answer

7. ?!! At the time, of course, I wasn't.

194

JACQUES JOUET

The Journey of the Large Glass

Le Voyage du Grand Verre

Translated by Ian Monk

●

Bibliothèque oulipienne 162

2007

I shall begin with the memory of a serious mistake I made during my previous career. It happened in 1975. I was running the Maison des Jeunes et de la Culture in Ris-Orangis, near Paris. It was very much a job with many different responsibilities. That evening, the cinema club was showing Eisenstein's *October*, and I was in the booth, at the controls of a 16mm Debrie projector, which was sending its beam through a thick pane of glass, put there to prevent the sound of the motor from drowning out the soundtrack. I glanced through the window to check the film and noticed, almost in the nick of time, that it was running backwards. The broken statue of Tsar Alexander III was rising back on to its plinth. What a disaster! The rental company had forgotten to wind it back! Lights on in the cinema, apologies, feverish rewinding… Phew! I started the film again. But it was still running the wrong way round. Crowds of determined proletarians were dashing backwards, away from the Winter Palace. I knew Lenin's adage: "One step forwards, two steps back", but, as an illustration, this was taking things a little far. Then someone in the audience came up to inform me discreetly that he knew this Eisenstein film well, and that it started with a rather technically naïve flashback, during which the broken Tsar rose back on to his plinth. I should have watched the film before showing it! Sheepishly I wound back the damned spool once again and finally started showing our film, which ran backwards, the right way round.

I was thinking of this bad memory while contemplating Marcel Duchamp's *Nude Descending a Staircase*, the famous 1912 painting, which had been rejected by the Salon des Indépendants, even though it included the cream of the avant-garde at the time (at the head of which were his own brothers, Jacques Villon and Raymond Duchamp-

Villon), a refusal which is generally seen as being the most fertile trauma in the entire history of modern art. Duchamp was not best pleased, and he turned his back on Art, to such an extent that he even took a job as an assistant librarian in the Bibliothèque Sainte-Geneviève. When will Duchamp's ashes be transferred to the nearby Pantheon, in a small signed box, shaped like a book?

One evening, under a mango tree, I was talking about all this with a very young assistant lecturer in French (or as he would have it "Francophone") literature at the University of Ouagadougou.

"Do you know what?" he said, "I view the twelve Oulipian *Voyages* to be the sole really convincing example of a collective novel."

"Really?" I replied, as interested as I was surprised, by what sounded like an utterly sincere compliment.

I must point out that I had met Mohammoudou Bakoungou a few days before, in difficult circumstances during which he had shown great courage. He was being confronted by a student who was trying to buy his degree from his teacher, but his teacher had refused and, raising his voice, was now creating a public scene, which is quite something when you know how much lecturers earn, when you know that the student in question was the son of a minister and that this kind of corruption, which is the gangrene of African universities, is unfortunately far from rare.

"Yes," Bakoungou told me, "your series of *Voyages* (correct me if I'm wrong) was initiated by Georges Perec, who never imagined — and never even wished for — such a continuation. His followers have been working as they want, when they want, without any obligation or imposed order. This is exactly the opposite of all those awful novels launched in August by the press during the silly season, in which everyone does their tedious little piece of homework under the name of a *cadavre exquis*, which is fallacious, given that it isn't one, since everyone has read at least one of the preceding episodes. But your novel is based on potentiality, and is a centrifuge. The end was not and has not been planned. Even Marcel Bénabou has no obligation to contribute. What a relief that must be for him!"

"You know Marcel Bénabou?" I asked.

"I haven't been able to resist reading none of his books," said Bakoungou, in a deliciously convoluted way. "But, if you don't object, let's get back to the point and your Duchamp."

"Of course," I said.

"The fact that, after his great let-down in 1912, Marcel Duchamp became a librarian must have some importance for Jacques Roubaud who, so far as I can tell, tends to place all of Duchamp's activities in the sole field of language…"

"There's a good chance of that," I confirmed.

"And he's quite right, Duchamp was a writer, not a painter, nor even a visual artist! For example," Bakoungou went on, clutching my arm, "I think — and am ready to prove it — that the term 'ready-made', which is apparently an English expression, was in fact taken from the French language, and more exactly from sixteenth-century French, and even more specifically from Rabelais."

"What makes you say that?"

"A passage in the *Tiers Livre*, chapter 19. Pantagruel and Panurge are trying to interpret the versified pronouncement of the Sybil of Panzoust, which concerns a young *briffault* (or begging friar), who is a rapist, who has impregnated a nun, and who answers to a name which the commentary in my edition describes as requiring no comment. His name is **Brother Royddimet**, to which the translation into modern French adds a further touch, putting it as: **Raide-y-met**."★

"How can I believe you?" I asked, as distrustful as I was amazed.

"It's not hard to check. Anyone can buy the *Tiers Livre* and, as I told you, it's in chapter 19. It's hardly necessary for me to remind you of the constant sexual allusions in Marcel Duchamp's poetic work, nor his statement that the expression *ready-made* 'pushed (him) into being herself'. What a good push, indeed — if not an erection, then at least an irruption. But that's not at all," Bakoungou went on. "Come to my office tomorrow. I want to show you something that may well have a certain bearing on Hugo Vernier."

Then he left me, groggy from the heat, impatient, and wondering how to cool down the hours that separated me from the next day.

★ Put-it-in-stiff. [Trans.]

Bakoungou lived in a small, tepid house in the district of Dassassogo, which is my favourite neighbourhood in Ouagadougou. He showed me in, introduced me to his smiling wife and four, shy children, and made some tea. Then he beckoned me into his office.

"Before showing you," he said, "let me share with you two points that leave me perplexed about the *Voyages* written by the collective novelist Oulipo who is, as I am well aware, also a collective character in the novel. Perplexity number 1: the idea that the *Voyage d'hiver* by Hugo Vernier (VH by HV!), read by Vincent Degraël in Normandy, should be coveted quite so much seems rather naïve to me. Obviously the book exists, or at least existed, in concrete terms; certainly the book is the subject of a novel, in concrete terms too. These two propositions are not contradictory and the colophon of Frédéric Forte's *Voyage des rêves* can stand as a sort of pre-stated conclusion. Perplexity number 2: why are you focusing to such a great extent on Vernier's tome, while neglecting all the other documents so much? Whether Vernier's book ended up in the stomach of a worm, in a burnt-out bunker, in J. Edgar Hoover's garter-belt drawer, or a safe in Key West has little real importance, in fact…"

"What other documents do you mean?" I asked with prodigious curiosity.

"Firstly, Vincent Degraël's notebook, which is mentioned in the first episode by Perec; secondly, Vincent Degraël's 'register' bound in black cloth (same source); thirdly, the 'vast pile of documents and manuscripts' which Degraël left behind and his students set about sorting through (the same source again); not to mention the 'school exercise-book belonging to a certain H. Vernier' which is mentioned by Hervé Le Tellier in *Le Voyage d'Hitler*; and so on and so forth… It is quite stupefying that Jacques Roubaud has not looked into all this."

"Oh, you know," I said with a shrug, "Roubaud and his Reine Haugure read what they want to read!… I think that Roubaud has never forgiven the Oulipians for not leaving him alone to get on with that hyper-novel with Perec and Calvino which Gorliouk has presented so marvellously."

"Perhaps, but it would be just to say that you yourself…"

Then he fell silent. There was a question I was dying to ask him, and which I sensed Bakoungou wanted me to ask before going any further. Putting aside any misplaced pride, I restrained the beating of my heart and murmured:

"Have you discovered something of importance?"

"Take a look at this," Bakoungou said, handing me a small sheet of paper in portrait format with hand-writing upon it.

I read: "Vernier-Duchamp: *Nude Re-ascending a Staircase Backwards to Get Dressed*, p.83, line 7." I stared at Bakoungou. I re-read the sentence.

"You're not going to tell me that Hugo Vernier had foreseen the slap in the face that Marcel Duchamp was to receive in 1912! I warn you that any attempt to turn Vernier into a sort of Nostradamus of late romanticism will come over as being highly suspect."

"That isn't my intention," Bakoungou said. "This piece of paper comes, and I can prove it, from Vincent Degraël's notebook, which I mentioned earlier. Perec wrote: 'Degraël made a careful note of the list of authors and the sources of their borrowings'. In this case, he spotted Duchamp."

"Where did you find this piece of paper?"

"What does it matter? In Paris."

"Which *arrondissement*?"

"That question is irrelevant. In the 4th."

"In the Bibliothèque de l'Arsenal?"

"Do you think I'm capable of stealing a document that belongs to your nation? No."

"So how did you find it, then?"

"Thanks to a combination of flair and luck. But, you know, when you're nuts, everything ends up looking like a cracker."

"And… what are your deductions?"

"All in good time. I could play the wise guy and tell you, without further ado, that Marcel Duchamp, once he'd been turned down by the Salon des Indépéndants in 1912, decided to re-title his *Nude Descending a Staircase* as *Nude Re-ascending the Staircase, Back to the Stairs, To Get Dressed*, a little like that Eisenstein film you told me about the other day, and that the Nude when getting dressed, obviously dresses as a bride with the sole objective of being stripped bare by her bachelors, even, who will then throw her back downstairs, her skin as white as porcelain, only to be refused once again in the form of a urinal, because you know that *Fountain*, the famous ready-made, was also refused by the exhibition committee of the Society of Independent Artists of New York (apparently, Duchamp was like us Africans, rather luckless when it came to Independences). But, my dear sir, I'm not writing a novel, and I'm not now writing the thirteenth chapter of the *Voyages*. I would just like to draw your attention to things which you might like to think over: in New York, Marcel Duchamp lived on Beekman Place for a short time in 1915 (I've just learnt this from Francis M. Naumann's *The Art of Making Art in the Age of Mechanical Reproduction*, Achim Moeller Fine Art, 1999-2000). Now, Beekman Place was also, much later of course, the New York address of Harry Mathews, of the Oulipo. The second point concerns *Fountain*, and here, too, don't bank on me to develop any extravagant views of dubious taste concerning this urinal, this *raide-y-met*, or whatever. No, what interests me is the signature: '**R. Mutt, 1917**'."

"Well?"

"Firstly, it is known that Duchamp bought this urinal from J.L. Mott Iron Works, in New York, like France's Porcher, if you will… Then J.L. Mott became R. Mutt. Why?"

"That's just what I was going to ask you," I said. "Some connection with Warren Motte, perhaps?"

"I don't think so. Using the signature of a manufacturer, or almost, and an industrial manufacturer at that, was no doubt a notion that fitted very well with the destructive ideas of Duchamp the artist, who was already a Dadaist at heart. Now, it should not be forgotten that, the following year, Marcel Duchamp painted an 'oil and crayon on canvas, with bottle brush, three safety pins and one bolt'. And what did he call it?"

"What?"

"'**Tu m'**', thus abbreviating '*tu m'emmerdes*', or 'you piss me off'. Now, if we turn it backwards, what do we get?"

"'**Mut**'," I suddenly said, as beaten down as I was exhausted. "But there's still a *t* missing."

"Rrose Sélavy was first spelt Rose…"

"True."

"That will be all for today. Tomorrow, I'll tell you more about Hugo Vernier and the voyage of the Glass, or rather *Le Voyage du Grand Verre*."

I felt like pinching myself. I couldn't believe my ears. I was utterly stupefied! (I love such expressions of narrative disbelief.) I hadn't come to Ouagadougou for nothing. In any case, you never go to Ouagadougou for nothing. I was there the next day, before the appointed time, on my dear Bakoungou's mat.

"Would you mind," he began, "if I first spoke to you about Jules Verne?"

"I came here for Duchamp, so I was hardly expecting him," I said. "But don't worry, I won't mind very much, as I have nothing but admiration for the greatest French novelist of the nineteenth century."

"So, on that point, you are in complete agreement with Raymond Roussel. But perhaps you haven't noticed that one of Jules Verne's African novels, *The Adventures of Three Englishmen and Three Russians in South Africa*, is without doubt the work which, prior to your collective novel, mentions the name of Vernier most often!"

"I'm dumbfounded."

"Yes indeed, and you're now going to get dumber and dumber, until finally you'll be so dumb that you'll reach the wisdom of the fool and glimpse the truth. The three Englishmen and three Russians were in South Africa on a scientific mission to measure the meridian. The method they adopted was triangulation. To obtain the greatest possible precision in their measurements, they used a vernier, which is a sort of sub-division of a ruler, allowing for the calculation of even minuscule dilations in the standard scale. The common noun, vernier, comes from Pierre Vernier, a mathematician from the Franche-Comté who invented the device in 1631. In a way, the absolute, fixed scale is always just slightly relative, and it is necessary to calculate any difference, any tiny little not-quite-right. 'This vernier,' wrote Verne, 'was also equipped with a microscope allowing estimates to be made of the quarters of a hundred-thousandth of a toise.' I have no need to tell you that Marcel Duchamp's *Standard Stoppages* plough the field of an analogous preoccupation. Let me sum up: we now have Pierre Vernier, a forgotten proper noun; vernier, a common noun; Hugo Vernier, a proper noun, completely obliterated by posterity until its rediscovery by Vincent Degraël, and then by Georges Perec! But what interests me personally is what happened before Degraël! And so it was that my research led me to Marcel Duchamp."

"I see."

"As we have seen, in 1915, Marcel Duchamp lived for a short time on Beekman Place, New York, and it was during this period that he hung his snow shovel from the ceiling, screwed his coat-rack to the floor, fixed a bicycle wheel on a stool and exhibited a grey, steel comb… all pre- or initial ready-mades… The relationship between the industrial object and a painting on an easel, or in a museum, is the same as that between a common noun and a proper noun. Duchamp radicalised this notion and invented the ready-made which, if he signed it, became in a way the proper noun of a mass-produced object. This is the great contradiction which Duchamp takes on: by reducing the value of artistic objects, he heightened the value of mass-produced objects. But he could not rob everything of its value. When, previously, Jules Verne dwelt so much on vernier as a common noun, he was doing something similar: Verne, a proper name and paronym of vernier, becomes a common noun, or a thing. It is the removal of value from a proper noun and, at the same time, an addition of value to an object, given that it is an instrument of measure, and so of poetry. Even better, it is a precision tool. Even better, it is for splitting exceptionally fine hairs, exactly as a novel does with respect to concrete existence."

"Assuming," I pointed out, "that Duchamp was familiar with the *Extraordinary Voyages*. But Verne does not appear in the index of Duchamp's library, as published in Marc Décimo's *La Bibliothèque de Marcel Duchamp, peut-être*, Les Presses du réel, 2002! However, Rabelais was certainly there…"

"You know," said Bakoungou, brimming with a false modesty tempered by self-mockery, "I'm a sort of Dupin, I'm interested only in deductions. One of these days, we'll see if the facts confirm them or not. For me, there is no place here for doubt. So I'll leave that to you. Anyway, in New York, on Beekman Place, Marcel Duchamp **must have** read Hugo Vernier's *Voyage d'hiver* (HV's VH). This is, in a sense, a necessity. He read it, and found the sentence attested by Degraël: '*Nude Re-ascending a Staircase Backwards to Get Dressed*'. At that moment, he got thinking."

"But how did he get hold of the book?"

"That's the sort of fact-checking that barely interests me at all. I guess that, if you attach any real importance to this detail, you should probably ask Harry Mathews."

"Er, this was in 1915… and I'm sorry, but at the time Harry Mathews was aged about minus fifteen, given that he was born in 1930…"

"Of course, of course… but he did already have a family. And already a family library. And his family was not the only one to live on Beekman Place!"

"True enough, and as true even as I am sitting here. In the 1980s I saw in Harry Mathews's home on Beekman Place his mother's beautiful library in the rotunda that looked out over the East River, and it was utterly marvellous."

"You're telling me."

"You wouldn't be adding grist to Frédéric Forte's mill, would you, by suggesting that Harry Mathews is the happy owner of the sole and unique copy of Vernier's book?"

"Maybe. But sole and unique? Not so sure! What interests me though are the motives. Marcel Duchamp was in Hugo Vernier's debt. And, unfortunately — I mean unfortunately in ethical terms — he did not want to honour this debt. But in that respect, he is not the only one in this tale, because from Bach to Baudelaire, by way of Perec himself, nobody has particularly shone in their attempts to cultivate the memory of this poor boy who had been of so much use to them! Duchamp did not want to recognise this debt, because being avant-garde is all that mattered during that accursed twentieth century. And that was his second mistake."

"The first one seems to have escaped me," I said.

"But the first one was quite simply to have trumpeted the contents of Vernier's book all over the place, I mean all over Beekman Place. At this point, I'm going to leave the world of conjectures and ask you to look at this."

Bakoungou then placed before my eyes a clipping from the *New York Times*, dated one fine day in 1931. The article was entitled: FATAL VOYAGE FOR THE LARGE GLASS.

"Don't worry," my host went on, "I'm quite aware that Harry Mathews was one year old in 1931, and cannot reasonably be considered responsible for transporting the *Large Glass* in a truck from the Brooklyn Museum to the house of its owner, Katherine Dreier, who had loaned it, and which resulted in the infamous breakage of this fragile work."

"The CIA sometimes recruit them right from the cradle," I jeered.

"Jeer not," Bakoungou said. "Anyway, as you're so fond of dates, the CIA was founded only in 1946. But just look at what this *New York Times* article has to say."

I read:"In Little Odessa, on the peninsula of Coney Island, a bride walking backwards, on emerging from City Hall, trapped her feet in her train, was caught by her page boys, who clumsily tore off her dress while trying to save her. She then dashed down the steps, and ended up on the road, where a transport truck from the Brooklyn Museum was forced to swerve to avoid her. Witnesses report having heard a sinister sound of breaking glass. All the shopkeepers came outside and saw that none of their store windows had been damaged. But, apparently, inside the truck, things were rather different."

"Was this done accidentally on purpose?"

"That seems to me to be possible, at the very least."

"Who was behind it?"

"Aren't you just full of questions?"

"Just one more…"

"Don't bank on me to spoon-feed you. Instead, why don't you take a look at the classified ads page, in the same paper?"

"There are three photos," I said, utterly fazed.

"Can you describe them to me?"

"Two brides and an object."

"Describe the object."

"A sort of slide-rule, with a graduated ring and a magnifying glass, which seem to be there so as to magnify the millimetres inscribed on the main scale…"

"It's a vernier. Bride number 2, the one who fell down the stairs, was the daughter of the king of verniers, in Little Odessa, the best manufacturer of this tool in the world."

"And what's written there, in black on grey, on the vernier? It looks like a signature…"

"Yes, it quite clearly says 'Marcel'. And 'Duchamp' can quite easily be deduced, don't you think?"

"Marcel Duchamp signed a vernier? But there's no mention of such a ready-made in his *catalogue raisonné*!"

"There are two possible explanations. Either the catalogue isn't as *raisonné* as all that, or else this ready-made is a fake," said Bakoungou. "In other words, the signature is false. I would favour the latter hypothesis, and it was probably the only ready-made Marcel Duchamp, as he was later so often to do, would never have agreed to make genuine."

REINE HAUGURE

H... Ver...'s Journey

Le Voyage d'H... V...

Translated by Ian Monk

●

Bibliothèque oulipienne 179

2008

● **1.** As soon as the Oulipo was founded, its President-Founder, François Le Lionnais, took care to draw its followers' attention to the need to keep their eyes obstinately focused, like Captain Hatteras staring towards the pole, or Paul Déroulède towards the blue line of the Vosges, obstinately focused, say I, on the Everest of the PERFECT CONSTRAINT.

2. "**The PERFECT CONSTRAINT**", said the President, is one that governs "**each page, line and letter of the ideal Oulipian text, which chooses each of its words, which places all of its commas, and dots all of its *j*s**".

3. He often repeated this maxim, in a variety of forms, particularly to new Oulipians, whose laziness he deplored, as well as their lack of literary ambition and tendency to overuse the "clinamen".

4. And it must be noted that, from the 'wild blue yonder' where he has been for over twenty years now, he must currently be worrying about the propensity of today's Oulipians to satisfy themselves with OULIPO-Lite activities, and thus squander their time with *"starter lists"*, *"chicagos"*, *"solicitudes"*, *"veiled rhymes"* or so-called *"sardinosaurs"*.

5. I am sure that it is unnecessary to recall that the President's maxim was taken more or less exactly from a famous short story by Henry James (no, HLT, not Marcel Proust!), "The Figure in the Carpet"? Unnecessary? Or not?

6. The Oulipo has used it on countless occasions in its public readings, educational activities, broadcasts on the radio or television, a reception speech at the Académie Française and in the text read out in its name in Stockholm by MB (Marcel Bénabou) after it had won the Nobel Prize,

7. but apparently without bothering to read the short story in its entirety.

8. We now have. And this has led us to an astonishing discovery which we shall now present.

9. We shall mention only those aspects of James's short story which are relevant to our demonstration.

10. In this perspective, the two main characters are: an author who, in the presence of a young man who admires him (the narrator), enigmatically evokes the fact that no one has understood how his *œuvre* has been built up. He claims to have a 'secret procedure'. He does not reveal what this is, but does provide a few indications which, according to him, will allow it to be deciphered. Here are the main ones:

a) *There's an idea in my work without which I wouldn't have given a straw for the whole job. It's the finest, fullest intention of the lot, and the application of it has been, I think, a triumph of patience, of ingenuity.*

b) *The particular thing I've written my books most for [...] the thing that most makes [a writer] apply himself, the thing without the effort to achieve which he wouldn't write at all, the very passion of his passion, the part of the business in which, for him, the flame of art burns most intensely? Well, it's that.*

c) *It stretches, this little trick of mine, from book to book, and everything else, comparatively, plays over the surface of it. The order, the form, the texture of my books will perhaps some day constitute for the initiated a complete representation of it.*

d) *It's the thing of the critic to look for.*

e) *I live almost to see if it will ever be detected.*

f) *My whole lucid effort gives him the clue —* ***every page and line and letter.*** *The thing is as* *concrete there as a bird in a cage, a bait on a hook, a piece of cheese in a mouse-trap. It's stuck in every volume as your foot is stuck into your shoe. **It governs every line, it chooses every word, it dots every i, it places every comma.***

g) *It's the very string that my pearls are strung on.*

h) [It is] *something like a complex figure in a Persian carpet.*

11. To a question asked by the narrator: "*Is it something in the style, or something in the thought? An element of form or an element of feeling?*" the author replies:

i) *Well, you've got a heart in your body? Is that an element of form or an element of feeling? What I contend that nobody has ever mentioned in my work is the* **organ of life**.

12. To another question: "*[unless it be] some kind of game you're up to with your style, something you're after in the language. Perhaps it's a preference for the letter P: ... Papa, potatoes, prunes — that sort of thing?*" The author does not answer.

13. But he then answers positively the question: "*Should you be able, pen in hand, to state it clearly yourself — to name it, phrase it, formulate it?*"

14. And he also affirms that *the figure* could be made explicit with a brief *exposition*:

j) ... *it would fit into a letter.*

15. As we know, in the end, the secret is not revealed.

16. An attentive reading of this short story, and above all a consideration of the passages we have just cited, leads to the following conclusion:

The author invented by James writes using PERFECT OULIPIAN CONSTRAINTS, according to the definition of President Le Lionnais. It is an ANTICIPATORY PLAGIARY OF THE OULIPO.

17. But Henry James was not an Oulipian author. So how was he able to describe so exactly what constitutes the irreducible singularity of the Oulipo, over sixty years before it was founded?

II

18. The first clue that set us on the track was the name of the fictitious Oulipian author chosen by James: **Hugh Vereker**.

19. This name immediately evokes another one: **Hugo Vernier**.

20. The two names have the following in common:
   a) the initial of the forename;
   b) the beginning of the surname;
   c) the number of letters in the forename and in the surname.
   If we write: **H... Ver...** we can easily complete it as Hugo Vernier.

21. As is well known, Hugo Vernier and his lost, essential work, *Le Voyage d'hiver*, attracted the attention of Georges Perec, and since then investigations have been carried out by several Oulipians (see fascicles 53, 105, 108, 110, 112, 113, 114, 118, 129, 139 and 162 of the *Bibliothèque oulipienne*), some of which, as is only appropriate, have attracted in turn our kindly yet severe critical attentions (BO 117).

22. Our hypothesis can be expressed as follows: **Henry James knew of Vernier's *œuvre* and used it as a source of inspiration for his short story**.

23. If we could establish the validity of this hypothesis, we would have made not only a decisive step forward in *Jamesian studies*, but perhaps even more importantly in *Vernierian studies*. Because we could then prove the following extraordinary fact, which none has suspected before: **Hugo Vernier INVENTED THE OULIPO.**

24. But we had first to identify James's informer. Our attention was immediately attracted by James's stay in Paris (1875-1876) and the (rather complex and conflicted relationships) he had with the novelists of the time, especially those in Flaubert's "circle".

25. It is known that these relationships were not warm.

26. James found Flaubert's disciples *extremely narrow*. In a letter to his mother, he wrote: "*They are a queer lot, and intellectually very remote from my own sympathies. They are extremely narrow and it makes me rather scorn them that not a mother's son of them can read English. But this hardly matters, for they couldn't really understand it if they did.*"

27. And, in a "literary correspondence" published in the *New York Tribune*: "*You ask a writer whose production you admire some questions about any other writer, for whose work you have also a relish*" and they will answer: "*oh, he is of the school of This or That. He is of the queue of So and So.*" or else: "*We think nothing of him. You mustn't talk of him here; for us he doesn't exist.*"

28. These sarcastic comments were aimed in particular at an author whom James greatly admired: **Gustave Droz**.

   (The disdain the Flaubertians felt for Droz or Cherbuliez, the author of *L'Aventure de Ladislas Bolski*, was not the only thing that disturbed James during his stay in Paris. In another letter he tells how shocked he was to see Turgenev, a writer he held in great esteem, crawling round a salon on all fours while playing a parlour game.)

29. To quote Leon Edel's indispensable biography of the author of *The Wings of the Dove*: "*The fictions of Droz, one of the last novelists of the Second Empire, delight Henry. They have French precision of thought and statement and the 'old Gallic salt of humour'. He is particularly struck by one which tells of the history of a watering-place.*"

30. James had discovered Droz in about 1870 and reviewed several of his novels, which had just been translated in the USA.

31. In his critical examination, James described Droz's work as follows: "*a genuine example of the better genius of the land.*" He compared him, favourably, to Balzac: "*Droz has resolved the social force of his own brief hour into a clearer essence than his great predecessor... of all the amuseurs of pre-Communal Paris, he seems to us to have been the most open-eyed. We speak not of his philosophy — we doubt he boasts of one — but of his clear and penetrating perception.*" High praise, indeed.

32. For him, Droz's art is "*intelligent realism*".

33. A serious examination of Droz's *œuvre*, which is now rather neglected, remains to be done. Our investigation has provided us with the necessary material. But we shall here limit ourselves to what is relevant to our investigations.

III

34. (Extract from the Wikipedia article): "Son of the sculptor Jules-Antoine Droz and grandson of the engraver Jean-Pierre Droz, he studied with a view to attending the École polytechnique, before electing a career as a painter and frequenting the studio of François-Édouard Picot at the École des Beaux-Arts. From 1857 to 1865, he exhibited at the Salon des peintures de genre, in a style that Jules Claretie described as being 'ironic and sentimental, like his future novels'.

Subsequently invited to work on *La Vie parisienne*, which had just been launched, he abandoned painting and as 'Gustave Z' signed a series of sketches of the intimate secrets of family life. His success was immediate. He was saluted by a member of the Académie Française as 'an exquisite raconteur' and 'a penetrating analyst'. In 1866, he brought together his articles in a volume entitled *Monsieur, Madame et Bébé*, the publication of which triggered a quite extraordinary enthusiasm. In Europe, as in the United States, his sales took off. In France, no fewer than 121 editions appeared between 1866 and 1884. Then, in the same vein, he brought out *Entre Nous* in 1867 and *Le Cahier bleu de Mlle Cibot* in 1868.

During the next few years, he published other, more elaborate books, 'still with a lot of wit, but with a hint of homily'. In 1885, after the death of Edmond About, he canvassed for a chair on the Académie Française. It was then that, to block his candidature, he was accused of having written an anonymous book charged with being obscene. Either out of pusillanimity, or for other reasons which remain unknown, Droz did not fight back. The chair was given to Léon Say and Droz put a stop to his career as a writer.

When this man of honour and talent, who was ever smiling, polite, welcoming and friendly, was asked what he was now doing, he would reply:

'I'm re-reading *Les Lettres d'un dragon!*'

'But that's by your son!'

'That's right, *Monsieur* and *Madame* are done with. Now it's *Baby* who's on the way up.' "

35. This article, which is not overly incorrect for once, needs to be completed and corrected on at least three points:

a) The number of editions of *MMB* (*Monsieur, Madame et Bébé*) far exceeded a hundred and something, and almost reached 300 (see our appendix).

b) More importantly: *MMB* is **a novel and not just a simple collection of sketches**. Droz previously cut it up into pieces so as to publish it in the press. Thus the major originality of the work remained unnoticed: *MMB* is **a novel with multiple narrators** (the multiplicity of viewpoints is not, in this case, limited by the conventions of the 'epistolary novel').

c) The book that was falsely attributed to him (and still is in some booksellers' catalogues) can be found in the *Enfer* of the Bibliothèque Nationale. Its title is: *Summer in the Country*. It has recently been republished.

36. Droz's success did not please everyone. (Wikipedia cont'd:) "The wave that lifted Droz's novels to the skies soon ran up against the condemnation of his most eminent contemporaries. Zola called his work 'vanilla-flavoured shit'. Huysmans, while evoking 'the unhealthily elegant art of the Second Empire', ironised about 'this coquettish boudoir where M. Droz's ladies flirt on their knees and aspire to mystical lunches'. Jules Renard was indignant about being described by a critic as 'Gustave Droz no. 2' and declared: 'We must shatter the sugar baby that all the Drozes of the world have given the public to suck'."

37. Zola's attack annoyed James, who answered in a letter, as follows: "*to Thomas Sergeant Perry: I prefer an inch of GD to a mile of Daudet. Why the Flaubert circle don't like him is their own affair. I hear Émile Zola characterizes his manner as ...* merde à la vanille.

I send you by post Zola's last — merde au naturel. *Simply hideous."*

38. Let us now give the reader an example of this *gallic wit* admired by James, taken from *MMB*: one of the many narrators in the novel is a childhood friend of "Monsieur", they have since lost touch, but bump into one other on a railway station platform. He is at once invited to a small château where the young couple ("Monsieur" and "Madame") have just set up home ("Baby" hasn't arrived yet). He finds the young woman very beautiful and very much in love with her husband, and yet feels worried about the way a distant cousin of the family keeps staring pointedly at her during dinner. (In James's short stories (one of the aspects of Droz's influence which has not been noticed) there can be found frequent variants of this type of character, who admires the heroine from a distance, without surrendering to love.) They serve melon, small melons from Trets which are among the best in Provence. Everyone appreciates these melons and eats abundantly of them, but they are a fruit which Olaf (his name) does not like. He refrains. Then he goes to bed. Olaf, highly troubled by "Madame's" beauty and the happiness of the cooing couple which she forms with his friend (as for him (another characteristic of 'Jamesian narrators'), he has remained single after an unhappy affair), cannot sleep. He leans over the balcony of his bedroom, in the moonlight. At some distance from the (not very modern) château stands a pavilion, which is more or less concealed by the shrubbery. Suddenly, he sees the young woman emerge, in a long white nightshirt, and head in that direction in a great hurry. A minute later, the "cousin" then emerges, whose unmentionable intentions Olaf had suspected. He then dashes after her. How? What? Olaf feels horrified. And now the husband appears, and runs after them. A brutal drama takes place. Olaf cannot take any more. He wants to save the young wife, the couple and avoid a scandal, or any violence that may be on the way. He rushes downstairs, tries to hold back his friend, who sends him packing, then runs in turn towards the pavilion, muttering "Oh, those melons, those melons!"

(It is easy to understand Barbey d'Aurevilly's praise for Droz in *Le Nain jaune* when the book came out: *"What should be written about him is that he's Light! He is one of those Light writers that I love, whatever the century, but whom I really relish in my own; because the Solemn, the Serious and the Puritans have absolutely ruined the nineteenth century for me; but with the Light, like M. Gustave Droz, we sometimes have superb flashes of depth."*)

IV

39. James the "Drozophile": *Autour d'une source* — Of the three books by Droz which James reviewed, *Monsieur, Madame et Bébé*, *Le Cahier bleu de Mlle Cibot* and *Autour d'une source*, the third one perhaps held most importance for him. In particular, its construction struck him: "*The fable is extremely ingenious, it has the advantage of a moulded plot. ...*". The character of the priest is the continental equivalent of many of James's narrators: he does not dare denounce the fraud of a "*bogus miracle*" attributed to the virtues of a source of mineral water, for fear of damaging the reputation of a countess, whom he cannot stop himself from loving. The plot is highly complex. But what motivated James's high praise is the fact that its threads are carefully concealed from the reader who, if he does not pay enough attention to everything which is not stated explicitly, could well reach the end of the book without having noticed the essential. He emphasises: "*the unfolding of those personal passions and motives, accidents which link beneath the surface of broad public facts, like the little worms and insects we find swarming on the earthward face of stone. ...*".

40. Droz's *œuvre* has been almost entirely neglected by critics in the second half of the twentieth century. Théodore Zeldin devotes three inept lines to *MMB* in his *Histoire des Passions Françaises*. This is all the more regrettable given that Droz's *œuvre* was undoubtedly a major influence on Henry James.

41. In her 1981 study, *The Literary Criticism of Henry James*, Sarah Daugherty noted: "*Since the minor French novelists have passed into oblivion, scholars have underestimated their influence on James, seeing this only on his early writings*". She clearly saw (without examining it in depth) the influence of Droz on the master's last novels and short stories, but strangely enough she failed to mention the work that depends most obviously on *Autour d'une source*, *The Sacred Fount* (1901; *La Source sacrée* (in a very poor French translation)).

42. And yet this is admitted, and even declared in the title! We shall devote a subsequent paper to the way in which, in this novel, James both imitated and transcended his predecessor. It seems to us that our analysis will shed unexpected light on this mysterious book, which has thus far defied all attempts at interpretation.

V

43. But let's get back to the point, which is to say Hugo Vernier. It became apparent to us, after an attentive re-reading of "The Figure in the Carpet", that James had certainly encountered this brilliant poet's work. So who was his informer? We might answer: Gustave Droz. This seemed to be the most likely name. But we still needed proof.

44. We found it after a long investigation, which required several trips to a large number of libraries, in several European countries and on the American continent, the consultation of numerous catalogues of old books, etc.… And how did we proceed? We examined the greatest possible number of copies of the numerous editions of Droz's three works which were most appreciated by James. The list can be found in our appendix. (It includes editions published after Droz's death, which were necessary for our future monograph concerning the novelist.) Our hope was to find an inscription in one of these volumes. We almost gave up, so thankless and expensive was the task. But our efforts were finally rewarded.

45. The copy of the 35th edition of *Monsieur, Madame et Bébé* in the Bibliothèque Municipale of Nevers contains the following hand-written inscription: "**To MY DEAR HENRY, this modest attempt at 'gallic' wit, along with the promised set-square AND ITS VERNIER.**"

46. What can we conclude from this?

   a) Droz sent James, along with his novel, a copy of Hugo Vernier's *Voyage d'hier* (its real title, as JR has shown).

b) This book had been "promised" to James, either when the two authors met, which must have happened in about 1875–1876, or in a letter (which could have been written earlier, as James's reviews date to 1871).

c) The allusion to a "set-square", an instrument which is quite naturally associated with a "vernier" (cf. this text by Arago: "Since it was impossible to place absolutely horizontally a four-metre-long ruler, it was necessary to determine with a spirit level the angle that the ruler made in each of its positions. What was used was a mobile measure set on a hinge and placed towards the tip of a wooden set-square. A vernier positioned in front of a graduation of 10° divided into 120 parts each of a value of 5', allowed the angle to be read. It was useful to turn over the instrument, from one end to the other, in other words placing foot A where foot D was, and *vice versa*, so as to read the double of the required inclination."), seems to indicate (this is just a supposition but, we think, a supposition that seems quite likely) that James had already started planning the writing of his short story. Why? Because the author's name is... **VER-EKER!** (*Ver-équerre*, or "set-square" in French.)

d) Let us add a final indication: the "journey" undertaken by Vereker, which concludes with his death, is pointless when it comes to the structure of the short story, and seems almost clumsy (which is rare for James). Yet it stands as a further allusion to Vernier's work (hence our title).

VI

47. *A few questions remain unanswered.*

Having arrived at the end of our demonstration, we have no choice but to recognise that certain questions remain open:

a) How did Droz get to know Vernier's work?

b) How did he acquire his copy?

c) Why did he talk about it to James?

d) Why did he give it to him?

48. A few possible explanations might be suggested:

(i) Droz wanted to exact revenge on someone, quite probably a poet in Flaubert's circle who, like so many others, had 'benefited' from Vernier's *œuvre*.

49. (ii) James published his short story in 1897, in other words, <u>in the year that followed Droz's death</u>. If, as we believe, he had written it much earlier, he perhaps put off publication so as not to undermine his friend's candidacy for the Académie.

APPENDIX I: *Concerning a false lead*

50. For some time, before our discovery of the inscription in Nevers (how did James's copy end up there? Yet another mystery), we had been stuck in a dead-end. We had noted that *Les Lettres d'un dragon*, the book by "baby", or Paul Droz, Gustave's son, was structured as a series of letters sent to a friend called "my dear Henry". Could this be James? Some of the book's passages could be enlightened by this hypothesis, for example, certain remarks that could have been used as the basis for a short story. Take for instance: "*Does man exist? — I don't think so. At least, I've never seen him.*" Or else the last sentence in the book: "*The army is the sole place where a man can enjoy a healthy freedom: I mean the freedom that consists in making big efforts in order to deserve new privileges and mount another rung.*"

51. We note as well that Paul Droz served in Louviers. And the second husband of Virginie, Hugo Vernier's widow, was a roadmender in that town! (see *Le Voyage d'hier.*)

APPENDIX II

52. *Editions of the works of Droz, consulted or identified*

Monsieur, Madame et Bébé
(The copies that have not been seen are in italics)

no. of the edition		
1		BNF, (*Galaxidion*), BM Troyes, Louisiana State U, Royal Library Nijmegen (Holland), BPU Neuchâtel (Switzerland)
2	1866	(*Amazon.fr*)
3	1866	BM Amiens, (*Galaxidion*)
4	1866	(*Galaxidion*)
.		
.		
7		(*Germany*)
8		(*Germany*)
.		
11		(*Germany*)
.		
13	1867	Erasmus U (Rotterdam), Bayerische Staatsbibliothek
.		
15		(*Germany*)
.		
17	1867	Arnhem (Holland)
18	1867	British Library, (*Germany*)
19		U Nijmegen (Holland), (*Germany*)
20	1867	BNF, NY Public Library, Royal Library Holland
21		U Groningen (Holland)
.		
23		(*Germany*)
.		
25	1868	U of California
26	1868	NL Italy (Florence), NL Sweden
.		
28		(*Germany*)
.		

30	1868	(*Amazon.fr*), (*Galaxidion*), (*Abebooks*)
.		
33	1869	Institut, BM Rouen, US Naval Academy
34		(*according to WorldCat*)
35	1869	Ste Gen, Yale, **BM Nevers**, BM Reims
.		
38		Tulane U
39	1869	(*Galaxidion*)
.		
.		
43		U of New Hampshire
44	1870	Ste Gen, Widener, Duke U
.		
.		
47		(*Germany*)
.		
49	1872	Brown U
50	1872	(*Galaxidion*), (*Abebooks*)
51	1872	Bibl Institut, BM Lille
52	1872	California State Library
.		
54		BM Lille
55		BNF
.		
57	1872	Widener, U Michigan (Ann Arbor)
.		
.		
.		
.		
63		(*Germany*)
64	1874	U Oxford, Barton College
.		
.		
67	1874	Norway (Bergen)
.		

69	1875	Bibl Institut, (*Germany*)
.		
.		
.		
.		
74		Neuchâtel BPU, (*Germany*)
75		BNF, (*Germany*)
.		
.		
.		
.		
80	1876	BNF
.		
.		
83	1876	Widener
.		
85	1876	NY Public Library, U of Chicago, (*Germany*)
.		
87		Staatsbibliothek Mainz
.		
89	1878	(*Chapitre.com*), (*le-livre.com*)
.		
.		
.		
94	1878	(*Chapitre.com*), (*Abebooks*)
95		(*Chapitre.com*)
96	1879	NL Denmark
.		
98		(*Germany*)
99		(*Germany*)
.		
101		U Iowa
.		
.		
.		
.		
107		(*Germany*)

.		
110	1881	Seattle U
111	1882	Troyes, (*Germany*)
.		
113	1882	(*Amazon.fr*)
.		
115		(*Germany*)
116	1882	BNF, BM Lyon, Basel UB
117		(*Galaxidion*), (*le.livre.com*), (*Abebooks*)
118		NY Public Library, British Library, Bayerische Staatsbibliothek
.		
120	1882	Yale
121		(*Germany*)
.		
123		(*Germany*)
124	1884	Widener, Boston U, U North Carolina
.		
.		
.		
.		
129	1884	Columbia, Institut de France, BM Lyon, U Lille III
130		Southampton
131		Widener
132		(*Germany*)
.		
.		
.		
136	1887	Yale
137		Widener
138	1887	Lehigh U
.		
140	1887	Oxford U, Bayerische Staatsbibliothek
.		
142		(*Abebooks*), Western Washington U
143	1888	Northwestern U
144		Tulane U
.		
146	1890	(*Abebooks*)

147	1890	U of Mass. (Du Bois College)
148	1890	(Abebooks), Leeds, British Library
149	1890	Widener
.		
.		
.		
.		
154	1892	Penn State U
.		
156		Rice U
.		
.		
.		
161	1894	BM Lyon
162	1894	(*Galaxidion*), (*Abebooks*)
163		U Rochester, U Chicago, U Rhode Island
.		
.		
.		
167	1895	NL Austria
.		
.		
170	1897	(*Chapitre.com*), (*Galaxidion*), (*Abebooks*)
.		
.		
.		
.		
176		Dartmouth College
.		
178		(*Germany*)
.		
.		
.		
.		
183	1899	NL Portugal
.		
185	1899	NL Austria

.

.

189	1900	Library of Congress, U of New Brunswick, Purdue U, Washington College
190	1900	Limoges Ufr lettres, (*Japan*)
191		(*WorldCat*)
.		
193		(*Germany*)
194	1901	U of Cincinnati
.		
196		Hamilton College
.		
.		
.		
.		
201		(*according to WorldCat*)
.		
.		
204	1904	BM Avignon, (*Abebooks*)
.		
.		
.		
208	1908	Bayerische Staatsbibliothek
209		Delft
.		
.		
.		
.		
215	1908	NY Public Library
216		U Wisconsin (Madison)
217		U Missouri, Seattle Public Library, Columbia
218		National Library of Wales
219		(*Germany*)
220		Tulane U
.		
.		
223		(*Germany*)

224		NL Finland Helsinki
225		(*Price-Minister*)
226		BN Quebec
.		
.		
229		Oberlin College
.		
231		St Olaf College
232		Bibl Ville du Locle (Switzerland)
.		
234		California State Library
.		
.		
.		
.		
240		U Toronto, U Minnesota
.		
242		Norway (Bergen)
.		
.		
246	1908	Cambridge U
247		Illinois Wesleyan U, Lawrence U, U Mass. (Amherst)
248		(*Galaxidion*), (*Abebooks*)
.		
250		Miami U, **my personal copy (Reine Haugure)**
.		
.		
254		(*Germany*)
.		
.		
.		
.		
.		
.		
.		

.
.
.
266   1924   BNF, Stanford
.
.
.
.
.
.

274   *(Japan)*
.
.
.
.

280   BN Quebec
.
.
.
.

286   *(Chapitre.com)*

53. *Editions mentioned by the* Journal de la Librairie

1866: 1, 2?, 3, 4, 5?, 6?, 7, 8
1867: 9, 10, 11, 12, 14, 13 (inversion), 15, 16, 17, 18, 19, 20, 21, 22, 23
1868: 24, 25, 26, 27, 28, 29, 30
1869: 33, 37
1870: 47
1871: ?
1872: 50, 55
1875: 72
1877: 86
After this date, the *Journal de la Librairie* does not mention a single new edition.

Autour d'une source

1	1869	Ste Gen, BNF, BM Troyes
2		(*Galaxidion*), Yale, U Texas (Austin), Michigan St U, U of Cal (Irvine)
3		BNF, British Library, (*Northern Germany Cat*), Smith College
4		Institut de France, BM Lyon, NL Austria
.		
.		
.		
8		(*Germany*)
.		
.		
11		(*Germany*)
12	1872	New York PL, NL Sweden
13		BNF, Widener, (*Galaxidion*)
14	1873	BNF
15		(*Galaxidion*), (*Abebooks*), U Glasgow
16		BNF
17		BNF, Rhine–Westphaly Cat
18	1876	Yale, *Rhine-Westphaly Cat*
.		
.		
21	1878	Yale, (*Booklooker*)
.		
23	1879	(*Abebooks*), NL Scotland, Oxford Union Lib, Northwestern U
24	1882	Widener, BM Le Mans, Cornell U
25		Temple U
.		
27		North–Westphalia
28	1885	BM Montpellier, (*Galaxidion*)
29		Southampton
30	1892	BM Lyon, *Northern Germany Cat*
31		Tulane U
.		
33	1897	NYPL, Library of Congress, Princeton
34	1907	Ohio State U? U North Carolina
.		
.		
.		

Le Cahier bleu de Mlle Cibot

1	NL Finland, BM Troyes
2	BN Canada
3	BM Rouen
.	
5	NL Holland
6	Italy (Bari)
.	
.	
10	UL Frankfurt
11	Arsenal, Italy (Varese)
.	
13	New York Public Library, Princeton
.	
.	
.	
.	
19	Harvard
20	BM Lyon
21	NL Denmark
22	Harvard
23	New York Public Library, Case Western U
.	
25	Arsenal
.	
.	
.	
30	(*WorldCat*)
31	NL Wales
32	(*WorldCat*)
33	Italy (Calgari)
34	BM Besançon, Yale
.	
36	(*WorldCat*), Penn Lib
.	

39	BL, BM Lyon
40	BN Canada, McGill
41	U North Carolina
42	Library of Congress

54. We have also consulted some of the extremely numerous translations of Droz's works, which can be found in all the languages of Europe, or nearly. Sometimes two translations are in competition for the same readership.

For example, in the USA the title of *MMB* is *Monsieur, Madame and Bébé*, while in the UK it is *Papa, Mamma and Baby* (the Bodleian, in Oxford, only has the British English version, as would be expected). Italians have the choice between *Lui, lei et il bimbo* and *Marito, moglie e bebé*…

APPENDIX III: *Perplexity*

55. When founding the OULIPO, President Le Lionnais must have known that he was plagiarising Hugo Vernier. He must have had a copy of *Le Voyage d'hier* in his possession.

56. But, neither in Georges Perec's short story (*Le Voyage d'hiver*), nor in the numerous sequels and prequels subsequently written by the Oulipians, **not once is this vital aspect of Vernier's work mentioned**. We confess our perplexity at this curious, anomalous absence.

57. We can only wonder if this is not a DELIBERATE OMISSION, if the Oulipians have not been trying to turn their readers' attention away, to draw a veil over their president's plagiary so as to conserve the idea of his absolute originality (is not the invention of the concept of **Anticipatory Plagiary** by François Le Lionnais a sort of avowal?).

58. Our hypothesis, which we will express with all the prudence we can, may elucidate a strange aspect of the Oulipo's history: the absence of François Caradec from the original group. For FC must have been the person who introduced FLL to Vernier's work. So, were certain people in Queneau's circle afraid that he might reveal the real origins of the Oulipo?[1] Was François Caradec's late arrival in the *ouvroir* accompanied by a promise of silence?

1. Is it not high time to examine more seriously the circumstances of Marcel Duchamp's death? Is it not clear that the version 'suggested' (oh so clumsily!) by JR, in the *Moments oulipiens*, is utterly fanciful?

HUGO VERNIER

Hell's Journey

Le Voyage d'Enfer

Translated by Ian Monk

●

Bibliothèque oulipienne 200

2012

● That evening, there was a meeting of the Oulipo, hosted by Mireille Cardot on Rue Jean-Pierre Timbaud, where even wan faces blossom; it was the 616th according to the most dedicated secretarial calculations. There was no guest of honour, or not officially at least. But then, an unofficial one rang at the door, while at the same time hammering with the knocker.

There entered a man of modest build, a woman dressed and transfigured to perfection, as if the famous stylist Pascale Lavandier had, one day, abandoned Mme Aline in order to concentrate on a more distant past. His hair was auburn, with a parting to one side, falling over her ear on the other. Paradoxically, her make-up gave him a white complexion brimming with health (I do not want to seem to protest over much, but we were on the street mentioned above, unless it were Rue Sébastien-Bottin, but what does it matter in the end?), her eyebrows were coal-black, while a slight moustache had been sketched in with a pencil. His shirt was of white poplin, the collar folded down, circled by a soft, white silk tie. Her woollen waistcoat was black, with the drooping chain of a pocket-watch hanging across it. His morning-coat was also of black wool with a turned-down satin collar, while her tweed trousers were chequered black and brown, with white piping. His caramel-brown ankle-boots were curiously out of place, because with such an outfit they should obviously have been black. Overall this person looked rather like Valérie Beaudouin. But, as opposed to her, he smelt slightly of humus.

While signing in on the agenda, under the pre-initial heading, he introduced herself and announced his name as follows:

"If I were Hugo Vernier, and if I had come to see you, my dear Oulipians of the Oulipo, then I should have dressed appropriately. I should have gone about changing this outfit radically, but in Hell, you know, our existences are rather limited: you wear a strip of fabric around your pelvis, a plain loin-cloth, and nothing more.

"If I were Hugo Vernier, and had come to see you, I would have chosen an evening when, according to your agenda, you would have been discussing, as ever, and in whichever direction you had taken, *the book*, with the sole intention of ripping you apart with a drunken flash of a wing, of knocking you out with your books, knocking you out with *the book*.

"If I were to knock you out with that book, if I were Hugo Vernier, and had come to see you, I would knock you out again with mine, which, if I have been informed correctly, has now for so long been the Grail of your quest...

"Since I am, let us suppose, Hugo Vernier, and as I wrote a long time ago (it was in about 1843 or '44, I think...), and since everything that exists does so for the purpose of creating a beautiful book, then I can only wonder which book that might be.

"If I were Hugo Vernier, this beautiful book, towards the creation of which the world in its entirety has been created, would not be just any book, it would be entitled for example, *Le Voyage d'hiver*, or perhaps *Le Voyage d'hier*, or perhaps *Le Voyage d'Hitler*, or perhaps *Hinterreise*, or perhaps *Le Voyage d'Hoover*, or perhaps *Le Voyage d'Arvers*, or perhaps *Un Voyage Divergent*, or perhaps *Le Voyage du ver*, or perhaps *Le Voyage du vers*, or perhaps *Le Voyage des verres*, or perhaps *Si par une Nuit un Voyageur d'Hiver*, or perhaps *Le Voyage des rêves*, or perhaps *Le Voyage du Grand Verre*, or perhaps *Le Voyage d'H...Ver...* (a list that remains open, I hope).

"For, in the end, if I were Hugo Vernier and could count on your complicity, I should have no hesitation about founding (no less!) a new civilisation of the book — it seems to me that I am in many ways the man for the job — even though I have little desire for a civilisation of just one book, even if it were mine.

"If I were Hugo Vernier, I should not have come like this, my face powdered, hands in the pockets of my vanished being, I should have taken on the appearance of one or another of you, to show my benevolence.

"But, as I am in fact Hugo Vernier (even in this state of weary bones under my crumbling skin), I shall not be so ridiculous as to sing the praises of my book which, if you would allow me to give you all a pat on the back, you, my dear Oulipians of the Oulipo, know far more about than I do, and which, I should even say, you have been filling up even more actively and tenaciously than I once did.

"And since I am perhaps not just Hugo Vernier but, in a certain sense, also one of you, and a lady Oulipian at that (which would delight me more than anything in the world), I could then stand easy in my sandals, or even my trainers or canvas boots, such trainers and canvas boots as can be found more often, it must be said, in the poems of Jacques Roubaud or Michelle Grangaud than, for example, in those of Yves Bonnefoy or Philippe Jacottet, even though I once greatly inspired them too!

"If I were Hugo Vernier, I should fall silent at once."

(*A 'minute's' silence*)

"But there we are. Am I Hugo Vernier? I wonder. (*A pause*) Apparently I do not reply to my own questions. No, I do not answer myself as much as I should.

"If I were Hugo Vernier, I should tell you that my book *Le Voyage d'hiver* contains all of yours. Not in the sense of the cliché: 'This has been done before!', but instead in the sense of another phrase which resembles it like a sister or a cousin: 'It will be done!' What you write has not *already* been written; this is not a question of fate, or predestination! But it will be one day; it will have been so. I should wager that Erik Satie would one day have spoken of 'retrospective precursors', then your François Le Lionnais of 'anticipatory plagiarists' and the Schlegel brothers would say that 'any historian is a prophet turned towards the past.'

"On a different level, when I shall have been Raymond Queneau, I shall not have failed to have sung that a poem is always *a tad extreme*, and that, like one and all in my generation having received the sort of education that I once did, I am an authority when it comes to non-phonetic spelling.

"If I were Hugo Vernier, I should automatically, in a gesture assisting reflection, pass my hand over my hair to smooth it down. There, it has now been done.

"If I were Hugo Vernier, I should tell you that the past and the future touch each other in the present.

"If I were Hugo Vernier, I should also tell you that extremes of any sort touch each other, and do so betimes lastingly, and that they even lie down willingly, sometimes together.

"If I were Hugo Vernier, I should tell you that these extremes that touch each other betimes, and always lie down, are the extremes of times, and of existence.

"The book of catastrophes is the first book, the supreme book, the untouchable book, the untranslatable book, the book that was not composed by any human hand, the unbookish book!

"If I were Hugo Vernier, I should say perhaps that it takes money to make moneyed books, but mine was never moneyed enough, while you, as servants of potentiality, escape from the idolatry of the basic present, the very thing which, if I were Hugo Vernier, I should not be able to bear.

"For if I were Hugo Vernier, oh! I could quite easily not speak to you about a journey (the one I undertook was no cakewalk, for I can tell you that the Hell from which I have just emerged is something quite other than the *Enfer*★ of the Bibliothèque Nationale!). However, I should be quite incapable of steering clear of winter, yes winter, season of serene art, lucid winter (I think I wrote that in around 1847–48), season of temporary constraint on the Earth, and of skeletal vegetation, which has nothing to do with death but with form, in other words, with the announcement of spring.

"If I were really Hugo Vernier, I should have brought you my book as a gift. *Le Voyage d'hiver*, which was published, as you know, in the town that lovingly looks after the *Séquence de Sainte Eulalie*, once known as the *Cantilène*, that is to say the fine town of Valenciennes, whence, I have heard tell, one of your brigades has just returned. Yes, *Le Voyage d'hiver*, 1864, published by Hervé Frères, printers and booksellers… But you know quite well that such a thing would be impossible. I no longer have my book. It has passed from me. Neither Pluto nor Cerberus allowed me either officially or surreptitiously to take it with me when I went. I explained just as much yesterday, to

★ In the French National Library obscene books are kept in a section called "*Enfer*" (Hell).

two hang-dog, scruffy individuals, a certain Dante Alighieri and his guide, Virgil, who seemed set on opening every door to me in the absurd aim of getting their hands on my book which, they said, overshadowed their own. How very funny. 'Overshadowing', in a world of shadows!… And 'opening doors', when what I needed was to bestride the Styx!… What utter nonsense…

"So, if I were Hugo Vernier, I should stop beating about the bush.

"And, since I am Hugo Vernier, let's be done, I shall quite simply hand my book over to you. If it be not made of ink, glue and paper, nor even of pixels, it is still as concrete as any other, as genuine as it is not a machination, no, but above all a machine, a machine to conceive and compose books, quite simply, a machine for writing and for reading.

"Here it is. I shall give it to you so that it might be of use. It is an utterly creatively creating creation.

"I am also giving it to you so that you do not stop in your splendid tracks. I recently read that Jacques Roubaud, in an article entitled 'Of an Oulipian Work Born of Chance' (in *Accident Créateur*, Master Edition, Université Paris-Sorbonne, 2009), had programmatically launched several titles: *Le Voyage d'Auvers*, *Le Voyage d'Anvers*, *Le Voyage à l'envers*, so why not an excursion to Nevers?… and that Marcel Bénabou had added to this list a series of books to be 'notwritten', for example, a *Voyage d'Homère* (outrageously claiming that his *Résidence d'Hiver* released him from any other Vernierian duties), that Anne F. Garréta intended to describe the entire series in a sensational synthesis, that Paul Fournel, that Daniel Levin Becker, that Michèle Audin, that Valérie Beaudouin herself, in whom I have embodied myself for an evening, would… But, in the end, where are they? Have they no pride, have they no personal or collective honour to defend?

"Forgive me, but the fact that you are leaving the door open to the likes of Reine Haugure and Gorliouk brings me down to a point I fail to fathom.

"Can you not in some way or other shake yourselves, and your comrades, awake?

"By publishing under my own name, as, for example, fascicle number 200 of the *Bibliothèque oulipienne*, my own *Voyage d'Enfer*, I exhort you to co-opt me as a full member, so that I shall become your number 38.

"I am fully aware that QB stands as a precedent, given that he is not mentioned in the official list of members. I am also fully aware that applying for membership of the Oulipo is the same as shooting oneself in the foot. I am not that stupid. If I am now swimming upstream like this, it is because I am not arriving entirely empty-handed, while the underlying idea that I have re-emerged from my infernal home, just for you, seems to me, concretely, to constitute a healthy exception to your rule.

"For, truly, sincerely, an idea has just occurred to me.

"Imagine to what an extent the Nobel Prize for Literature, or else the Peace Prize, or even, for once, both, both at once, awarded to the Oulipo, to what an extent this decision would be rich with benefits:

"1) It would be the opportunity to reward a group, and not just another dumbly blinkered individual.

"2) It would be the opportunity to reward something other than simply the inhabitant of a narrow country or even of a single continent.

"3) It would be the opportunity to reward at once several literary languages, and not just one.

"4) It would be the opportunity to compensate for several of the overlooked, who still make the Stockholm jurors lose sleep at night: François Le Lionnais, Raymond Queneau, Georges Perec, Italo Calvino, Marcel Duchamp, Oskar Pastior... thus reforming the Pantheon.

"5) It would be the only way to honour authors who, on their own, would quite clearly never have deserved such glory, and would thus cast light on all those writers in the wings, who are so very useful to the stars (I do not want to upset anyone, and so shall name no names, but it is quite clear that those people who should feel targeted are those who have not even bothered to add a chapter to our 'hyper-novel', to use Calvino's term).

"6) In the end, this would be the right way for me, and for you by my side, to win the Nobel Prize, which was established long after my death, thus implying, it seems to me, that I deserve its homage more than anyone else."

MICHÈLE AUDIN

IV-R-16

IV-R-16

Translated by Ian Monk

●

Bibliothèque oulipienne 209

2012

There are too many dullard verses
But this is pure prose, you fool!
Molière, *Le Bourgeois gentilhomme*

1 March 2012

● I finished the minutes of meeting number 616 and sent them to my friends in the Oulipo. It was late. "Gute Nacht", sang Fischer-Dieskau on the radio. I opened a fat hardback book and turned the pages. It was Report R covering the fourth year (1936–37) of the seminar on mathematics, devoted to the work of Élie Cartan. What, in 1937, was the vision of the structure of infinite groups (this being the title)? The physical aspect of the presentation was worth describing: the text was typewritten on a stencil, the mathematical symbols had been added by hand and the pages had yellowed. As for groups, Élie Cartan informed us that definitional equations stood as a departure point for his research. This viewpoint, though dated, was thrilling. The pleasure of reading it made me forget the slight irritation I had felt at the idea of co-opting Hugo Vernier into the Oulipo, which Jacques Jouet had tried to justify during our meeting the day before yesterday (this irritation had been caused by such a futile reason that I'd never admit it: the childish desire to remain "the last Oulipian born before the foundation of the *ouvroir*" (symmetrical to "the first Oulipian born after the foundation of the *ouvroir*", Anne Garréta, which was a definitively definitive position)). Groups filled me up, while on the radio the great Dietrich had just begun "Der Lindenbaum". I had now read a good fifteen pages; these definitional equations perhaps contained a certain number of relationships, I turned over a page, and then… an undetermined formation… What? There was a page missing. Page IV-R-16 to be precise. The page numbering of this seminar publication was quite bizarre: IV stood for the fourth year, R was a sort of reference letter alluding to the order of other, various presentations, and 16 marked (or in this case didn't) the sixteenth page. I tried to interpolate and guess what Élie Cartan must have said. I could see quite clearly what I would have said personally, between "a certain number of relationships" and "an indeterminate formation". But what about him? It was another era and another style. So how to be sure? I turned off the radio before the end of "Wasserflut" and went to bed.

2 March 2012

I got up, checked my diary and saw that I wouldn't be spending a working day in Paris before the end of the month, then, as always, I made some coffee (far from being cheap instant coffee mixed with lukewarm water, I use Arabica in an Italian coffee-maker), opened my (electronic) mail box and sent a message to the librarian of a Parisian institute:

> Dear Brigitte
> I'm working on some old seminar presentations. There is a page missing from the volume in your library. I'd be infinitely grateful if someone in the IHV library could send me a scan of this page, because I cannot drop by until April. The volume's reference for you is K 998 53 IV
> and the page I need is IV-R-16
> Many thanks
> All the best
> michele

I poured out some coffee. As well as Hervé Le Tellier's *billets* for *Le Monde*, there was a message in my in-box from Jacques Jouet:

> Dear Michèle
> Here's the text as requested.
> Thanks for the minutes. But we will have to deal with the HV question seriously sooner or later.
> jj x

I decided to ignore the criticism and take the kiss for breakfast, along with the text, which was a rumination on libraries. I could easily imagine contributing library-loving texts to the Oulipian corpus. In fact, rather libraries than Hugo Vernier and his *Voyage d'hiver*. The adventures in those volumes of the seminar in the 1930s… Or the *ex-libris* of Kurt Hensel, his violin and elliptical curve on the books in his own personal library, with their fawn bindings, the story of Hensel, and of his grandmother Fanny, *née* Mendelssohn, his p-adic numbers, and his death in 1941 which, no doubt, meant that he avoided an even worse fate and also that we had possession of his books. The sun was rising. C was too. I made some more coffee and we chatted (about something else).

A little later, I made two mistakes. Firstly, I answered JJ, and my reply contained the following sentence: That's given me a few ideas.

Then, I wrote to Olivier Salon and Frédéric Forte inquiring about the last six issues of the *Bibliothèque oulipienne* which had been devoted to HV (as JJ put it, I think, in anticipation of a co-optation — but all in good time). In any case, I now really had to become better informed about this Hugo Vernier. The result was a series of blacked-out, illegible pdf files, followed by a few legible text files, thus allowing me to familiarise myself with a certain number of these journeys. One of my messages had wound up being forwarded to JJ, and I sensed his jubilation (anyone who knows JJ can easily imagine the particular form of his jubilant smile) on reading his reply:

Dear Michèle,
Please find attached a pdf of the BO Castor Astral collection, volume 8 (which contains several Journeys), as well as a word doc of Gorliouk (but there were almost certainly some corrections made to it before publication, though I can't remember what…)
If I understand things correctly, you're relaunching the affair… I'm impatient to see.
jj x

3 and 4 March 2012

The next day was a Saturday and (oddly enough) the day after that a Sunday. There was a series of family problems, which were not particularly unpleasant, and between which I took time out to read or re-read the various journeys.

Everything had already been said (I might even say, said and re-said). To the fourteen (14! — this is an exclamation mark, not a factorial, although, given the speed at which some of the contributors write…) chapters which had already been published of this so-called collective novel, it would now be necessary to add the *Voyage d'Enfer*, which JJ (yes, him again), who, if my sums were right, had already fathered three, had just written and signed under the name of… Hugo Vernier. But I still answered JJ's impatience:

> You shouldn't be. I'm thinking of acting in this way to protest against HV's request to be co-opted…

For I had at last found a decent argument: Hugo Vernier would certainly not take down the minutes of our meetings.

I soon noticed that not everyone had contributed. Marcel Bénabou, for example, had not written anything yet. But whom could I hope to convince that, from a scribbling point of view, I was distinctly on Bénabou's territory? Picking on Olivier Salon (a mathematician), or even Anne Garréta and Valérie Beaudouin (women) seemed to be a far better policy. And then there was the presidential silence.★

I then spent a good deal of my day in the library (which was, of course, closed, I am not at Johns Hopkins but Strasbourg, however, I have the key, which means I can go there whenever I want (at times when even American libraries are closed)).

5 March 2012

In Paris, the (winter) holidays were over, and so it was that I soon received the

★ Paul Fournel was, and is, the President of the Oulipo.

following message:

> Hullo Michèle,
> Pages IV-R-15 and IV-R-16 are missing from our copy.
> Best wishes
> The Library

How surprising. As well as loving libraries, I also have a good network of acquaintances, some very close, among their librarians. So I sent out a few more messages. In the maths libraries that had copies of the seminar, they looked, in general found the doorstopper in question, blew off the dust, turned the pages, and then, in amazement, a message followed:

> We don't have page IV-R-16 either.
> Best
> Odile

> Sorry, but I can't help you: one of our copies is being rebound, the other is missing (noticed during the last indexing).
> So sorry
> Liliane

> Hello
> Thanks to you, I have now noticed that presentation IV-R is missing from our copy of J-87 912-4
> Best wishes
> Anne

and so on. For some years I'd known which libraries had which copies: I'd done a lot of work on the, let's say, archaeological aspects of this seminar. I knew where the copies in Nancy and Grenoble came from. I also knew that all the copies were different. I'd seen the archives of several mathematicians, who had not kept their copies of the seminar. I'd pinpointed volume III, which is hard to pinpoint, in the reserve stock of the archives of the Académie des Sciences. I thought that I knew a great deal about the subject, but I hadn't dug deep enough: I didn't know about these absences.

In Göttingen, where I had been at the beginning of the winter, I'd read the letters of a German mathematician called Wilfried Gauger, who had gone to Paris to give some lectures during the very same seminar of May 1939. This correspondence (three letters in just the last week of August 1939) concerned the texts of the lectures, which Gauger was meant to send to Paris, though the war had presumably prevented this. It was to a certain Robert Petit (fact is stranger than fiction) that he was about to send (or had sent) his text. I knew that, at the time, Petit was acting as the seminar's secretary, that he had subsequently been a prisoner of war, that his knowledge of mathematics had been exploited in Berlin and that he had been appointed to the university of Besançon in 1945. It was high time I found out what had happened to his archives.

I then did three simple things, which were followed by a minor miracle. Looking up the site that listed former students of the ENS provided me with the date when Petit started at the school: 1931. So he must have been born in around 1912. I then learnt from a specialist site that his last maths article had been published in 1953. The third easy (but slightly more time-consuming) thing was to check through the directories which the Société mathématique de France used to publish at the end of its bulletins (a journal that has now been fortunately digitised). There I learnt that he had become a member of the society in 1937, and had still been paying his dues in 1974, when the directory noted that he was an "honorary professor" at the university of Besançon (which meant that he had not died in 1953, but had continued his career, though without publishing anything, for a good twenty years) while providing his address, all in just one line:

1937. PETIT (Robert), Prof. Hon. Univ. Besançon, 53 rue Théophile Gautier, 25290 Ornans.

Ornans, in the *département* of Le Doubs, sure enough, with the burial, Courbet, the origin of the world, the studio, the fall of the Colonne Vendôme. Ornans. Far from Le Havre, far from Normandy, where the authors of these *voyages* were trying to draw me.

This little miracle had been the result of a flash of inspiration. Of flair and fluke. A quick check in the telephone directory: Petit, Ornans, and I found:

Petit Reine,
53 r Théophile Gautier
25290 Ornans
03 81 62 06 44

It was all too neat and too easy. Feeling that I just had to put off such a pleasure, I did so until the next day.

Tuesday, 6 March

I even managed to wait till the following afternoon. I'd had a perfect night's sleep. JJ's insistence had triggered off no nightmares. I seemed to be in better shape than Frédéric Forte, who had dreamed of his Hugo. Talking about JJ's insistence, the word harassment would have been inappropriate (anyone who knows JJ would agree), such insistence could even be described as being gentle (anyone who knows JJ would understand), a gentle insistence — gentleness heightening the insistence. And of course, I had noticed at once that the forename Reine was contained in the surname Vernier and I had had no need of a set of scrabble letters to be able to form Reine Hogruve (the cousin of the Roubaldian Haugure).

At about five past two, I cracked. The telephone rang several times, then a voice answered. It sounded like the voice of an old woman. I apologised for disturbing her, then asked if she was indeed Madame Petit (I didn't dare utter her husband's forename, I was terrified of breaking into a fit of giggles thinking about the *Petit Robert* dictionary), then introduced myself by my name and job title, before asking about her precise relationship with Robert Petit.

"I was his wife," she said, "or to be more exact, his second wife."

Then she told me that he had died in 1982, and that he would have been a hundred this year (which confirmed my estimation). I explained that I was interested in the archives of mathematicians, and in particular those of her husband, before qualifying the role that he had played as being especially important (which was not a total lie, because the fact that he might have owned a page IV-R-16 did have a certain importance, at least for me). She then told me that there were a number of boxes in the cellar but she didn't know what they contained, that she understood nothing about such things and that, anyway, she was far too old to go down there. "I'm seventy-nine," she said. So, he had been twenty-one years older than her. But, at least, she clearly hadn't been one of his students. "You should see about that with his daughter," she said. And she gave me the mobile phone number of a certain Valérie Petit-Huet. I in turn left my contact details.

I taught until half past six (no, I don't spend my entire life hanging around in libraries), dropped into my office, then went home, dressed in pure probity and (above all) white chalk. The telephone rang. This generally happens when I get back, and it's nearly always Nicole Dupont trying to sell me frozen food. Sometimes I even answer. But this caller did not have a Chinese accent and introduced herself as Valérie Petit. She was cordial, almost joyful. "It seems that we're colleagues." "Yes, I'm a professor at the university of Besançon. Like my father before me, but of literature. My speciality is Hugo…" (I gulped back my saliva.) "Does that surprise you? You know, Victor Hugo, what with being in Besançon, isn't that original?…" (I got my breath back.) "My stepmother told me that you wanted to see my father's papers. You don't live that far away, if I've understood things correctly…" We arranged to meet the following Friday (9 March) at her stepmother's.

Of course, a cellar in Ornans was less 'sexy' than Key West, Marathon, Hoover's drawer or Hitler's bunker, and I shall write nothing about my journey to Ornans (or to anywhere else for that matter)…

7 and 8 March

Forget about my lessons on Wednesday. But a word or two about Thursday, the day when I worked in the library. At least in theory, because it is a place that favours both work and the wandering of ideas. It has to be said that the wireless connexion, which is indispensable to documentary research (looking for a source on the web, then reading it on the hard copy owned by the library, is a real luxury — of course, you have to be in the right library, but this was very much the case), also allowed emails to arrive on a regular basis (you might object that I could have turned off my mailer, but nobody's perfect). Among them, for example, there was:

> Dear Michèle,
> What's new?
> jj

Of course, Jacques was alluding to one of my family problems, as mentioned above. But I could still hear (if speech can, in a sense, be heard in this kind of message) that gentle insistence I have already evoked. There were other examples:

> Dear MA,
> Have you managed to get hold of all of the Hugo-Vernian BOs? Don't hesitate to ask JR for his.
> FF x

No, no and no again, I was not going to write a *Voyage d'hiver*. Everything had already been said. Of course I, too, could invent a twisted tale in which the mountain in the background of Hensel's *ex-libris* would hide a deeper meaning, associated with Fanny Mendelssohn, the composer, to be precise, and her grandson, then with Hugo Vernier and Vincent Degraël (who I had never even met at the Lycée d'Étampes) — but, enough extravagant yarns had already been spun. Or, I could suggest that Fanny Mendelssohn (yes, I'd like to write something about Fanny Mendelssohn) was the real author of *Winterreise* (and not Schubert), but in terms of the dates, this would be hard to pull off, and in any case musical anticipatory plagiary had already been used (by JJ...). I could slip in Sofia Kovalevskaya's burnt letter, discovered by a German historian, a lovely story which I hadn't dared include in the book I'd written about her. I could also put to good use the detailed knowledge I had acquired of how Jewish writers had been eliminated from scientific publications during the Occupation, while pillaging the content of Gauger's letters I'd read in Göttingen — I'd be really close to the subject in that event, but did I really want to add footnotes to the *Voyage d'Hitler*? Along the same lines, I could also write an offshoot of this story which would take place in the mud of the trenches, which was just as valid as the sands of Dunkirk. And I'd call the mathematician involved Hélie Vartan, one of whose articles I was then reading.

I returned without any real difficulty to my main areas of interest. I found that the ideas Élie Cartan had had were not just exciting, but also highly impressive.

Shortly after joining the Oulipo, JJ had whispered to me: "You'll now have to write your *Voyage d'hiver* too". I really liked the idea of adding a chapter to a collective work. I thought about it and found a title, given that *Voyages Divers* was quite clearly missing from the list of contents. I had even found an epigraph in "There are too many dullard verses". But that was all. Even two-bit provincial poets had now been called in. Of course, I'd have loved to write something about Julio Cortázar's *Hopscotch*. The subject might even lead me to Scotland: the bookshop in Ullapool would have made a perfect setting. But it had already been done (without the bookshop, but this would once again be no more than infra-folio jottings on a text that had already been written). The worst part of all was *If on a Winter's Night*. That book was mine, that was all there was to it, Calvino had written it for me. I am the reader in *If on a Winter's Night a Traveller*. And they had now succeeded in introducing my book into their stories.

So what on Earth could I do? Write a piece of Oulipo-lite? Or a chapter 16? But it wasn't even a Queneau number! Put words into the mouth of a male character in the first person? Take on a role that wasn't mine?

In the end, once I had enumerated (for myself) all these arguments, I felt quite at ease with my Oulipian conscience, took off my shoes to feel at ease about everything else, and concentrated without making any great effort on Cartan and his infinite groups. Forgetting about Hugo, Schubert and the rest.

9 March

And then came Friday, and my visit to Ornans. Along with Hervé's *billets*, which had arrived much earlier, I found Jacques Roubaud's answer concerning my request for BOs by Reine Haugure:

> Unfortunately, I have nothing on my computer (an electronic disaster preceding the more recent one).
> Have a good weekend.
> jrjr

I loved this tautology. JR's hard drives deserved a novel of their own.

But, on to Ornans. I was impatient. Obviously, I was hoping to find page IV-R-16, but it was above all a curiosity about everything else that was so thrilling. Opening a box of archives is always something of an adventure. I wouldn't find Hugo Vernier's *Le Voyage d'hiver* there, nor Vincent Degraël's black, clothbound register. But maybe there would be other black, clothbound notebooks from the 1930s, full of jottings about the organisation of the seminar. Or else letters.

I set off at about noon. In the car, I put on some music. I knew that it took about two hours to reach Besançon (maybe I drive a bit too fast), then there were the twenty-five kilometres to Ornans, so there would be plenty of time to listen to Hans Hotter singing "La Belle Meunière" and "Le Chant du cygne" while nibbling some Figolus (me that is, not Hans Hotter). It was still winter, as could be seen in the forms of the bare trees. I easily found Rue Théophile Gautier, parked in front of number 53 and rang the doorbell. Two women opened the door, we introduced ourselves, I accepted a cup of tea, which was more than welcome after all those Figolus, we chatted for a while, then Valérie (we had agreed to be on first-name terms), who was quite aware that I had not come to Ornans just to drink tea, took me down to the cellar.

There was a trapdoor, a steep staircase, a naked light-bulb casting a pale light, to sum up, it was more than just a cellar, it was an absolute cliché of a cellar, with dust, cobwebs, and even an ancient coal bin, alongside a variety of unused objects, the frame and posts of a cabin bed, some ancient skis, then tennis rackets in their heavy trapezoid presses, an old illustrated *Petit Larousse* ending at VERNE, Jules, beside piles and piles of old periodicals, including a set of the *Bulletin de la Société mathématique de France*. At the far end, some metal shelves contained boxes of bottled Vichy (the mineral water, that is). Valérie turned on another lamp, and I was able to make out what was written in black marker on the boxes: VALÉRIE REGISTRY HUGO VERNIER…

"What's that?" I blurted out.

"The land registry, you know, endless problems with the tax office. Mostly papers dating from the previous owners."

"No, I mean that, over there."

"Ah! That's my thesis," she laughed. "Paralipsis in the works of Victor Hugo. And then there's my father's book."

"His book?"

"About Vernier. That's what you wanted to see, wasn't it?"

There then followed a rather long explanation, which I shall sum up: on moving to Ornans at the beginning of the 1950s, after spending a few years in Besançon, Petit had become extremely interested in another local celebrity, Pierre Vernier (1580–1637), and had started bringing together the necessary sources in order to write a biography of this mathematician (Pierre Vernier had given his name to the vernier, an instrument allowing measurements to be made which are accurate to the tenth of a millimetre, which is obviously now an anachronism). For over twenty years, he had worked night and day on this project. By the early 1970s, he had still not yet quite finished drafting the final version of the results of his research, but decided to start contacting various publishers, who had then seemed so unenthusiastic about the project that he had dropped it at once. Since then, the unfinished manuscript had remained there.

After being informed of all this I obviously opened the box, which contained nothing more or less than it should have contained, all neatly ordered. A second box was less tidy. My hopes were revived. There were stacks of notebooks (orange, blue, white, all yellowed), registers (even some black, clothbound ones), various notes, as well as a typescript (an algebra lecture, concluding with a demonstration of

Wedderburn's theory) but nothing from before the war, no page IV-R-16 (nor any other pages from the seminar), nor any notes by Gauger.

I thanked her, turned down a second cup of tea, said goodbye, got into my car, lost my way, ended up on Rue Pierre Vernier which led to Place Gustave Courbet, then the road to Besançon, and finally the motorway. I began to think that, maybe, as they had missed out on Pierre Vernier, with his vernier and its use in other instruments, for measuring the meridian for example, this book written by a former prisoner of war, along with the burnt letter and the page missing from the archives of the seminar, and perhaps a little-known novel by Jules Verne, plus Hensel's violin in Nazi Germany thrown in for good measure, with all this then I could maybe come up with something. It would soon be spring, as could be seen from the buds on the bare trees. I put *Les Nuits d'été* into my CD player (talk about dullard verses).

At home, C was cooking dinner. We drank a glass of Oban while I told him about my non-discoveries of the afternoon. I might now write a winter's journey about this Pierre Vernier, I added, while going to fetch the copy of *The Adventures of Three Englishmen and Three Russians* from my Jules Verne collection. Later, before going to bed, I looked at my emails:

> Good evening Michèle,
> The volume that was borrowed has been returned. Herewith a scan of page IV-R-16. Have a good weekend
> Liliane

But also:

> Dear Michèle,
> It seems to me that I forgot to send you *Le Voyage du Grand Verre*, here it is. As you will see, it touches on a mathematician called Vernier (mentioned in *The Adventures of Three Englishmen and Three Russians in South Africa*). It might give you a few ideas.
> jj x

PAUL FOURNEL

Hébert's Journey

Le Voyage d'Hébert

Translated by Ian Monk

Bibliothèque oulipienne 211

2012

● It was just after the mid-term break in November 1819 that Monsieur Hébert, a teacher of rhetoric, stood up to his full height on the dais in front of the blackboard and addressed his pupils as follows:

"Gentlemen, before beginning our lesson, I must speak to you of something of which you have no doubt heard talk — by nature, man is not a modest creature, and a young man even less so — but the details of which you are doubtless unaware."

In order to heighten the suspense and adopt a fitting posture, he pulled down the cuffs of his white shirt, which emerged from his grey morning-coat, checked the correct position of his tie, smoothed down his goatee, then went on:

"We now have a poet amongst us. And a published one at that, for here is the collection of poetry with which he had the audacity to entrust me, before our autumnal break."

Then, like a magician conjuring up a dove, he produced from his briefcase a small, beautifully bound book, the dark, blank cover of which he then brandished before everyone's eyes.

"He applied to me as an expert, asking me to be honest with him and give an opinion from the vantage point of the intimate knowledge of French poetry that is mine… Stand up, Vernier! I shall now tell you what I think, and do so before your fellow pupils, for whom a lesson in poetry will not be amiss."

A slim, dark-haired boy stood up timidly behind his desk, his arms flapping and his eyes focused on the tips of his shoes. The whole class turned round towards him. Vernier, who was so taciturn, Vernier who was so shy, Vernier who was so withdrawn, was also apparently a poet. What is more, he had not boasted about the fact at all. His fellow pupils could not really see Vernier as a poet. Vernier could not really be seen as anything. He went by almost unseen in fact. He watched their games from a distance, seemed to enjoy a good joke, but never dared to crack one himself, kept himself to himself, and wanted to remain average all round, so as to avoid attracting either praise or criticism. The fact that he was a poet, then, was the major revelation of the year. An astonished murmur arose from the entire class, which Monsieur Hébert stifled with a brusque gesture.

Vernier was in torment. He had hoped for some discreet advice, whispered in a deserted school corridor after lessons, but now he was on trial. He clasped his sweaty hands behind his back.

"Vernier," Monsieur Hébert went on, "your book is quite beautiful. The binding, albeit amateur, is utterly irreproachable. You have produced an object which is perfectly parallelepipedic and dark, which resembles in every way a little coffin. It is the All Souls' Day of poetry that you are celebrating here! Its decline and death at the end, God be praised, is from an extremely brief illness. It is always very dangerous, Monsieur Vernier, to write poems when you have read none. Turning one's back on the masters is a childish solution that leads to the derangement of both thought and form. I shall not read out any of your verses, nor any of your confessions in prose, and shall not distribute your opus among your fellow pupils, for it contains several revolting passages, from which it is my duty to protect them. You will not hold this against me, and will surely agree that I am doing you a favour, assuming that you want to keep their affections to any degree."

Hébert then paced back and forth for a time on his dais, apparently deep in thought, then came to a halt in front of the blackboard.

"Last night, I thought of a second baptism for you. I thought that, from now on, it would be better to call you…"

He picked up a stick of chalk and wrote in large, straight letters:

HUGO VERS NIAIS

The class laughed at this pun on their fellow pupil's surname and "dullard verses", but only softly, just enough so as not to annoy their teacher, and not too much so as not to crush Vernier, who had visibly buckled as the butt of this joke. Those closest to him saw his lips start to tremble and tears fill his eyes. 'Père Hébert' could be awful when he picked someone out, and anyone might be the target for such treatment.

Pleased with his pun, Hébert flicked at a lapel of his morning-coat, turned round and opened the book at random.

"What do we find on page 4? *J'aime à revoir encor pour la dernière fois ce soleil pâlissant dont la faible lumière perce à peine à mes pieds l'obscurité des bois.*[1] 'For the last time…'? Have you taken a look at yourself, Vers Niais? With your pink cheeks, slim build and budding moustache already twisting up in arrogance? Who is supposed to believe in such suicidal moods? Nothing in a poem is more dangerous than a posture. For whom do you take yourself, when talking in this way? What is your little self doing here, bursting into the world of poetry in this way? What has got into your head?"

Vernier did not move an inch and kept his eyes down during this attack. His fellow pupils watched, only too pleased not to be under fire themselves.

"If I believe my eyes, as well as page 16, I now find myself in a jumble, which could never stand as a poem:

> *Ô vie, énigme, sphinx, nuit, sois la bienvenue!*
> *Car je me sens d'accord avec l'âme inconnue.*[2]

"Rubbish! What have you done with the lessons of your masters? Where is the brilliance of Diderot's intelligence? The immortal versification of Voltaire? What is this sudden limpness, this taste for the vague?"

Vernier shrugged his shoulders. "*Merdre,*" he said to himself. He had little to say to such questions, and the attack was so brutal that he could not see any real way to explain himself. He had written his poems from a feeling for difference, from a refusal of the sort of similitude his master was demanding.

"The clumsiest part of your work is when you directly offend common sense.

1. *I like to see once more for the last time this pallid sun, whose feeble light barely pierces at my feet the darkness of the woods.*
2. *Oh life, enigma, sphinx, night, be welcome! / For I feel in agreement with the unknown soul.*

When you offend the geniuses of your time, or when you offend your teachers, one can understand it, but what about common sense? Here we find: '*ses ailes de géant l'empêchent de marcher.*'[3] Where did you learn that giants have wings? We have studied mythology, you are a sensible student, you learnt what there was to learn… And then? For even if your giant did have wings, why would that stop him from walking? You there, Courbon, instead of scratching your nose, can you tell me why your giant's wings would stop you from walking?"

Young Courbon wriggled in his chair. He glanced sideways at his fellow pupil and said nothing.

Monsieur Hébert shrugged and pressed on.

"Even if I have to admit that your verses are often metrical at the beginning of your work, it must be said that the haste, which seems to have pushed you into finishing it, was a poor master. Would you be so good as to scan these two lines, which can be found on page 57?

> *Ô le frêle et frais murmure*
> *Cela gazouille et susurre*[4]

"But that would be quite clearly impossible, would it not?"

Vernier raised an eye and, strangely as it seemed to Monsieur Hébert, looked amused. He was laughing to himself, because these were the two lines he liked the best in his book, the ones that most fully gave him the feeling that he was being playful, different and provocative — and now he had the proof. He shrugged and made no answer.

Monsieur Hébert was now feeling rather alone in this attack. If an adversary refused to resist, then warfare lost both its meaning and its value. What he had hoped for was a head-on struggle, with positions gained and lost, strategic retreats, brutal opinions and decisive arguments. But he now had to accept that this apprentice poet was also rather weak, when it came to his defences. So he decided to strike a final blow

---

3. *Its giant's wings stop it from walking.*

4. *Oh, the frail and fresh murmur / It twitters and whispers.*

which would put this arrogant young man firmly back in his place.

"Even better, in the final text, which reaches fresh heights of absurdity, you write (if you can call this 'writing'):

> *Je trône dans l'azur comme un sphinx incompris*
> *L'azur, l'azur, l'azur.*[5]

"There, I am sorry, but I could teach you better and more discreet ways to fill up a line! To keep yourself in practice, Vers Niais, I am giving you thirty lines of *azure* for tomorrow morning…"

Upon which, he flung the book down on his desk scornfully, then opened his arms, thus inviting the class to get down to more serious business.

Now standing bolt upright, Vernier suddenly seemed no longer interested, as though his poetic soul had just perished and all of this business had not the slightest importance any more. He watched his teacher busying himself, becoming animated like a vaguely ridiculous windmill. But he was no longer aware of what was being said.

His class, too, soon lost interest. After all, poetry was only a minor matter and they all had far more serious things on their minds. Over the next few days, all that some of them noticed was that Vernier started to display a greater interest in mathematics.

Back home, young Hugo had no problem in getting back the copy he had bound in pink cloth for his mother. As well as the red copy for his father. Both were intact and unopened. The white one he had made for himself was still on his bedside table. All were consumed by the fire with relief. They were only too pleased to be crackling there, along with the manuscript, in the hearth, and vanishing into a grey dust whose origins could as easily have been a poem or a pig. But he lacked the courage to ask Monsieur Hébert to give him back the black copy. He feared a further poetry lesson, administered like a spanking, and decided to forget about it, convinced that such

---

5. *I am enthroned in the azure like a misunderstood sphinx / Azure, azure, azure.*

loathing had destroyed the book just as surely as a flame.

A little while later, Monsieur Hébert had to go away for a few days, to attend a funeral, and so had to take the coach. As he was not a great traveller, he felt distinctly apprehensive about having to spend so much time in the close proximity of perfect strangers. He had a rather high opinion of himself, which the seriousness of his profession alone justified, to his mind at least, and so he did not really like the idea of mixing with people who would certainly be vulgar, or at the very least different. Thus, he chose to sit in a corner in the coach, so that only one of his shoulders would be shared with a neighbour of the male or, even worse, of the female persuasion. With this in mind, he tipped the coachman, who arranged things accordingly. The coach soon filled up, with trunks stacked up on the roof-rack, then the coachman cracked his whip.

There then followed a period of silence, during which everyone scrutinised everyone else, trying to place each passenger on the social ladder. Monsieur Hébert had no difficulty in working out that the soldier with the reddish moustache was a captain, while the nun's outfit spoke for itself, and the noisy fat man opposite him was a merchant. Meanwhile, the dark lady modestly dressed was a member of the bourgeoisie in disguise. On his side, at the far end there was a doctor, who had revealed himself thanks to his black leather bag, which he held on to and which looked just like Hébert's own doctor's bag. The woman to his side, who was as round as a ball, was a lady of the night; he sensed the fact quite simply from the weight of her shoulder against his, the curve of her hips, which could be guessed at under her flowery dress, and the futile intrusiveness of her perfume. And it was her that started up the conversation, by remarking that it was time to eat, and that she was very hungry. She pulled out a hamper from beneath her legs and opened it on her lap. Her perfume faded away, replaced by the smells of her victuals and, soon enough, as if an expected signal had now arrived, hampers emerged from all sides. The atmosphere in the coach became merrier. Soon, they were all handing round white puddings, swapping ciders, sharing cold poultry and trying out stewed fruits. As food evoked yarns of eating and drinking, each of them told a delightful tale of a festive meal, a disastrous dinner or an imaginary banquet, and they all laughed out loud when the bumps in the road liberated a sausage, rolled a piece of fruit across the floor or brought dribble to the lips of someone who had drunk at the wrong moment. Such little pleasures obscured, for a time, the discomfort of the journey.

At the end of the meal, the teacher's neighbour, who declared that she was forenamed Elisabeth and surnamed Rousset, sang a sea shanty full of vigorous, sad expressions. Upon which, the merchant recounted his memories of the day Napoleon had hugged him on a battlefield. The nun moved her lips in silent prayer. The doctor told how, under bombardment from grape-shot, he had stitched up the arm of a cavalryman, who then charged back off at once. Monsieur Hébert, sensing that it would soon be his turn, felt rather at a loss, unused as he was to talking in such a way, without rhyme or reason. He could hardly give them a grammar lesson — though, to judge by the tales he had just heard, it would scarcely have been amiss — nor did he feel up to singing the praises of Diderot, even less so poetry… He had reached this point in his hesitations when he removed from his pocket young VH's little black book and started sarcastically reading out the poem chance had set before his eyes.

"You write beautiful poetry," his lady neighbour said. "It contains a great sensation of beauty, and creates more feeling than it does thought."

"They are elevated verses," added the nun, whose voice had not yet been heard.

As for the soldier, he pointed out that poetry was not his strong suit. To which the merchant replied that soldiers had to be strong in both suit and uniform. He laughed loudly at his joke, which sank into the silence that had fallen once again in the coach. It was now time for a rest, and they all snuggled down as best they could.

Monsieur Hébert leant his head back and closed his eyes. The bumps in the road were making him feel travel sick. The white pudding and cider were dancing a waltz. He was also forced to admit to himself that reading out the poem and the doubts that assailed him afterwards were contributing to his malaise. The verses stayed on the tip of his tongue, and were threatening to burst forth. In his half-sleep, he felt like giving up something, but what, and to whom? Every time the wheels hit a stone, he felt his stomach heave. Entire lines came to his lips, lines he had scorned and that were now haunting him. What was the precise meaning of *ton souvenir en moi luit comme un suspensoir?*[6] And what was the meaning of the word *nonchaloir,*[7] which was now drumming at his temples? And that *bouquetier de cristal obscurci?*[8] And that *lampadophore,*[9] which rang out luminously amid his neighbours' snores?

They had nearly reached Andé, in pitch darkness, when the coach hit a rock that had rolled down from the cliff. The sleepy coachman was powerless to prevent the vehicle from tipping over and coming to rest on its side in the rubble. The horses whinnied, the driver yelled. The fallen coach was dragged along for several metres.

Inside, crushed by the weight of the lady of the night, the doctor and the merchant, the teacher's ghost gave itself up. It fled his body through the broken window and no one, not even the doctor, nor even the nun, thought of holding it back as it flew. A great nocturnal confusion ensued. The wounded were carried on the backs of the unscathed to a hospice, the horses were freed from their reins, the coachman picked up his whip, while the corpse remained there, in the cool of the night, since its state required less urgent action. Early the next day, it was collected in the hope of returning it to its kith and kin. Its trunk had been shattered, so the contents were transferred to a box. The undertaker who dealt with things found a book in the pocket of the black overcoat, and opened it. It was signed "Hugo Vernier" and modestly entitled *Poèmes.* Not being much of a reader, he put it into the box, among the clothes, thinking that it might have some importance for the dead man's family, and for those who might read it later. But he doubted it.

6. *Your memory gleams in me like a jockstrap.*

7. *Nonchalance.*

8. *Pierced vase of darkened crystal.*

9. *Lamp-bearer.*

MARCEL BÉNABOU

The Forthcoming Journey

Le Voyage disert

Translated by Ian Monk

●

Bibliothèque oulipienne 212

2012

There is no less invention in correctly applying a thought found in a book than in being the initial creator of the thought. It has been said that Cardinal du Perron found the felicitous use of a line by Virgil to be worthy of being called talent.

Stendhal

The Russian Church, which talks in such magnificent terms of the prince of the apostles, is no less forthcoming about his successors.

Joseph de Maistre

The men of letters and the erudite of the time hung on people's lips for the old and beautiful phrases that would emerge.

Lucien Febvre

● Let us suppose that someone, for example, one of my Oulipian friends (Jacques Jouet, for instance, of whom I think first and foremost, of course, because of the phrase "let us suppose", which he has used, just like Perec with "I remember", as a fertile trigger and turned into a genuine form, which, as one and all can see, I have no hesitation about adopting), or else one of my readers (and why not? There must still be some, somewhere, some people, who I like to imagine as being patriarchs with hoary brows), or even just someone who is curious (if such people still exist in our societies saturated with unsolicited information),

let us suppose, then, that someone having been suddenly gripped by the desire, which he or she sees to be quite legitimate, and thus irrepressible, to know (for, it must be admitted, desire is often irrepressible, and most often the desire to know, described by the learned as *libido sciendi*), to know why, why indeed, I have now decided to publish these few pages, given that I, as everyone knows (for I have proclaimed the fact, *urbi et orbi*, on numerous occasions, both orally and in ink), that I suffer from, if not total agraphia, which would have excluded me permanently from the world of writing (which is not as yet, I think, quite the case), then at least from acute oligographia (a vital word, which is as yet unknown to any dictionary, but which should certainly be used in preference to many others, with less of a ring to them, such as oliguria or oligospermia), from, then, the illness which means that I reduce opportunities to write to the absolute minimum,

let us suppose, then again, that someone ventured to ask me the difficult question as to why now, which always sounds just as embarrassing, to me as it does to anyone else, as to how,

here then, I think, comes what, after due thought, I might have tendered as an answer.

A long time ago, or to be quite exact, just after the publication, twenty years back (quite a while, then), of Jacques Roubaud's charming work entitled *Le Voyage d'hier*, which had fittingly rounded off Georges Perec's *Le Voyage d'hiver*, I had thought of explaining why this Roubaldian initiative had made me feel rather disturbed, edgy and uneasy.

Of course, I do not in any way disapprove of this step, nor do I consider that his idea of using a text by Perec as the generator or trigger for a further text is in any way condemnable or contestable. On the contrary. I was, I think, one of the first to show Perec's powerful ability to incite creation, his aptitude to provoke among his readers a desire, or even a need, to write, while providing them, most often, with the basics for being able to satisfy this need.[1] Please forgive me, then, if I summarise the following points, which can easily be verified:

— in 1978, when I discovered with surprise that *Life a User's Manual* contained only 99 chapters, I decided to write the hundredth one, which I intended to call "Le chapitre (ab)cent";

— in 1983, shortly after Perec's premature death, I published this brief tale under the title "L'appentis"[2] (or "The Lumber-Room"), which corresponded to this project, albeit obliquely. I note in passing that, when so doing, I was wrong not to take into account the words of Pindar, who proclaimed that: *Happiness does not blossom for those who follow an oblique path.*[3]

— in 1987, on publishing a new, revised and augmented version of this text, now entitled "L'appentis revisité",[4] I took the precaution of adding, as an epigraph, the

1. Take, for example, the blank pages provided for the reader at the end of *Je me souviens*.

2. In *Littératures*, Université de Toulouse-Le Mirail, 7, 1983, 105-110.

3. *Isthmian Odes.*

4. Or "The Lumber-Room Revisited"; an English translation is available here: http://www.drunkenboat.com/db8/oulipo/feature-oulipo/oulipo/texts/benabou/lumber_en.html.

following declaration: *For those who know how to approach them, Georges Perec's writings not only provide a rare pleasure, they can also sometimes offer an even rarer gift: a sort of light, yet tenacious fever from which the only means of recovery — almost with regret — is to take up a pen.*[5]

So, as can be seen, I was in no way reticent, in principle, about Roubaud's initiative. It was clear in my mind that the extremely short, fascinating and enigmatic *Voyage d'hiver* was a perfect example of an incitement to go further, and provide it with a complement.[6] If I had any regret on this point, then it was that I had not thought of taking this step myself, given that I could flatter myself with the fact that I had a particularly close connection with Perec's short story, given that I had in my possession the first drafts,[7] which their author had given me. To explain this connection, it is necessary to go back to the years 1965-1967, a rather euphoric period that had succeeded the unexpected success of *Things*: Perec and I had become accustomed to meeting up in his new flat on Rue du Bac, so as to devote a few hours every week to working on our shared literary projects.[8] Among these projects, apart from *PALF-LSD* and *The Universal History*, was the writing of a book which was to be called *The Novel in the 19th Century*. The scheme was as follows: the construction of an immense tale, written in the first person, in which would be included, in the order in which they appeared, all of the extracts from the novels included in the nineteenth-century volume of the school manual *Lagarde et Michard*. Some may remember that this book, which aimed at being both an anthology and a text-book of literary history, was highly fashionable in our *lycées* and acted as a sort of cultural yardstick. The idea was thus to create a framework, which would be as light as possible, in which we could, innocently and unscrupulously, recycle, having simply modified a detail or two, the

5. *Le Genre humain*, 15, 1987, 61-73.

6. See Claudette Oriol-Boyer, "Le Voyage d'hiver (Lire/écrire avec Perec)", in *Cahiers Georges Perec*, 1, 1984, 146-171.

7. These drafts can be found in the appendix to the article by Claudette Oriol-Boyer mentioned above.

8. Concerning this period, see "Presbytère et Prolétaires, Le dossier PALF", in *Cahiers Georges Perec*, 3, 1989.

finest fragments of the greatest classics. What a vast and thrilling programme! To my bitter regret, we did not have enough time to bring this project to fruition, and it was to remain, like many others, unfinished. However, after completing *Life a User's Manual* (and as a relaxation after erecting such a monument), Perec took over the idea for himself. But he was sufficiently cunning to make three major changes to it: he shifted from the novel to poetry; he adopted the eminently Oulipian notion of "anticipatory plagiary", in order to conceive a paradoxical work which is a "premonitory anthology"; and he turned this 'premonitory anthology' into a ghost book, and the object of a doomed quest! I had nothing but admiration for the final result of what had once been a shared project, but felt bad about the fact that, having been so preoccupied about providing a complement to *Life a User's Manual*, I had neglected doing the same for *Le Voyage d'hiver*.

This regret did not prevent me from being highly appreciative of Roubaud's work, and in particular of some of the choices he had made when it came to grafting himself on to Perec's story, which he had done quite judiciously, I thought.

— He had had the right instinct and had not imitated those who, like Quintus of Smyrna who picked up the tale of the *Iliad* just where Homer had left it, attempted to write the sequel of a great work from the past.[9] Instead, he had done quite the opposite: using a process that Gérard Genette would no doubt place in his category of "analeptic continuations",[10] he had gone back one step in the story, and reconstituted in great detail the genesis of Vernier's opus.

— He had had the daring to go further than Perec, by highlighting even more the importance of the role played by Hugo Vernier in literary history. In what way? By deciding to add to the young poet's *œuvre* an initial collection, of which he even provided ample and highly instructive extracts. This collection was to turn out to be almost as important in its own way as the future *Voyage d'hiver*, because he made Vernier the incontestable master of "combinatory poetry", by far surpassing, as he

9. Concerning the literary tradition of "sequels" and "continuations", see Gérard Genette's excellent analysis in *Palimpsestes*, Seuil, 1982, 195-233.

10. Gérard Genette, *op. cit.*, 197, provides several examples.

himself emphasised, "(his) illustrious predecessors [...] Meschinot, Puteanus, Kenellios, Kuhlmann".[11]

— He had had the delicacy to introduce, into the overwhelmingly male world of Hugo Vernier, several movingly gracious female characters, thus providing his tale with an indispensable sentimental touch, which was perhaps lacking in Perec's text.

— Finally, he had not hesitated to introduce Perec in person, by evoking an episode in his life (his stay in Australia during the summer of 1981), as well as one of his works (the novel he was writing, *"53 Days"*).[12]

All of this seemed to me to be in perfect harmony with the image I had long ago formed of Perec's work. If his *œuvre*, I thought, was a construction site which could be exploited in order to rebuild on it, this meant that the elements that made it up were solid enough to bear being transferred and recycled.

"But then," you might say, *"why did you then feel disturbed, or ill at ease, as you stated at the beginning of this text?"*

The reasons were, apart from a few details which I shall not deal with here,[13] linked to three extremely precise points which I could not fail but notice about *Le Voyage d'hier.*

— Firstly, there was the great disparity of size between Perec's and Roubaud's texts: while Perec had told his tale in 13 pages, Roubaud's complement took up 41, or three times as many.[14] This flagrant imbalance of course had its reasons (new characters, new episodes, new directions), which I was ready to accept. That said, I could not free myself from the feeling that the marvellous purity/simplicity, which was one of the charms of Perec's text, had thus been altered, or even upset, by the overwhelming complexity of Roubaud's addenda.

11. I obviously appreciated, inevitably in this context, the inclusion of the glorious Kenellios.

12. A work by Perec that he knew well, having, along with Harry Mathews, scrupulously edited it.

13. Mainly a few uncertain points about its chronology.

14. This calculation is based on the following volume: Georges Perec, *Le Voyage d'hiver* [suivi de] Jacques Roubaud, *Le Voyage d'hier*, Le Passeur, Cecopof, Nantes, 1997; *Le Voyage d'hiver* takes up pages 17 to 30, *Le Voyage d'hier* pages 33 to 74.

— Then comes the mistake concerning the nature of Hugo Vernier's masterwork, which is presented in Roubaud's text as a "slim volume of verse".[15] This description does not correspond in any way with the information explicitly provided by Perec. He may start by evoking a "slim volume", but he then specifies that: "*The Winter Journey* was a sort of **narrative** written in the first person",[16] "the book was divided into **two parts**",[17] the second one being "a **long confession** of an exacerbated lyricism, mixed in with poems, with enigmatic maxims, with blasphemous incantations".[18] *Narrative, two parts, long confession*: all of these indications clearly showed that it was a real book, with complex contents, and not a "slim volume of verse" as described by Roubaud's narrator.

— Finally, there was the dubious nature of the correction made to the title of Vernier's tome: Roubaud, basing himself on the misprint in the original edition of Perec's short story, claims that the real title of Vernier's book was indeed *Le Voyage d'hier*. This hypothesis does not stand up. It is hard to understand why Perec would have had the strange idea of entitling his own story *Le Voyage d'hiver* if its subject, Vernier's book, had in fact been entitled *Le Voyage d'hier*. On the contrary, Perec (accustomed as he was to this kind of procedure) was quite clearly using, as a shift in perspective, the strictly identical titles of three works: his own short story, Vernier's book and (which should not be forgotten!) that of the "thick register bound in black cloth" included among the "vast pile of documents"[19] found among Vincent Degraël's possessions after his death.

Are these failings enough to remove any value from Roubaud's precious work? Of course not. But they do cast a certain suspicion over his series of claims most of which, no matter how appealing they may sound, cannot be confirmed. I was thus led to ask myself two questions:

15. *Ibid.*, 36.
16. *Ibid.*, 18.
17. *Ibid.*, 20.
18. *Ibid.*, 20.
19. *Ibid.*, 30.

— Was Roubaud right to take Perec's narrative at face value, and treat it as a genuine historical document, without applying to it any of the basic rules of textual genetics or criticism?[20]

— Furthermore, had he not, no doubt in perfectly good faith, given too great a part to his own imagination in this reconstruction of the genesis of Vernier's book?

These questions became increasingly pressing and turned into genuine obsessions for me. So, without saying a word to anyone (Pindar having taught me that *silence is mankind's greatest wisdom*),[21] I decided to undertake a comparative examination of the two texts, based on a new approach. As usual, I started to note down my critical observations on small cards, which I piled up on a corner of my desk. My plan was to build up enough material to be able to draft a friendly, but firm contestation[22] of some of the "revelations" in *Le Voyage d'hier.*

But soon this work, which was rather painstaking, it must be admitted, started to seem futile. What was the point, I thought, of limiting myself to a form of criticism, which could only be sterile? And, above all, when it came to the work of a friend? A larger, more appealing project then occurred to me. Given that I did indeed recognise the legitimacy of adding complements to Perec's narrative, and given that Roubaud's complements did not seem to me to be completely convincing, why not try to provide different ones? And, in this case, why just limit myself to one proposition? Why not aspire, as Descartes desired, to "general reviews" and "full censuses"? I could already glimpse the existence of a grandiose construct, something like an 'attempt at exhausting' the complements that could possibly be added to *Le Voyage d'hiver*, a sort of huge arena, with multiple entry points, summing up all of the possibilities for extending Perec's text. It would be a work of systematic exploration, and this seemed to me to conform perfectly to the spirit of the Oulipo…

But I still had to find the right angle of attack. After a few hesitations and several

20. On this subject, see Claudette Oriol-Boyer's remarks in the article quoted above.

21. *Nemean Odes.*

22. Is it necessary to recall that one of my favourite aphorisms has always been *Amicus Plato, sed magis amica veritas*?

false starts, the method I needed to follow soon established itself. As Roubaud had done, it was necessary to find a title for each new text, which would be just as eloquent and suggestive. Had not Antoine Furetière rightly said that fine titles are true procurers for books?[23] To do so, I decided to adopt a principle inspired from the "homophonic variation":[24] thus, starting from the title of Perec's short story, I kept as an invariant base the sequence of *le Voyage de* (or *d'*), and followed it with a variable element, which was more or less phonetically close to the word *hiver*.

From this expedition into the world of paronyms, which I undertook step by step, while leaping from one to the next, as with a word ladder, I rapidly brought back a rich harvest of titles. Here are some of them, which respect more or less the structure of my model:

Le Voyage divers, *Le Voyage d'Yves Hayres*, *Le Voyage d'Yvert*, *Le Voyage dit vert*, *Le Voyage du ver*, *Le Voyage du vers*, *Le Voyage du vert*, *Le Voyage du Vair*, *Le Voyage du Verbe*, *Le Voyage des verres*, *Le Voyage du maire*, *Le Voyage du Fer*, *Le Voyage du serf*, *Le Voyage du père*, *Le Voyage du pair*, *Le Voyage d'Hitler*, *Le Voyage d'Hoover*, *Le Voyage d'Homère*, *Le Voyage d'Hubert*, *Le Voyage d'Hébert*, *Le Voyage d'Ampère*, *Le Voyage d'Arvers*, *Le Voyage d'Auvers*, *Le Voyage d'Anvers*, *Le Voyage d'Ambère*, *Le Voyage d'Himère*, *Le Voyage d'Isère*, *Le Voyage d'ivoire*, *Le Voyage d'Issoire*, *Le Voyage d'envers*, *Le Voyage d'Enfer*.

Each of these titles provided me either with the name of a character (Yves Hayres, Hitler, Hoover, Arvers, Hébert, Hubert, etc.), or a place name (Anvers, Auvers, Ambère, etc.) or else an element of a quite different sort. As a second step, all I would then have to do would be to place these new factors in relationship with elements in Perec's narrative and, as a priority of course, with the theme of 'anticipatory plagiary', so as to obtain a new branch of the story. *Le Voyage d'hiver* would thus become, in a way, the centre of a circuit to which each new title would add a fresh ring.[25] I shall here

---

23. *Le Roman bourgeois*, Gallimard, Folio, 1981, 233.

24. Many classic examples of which appear in the volume *Vœux*, Seuil, 1989.

25. I could not stop myself from seeing, in this approach, a sort of analogy with the way in which the Greek tragedians had used Homeric legends: from the overall framework, each had selected a character or an event which they then used as the theme of their plays.

provide one or two examples, which seem to me to be particularly eloquent.

Knowing the importance of references to the Second World War in the life and work of Perec,[26] I was tempted to explore the avenue offered by the title *Le Voyage d'Hitler*. So I devised a rather simple scenario, thus:

At the time of the arrests made during the Vél d'Hiv round-up, the German authorities learnt of the existence of Hugo Vernier's book, and the distinctly inglorious light that it shed on the cream of the French poets of the second half of the nineteenth century, reducing them to the rank of vulgar plagiarists. This was a sledgehammer argument which the members of the Nazi Party, up to the highest level, wanted to exploit in their propaganda against the French, who were so proud of their cultural heritage. Hence the creation of a Hugo Gruppe, with the responsibility of recovering the sole surviving copy of the work, in the greatest secrecy. Once discovered, it would be presented to the Führer in his bunker, where it would become his favourite book, until he realised that, in the same way as for their French counterparts, the finest verses of the great German poets had also been quite simply borrowed from Vernier…

For *Le Voyage d'Hoover*, my scenario of course brought in the CIA and its head with his scandalous reputation. The tale essentially involved a fifteenth-century manuscript which included most of the plays which Shakespeare was to publish under his own name two centuries later.

Day by day, the same procedure allowed me to produce a whole series of different scenarios. In general, they were extremely brief: just a dozen lines, at most. Once noted down, I put them carefully to one side, waiting to have the time and energy to use them for the fascinating narratives of which they were just sketches, or sometimes the starting point. As I had not yet, as Pindar recommended, *exhausted the field of the possible*,[27] at the time it seemed sufficient simply to carry out a thorough preparation

---

26. See, of course, *W or the Memory of Childhood*, and the countless commentaries that have been made on this book, while not forgetting that the Second World War is also present in the short story itself.

27. *Pythian Odes* III, 61-62. The complete couplet, which Paul Valéry used as an epigraph for "The Graveyard by the Sea", and Albert Camus for *The Myth of Sisyphus*, has been translated as follows: "O my soul, do not aspire to immortal life, but exhaust the field of the possible". This translation is debatable, but that is another story.

of this territory. After all, there was no hurry, and so many other texts were waiting to be written…

It is thus easy to imagine my stupefaction when suddenly, in 1999, Hervé Le Tellier succeeded Jacques Roubaud, after a delay of a few years (but as is well known, this kind of gap in time is frequent in the Oulipo),[28] and published a fascicle entitled *Le Voyage d'Hitler*, whose scenario seemed to be based on mine, with the exception of a few details! Almost everything was there: the Hugo Gruppe, the Führer, his bunker. All that was missing was the *Vél d'hiv*, whose initials (V. H.) should have occurred to Le Tellier's subtle mind. This was a heavy blow. Of course, I could hardly accuse Hervé Le Tellier of having stolen one of my ideas. And for two excellent reasons. Firstly, just as theft cannot be committed between spouses,[29] there can be no thefts of ideas between Oulipians. As everyone knows, the Oulipo is a place for voluntary sharing. But the second reason was even more decisive: I was certain that I had never mentioned, either to Hervé or to anyone else, the vast navigation that I had undertaken around Perec's *Voyage*. I could easily have included it in the agenda of a meeting of the Oulipo, as a perfect communication in the "rumination" section. But I had not done so, for obvious questions of security. I had not even created a file or document on this theme on my computer. I then had to face the fact that my scenario was not as original as I had thought, given that another Oulipian had managed to come up with an extremely similar one.

Of course, I said nothing and kept this let-down to myself. Then, in a fret, I waited for what would happen next. Something (though I would have been incapable of saying exactly what) told me that this unhappy coincidence was probably not going to be the last. So it was that my worst fears were confirmed as, between 1999 and 2001, an entire series of *Voyages*[30] appeared in a flash, most of whose titles[31] and

28. The same phenomenon would occur again a few years later with the series of "self-portraits". See Oulipo, *C'est un métier d'homme*, Mille et une nuits, 2010.

29. The famous article 311-312 of the *Code pénal*.

30. Here is the list: Jacques Jouet: *Hinterreise et autres histoires retournées*, 1999, BO 108; Ian Monk: *Le Voyage d'Hoover*, 1999, BO 110; Jacques Bens: *Le Voyage d'Arvers*, 1999, BO 112; Michelle

scenarios were disturbingly similar to those I had concocted myself. It would be pointless and pernickety to draw up a complete list of all of these coincidences here. But what does seem interesting to point out is the fact that the way these various elements were used did not correspond at all to the use I would have made of them myself, if I had made the effort to write all of these texts.

An attentive reading of the entirety of this production revealed to me the extent of the perhaps irreparable damage that had been caused to other Oulipians, and some members of their entourages or else their supporters (whose existence was news to me, having been previously carefully concealed), which a certain Reine Haugure (one such creature who had arisen, just like that, from the void, to take part in the galaxy of the *Voyages*, with a fascicle or two of her own) had rightly called *a Verniereal disease*.[32]

For this verniereal disease, this headlong gallop, in which each fresh author picked up on one or more fragments of their predecessors' texts, turning them into the centre of their own narrative, had led to a frenzied jostling over supposed discoveries, most often obtained thanks to unlikely telescoping effects: a telescoping of eras here, a telescoping of characters there, or telescoping of situations left, right and centre, with an even greater telescoping of characters…

For this verniereal disease, with its burgeoning, dense, inextricable productions, and their endless pseudo-scholarly claims and purely fantastical considerations, had even triggered off more or less bitter debates, even leading to an actual settling of scores.

The sad truth was all too clear to me: all of these zealous commentators/ continuers, while claiming to provide original illumination, were in fact simply trying to bring out the extent of their own knowledge, their erudition or, most often, their subtlety. To sum up, they all had just own goal: looking after number one, as the saying

---

Grangaud: *Un Voyage divergent*, 2001, BO 113; François Caradec: *Le Voyage du ver*, 2001, BO 114; Reine Haugure: *Le Voyage du vers*, 2001, BO 117; Harry Mathews: *Le Voyage des verres*, 2001, BO 118.

31. I say most, but not all. I must admit that I had not thought of such titles as *Hinterreise* or *Un Voyage divergent*, whose inventors I acknowledge to be Jacques Jouet and Michelle Grangaud respectively.

32. Reine Haugure: *Le Voyage du vers*, 6.

goes. Once again, a legitimate and fertile exploration of virtuality had given way to a self-congratulatory exhibition of virtuosity, which is something I had often deplored in other circumstances.

I was only too pleased to have escaped from this epidemic, given that my sole ambition was to carry out systematic research into the potentialities of Perec's text. It is easy to understand that the woeful contemplation of this closed territory, or rather this minefield, which could very soon turn into a wasteland, had removed any desire for me to continue. They have so overloaded the boat, I said to myself, that, in the end, it was bound to capsize and tip the entire business into the deep blue sea. So I left my initial project to slumber in a drawer, continued to remain silent about it, despite the various digs I received from my friends, who were surprised or disappointed about the fact that I had not joined in with their waltz. But I took some satisfaction from the thought that, if these *Voyages* would one day come to an end, and make up a huge narrative jigsaw puzzle, in the spirit of Perec, it would be better if one piece were missing. What is more, had I not myself asserted that there are works whose value comes from the very fact of their being unfinished?[33]

But the truth had to come out one day or another.

And now it has.

---

33. "Make an unfinished and unfinishable book, not into an unfortunate accident down to my incompetence, but instead into a genuine literary genre, with its own norms and precepts", *Jacob, Menahem and Mimoun. A Family Epic*, Stages, 2001.

ÉTIENNE LÉCROART

Various Journeys

Divers voyages

Translated by Ian Monk

●

Bibliothèque oulipienne 213

2013

H. Vernier

Divers voyages

INTRODUCTION

● On Friday, 24 November 1995, at a jumble sale on Rue Valentin Degrec in Hurvige (Orne), Jean-Pierre Mercier, scientific advisor for the Musée de la Bande Dessinée d'Angoulême, spotted and bought a large batch of old cartoon albums, some of which were first editions. The seller said he had inherited them from his grandparents in Paris.

On examining them the next day, he discovered between the pages of a volume of Strapontin a small black notebook written in a fine hand and decorated with drawings, of which just the first 12 pages remained. On the cover was handwritten in white ink: "H. Vernie… Divers Voyages".

Knowing nothing about this person, he indexed the batch and put it away in a drawer in the museum. It wasn't until 16 years later, when carrying out an inventory, that he rediscovered this notebook and, inspired by a legitimate, albeit tardy curiosity ran a quick web-search. He thus discovered the existence of Hugo Vernier and his connections with the Oulipo. Knowing of my involvement with the group, he spoke to me about it over dinner, at his home, in the company of our partners Pili Muñoz and Aline Calendreau, on 23 December 2011. Initially dubious, I finally had to admit that the coincidences of names, dates and places were, at the very least, disturbing.

I talked to Jacques Jouet and Frédéric Forte about it immediately afterwards and they enthusiastically encouraged me to publish this find as quickly as possible. Since these few pages are, to date, the only ones known to have been written by this author, assuming their authenticity is confirmed, it is of vital importance that their discovery should be made available to one and all and in so doing allow our research to continue.

Hugo Vernier's text will add little to the state of our understanding of the underlying features of this enigma. It does not shine either by virtue of its graphic or its literary qualities. It is all quite flat and purely informative. On the other hand, it does enlighten us about its author's character. We here discover an adventurous spirit, a real, solitary explorer, with innovative ideas, who did not hesitate to call into doubt the conventions of his era. A personality which, it must be said, fits perfectly with the precursor who was Hugo Vernier.

Étienne Lécroart

Corsica

14 July 1850: the end of my holidays in Erquy.[1] It is Bastille Day. I spend the morning playing with the village children. Preparations for the evening's festivities. Arrival of the various delegations from France and elsewhere. Drinks. I do not know what they put in them, but, as though by magic, we are all suddenly in excellent spirits. A big parade. I see J.R. in fancy dress as the King of the Baobabro'ms.[2]

During a row with some Italians from Rome, at the end of the day, I make the acquaintance of a Corsican, named B.O. After a brief disagreement with my friend O.B., they make up. We have dinner together. A song in honour of B.O. A friendly atmosphere. B.O. invites my friends O.B. and A.S. to go back with him to Corsica.

They accept at once.

15 July: O.B. suggests that I go with them. A.S. is reluctant to take responsibility for me given my young age. B.O. finally takes me under his wing. I inform H.V. and S.J.,[3] pack and bid my farewells. We leave around noon in a Huderni omnibus for Angers. An unremarkable journey.

16 July: train to Orléans, then Nevers.

17 July: from Nevers, we take the Gault–Ciseaux coach to Alès.

18 July: the train to Marseille. Arrival at about 4 p.m. Thanks to a Corsican friend of B.O. and his (voluble) wife we find a boat going to Corsica. We embark that evening. An unremarkable crossing apart from the inscrutability and wiliness of the crew who, I think, took us for fools.

1. Seaside town in the Côtes d'Armor.

2. Tribe of the former Belgian Congo.

3. Perhaps Hippolyte Véron Vernier and Sarah Judith Singer, Hugo Vernier's parents (see Jacques Roubaud, *Le Voyage d'hier*, BO 53 and Hervé Le Tellier, *Le Voyage d'Hitler*, BO 105).

19 July: arrival in Bastia. Discovery of the local cuisine. A new understanding of the adjective "coarse". A swim in the sea. Coach trip to Aléria. Arrival after sunset. A quiet night.

le village de Marinella - 20 juillet 1950

20 July: a long walk through the scrubland. Heard a loud explosion coming from the coastal region early in the morning. Cause unknown. A bandit? A Corsican partisan? This is normal here apparently. I do hope that this obsession with explosives will soon be abandoned on this irenic island. Arrival in B.O.'s village of Marinella.[4] Picturesque, almost too much so. People are saying the whole of Corsica has now been occupied by continental tourists… The whole of it? Not quite! One village, at least, still resists the invaders. A find of four fine fossils at the entrance to the village. We dine at C.A.'s home, who is a friend of B.O.'s: wild boar and chestnuts. Several of the natives make fun of how short I am. Should I remind them of Napoleon's height? I try to understand the subtle threads in the rivalries between the various Corsican clans. In vain.

21 July: the constabulary here is made up of expatriates (Italians for the most part) who are generally rather indolent. This morning, an altercation between C.A. and a young brigadier. I fail altogether to understand what it's about. Some obscure issue concerning their taste, or lack of, for sausages…

Then back to the scrubland for a few days, with B.O., A.S. and O.B. For a brief

4. Ancient village in Upper Corsica.

while I manage to become lost. Then I find my friends again, without any help from the utterly useless constabulary. A rough campsite. Wild boar on the menu again, shot by O.B. I can't get enough of it.

22 July: a lazy morning. I see almost nobody apart from S.A., a loon who wants to become a civil servant. Bumped into a notary's clerk from Paris, called J.P., lost in the Corsican scrubland. He tells me an extravagant story: he is searching for a certain A.L., because of an inheritance, and has now found himself caught up in an improbable mishmash. I have noted down his tale in my notebook under the title "Corsican File".[5]

O.B. et A.S. en Corse - 23 juillet 1850   H.Y.

23 July: I meet several of B.O.'s friends in various villages. O.B. subsequently suffers from a terrible migraine. Maybe owing to the heat. A very calm night.

24 July: departure at dawn with some of B.O.'s friends to pick chestnuts. A beautiful panorama of Aléria which O.B. keeps calling Alésia. At least he does not seem to be confusing Julius Caesar with Napoleon…

25 July: I meet O.L. with whom B.O. is on very bad terms. Not interested in their conversation. We visit Aléria.

Saw four fine antique vases when we got there. Several not particularly striking Roman ruins visited on the trot. I see our "loon" again, who is utterly deranged. We

5. No trace has been found of this notebook.

conclude the proceedings with a short boat trip and a dip in the pool at Diane.[6]

26 July: Aléria. A day spent in Napoleon's footsteps. In the evening, B.O. organises a large banquet for our depart-ure. A large number of guests. Even O.L. was there. Yes, even Corsicans can overcome their diff-erences. Soon all these absurdly prehistoric quarrels between clans will be just a distant memory.

Vue d'Aléria - 26 juillet 1850

27 July: departure for Bastia with B.O. An unremarkable journey.

2 August: arrival in Erquy. A moving evocation of friends encountered during the trip. Big get-together for a meal, very merry, but no singing. Slept deeply.

Oklahoma

28 March 1889: coach trip from Vimy[7] to Vernon[8] with V. and V.[9]

31 March: the train from Vernon to Le Havre.

---

6. Towards the north of Aléria. The former site of a Roman port.

7. Town in the Pas-de-Calais. Reported birthplace of Hugo Vernier (see Georges Perec, *Le Voyage d'hiver*).

8. Reported to be the home town of Hugo Vernier (see Jacques Roubaud, *Le Voyage d'hier*, BO 53).

9. Perhaps Virginie and Vincent, Hugo Vernier's wife and son (see Jacques Roubaud *op. cit.*).

1 April: departure from Le Havre for America aboard the *Daisy Belle*. An uneventful voyage.

10 April: arrival in Washington. I am here to witness the opening of the Indian territory in Oklahoma to settlers. These lands had been granted to the American Indians by the federal government, according to the terms set down in the Indian Intercourse Act of 1834. But under the pressure of white settlers, led in particular by D.L.P. and W.L.C.,[10] they have been constantly reduced and many tribes have been forced to settle elsewhere, without any respect for their most basic rights. I want to see the extent of this ignominy for myself.

From 11 to 15 April: journey by train with the Santa Fe Railway Company to Arkansas City[11] (Kansas) via Saint Louis (Missouri) and Junction City (Kansas). The nearer I approach my destination, the more the second-class coaches of the train fill up with migrants heading for this new world. Meanwhile, alongside the tracks, lines of paupers carry their few miserable belongings, a tent, a blanket, various tools, an axe and enough provisions for a few days. In their eyes could be read the half-concealed hope for a better life. Whatever the price.

16 April: in the "Maurice Sinigaud" saloon in Arkansas City I meet the chief organiser of this migration: L.L., the Coordinator of the Surveillance Committee set up by the Senate. He is young, brash and arrogant. He boasts of his offhand methods for chasing away the "sooners"[12] from his territory. L.L. has even imprisoned a "sooner" in his own house for several days, trapped many others by passing himself off as an ambulant liquor merchant, and shot one in the middle of the night, by firing at random. He claims to be able to shoot faster than a shadow, which he seems to find funny.

10. No doubt Captains David L. Payne and William L. Couch.

11. Departure point for the great gold rush in Oklahoma in 1889.

12. The term for illegal settlers before the territories were opened up.

17 April: I meet D., a courageous settler, who hopes to find a quiet place where he can set up home. He asks if I can help him. I just advise him to make his voice heard.

18 April: I ask L.L. for a pass allowing me to go and observe more easily the conditions of the

Le village de toile - 17 avril 1889

first settlers. I should have done better making myself scarce: L.L., suspecting that I was a sooner, puts me in preventive detention for 4 days. D. tries to get me released, but in vain. He is then even arrested himself, completely illegally!

19 April: the atmosphere heats up; I overhear a huge brawl in the saloon concerning a case of cheating.

20 April: I hear various rumours: drugging, sabotage, etc. The mood is electric.

21 April: all is set for tomorrow. I hear preparations being made all day, then an official speech.

22 April: at noon, I hear the sound of the bugle announcing the settlers' departure. Then *Rintincan Tirelire*,[13] off they go. I am furious not to see anything! I get freed about 4 p.m. What I then see is quite incredible: there are tents pitched everywhere, with signs apparently indicating their owners. Lawyers, who have arrived for this very

13. A reference to the popular song "Le Corniaud".

L.L. en Oklahoma - 23 avril 1889

reason, are recording the owners' title-deeds and settling complaints for a few dollars. I too have to pay up in order to find a place to sleep.

23 April: arrival at Deer Creek, now re-baptised Guthrie.[14] Already 15,000 title-deeds have been recorded! The town is being built before my very eyes! Restaurants, hotels, schools, saloons, banks… with, at the same time, a blossoming of crime and criminals. This rule of gun law does not seem to worry the authorities.

24 April: D. suggests to B.B., a friend met in prison, that they should become partners in the setting-up of a small fizzy-drink factory. I decide to follow their project. The company is set up that very day. A visit from L.L. who suggests that they work for him. They refuse. He leaves in anger.

25 April: business is progressing nicely for D. and B.B.

26 April: customers start arriving.

27 April: a rumour runs

Guthrie - Luke's Avenue - 26 avril 1889

14. First capital of Oklahoma.

around town according to which D.'s and B.B.'s drinks are unsafe. L.L. takes advantage of the situation and has their establishment closed down. I should not be surprised if he had started these rumours himself.

28 April: organisation of the local elections in Guthrie. There are numerous candidates using the most varied slogans. D., now idle, considers standing. I encourage him. L.L. sarcastically notes down his candidacy.

29 April: the local elections. Despite all of L.L.'s plots, D.[15] is elected. I faint from the emotional shock and the heat. I fear that L.L. will try to bribe D. to get him to work in his favour…

30 April: I help B.B. to set up a public works company.

Beginning of May: drought and starvation in the town.

21 May: B.B. closes down his company and opens a small printer's. I assist him.

23 May: stormy weather. A sand-storm.

24 May: I meet an extraordinary Belgian naturalist, returned from the Amazon jungle. He tells me about the astonishing creatures he has observed there. Among others, there is a strange marsupial that lays eggs,[16] and which is incredibly strong while being equipped with a long, prehensile tail. He also tells me about a tribe of tiny natives with bluish skin, whose language is stuffed with repetitions. I am unsure how much to believe all this. But I still write it all down in some of my other notebooks.[17]

---

15. D. would thus seem to be Dalton A. Simpley, the first governor of Guthrie.
16. It is thus rather a monotreme.
17. No trace has been found of these notebooks.

End of May: the town is still growing extremely quickly. Property speculations.

2 June: I decide to leave this town, which I no longer recognise. I close my bank account.

3 June: D. organises a little party in my honour; fireworks and dancing. I leave that evening. D. and B.B. accompany me for a while. L.L. has also decided to leave, with J.J. I hope we do not run into each other.

I suddenly realise that, during this entire journey, I have met only about ten women (and only heard one speak, on two occasions). It makes one wonder how these settlers manage to reproduce so rapidly…

I come across a few Indians on the way. They are the great losers in this ignoble business. I am afraid that this miserable page of history may later be transformed into the glorious legend of the Wild West. Or, even worse, made into a mockery. During the entire journey back, I have an old nostalgic air in my mind. I have no idea where it came from.

Congo

21 October 1899: I rise early, weary from the festivities the day before. I am starting to feel my age, it seems. I take the train from Vernon[18] to Antwerp, via Paris and Brussels.

23 October: I leave Antwerp aboard the *Karaboudjan*. A calm sea.

30 October: we pass Tenerife.

1 November: we pass Dakar. I overhear a violent argument during the night coming from a neighbouring cabin. An exchange of curses.

2 November: I discover my neighbours, 2 Belgians called T. and S. The latter bears

18. See note 8.

traces of blows. It was presumably him who was fighting the previous night. I do not know who with. They seem pleasant enough, though rather full of themselves. S. comes to speak to me in my cabin that afternoon: what a bore… Then he goes to do some fishing with T. Hardly a bite, apparently. I see a shark.

6 November: stopover in Banana.[19] It has been almost 39 years since I last set foot on African soil.[20]

7 November: arrival in Matadi.[21] A local welcoming committee is awaiting the passengers. T. and S. take this as having been arranged for them personally, and appear enchanted. I take the brand new train[22] to Leopoldville. During the journey, T. and S. suggest that I travel on with them. After some hesitation, I finally accept. I am not sure if this is a good idea. A sleepless night in the hotel: heat and mosquitoes.

8 November: breakfast with T. and S. T. has decided to go on a safari and write a report of it for a newspaper. For the moment, no one seems interested except for a small, obscure Belgian paper.

He starts looking out for a servant and some porters. He completes the task that afternoon: the former is very young and servile, the latter are far older and unruly. That evening, we draw up our itinerary.

9 November: we leave together that morning for a trip lasting several days in the brush. I leave T. and S. beside the River Cutts[23] to go "crocodile hunting" with C., their servant. I continue exploring the locality. One of the porters hurts his foot. On

19. Port in the former Belgian Congo.

20. This seems to corroborate the date of Hugo Vernier's journey to Egypt in December 1860, mentioned by Harry Mathews (see *Le Voyage des verres*, BO 118).

21. Port in the former Belgian Congo.

22. Railway line inaugurated in 1898.

23. Unknown. No doubt a mistake.

my return, I receive a dressing-down from T., who is furious about my being late. In reality, I think he is angry most of all because of the results of their hunting trip: they ran out of cartridges without hitting the slightest crocodile and have even lost a gun... To calm down, while camp is being pitched, T. goes off to hunt antelopes. A real massacre: 15 of them shot! Not to mention an ape, whose skin he wanted for a fancy-dress party. His childish behaviour finally makes me decide to complete this trip alone.

T. au Congo - 9 novembre 1899

10 November: by my own means, I reach the country of the Baobabro'm tribe,[24] whose praises had been sung to me by my friend J.R. Sure enough, I am warmly welcomed by them. I am given lodging by Muganga, a witch-doctor with a warm nature and bright intelligence. We have long discussions together. I discover their vast, traditional culture based on humanism and a respect for foreigners.

11 November: this moment of calm does not last long. T. and S., one of whose porters has been slightly injured while running into a convoy of natives, are also to be lodged here, while the porter is being treated. The Baobabro'ms then show that they fully deserve their reputation for hospitality given that, after this accident, T. and S. behave like arrogant colonists. For the first time since the beginning of this journey, I meet a woman. They seem to be very scarce here, too.

12 November: T. and S. have decided to join a lion hunt which the king has organised in my honour. After some hours spent tracking, the natives manage to drive a young

24. See note 2.

male towards our group. But, just when T. is in the right position to shoot it, he faints in panic. Luckily, several of us react quickly enough to kill the animal. S. then absolutely insists on being recognised as the person who fired the fatal shot. To please him, the king has to present him with the beast's tail as a trophy. This calms him down at once, but ignites T.'s jealousy. He then demands a similar trophy. Since our lion is not bicaudal, the king can do nothing about it. T. swears that this will not be the end of the matter.

13 November: I am awoken by cries of distress from among the tribe. I learn that their sacred fetish has disappeared during the night. After a rapid investigation, we find it hidden in T.'s hut. He pleads his innocence. But everything points to the opposite conclusion. What the Devil was he intending to do with it? A council of wise men is assembled to decide on his fate. He owes his eventual release, that evening, to the clemency of the witch-doctor and his understandable distrust in the justice of the local authorities. While talking, as usual, with S., I notice T. pacing about and grumbling, as though planning some other misdeed.

14 November: T. organises a projection show this morning, using a small magic lantern which he has brought with him. He claims to be doing this in order to enlighten the natives. But I wonder if he is not in fact trying to gain some ascendancy over them… S. suggests that we visit several neighbouring tribes together, for a few days. I accept his proposal with delight. We leave that evening.

15 November: we arrive among the M'Havoutous.[25] A warm welcome. While S. participates in the customary meeting under the palaver tree, I treat several cases of malaria.

16 November: a long meeting with the king. He explains the subtle system of rituals used to settle conflicts between neighbouring tribes. It is based on pacts and sacrifices of hens, by drowning. This seems to work perfectly, the best proof being the pathetic

25. Tribe in the former Belgian Congo (province of Rawapoulata).

state of their weaponry: a few bent arrows and spears, and some ancient muskets, which would be better off never used…

S. tells me about the secret society of the Aniotos.[26] They are involved in the fight against colonisation. Having seen the appalling state of their local institutions, I can quite understand their legitimate reasons for this struggle, even if I have my reservations about the methods they use.

That night, we go leopard hunting. Nothing shot, except a large snake that almost bit S. A terrible thirst. At dawn, I emptied two gourds beneath a baobab.

la rivière Zorrino - 17 novembre 1899

17 November: I go crocodile hunting with Father C. from the nearby mission, using live bait hanging from a tree. Four kills. I observe a python digesting its meal, probably a small mammal. The appetite of these snakes is astonishing: it has been claimed that, when food is scarce, they even consume themselves. To be confirmed. I visit the mission with Father C.: a school giving classes in arithmetic, zoology (with J. Mc D., an American) and experiments in physics.

18 November: elephant hunting with Father C. My scalp is now sunburnt. A nap. One animal killed, I do not know by whom. On my return, I discover T. and S. who seem

26. The Aniotas, Anioto or Anyoto, also called "leopard men": a secret society of animists, active in the former Belgian Congo (Babali region of the Upper Aruwimi), who practised ritual murders by simulating a leopard's attack.

to be following me everywhere. T. absolutely insists on buying the creature's tusks, no doubt to claim them as his own trophies on his return. Fortunately, they leave to go canoeing and climbing with Father C. that afternoon, while I go hunting on my own. I shoot nothing. I dip my head in the stream. A night in the brush.

les chutes de Gibbons - 18 novembre 1899

19 November: on my return, I learn that T. and S. have gone to visit a neighbouring tribe. No doubt they consider that they are not being sufficiently well respected here.

20 November: I decide to continue my journey towards Kalabelou,[27] where I am to meet the commander of the garrison. Great festivities in my honour before I leave. Dancing.

21 November: arrival in K. I find T. and S. once again, disguised in a ridiculous way. They seem angry with me. I do not know why.

A meeting with Commander Audaque. In particular, he speaks to me about the problem of smuggling precious stones, over which a variety of criminal organisations want control. That evening, he is to conduct in person an operation against a gang from Chicago.

27. Former name of Jauga (province of Bandundu).

22 November: rest and relaxation in K. before my return to Europe. Nothing much to relate, apart from my encounter with C.M., a Maltese sailor on his way back from Ethiopia. He tells me of his countless journeys around the world: Manchuria, the Pacific isles, Guyana, Brazil, Honduras, the West Indies, Venezuela, Nicaragua, the Caribbean, Venice, Montenegro, Dublin, Stonehenge, Picardy, China, Mongolia, Turkey, Russia, Iran, Argentina, Switzerland, Easter Island, etc. All are remarkable. I have described them in detail in twelve separate notebooks.[28]

23 November: on the train back to Matadi, I bump into T. and S.! They tell me about a "memorable" safari they have just been on: leopard hunting with a kind of lark mirror, giraffe hunting with a snare, rhinoceros hunting with explosives, buffalo hunting with a sling… They even claim they flew in Tatin and Snowie's plane.[29] How absurd! It is just as if they claimed they walked on the moon! Fortunately, I am able to leave them on arriving and I hope that I shall never hear from them again.

24 November: departure from Matadi. I pass by Banana that evening. The sea is rather rough.

Iran

3 September 1902: family birthday celebrations[30] with V. and V.[31] before leaving from the Gare de l'Est, on the Orient Express, for Iran. I have been invited there by my lady friend M.S. who lives in Shiraz, near the ancient site of Persepolis. For some years now, she has been suggesting that I should go there, so that she can show me around this beautiful country, scarred by centuries of conflicts and autocratic regimes.

28. No trace has been found of these notebooks.

29. More exactly, Victor Tatin and Charles Richet, who built an aeroplane in 1897.

30. Possible allusion to his birthday: Hugo Vernier was born on 3 September 1836 (see Perec *Le Voyage d'hiver*). He must then have been 66 and did not die young, as claimed by Roubaud in *Le Voyage d'hier*.

31. See note 9.

8 September: Constantinople. Start of…

(Subsequent pages have been torn out)

M.S devant Persépolis- 10 avril 1902

PAUL BRAFFORT

Yvert's Journey

Le Voyage d'Yvert

Translated by Ian Monk

Bibliothèque oulipienne 214

2013

Auto-, hetero- and pseudo-biographical narrative in 4,939 words and 8 images

● It was 31 December 1983 in Namur, during the first International Cybernetics Congress, that I had an important conversation with **FRANÇOIS LE LIONNAIS**, the co-president of the event, concerning a subject that had long been his own, and which was now mine: the **disparate**. During a coffee break, we discovered that we were both readers — and admirers — of a book by Michel Petrovitch (1868-1943): *Mechanisms Common to Disparate Phenomena*, published in 1921 by the bookseller Félix Alcan in the Nouvelle Collection Scientifique directed by Émile Borel. For the philosopher Léon Delpech had mentioned Petrovitch in his paper "Cybernetics and Philosophy" presented in the Principles and Methods of Cybernetics section at the congress.

I could easily be drawn into a long digression concerning Petrovitch, but this would have little to do with Louis Yvert, who is after all the main subject of this essay. I shall thus limit myself to referring the reader to the article I devoted to this Serbian mathematician, who was at once a phenomenologist, an analogue engineer, a qualified professional fisherman, a violinist and conductor of folk music, while also being a sailor, long-distance traveller and naturalist.[1] Educated at the ENS from 1890 to 1893, Petrovitch also wrote poetry (in French) while composing his thesis on *Zeroes and Infinites in Integrals in Algebraic Equations.* I am now looking out for his poems, just as **MICHÈLE AUDIN** searched out the elusive page **IV-R-16** of Élie Cartan's seminar of 1936-1937.[2]

1. *La deuxième vie de Michel Petrovitch*, Epistémocritique, 2003-2004 (www. epistemocritique.com).

2. Michèle Audin: *IV-R-16*, BO 209. Unlike Michèle's extended search, my attempts have not yet been crowned by success.

As is well known, François Le Lionnais was a member of a very large number of associations: the Mathematical Society of France, but also the Friends of the Rat, Les Amis du **JOUET**, the French Society of Conjurers and the little-known Society of Collectors of Triangular Cape Stamps.

It is impossible, of course, to mention these famous triangular stamps without evoking Edward Stanley Gibbons (Plymouth 1840 – Kensington 1913) who, in 1863, purchased for five pounds sterling two bags of triangular postage stamps from the Cape, and then managed to sell them on for five hundred pounds. After this success, he set himself up in the stamp trade and published a list of sixteen pages, which was the first version of the future *Stanley Gibbons* catalogue. After his father's death, he moved to Plymouth Hoe where he produced albums for keeping stamp collections.

In 1874, he set up home in London, where he founded a monthly philately magazine, which was a great success. Never having left Great Britain before, Gibbons then started travelling widely in the United States and the Far East.

Triangular Cape Stamp   Triangular Nepalese Stamp

The unusual and precious nature of these triangular stamps made their possession a natural subject for adventure stories and detective novels based on a "mystery", such as those that delighted both FLL and me from the 1930s. But other postage stamps have also featured in detective stories, particularly in Ellery Queen's famous *The Chinese Orange Mystery*.

As is often the case with Ellery Queen, the solution to the mystery lies in the decipherment of an example of homophony, or semantic ambiguity. In this case, the expression "Chinese orange" can mean either a rare stamp, or else a mandarin (to be more precise, a tangerine).

François Le Lionnais founded the Oulipopo (*Ouvroir de Littérature Policière Potentielle*) in 1973, the first of the series of Ou-*x*-Po (there are now dozens of them). As early as 1971, Paul Gayot, Jacques Baudou, François Guérif and **JACQUES BENS** had started to research the potentiality of detective themes (sealed rooms, time paradoxes, etc.). For example, in *Ten Days' Wonder*, there appears a certain Salomina, whose name contains both that of the heroine, Lia Mason... but also Mona Lisa![3]

Despite the various leads I tried in vain to follow up, my detective investigation into Petrovitch's poetry produced only one disappointing result: all I received (anonymously) was a simple ten-line poem, "Le Voyage (dix vers)", which I reproduce here:

> The Journey
> (ten verses)
>
> Leave
> on a barge which
> serves the Isles of Sandwich
> though you aren't rich
> Leave
> on an old cargo
> to deepest Ohio
> to Santiago
> or Mexico

---

3. "Ellery Queen, in his own way, is the last of the Great Rhetoricians!", wrote Thomas Narcejac, a guest of honour of the Oulipopo, in *Une Machine à lire: le roman policier* (Denoël-Gonthier, 1975, p.124, preface by FLL) where, a little further on, he also mentions *The Chinese Orange Mystery*.

Punctilious critics might point out that this ten-liner contains just *nine* verses (could a clinamen be at work here?), and that it seems aesthetically closer to the poetics of Georgius than to the supposed work, albeit still unknown to me, of Petrovitch.

In Great Britain, Gibbons's magazine became increasingly successful, and soon crossed the Channel, inspiring imitators in the Netherlands, Belgium and France. And it was in the very year 1866, at the same instant when Gibbons started to gather the profits of his "triangular gambit", that Louis Yvert was born, the man who was to become his worthy successor. The son of a lawyer and a singer, Louis moved to Amiens with his parents, who had inherited the family's printing business. He was a brilliant student (a *baccalauréat* in both sciences and literature), then joined the army, becoming a sub-lieutenant in the reserves.

He was also a successful piano-player and cellist, and led the dissolute life of a dandy, but this did not prevent him from passing a law degree in 1889 with flying colours.

Louis then returned to Amiens, where he assumed general control of his father's newspaper *L'Écho de la Somme*, even though he hated its legitimist editorial line. There, he befriended Théodule Tellier,[4] the head printer (and inventor of the famous "committee") and editor of *L'Écho de la timbrologie*. In 1895, Yvert left *L'Écho de la Somme* for good, and launched the *Catalogue prix-courant des timbres-postes par Yvert et Tellier* which became increasingly successful and later turned into the *Catalogue Yvert et Tellier-Champion*. Tellier retired in 1913, but Yvert, who bought up his shares, kept his colleague's name in the title. He died in 1950.

The catalogues of Yvert and Tellier sometimes look like exhibition catalogues, above all when they contain stamps that reproduce works of art, marking an anniversary or an exhibition. They thus include such celebrated masterpieces as da Vinci's *Mona Lisa*, Michelangelo's *The Slave*, Millet's *Angelus*, Greuze's *Village Betrothal*, etc., as well as the two remarkable (and rare) stamps here:

4. Not to be confused with **LUC ÉTIENNE** Tellier who signed his name L. E. TELLIER.

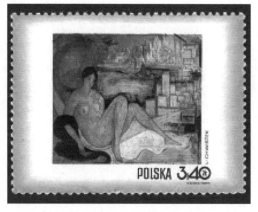

Left: Luitzen J. Brouwer, *Self-portrait.*
Above: Leon Chwistek, *Portrait of a Woman.*

The photo and the painting that illustrate these two stamps refer to Luitzen Egbertus Jan Brouwer (1881-1966) and Leon Chwistek (1884-1944), two great logicians, the former Dutch, the latter Polish (the two leading nations when it came to logic at the beginning of the twentieth century). The first stamp shows a photo of Brouwer when young and the second a reproduction of a painting by Chwistek himself: a portrait of his wife Olga, the daughter of the mathematician Hugo Steinhaus. Chwistek is the only mathematician to have his work displayed in a national art museum and to have had articles published in the *Journal of Symbolic Logic*.[5]

Brouwer and Chwistek were among the first "constructivist" logicians, a current in logic anticipated by Poincaré and which is now dominant. I wanted to bring them together in this narrative of an imaginary journey because their work lies at the origin of one of the (only) two original concepts in mathematical logic[6] devised by myself:

5. Just as I am the sole logician (?) who has also been published there while having sung at the Olympia (in 1958, on a programme where the leading act was Helmut Zacharias and his enchanted violins).

6. I shall say nothing about the second one, for obvious reasons of security.

the **dichome**.

I was fortunate enough to meet Luitzen E.J. Brouwer in 1961, in Blaricum (Holland), during a symposium entitled "Computer Programming and Formal Systems", organised by David Hirschberg and me at IBM's European Centre of Education.[7] I then discovered that my ideas in various fields (especially when it came to philately, but also pleasure trips and religion) were not incompatible with his, and how proud this made me feel!

CLAUDE BERGE, who was to become famous thanks to his work on graph theory (1970), was also present, as too were the logicians Hao Wang, Abraham Robinson, Evert Beth, etc.…

Brouwer, a famous geometer, was a fascinating, ultra-rational mystic. Apart from the polemic he created around the *Principle of the Excluded Third*[8] which founded *intuitionistic logic*, he set about formally analysing the phenomena of thought and language down to their final primitive forms. In his thesis presented in 1907, he stated:

> *Mathematics is created by a free action independent of experience; it develops from a single aprioristic basic intuition, which may be called <u>invariance in change</u> as well as <u>unity in multitude</u>.*

He then developed a sort of "phenomenology of empty thought" using an "elementary dichotomous process" considered as an "atom of thought":

7. The work of this seminar was published in *Computer Programming and Formal Systems*, Studies in Logic and the Foundation of Mathematics, North Holland, 1963.

8. The formal expression of this principle appears on the stamp that was dedicated to him (see above).

If we now attribute identifiers to the trees that have been thus defined (A_1 and A_2), the action that Brouwer calls "*the mental creation of two-icity of two mathematical systems previously acquired*" can be seen as the constitution of an "over-tree" (and so on recursively):

It should be noted that a linear representation of dichotomous trees is possible in three ways, corresponding to the usual representations of the laws of internal composition in algebra: if we represent symbolically "*the first act of intuitionism*", in Brouwer's sense, by the sign ★ the schema, and its preceding tree, can be represented by one or other of these expressions:

★A_1 A_2 (prefixed or "Polish" representation)
A_1 ★ A_2 (infixed representation — as usual in algebra)
A_1 A_2 ★   (postfixed representation — familiar to computer scientists)

Polish representation is the one, following Lukasiewicz and Lesnewski, Chwistek was to choose (as did most Polish (and Irish) logicians).

I never met Leon Chwistek but in 1946 I discovered his short work, written in French and published by Hermann under the ambitious title, which he was to cite so often: "La méthode générale des Sciences positives. L'esprit de la Sémantique".[9] Amongst his numerous publications, dating from 1912 to 1944, he developed a complex formalism susceptible of representing totality. All the concepts were represented by "little moons" and "stars": **c** and • and their adjusted assemblies.

Just as fascinating as Brouwer, Chwistek was one of three geniuses originating from

9. *Actualités Scientifiques et Industrielle*, 1014 (1946).

Zakopane, along with Bronislaw Malinowski (1884-1942) and Stanislaw Ignacy Witkiewicz (1885-1939). Malinowski became a famous anthropologist and Witkiewicz a scandalous novelist, playwright, philosopher, painter and all-round *provocateur*. His admiration for Chwistek was such that he turned him into a character in his novel *Farewell to Autumn*, and eulogised him in an article entitled: "Leon Chwistek — demon intellektu". Chwistek was also a novelist, playwright, graphic artist, painter, critic and philosopher as well as a logician.

At the end of his career, he concentrated on logic and found two young collaborators, W. Hetper and Jan Herzberg, who, being Jewish and communists, were arrested by Colonel Beck's henchmen and handed over to the Nazis, who then executed them.

His diverse (disparate, one might say) interests led him to travel widely, both in winter and summer. In London, he met Bertrand Russell. In Heidelberg, he conversed with Henri Poincaré. From 1910 to 1914, he lived in Paris (on Boulevard Saint-Michel, then at 47 Rue Dauphine). He worked on his drawing and painting at the Académie de la Grande Chaumière where he sketched this portrait of Olga Steinhaus:

Olga Steinhaus drawn by Leon Chwistek (1914)

He also met there the physicist Joseph Boussinesq, the mathematician Gaston Darboux, the sculptor Bourdelle, discovered the art of Boccioni... and fought a duel with Wladislaw Borkowski. As the instigator, along with Witkiewicz, of the *Formist* school, he wrote a novel: *Palace Boga* ('God's Palaces'), one of whose characters, Cardinal Poniflet, was to inspire Stefan Themerson, the translator and publisher of **RAYMOND QUENEAU**. He taught in Krakow, then in Lwow, before fleeing to Tbilisi and subsequently Moscow so as to take part in the Union of Polish Patriots.

Wanting to gain a deeper knowledge of all this, I too had to **journey**. I seized on the opportunity presented by the Warsaw Logic Conference (August 1972)[10] and made the acquaintance of Zbigniew Zwinogrodzki, who had just completed a thesis on Chwistek. I then went with Zbigniew to Krakow, where I was welcomed by Professor Karol Estreicher who was chief librarian at the celebrated Jagiellonian University; once upon a time he had been a friend of Chwistek's and had also written a seminal book about him.[11] I was also very warmly welcomed by Alina Davidowicz, the daughter of Leon and Olga Chwistek (and mother of a young Bourbakist mathematician) who entrusted me with a number of precious manuscripts and offprints (but no poems by Petrovitch!).

My philatelic-mathematical-literary researches then led me to Vulcano, one of the Lipari Islands (to the north of Sicily), to visit Silvio Ceccato, another universal genius whom I was to meet again in Blaricum.

In his little house in Vulcano, where we were baking in the heat, Silvio explained the principles and formalism of his semantic analysis, which had been developed by the Scuola Operativa Italiana which he had founded; this formalism was also capable of generating a number of variants.

Thus, the word *punto* (point) can be translated into different notations as:

a) "musical"[12]

---

10. I presented a paper entitled: "Leon Chwistek and Computer Science".

11. *Leon Chwistek: Biografia Artysty*, Pantswowe Wydawnictwo Naukowe, Krakow, 1971.

12. Which I shall not illustrate here, for obvious security reasons.

b) "Hilbertian" (using the "vinculum"):

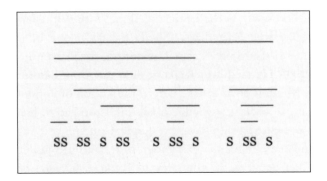

c) or "Polish", following Chwistek:

$$\star\star\star_{SS}\star\star_{SS}\star\star_{S}\star_{SS}\star\star_{SSS}\star_{S}\star_{SSS}$$

Silvio Ceccato (1914–1997)

I had brought along my banjo and Silvio liked it when I sang a few distinctly epistemological songs, such as:

Vernier Hugo
Slow waltz

Vernier Hugo,
an eye-tie, a yugo,
a polack, an a-rab, a chink, or towel-head.
Hugo Vernier,
till the last day,
rasta or wog, the vermin bred.

Let them drop the bomb,
or let the plague come:
then eulogies will be said!
Let the beast die,
if life's a party then my my
it's just for bums, Oh
fit for Vernier Hugo!

My repertoire also included "La Servante" by **DU CHÂTEAU**, "Besame Taïaut" and **JACQUES ROUBAUD**'s hit "Tycho Tycho Brahé" as well as texts by **IAN MONK** set by Michel Le**GRAND, GO**raguer (Alain) and a few others.

In studying Ceccato's semantic formalism I was naturally drawn in particular to the (poetical-cum-mathematical) theoretical work of Roubaud: here I mean his research into the theory of rhythm, which he has conducted since 1973 with Pierre Lusson,[13]

13. Pierre Lusson: *Notes préliminaires (II).* in *forme & Mesure. Cercle Polivanov: pour Jacques Roubaud / MéLanges.* MEZURA 49 (2001), p.279.

and which is also associated with formal verse expressions such as this iambic segment:

$$(((\star\star)) ((\star\star) (\star\star)) ((\star\star) (\star\star) (\star\star)))$$

or this fractal iamb:

$$((((\star\star)(\star\star))((\star\star)(\star\star)))(((\star\star)(\star\star))((\star\star)(\star\star))))$$

I shall not go into greater depth here: the (epicene) reader will surely, with reference to Brouwer, Chwistek, Ceccato and Lusson, be more than capable of developing his or her own **dichomology**.

Meanwhile, the relative failure of my research into Petrovitch's poetical works had not discouraged me, and I decided to broaden the field of my inquiries. I sought out information about the War of the Two (or more) Roses: the rose of Monsieur Beaucaire[14] and the rose of Heiningen (after all, roses are life!). The aesthetic mysticism of these two works naturally led me to Meister Eckhardt, whose hall I had frequented when, in Chicago along with **DANIEL LEVIN BECKER**, I attended the cartoon-strip lessons given by Chris Ware at the Art Institute. This building had also housed Enrico Fermi and Leo Szilard[15] who were preparing their famous experiment, derived from the work of Irène and Frédéric Joliot-Curie.

Leo Szilard leaving Eckhart Hall

14. This masterpiece by André Messager was performed by André Baugé, Marcel Merken… and Jacques Martin… But we should not forget *Les Roses de Picardie* (Frederick Weatherly and Haydn Wood).

15. Along with Paul Langevin and Léon Brillouin, Leo Szilard is one of the great non-winners of the Nobel Prize, despite the scientific importance of the **Szilard effect** and **Brillouin zones**.

Among the diverse roses mentioned above (each being of course a **ROSE EN STYLE**) it will doubtless be necessary to return to the *Rose of Heiningen*,[16] for this rose is in fact a tapestry (measuring 7 x 7 metres!), made by monks in 1516, and which presents, in its magnificent colours and with exceptional skill, an **image of philosophy**,[17] which is a sort of encyclopaedia of the knowledge of the time:

> — the central circle provides a symbolic representation of *Philosophy* surrounded by four medallions depicting respectively *Theory* and *Logic* (to the left), *Practice* and *Mechanics* (to the right), with also a semi-medallion lower down symbolising *Physics*;
> — the outer circle evokes no fewer than fourteen fields: the seven liberal arts and the seven gifts of the Holy Spirit (this time embodied by male figures such as Pythagoras, Jubal, Priscian, etc. for the arts, and Solomon, Samson, Achitophel, etc. for the gifts);
> — this circle is set in a square (itself set in a larger square), thus producing four triangular spaces containing respectively Ovid, Boethius, Aristotle and Horace;
> — numerous texts can be read on the tapestry around the perimeter of the circles and squares, or as phylacteries floating in the composition, among which there is a long text by Bernard de Clairvaux (an author particularly dear, as is well known, to **BERNARD CERQUIGLINI**. There are also the names of the fifty-nine monks who made this masterpiece, as well as those of numerous donors behind it.).

Among those who inspired the texts, reproduced on the tapestry, can be mentioned Joseph of **ARIMATHEA** (member of the Sanhedrin), **WHOSE** work was particularly highlighted, and, among the commentators, the aptly named Elizabethan

---

16. Lucien Braun: *L'Image de la Philosophie. Méconnaissance et reconnaissance*, Presses Universitaires de Strasbourg, 2005. Lucien Braun is of course, just like **M.A.**, a fleuron of the University of Strasbourg.
17. "It was the last one" declared **OSKAR PASTIOR** in his thesis.

IAN MONK. But any resulting controversies were argued with courtesy. Even during the most hotly disputed, there was no **BANE ABOU**t the slightest thing.

The figure of Joseph of Arimathea was also introduced into the Arthurian cycle by Robert de Boron in his romance *Estoire dou Graal* or *Joseph d'Arimathie*, written between 1190 and 1199. According to legend, Christ's last supper was given in Joseph of Arimathea's house. Joseph kept the goblet that was used, in which he later collected a little of Jesus's blood, before placing it in his sepulchre. Joseph then travelled to Brittany, where he carefully conserved the Holy Grail.[18]

As for me, I was not really attracted by metaphysical debates containing such **BLABLA VA** museum dustiness (nor sporting contests), but was only too keen to take part in political or ideological discussions. As a commun**AR**d — **NO**torious at the time — I discussed such issues in my **CAR RADEK** with **JEAN QUEVAL**, the brilliant editorialist of the *Gazette de Verviers*.

Louis Yvert, as you no doubt recall, was keen on music. As an amateur pianist and cellist, during his travels he went to concerts, **SALON**s and museums. In Geneva, he listened to Ernest Anser**MET, I** think, and elsewhere Wilhelm Furtwängler. In museums, he sought out little-known painters, each one of whom was a brilliant **CHAP** whose talents **MAN**ifestly eluded most critics, such as Ivan Albright, **ÉTIENNE LÉCROART**, Paul-Louis Mestrallet, Ernest Hébert or Jean Margat. He also had a charming voice and in a timbre *FORTE ma non troppo*, together with Théodule Tellier (in the style of Charpini and Brancato), sang the "Duo de l'escarpolette" by André Messager as well as the setting by Fauré of a poem by V. Rémy:

> *Assise **LA TIS**seuse au bleu de la croisée*
> *Où le jardin mélodieux se dodeline*[19]

He also fell deeply in love with Danielle Darrieux whose delicate **CHAMBER S**ongs

---

18. My thanks to **ALBERT-MARIE SCHMIDT** and his erudition for this information and his encouragement.

19. *Sitting, the weaver in the blue of her window / Where the melodious garden sways.*

rocked our adolescence (and even our later life!).[20]

His library was of course full of such celebrated, or little-known works as:

The Light Red Colossus, by Cratus

The Worst of Guardians, by Angelo Essermos

The Recurrence, by **ANNE GARRÉTA**, illustrated by Massin

I & J: Two Combinators and Totality, by Walter Henry, illustrated by the author

The Conquest of Algeria, by Claude Bonnal

Oedipus Rex V, by Hector Fragel

The Skinflint's Nap, by Errou

A Short History of Fairies, by Escieur

*Paying Your **DUE: CHAMP**ion Plagiarists*, by P.P.D.A.

A Gallery Portrait, by Sebastian Knight

The Hundred Duties of Cabalistic Analysis, by Kallour

A Complaint against Rigour, by Meroc (alias Mélanchon)

The Procrastinations of Nature, by Varancourt

The Beneficial Deceptions of Octul the Wise, by the Brothers Bogdanov

… and above all

The Voluptuousness of Plants, by Plassas, magnificently illustrated by Brenner,

… what an utterly topsy-turvy collection!

The *Voyage d'Yverdon* was an unexpected consequence of his literary tastes. Fascinated by Pierre Versins's encyclopaedic knowledge of science fiction, he wanted to visit the *Maison d'ailleurs* Versin had founded in a small town in the Jura in 1976. To the 70,000 documents donated by Versins can now be added the 20,000 from the

20. More than "Premier rendez-vous", I am here thinking of "Si vous n'osez pas me dire (Je vous aime)", which, thanks to Wal Berg's beautiful setting of Françoise Giroud's lyrics, magnifies Danielle's astonishing tessitura.

Espace Jules Verne, donated in 2003 by Jean-Michel Margot and curated by Baroness DuraFOUR *NÉE* Lusson, the foundation's president.

In effect, a library brings together tomes, pages, words, letters, graphemes, etc. but also, implicitly, places and characters, thus creating sometimes unexpected networks. Such webs also exist, potentially, in the world around us, drawing out the most varied virtual pathways. A fascinating phenomenon then occurs which, like many others, I observed during my youth, but whose existence was mentioned for the first time by the Hungarian writer Frigyes Karinthy (1887-1938) in his short story "Lancszemek" ('Chains') published in 1929.[21] In this text, one of the characters bets that any two inhabitants of our planet, in preference alive, can be connected by at most five people known and encountered by the succeeding person on the list.[22] For example, it can be seen that Adolf Hitler and **HERVÉ LE TELLIER** (who, what is more, wrote *Le Voyage d'Hitler*, published in 1999 as *Bibliothèque oulipienne* 105) can be connected by the following chain:

Adolf Hitler — J. Von Ribbentrop — Paul Baudoin[23] — Alfred Grosser — Jean-Marie Colombani — **HERVÉ LE TELLIER**

Another interestingly significant chain is:

Joseph Stalin — Ilya Ehrenbourg — Louis Aragon — Tristan Tzara — Christophe Tzara — **PAUL BRAFFORT**[24]

21. In his forty-sixth collection: *Minden masképpen van* ('Everything is Different').

22. Oddly enough, Duncan J. Watts, who has published on this subject *Small Worlds* (1999) and *Six Degrees* (2003), only mentions the sociologist Stanley Milgram as the discoverer of this phenomenon (in 1967). But then it was the mathematician Albert-Laszlo Barabasi who, in *Linked*, published in 2002, gave due acknowledgement to Frigyes, while also citing his influence on his compatriots, such as the mathematicians Paul Erdös and Alfred Renyi, who had read him in Budapest.

23. For studious readers: construct a chain from Karinthy by way of Paul Baudoin to **VALÉRIE BEAUDOIN**.

24. Author of a "Hymn to Stalin" (1949) which has remained little known, as opposed to the "Minuet for the Giaconda" (1958) and "My Own Library" (2005).

For the two examples above, shorter chains could of course be constructed, but they are here presented as mere tasters.

As the finest authors have shown, libraries are models of our universe and of a universe in rapidly accelerating expansion. To mention but a few examples: Jorge Luis Borges, Alberto Manguel, Georges Steiner, **GEORGES PEREC**, **JACQUES ROUBAUD**, **OULIPO**[25] and, last (but not least!), **PAUL BRAFFORT**.[26]

In our anxious hurry, we sometimes shake up such-and-such a universe, and this is why any given preceding pages, in their heightened realism, might create an impression of disorder, and even confusion. Thus it is that, in order to go from Namur to Verviers (two towns in Wallonia which are just fifty miles apart), it is necessary to go via Plymouth, Cape Town, the Sandwich Islands, Santiago, Amiens, Blaricum, Geneva, Krakow, Vulcano, Heiningen and Strasbourg (to name but a few!). We have also encountered one hundred and forty people, living or dead (such as Louis Yvert) including twenty-one mathematicians, living or dead (such as Michel Petrovitch), as well as the thirty-eight Oulipians, living or excused.

It might be remarked here that $38 = 31 + 7$, which is a further verification of Goldbach's conjecture. But what is the real reach of such a verification? Is arithmetic really reliable? As early as 1931 (on 8 September), Kurt Gödel demonstrated the undecidability of Hilbert's second question:[27]

> *Can one prove the consistency of arithmetic? In other words, is it possible to prove that the axioms of arithmetic are not contradictory and, subsequently, are they independent?*

Doubts could then arise (and did!). And yet, the previous year, on 8 September

---

25. BO 71: *Les Bibliothèques invisibles, toujours* (1995).

26. BO 130: *Les Univers bibliothèques, visibles invisibles réel(le)s virtuel(le)s* (2004).

27. One of the twenty-three problems posed by Hilbert at the Paris Congress, in August 1900.

1930,[28] Hilbert had declared:

> *Wir dürfen nicht denen glauben, die heute mit philosophischer Miene und überlegendem Tone den Kulturuntergang prophezeien und sich in dem Ignorabimus gefallen. Für uns gibt es kein Ignorabimus, und meiner Meinung nach auch für die Naturwissenschaft überhaupt nicht. Statt des törichten Ignorabimus heiße im Gegenteil unsere Losung:*
> Wir müssen wissen, Wir werden wissen.[29]

Herewith an approximate translation:

> We should not believe those who, today, on a philosophical note and in a superior tone, prophesy the end of culture and accept "*Ignorabimus*". For us, there is no *Ignorabimus*, and, in my opinion, nor is there any such thing in the natural sciences. In contrast to *Ignorabimus*, I suggest this rallying call:
> *We must know, we shall know.*

This wish — or affirmation — echoes the words of the German physiologist Emil du Bois-Reymond, who developed the theme in *Über die Grenzen des Naturerkennens* ("On the Limits of our Understanding of Nature"), published in 1872, which is reminiscent of the statement by Thomas Paine (1757-1809) which I shall never forget:

> The most formidable weapon against errors of every kind is reason. I have never used any other, and trust I never shall.

But the twentieth and twenty-first centuries have unfortunately witnessed the

---

28. I owe this information to Étienne Ghys from an article published in *Images des Mathématiques*.

29. This phrase was engraved on Hilbert's tomb in 1943 (see above).

misfortunes of reason[30] in several fields, such as:

> Logic, with the theorems of Gödel, Kleene, Turing, Chwistek, etc.
> Theoretical Physics with Einstein, Planck, etc.

fields in which many commentators with philosophical pretensions have added one gloss after another, often lacking in any relevance. Fortunately enough, there are some counter-examples.[31]

In the field of logic, after Lukasiewicz, there have been developments in trivalent and modal logics,[32] alongside the intuitionist approach. But their common ancestor, Chrysippus, like most Stoics, saw philosophy as the "search for plain reason" and dialectics as the "science of true things, false things, and things which are neither one nor the other". Chrysippus was thus an anticipatory plagiarist of Paine (for the first of these quotations) and of Graham Priest (for the second).

For Priest now promotes a philosophy that proclaims the compatibility of an assertion with its negation, an approach he has called "dialetheism". Based on theories of limitation, and opposed to Aristotle, Priest has established limits: limits of expression, limits of iteration, limits of cognition and limits of conception. The title of his latest work[33] quotes Rex Stout's injunction: *Doubt truth to be a liar.*[34]

---

30. See André Régnier: *Les Infortunes de la raison*, Seuil (1966), as well as Dominique Suriano: *L'Abbé de Saint-Pierre (1658-1743), ou, Les Infortunes de la raison* (2005).

31. In particular the article by Jacques Spitz: "La Théorie quantique et le problème de la connaissance", in the first (and only, for that matter) issue of the review *Inquisitions* founded and edited by Tristan Tzara in June 1936... nor should we forget the startling contribution by Marcel-Paul Schützenberger at the Sorbonne, on 14 May 1993, during a debate led by Gilles Cohen-Tannoudji, and the worldly André Comte-Sponville. This intervention by Marco, faithful to Paine's **reason** and Chwistek's **common sense**, burnt many an eminent author to a crisp.

32. With Jean-Louis Gardies, in particular.

33. Oxford University Press, 2005.

34. In *How like a God* (Act II, scene II), Vanguard Press, 1929.

And what better end could there be to this essay than a reproduction of a projected stamp which, not having been approved by the Post Office, appears in none of the *Yvert et Tellier* catalogues:

Stanley Chapman, *Design for a Stamp for the Oulipo,* based upon Leonardo da Vinci's *Last Supper* (1965)

So it goes…[35]

---

35. Kurt Vonnegut: *Slaughterhouse Five*, Delacorte, 1969.

DANIEL LEVIN BECKER

The Obscure Journey

Le Voyage obscur

Yet to appear in the Bibliothèque oulipienne

(Written 2013)

Georges y avait pensé.
(Traditional)

● In the last week of August 2012, I was putting the final touches on the manuscript of an English translation of Georges Perec's dream journal, *La Boutique obscure*. I had been a devoted admirer of Perec and his work for almost exactly ten years, since the day I learned of his existence in a French–lit seminar during my first semester of college. In the interim I had translated some of Perec's minor texts, written on his place within the Oulipo, and, surely the primary qualification in the eyes of the Brooklyn publisher who commissioned this translation, become an Oulipian myself — the fruition of a dream, certainly, though not the kind one writes down in the small hours of the morning.

La Boutique obscure was one of those books that I had always vaguely promised myself I would read, but that I had always, even in well-stocked bookstores and libraries, passed over in favour of something else. Published by Denoël in 1973, the book is a compilation of 124 dreams, recorded (and, per Perec's preface, polished too carefully) between 1968 and 1972, featuring a number of characters who will be familiar to readers of David Bellos's biography *Georges Perec: A Life in Words*. Having read Bellos's biography some years before, I considered myself equipped and, without bothering to verify that I had time to undertake the translation project — I did not — accepted the assignment immediately.

During the months I spent translating the book, my own dreams, which have always tended to disperse irretrievably the moment I wake up, became gradually more and more notable. Not in the sense that they were any more curious or improbable, only that they were easier to notice and notate. They were standard dream fare — odd narrative variations on the characters and settings of my waking life — but their dramatic action was so blandly familiar, so procedural, so *plausible*, that in the morning it was difficult to separate dream from reality. Sometimes I would dream of waking up, getting out of bed, showering and dressing — all before actually waking up and, muttering in somnolent indignation, having to repeat the whole routine again.

During these months there was also a phrase that rattled around in my head, a phrase whose origins I could not place — it always came when I was in the shower, or half-asleep, or otherwise unable to write it down or look it up — but whose meaning seemed generally manifest, dare I say obvious: *je est un autre* — I is another.

· · ·

But back to the last week of August, when I found in my mailbox a kraft paper envelope containing five new (well, recent, given the abominably slow postal service between Paris and San Francisco) volumes of the *Bibliothèque oulipienne*. Among them, two new instalments in the series of sequels to Perec's 1979 short story "Le Voyage d'hiver".

I had studied the series at length in college — the *Voyage d'hiver* had in fact been my first encounter with the Oulipo — and written a long essay on it, documenting all the typos, echoes and buried references I had ferreted out and hypothesised to be significant (for instance, the French national library code attributed to Hugo Vernier's *Voyage d'hiver*, Z87912, whose digits (letting Z = 26, for evident reasons) add up to 53, a number of particular importance for Perec, and the fact *moreover* that this datum appears (at least in the edition (Le Passeur, Nantes, 1992) that includes Jacques Roubaud's sequel) at the very end of the spread of pages 26 and 27 (whose sum is, not to belabour the point…)). So by the time I had finished the two new episodes, the stirrings of a familiar obsession sent me almost unthinkingly back into the whole series. Thus did I find, only a few pages into the *Voyage d'hiver*, that the tenacious *je est un autre* came from Rimbaud, via Vernier.

But the satisfaction of finally scratching a long-inaccessible mental itch was short-lived. For I had hardly begun re-reading Perec's story when I felt a vague sense of unease that grew sharper as I turned each page. It was as if Perec, describing Hugo Vernier's *Voyage d'hiver*, were really evoking his own dream journals: "a sort of narrative written in the first person, and set in a semi-imaginary country"; the collected traces of an "at once precise yet blurry memory" — of which there remains, in the light of day, no evidence.

I will be the first to admit that my mind was too saturated with dreams for me to evaluate these echoes rationally — but then one does not become an Oulipian by taking coincidences at face value. So, impelled by that reflex of the young researcher who never consults a work without remarking the bibliographical details — I am guiltiest at museums — I verified, heart at a steady resting pulse, that Perec had published his story some seven years after the last of his recorded dreams. The "Voyage d'hiver" did not prefigure *La Boutique obscure* by any means. But did it refigure it somehow? Was there, as dream no. 69 puts it, "another text too, hidden beneath the first"? Was Perec his own anticipatory plagiarist? Was the elusive Hugo Vernier merely an older version of himself, lost to the passage of time?

Je ne suis pas le héros de mon histoire, Perec had written in *W or the Memory of Childhood* (Denoël, 1975): I am not the hero of my tale. Had he found a way to remedy that feeling?

I spent the next hour or two inventorying the intersections between Perec's dreams and Vernier's fantasy. *La Boutique obscure* contained bridges, parental surrogates, transient homes, overwrought meals, even an actual winter journey or two. There was a whole dream devoted to a pile of books — "exactly the books I've been searching for for a long time" — that the dreamer can see but is prevented, twice, from laying his hands on. There is a crossword puzzle clue — "his most famous children didn't take his name" — whose correct answer turns out, after some initial misdirection, to be VERNE.

Hardly conclusive proof of anything, but the echoes intoxicated me none the less. The inevitable hangover followed: surely I was not the first to notice this. And yet — wasn't I more versed than most in the scholarship and arcana surrounding these two works? If their connection was news to me, could it really have resisted the spilling of so much scholarly ink about Perec's *œuvre*?

No, of course — Frédéric Forte's whole episode of the Journey series was about dreams. Feeling both disappointed and vindicated, I returned to the *Bibliothèque oulipienne* volumes splayed out on my living-room table and picked up *Le Voyage des rêves*. To my astonishment, I found no mention of *La Boutique obscure* therein —

references to Perec and dreams, certainly, and even the same notation to indicate voluntary omissions (//). Even a boutique! But no outright connection was made. Had Forte happened upon the theme of dreams by chance, failing to grasp the extent of the dialogue between the two works? Or had someone else gotten there first?

This seemed like a query to submit to the listserv run by the Association Georges Perec, which had served me well for this sort of lacuna in the past. I would either get a response from a professional Perecophile, referring me to some academic essay drunk on words like *oneiric*, or the collective membership of the Liste Perec would declare my observation a pioneering insight and clamour to publish my as-yet-unwritten explication. Either way, the issue would be resolved.

Morning was encroaching as I drafted an email to the Liste. I laid out some of the affinities between *Le Voyage d'hiver* and *La Boutique obscure* and solicited thoughts about the two texts in conjunction. Only after I hit send did I realise I had pulled an unintentional all-nighter. I stood up, stretched and went to brush my teeth and feed the cat.

When I returned to the living-room to shut down my computer, there were already three responses in my inbox. (The occasional joys of doing business with another time zone!) Encouragingly, all three pointed me to articles by the likes of Eric Lavallade, David Gascoigne, Claude Burgelin, Claudette Oriol-Boyer, etc. — all of which I had read, and none of which considered both works at once. As I was reviewing the last of these responses, a metallic ding announced a new message, this one addressed directly to me from none other than David Bellos:

> Dear Daniel,
>
> It is a fetching idea but I confess I am not persuaded. There is a resemblance between *Le Voyage d'hiver* and at most a dozen of the 144 dreams in *La Boutique obscure*, but even then it is a weak and circumstantial resemblance.
>
> Yours ever
> David Bellos

My heart sank. Who better than Bellos to refute my hasty theory? Two more responses had trickled in, but I left them unread. I decided to call it a night, or rather a morning. I closed my computer and shuffled sullenly off to bed. I dreamed of a religious ceremony in which several cats were drowned, one by one.

• • •

I woke up early the next afternoon residually discouraged, though relieved to have dreamed about something besides my morning ablutions. Still yawning, I returned to my email and deleted the usual fluff from my inbox, including some further responses to my question — "have you read *Dormi pleuré* by Queneau??" — and forced myself to look at Bellos's message one more time before consigning it to the archive.

Wait a minute.

144?

I was wide awake now. I checked both the French paperback on my desk and the nearly completed English manuscript on my desktop: *La Boutique obscure* contained only 124 dreams.

Logically, it had to be just a mistake, a typo — but then one does not become an Oulipian by being satisfied with logical explanations. What were the odds that Bellos, of all people, would get that detail wrong? (What were the odds that Perec's biographer ever committed *typos*?) What if he had meant to let slip an important clue? Was that why he had responded to me alone, rather than to the whole listserv?

And then, come to think of it, why *not* 144? According to Bellos's biography, Perec was unsatisfied with the psychoanalytic value of his recorded dreams, so why would he publish them as they were? Given his fastidiousness as a writer, and his clear predilection for squares as a structural aid — the chess-board layout of *Life A User's Manual*, the sudokuësque letter grids of his *ulcérations*, the schema of his "Places I've slept" project — didn't some kind of 12-by-12 scaffolding really make more sense than not?

And if so, how did 20 dreams turn up missing?

I was loath to bother Bellos again, but I had to be certain. I dashed off a quick and apologetic note "just to be sure," I said, that he had meant to type 124, not 144. I agonised for a moment about whether I was the kind of person who would send such an email. Then I sent it.

This time the response was practically instantaneous: an automatically generated message from a mailer-daemon informing me that the email account I had tried to contact did not exist.

● ● ●

In the weeks that followed I finished the manuscript, sent it to the publisher, exchanged a handful of edits and moved on to other projects — but the resonances between *La Boutique obscure* and *Le Voyage d'hiver* had taken up comfortable residence in the part of my brain where *je est un autre* used to be. Every so often Bellos made a cameo in my dreams, usually wearing a toque and brandishing a platter of cupcakes with green frosting.

● ● ●

In early October, I had occasion to spend a week in Paris. My visit did not coincide with a monthly Oulipo meeting, and the *jeudis de l'Oulipo* series had not yet started for the year, but I did set aside my last afternoon there to call at the Association Perec, located in a stately glorified alcove at the Arsenal branch of the French national library. I was received by Raoul Delemazure, who tactfully withheld judgement about the originality or validity of my theory, remarking only that the mindset of the Perecophile was indeed tilted down a slippery slope towards that of the conspiracy theorist.

Delemazure left me to pore over the respective paper trails of what had become *La Boutique obscure* and *Le Voyage d'hiver*. (I was tickled when he listed my college essay about the Journeys among the Association's holdings, but I declined to view it.) An hour and a half later, I had pulled six dreams, or notes thereon, that I did not recognise from the paperback edition. Delemazure explained, when I showed them to him, that two had been published in a small literary journal before *La Boutique obscure* came out; one had made it into the book, but with its entire contents replaced by a //; and one, he was pretty sure, actually was in the book. (He was right. I am only human.) In the case of the remaining two, however, he could not say why Perec or his publisher, Denoël, had not included them. He suggested I ask David Bellos.

● ● ●

I left the Association at four, the end of its public hours, with fresh photocopies of the two mystery dreams. I had dinner plans across town at seven, and saw little point in returning to my hotel in the opposite direction, so I settled at a table outside the small café across Rue Sully from Arsenal, ordered a beer and began reading.

The first dream, typed out neatly on graph paper with a handful of manual corrections, was a short piece without any sense of pacing: it begins in a doctor's office, where the dreamer is diagnosed with a rare kind of cancer, and suddenly pivots to an aeroplane that the dreamer is somehow both piloting and hijacking, with designs on crashing into the Eiffel Tower. The dream ends abruptly before the crash, with one of the passengers overheard discussing the use of sulphuric acid in waste-water processing.

The second was far longer but equally disjointed; its central narrative involves the dreamer taking a position as a secretary for an older writer (who one vaguely surmises is Marshall McLuhan), who is drafting a novel about a concentration camp on an island in the Pacific where a whole race has been enslaved to maintain a volcano that has been converted to a nuclear power plant. The perspective is jumpier than any single dream in *La Boutique obscure*, but almost Roussellian in its sense of underlying order, which seems too great not to have been tinkered with during transcription.

I am far from the most attentive or well-versed reader of contemporary literature, but I felt a frisson of recognition almost as soon as I dived into the dreams, a strong sense of *déjà lu* akin to the premonition that had begun this whole journal-journey business. There was something about them — not the style but the raw narrative elements — too familiar to ignore. But where had I encountered them before? And how would I even begin to find out?

When I surfaced from my reveries it was nearly six, and there was a man looking intently at me from the neighbouring table. He was in his sixties at least, and elegant in an essentially French way: clean-shaven, ascot disappearing under a starched collar, a severe aspect to his face but a trace of laughter in his eyes.

"Monsieur Levin Becker," he said.

I straightened my spine and searched my memory for a place where I had met the man before. "Good evening," I said. Arsenal? Bourges? A *jeudi*? An ex-neighbour? Nothing. "Forgive me, have we met?"

He smiled. "I don't believe so. I read the Liste Georges Perec, to which you wrote in recently, yes? I have some information that may aid you in your… quest."

"That's very kind, although I don't know that I'd call it a quest," I said. "And may I ask how you recognised me?"

A glow passed through his eyes, which were focused almost disconcertingly on mine. "What if it became a quest?"

A moment of silence followed, then his face softened and he looked down. "Excuse me, my manners are poor. I've been cooped up in the library all day. My name is Bruno Deronda. I'm a Perec… not scholar, but a follower, you might say."

"Pleasure," I said, hoping to sound both guarded and intrigued. "Then you work with the Association Perec?"

"Not exactly," he said, removing a pack of Gauloises from his breast pocket. "Our paths intersect occasionally." He tilted the pack at me; I waved no. "I was an intern at Denoël when they published some of Perec's work."

"Including *La Boutique obscure*?"

He lit his cigarette. "Including *La Boutique obscure*."

"Did you know Perec?"

"No, no, I was just a fan. I mean, I'm still a fan."

"Of course." I took a pointedly leisurely sip of beer. "Please, go on."

"Well," he said, getting up and settling into the vacant seat at my table. "I was in the office when his manuscript for *La Boutique obscure* arrived. As I say, I was a fan, so I was eager to read it. I couldn't resist slipping it into my bag and taking it home."

My pulse quickened. "And?"

"And I read it that night and brought it back the next day. It wasn't a particularly organised office. It's not like anybody missed it."

My pulse slowed again.

"Anyway, I enjoyed it for what it was, though I couldn't entirely tell what it was. A bit over my head, I suppose. Perec always has been. You could tell there was more to it than met the eye, the way the stories differed so much in length and subject matter."

"I should think that's par for the course for dreams, no?"

"Ah," he said, jabbing his cigarette in my direction. "I didn't realise at the time that they were dreams. There was no preface, and no sub-title. It was just a book called *La Boutique obscure*. There were many dreams in it, obviously, but it seemed like… more."

"Interesting. And so?"

"So I brought it back and left it where I had found it, and then the usual stuff happened. My work at Denoël was mostly clerical, so I had little to do with the actual production of the book. I didn't even think of it again until a few months after it came out, when I happened to read another book — a novel, very popular — and it was the funniest thing: the plot just seemed so familiar. I couldn't figure out why until I realised it was practically identical to something I had read in Perec's manuscript."

I swallowed mid-sip, making a small and relatively containable mess. "Which dream?"

"That's just it — I'm sure you haven't read it. I took a finished copy of *La Boutique obscure* from the office to make sure I wasn't just hallucinating, and it was gone. Not a trace of it. I read the book from cover to cover. Nothing."

"What was the other novel?"

He pursed his lips apologetically. "It's a bestseller, that's all I'll say. You've probably read it."

"Curious," I managed.

"Yes," he said, looking at me steadily. "Isn't it?"

"So did you say anything?"

"No. I mean, I was just an intern. And I couldn't prove I wasn't just… imagining things. Which is what I ended up convincing myself. For a time, anyway."

"But since then?"

Deronda smiled grimly. "There have been other coincidences."

"How many?"

"Oh, I don't know. At least a dozen."

"A dozen cases where you recognised something from Perec's dreams in another book?"

"Yes. And where I couldn't find any trace of it in the published edition of *La Boutique obscure*. Where the initial dream had… vanished, as it were."

"And become these other books?"

"Somehow, yes."

There was a long pause. "How?" I said finally, probably peevishly.

"I've been wondering that for years. Whatever happened, it happened between the day I read the manuscript of *La Boutique obscure* and the time it was published, which suggests someone at Denoël was involved. Personally I've always suspected Roger Dubois, the editor in charge of the project, edited out a handful of the dreams without telling Perec, and sold them to other writers. But of course, again, I couldn't prove it."

"Is Dubois still with Denoël?"

Deronda looked past me for an instant. "No, he's been dead for decades."

I turned to find the waiter behind me, and ordered another beer. Deronda kept his gaze on me the whole time.

"So what did Perec do when he found out?"

"It's hard to say whether he did find out. If he did, he never let on, as far as I know. For a while I thought he'd just never noticed, or maybe that Dubois paid him not to say anything. Or even that he was in on the deal — ghost-writing novels without even having to write them." He smirked. "Without even being awake."

"I don't know," I said, "none of that seems plausible to me. If a dozen dreams from his book just vanished, I can't believe he didn't notice. Or that he didn't say something."

"Well," Deronda said, putting out his cigarette daintily, "I've recently started to think he did."

The waiter returned, set my beer down in front of me, added a new bill to the old one, scowled at everything and disappeared.

"You mean *Le Voyage d'hiver*."

Deronda looked around and lowered his voice. "Yes. I think it contains clues to this whole affair. To what happened between Perec and Dubois, or–" His voice broke. "To how to find the rest of the dreams." He eyed me tentatively, then slumped down and sighed. "I'm sure this will sound silly, but it's become sort of an obsession of mine, trying to track down where all those dreams went."

"Doesn't sound silly to me," I said. "Sounds… Perecian."

"Yes, but I didn't even dream them myself, just read them once forty years ago. And it's not like each dream just corresponds to one novel — I find bits of them everywhere. In novels, poems, movies, television. In advertisements! And not just in French: I've found traces in things originally in English, Spanish, Russian, American, Hebrew. The older I get, the harder it is to tell whether I'm really recognising echoes of the dreams or just inventing them. Sometimes I think I've found a fragment of a Perec dream and it turns out to be something that happened in my own childhood." He chuckled morosely and looked at his feet. "I guess I've always regretted that I couldn't remember them all."

I had become aware while Deronda was talking that I needed to leave to make it across town for dinner, and he looked up just in time to catch me fiddling with my phone. I smiled weakly. "I'm sorry, this is a lot to take in. I'd love to help in whatever way I can, but I don't believe Perec would have taken, what, five, six years to react? If what you're telling me is true, there has to have been more going on."

"Well," said Deronda, straightening up. "I suppose, being an Oulipian, you might have an easier time finding out what that was."

"I'll see what I can do," I said, standing up and fishing in my pocket to pay my bill. "But I'm afraid you'll have to excuse me." Without rising, Deronda reached into his coat and produced a ten-euro note clipped to a card with an email address on it.

"Please," he said. "Allow me."

I thanked Deronda, assured him we would be in touch, and set off briskly down Rue Sully toward the Métro. Once aboard, I looked again at his card, on the back of which was an illustration of a cat primly licking what looked like a human femur.

• • •

Paul Fournel emailed me in early November to say he would be in San Francisco the following week, visiting friends he had made during his ambassadorial stint here. We arranged to have dinner in Hayes Valley on Wednesday. I had not found time to contact

Deronda since our encounter, nor had I spoken of it to the other Oulipians; responses to my query from the denizens of the Liste Perec had long since ceased as well. In other news, my dream life had returned to an innocuous brand of workaday surrealism.

Fournel was in fine form, as always. We compared notes on bicycling in San Francisco and on the vagaries of the local microclimates; he told me with excitement that David Bellos had signed on to translate his recent novel *La Liseuse* (which I had brought back from Paris but not yet found time to read), and shared groaning tales of the Oulipo's perennial publishing headaches. I might even have forgotten to bring up the Perec affair had Fournel not asked whether I had finally received the latest volumes of the *Bibliothèque oulipienne*. Yes, I told him, and funny he should mention it in light of what one Monsieur Deronda had recently told me about *La Boutique obscure*.

At this, a cloudy look passed over his face. "Have you been in touch with him?"

"Not since the day we met in Paris."

"Good. I don't want you talking to him." Fournel scanned the restaurant, then leaned in. "He's not who he says he is."

"He didn't say he was anyone, really. Just seemed like a Perec fan with a pet theory. I thought he was a harmless crank at first, but a lot about his story adds up."

"Crank perhaps," said Fournel. "But hardly harmless. He's in league with Dubois."

"Dubois from Denöel? I thought he was dead."

"Roger Dubois is dead. But his son is in publishing too. Has a respectable little imprint that's been around for a decade or two, mostly publishing small esoteric titles. Nothing you'd have come across. It was about to go under a few years ago, until suddenly Dubois *fils* got into digital publishing and started releasing these wildly successful books by no-name authors."

"I don't suppose those books have plots that bear strong resemblances to…"

"Perec's dreams. Yes."

"So then Deronda isn't a crank at all — Dubois stole pieces from the original manuscript of *La Boutique obscure* and sold them off?"

"Yes."

"Then why didn't Perec ever say anything?"

Fournel regarded me for a moment. "It's a long story," he said, as though still undecided about whether to tell it. Finally his face softened. "Have you ever wondered why it's called *La Boutique obscure*?"

"Of course."

"Well, let's just say there's more to it than what's in the book that got published. *La Boutique obscure* isn't a dream journal. It's a novel."

"Oh?"

"Yes. It was a novel in vignettes, strung together by an elaborate narrative mechanism. Each 'dream', as you know it, was supposed to be one piece in a puzzle that the reader had to solve in order to reveal the complete story."

"Was the puzzle a 12-by-12 grid?" I said, a little too eagerly.

Fournel paused. "Deronda told you that?"

"No, nobody did. But I got an email from David Bellos where he alludes to 144 dreams instead of 124. I thought it was a typo, but then I thought about Perec's aesthetic and—"

Fournel cleared his throat. "Yes, well done. Anyway, yes, *La Boutique obscure* was a 12-by-12 grid of scenes. Some short, some long, some dreams, some not, some first-person, and so on. Now, the key to putting the pieces together was to be hidden from the outset, attainable only once the reader had examined all of them. If then."

"Fair enough."

"That's easy for you to say. Perec finished the novel in 1971, only about a year and a half after *La Disparition* had come out and earned him a reputation as an alphabetical acrobat. Dubois wanted to use that reputation for publicity — include the key on the first page like they do in *Hopscotch*, have a big 12-by-12 grid on the cover, who knows. But Perec had decided he didn't want to be pigeon-holed. He wanted readers to really *read* the novel, not treat it like a puzzle to solve above all else."

"How Mathewsian."

"I suppose. But Dubois didn't see things the same way. He and Perec argued about how to package the novel — at first just normal writer-editor bickering, but then it escalated and they said some nasty things to each other, Perec especially. Finally he tried to get out of his contract with Denoël and publish *La Boutique obscure* elsewhere, but Dubois wouldn't let him."

"On legal grounds?"

"Well, that and Dubois happened to have a brother-in-law named Jean-Bertrand Pontalis. Heard of him?"

I searched for a moment. "Perec's *analyst*?"

"Bingo. So Dubois had what you Americans call *leverage*."

"That's disgusting."

"Well, Pontalis was a dirtbag. But Dubois was truly a bastard — a vengeful one. He kept Perec's manuscript, but he didn't publish it the way Perec wanted. He didn't even publish it the way *he* wanted: he picked a couple of dozen scenes at random, cut them from the novel, put the remaining pieces into a made-up chronological order and published it as a dream journal. He happened to make a pretty penny selling off the texts he cut, but that wasn't the point — he did it for the insult. He did it so Perec would see this complex machine of a novel stripped of its nuance and structure, its *soul*, and brought out destined to flop. That's how committed Dubois was to screwing Perec over."

"Jesus," I murmured. "Just because of that disagreement?"

Fournel took a sip of wine. "Perec might have also slept with Dubois's wife."

"And Perec had no recourse at all? He couldn't say anything because Pontalis was giving Dubois dirt on him?"

"Okay, Perec might have also slept with a few other publishers' wives. But yes, it was through Pontalis that Dubois knew enough to credibly threaten to ruin Perec's career in French letters."

"Credibly? I thought you people were too libertine to care about who slept with whom."

Fournel smiled and shrugged. "I suppose the dirt wasn't all so glamorous."

"So what did Perec do?"

"Well, he stewed about it for a while. Eventually he cut his losses and started over, essentially from scratch, and wrote *Life A User's Manual*. He published it, got the Médicis for it, everyone was happy, Hachette especially. But he wasn't truly satisfied. I don't think he ever got over the disgrace of seeing *La Boutique obscure* wrenched from him and turned into a passably interesting exercise in navel-gazing. Oh!" Fournel looked up at me cheerily. "Great news about your translation, by the way."

I took a long drink of wine and refilled my glass. "Thank you. So then what about *Le Voyage d'hiver*?"

"Roger Dubois died in 1977, before Perec could rub his nose in the critical reception of *Life A User's Manual* and show how badly Dubois had failed at ruining him. He didn't even know yet whether it was going to be a success — he believed in it, but he was still hung up on *La Boutique obscure*, which had assumed this sort of mythical status in his mind. He liked to think that even as an incomplete text, even with pieces of it amputated and scattered and usurped by others, the idea of it was strong enough to alter the course of literature for centuries to come."

"Just like…"

"Exactly, just like Hugo Vernier's book. In a sense *Le Voyage d'hiver* is an elegy for *La Boutique obscure*, because Perec knew the potential of that mythical book would never be realised. But it was also a way of sticking his tongue out at Dubois for missing out on what could have been. No matter that Dubois was dead. He wanted the last word."

"Except technically Dubois's son got the last word, right?"

"I suppose so. But not as far as Georges was concerned."

"Okay, but then where do Deronda and I fit into all this? If Dubois's son is still making money off of Perec's dreams and nobody can prove anything, what's the issue? What do they want from us?"

"The issue is that *Le Voyage d'hiver* worked too well as a provocation. The mythical status Perec bestowed on *La Boutique obscure* in his own mind came across too convincingly. Robert Dubois is just as unscrupulous as his father, but he's much more refined — he's figured out that publishing the novel as Perec had intended could bring him a great deal of success and prestige. So now he wants to bring out *La Boutique obscure* in its original combinatorial glory, no matter what it takes."

"What's stopping him?"

"The user's manual." Fournel smiled. "His father gave him the dreams he stole, but he obviously doesn't have the key to put all the pieces together."

I leaned in. "Do we?"

"That," said Fournel, raising his arm to signal for the check, "is an excellent question."

• • •

Go figure, I managed to remember the dream I had that night.

> An Oulipo meeting at Fournel's apartment. The table is square and checkered like a chess-board, twelve foot-long squares by twelve. (Even in my dream I am appalled by my subconscious's lack of subtlety.) Around it, the usual cast: Forte chattering excitedly, Jouet waiting patiently to speak, Audin drawing something on her notepad, Monk wisecracking, Bénabou shushing Monk, Garréta arguing with Bénabou, Roubaud looking balefully at the salad bowl. Bellos is there too, apparently as our guest of honour. Fournel is there, of course, presiding, but he has shaved his moustache. "*Je est un autre*," he says, as though bringing the meeting to order. Nobody responds.
>
> And across the room Perec is sitting in an armchair, a glass of wine at his side and a halo of smoke around his head, taking everything in. I can barely make out his face, but the twinkle in his eye is unmistakable. When I look over he grins at me, a wonderful, melancholy grin. "*Je ne suis pas le héros de mon histoire*," he says.
>
> I get up from the table, excusing myself to nobody in particular, and approach. On a notepad at his feet is what appears to be a large grid — 12 by 12, surely? — in which only maybe two dozen squares are filled in. I can't make out anything else.
>
> As I come over, Perec gestures, glass in hand, at the rest of the Oulipians, who are ignoring us. "*Si j'écris leur histoire*," he says, "*ils descendront de moi*." If I write their story, they will be my descendants.
>
> And then I get it. All this time we've been searching for the key to his

puzzle, the pattern behind his phantom work, we've been missing the point. None of this is unscripted. Not even close. Perec thought of everything, as usual: what seems to be the chaos of our chasing and misdirecting and leapfrogging over one another is in fact the patient unfolding of a meticulously plotted novel, one in which Dubois or Deronda is no less a character than Hugo Vernier or... me. What seems up close to be random — all the twists and turns, all the stories we've been stacking atop and against all the other stories — will reveal, upon zooming out, the very pattern we've been searching for all along.

I nod. Perec nods back, picks up his pad and darkens one more square in his grid.

"By the way, you got that wrong in your book," he adds. "It was Alfred de Vigny who said that, not me. But I won't tell anyone."

• • •

At the end of the dream I wake up in San Francisco and start the day, but this time I am happy to wake up: it's raining outside, the cat is snoozing at my feet and I have a stack of books on my bedside table and nowhere to be. I reach over and pick off the top book — *La Boutique obscure, sans sub-title* — and begin to read.

When I really did wake up, it was nearly 2 p.m. and the sun was shining. On my bedside table I found not *La Boutique obscure*, of course, but a paperback whose rear cover had been bent back and folded over in evident half-awake haste. On the inside of the cover, upside down, in what was unmistakably my handwriting, the following:

> the key to perec's puzzle isn't hidden in the journey series
> the key *is* the journey series

I closed the book, which turned out to be my copy of *La Liseuse*.
I knew what I had to do.

For a complete listing of all titles available from Atlas Press
and the London Institute of 'Pataphysics see our online catalogue at:
www.atlaspress.co.uk
To receive automatic notification of new publications
sign on to the emailing list at this website.
Atlas Press, 27 Old Gloucester st., London WC1N 3XX